ENDO

Ian O'Neill

BookStrand
www.BookStrand.com

A SIREN-BOOKSTRAND TITLE
IMPRINT: Romance

ENDO
Copyright © 2008 by Ian O'Neill

ISBN-10: 1-60601-172-3
ISBN-13: 978-1-60601-172-0

First Publication: December 2008

Cover design by Jinger Heaston
All cover art and logo copyright © 2008 by Siren-BookStrand, Inc.

Printed in the U.S.A.

PUBLISHER
www.BookStrand.com

To my mom, Alice O'Neill, who always encouraged me to walk my own path.

Acknowledgments

Contrary to popular belief, writing is not all that solitary. There are many people who have helped me along the way. A huge thank you to my wife, Sandy, for everything. Thank you to my editor, Marie Maddiss, who made this work better. Thanks to Kelley Armstrong, a fantastic writer who is always willing to listen and offer guidance. To Susan, Raina, John, Amy, Diane, Kym and all the other members of the OWG, a great big thank you for the fantastic critiques – I'm a better writer today thanks to all of you. Thanks to Maurice 'Rags' Ragogna for his invaluable help with police procedures. Thanks Jesse, for kick-starting the creative. Thanks to my publisher, Diana, for taking a chance.

My biggest thanks goes to you, dear reader. I hope you enjoy reading *Endo* as much as I enjoyed writing it.

ENDO

IAN O'NEILL
Copyright © 2008

Prologue

Pepe just earned his paycheque.

Todd pulled the small lever under his handlebars with his right index finger like he was rapidly firing a gun. The gears on his bike changed fluidly. His calves tightened and the slim, unseen muscles lining his shins clenched as he pushed and pulled to create fluid circles with his clipped-to-pedals feet. His bike responded nimbly with greater speed.

Excitement welled in him with every pedal stroke; pro or not, there was no better place than in the saddle.

Pepe had removed the front tire from the rim, spun it around and put it back on with the tread facing in the opposite direction. The tread had greater grip and that was the right move at this time of the night. Moist air was settling on the trail and the dirt would allow a deeper bite without relinquishing too much of its skin. He would thank Pepe when he finished this lap. His mechanic's decision was, as usual, the right one.

He clicked twice more on the small lever and urged his bike forward with ease over the flattest part of the course. It was never boring, but the sight of the dim blinking light a hundred yards up the trail was an excitement that fueled Todd through the least technical section of the off-road trail. Here it was flat with no logs or roots or rocks or drops – nothing to challenge him, except catching the blinking light.

"You can ride," he said to the night, "but you can't hide."

The light was unmistakable. The bike it was attached to was being driven by Kira, his former girlfriend. Where most riders had a series of blinks from their rear warning light, Kira used a light that spun, like a psychedelic painting from the Sixties. He pushed as hard as his body would allow. This was lap nine in hour twelve on a long course. He needed to be cautious about his pace if nothing else. A riding partner would be great for the rest of the lap, he thought and chuckled as he closed in on the little red swirling light.

It turned left, away from the course.

"What the hell?"

His headlamp shone strongest to about twenty feet and dimmed sharply beyond, fading to form a kind of soft halo, unable to penetrate the denseness of the deep forest and the night. Kira's rear swirling light disappeared and Todd coasted along the trail, searching for a way off the course. He slammed on his brakes, skidding, then made a quick twitch of the handlebars. His bike leapt left, just missing the first of a line of birch trees through which was woven yellow tape, not unlike what you'd find at a crime scene. This marked the edge of the course and the beginning of Todd's incredulity. If any other rider had gone off course he wouldn't have given them a second thought – this was a race and he was paid to win. Kira, however, wasn't any other rider.

"Kira?" he called out. "Where the hell are you going?"

He manoeuvred his machine through a few more trees, over a stretch of ragged, exposed Canadian Shield rock then unclipped his shoes from his pedals and swung free of his bike. He wasn't going to ride too close to the edge of the cliff. The organizers were smart to keep the course twenty or more yards away from the edge. He carefully placed his bike on the ground — it was a part of him and he respected it. The chain jangled a gentle thanks.

"Kira, are you—"

"Please, Todd, go. It isn't safe here."

He turned his head in the direction of her high-pitched, panicked voice and was nearly blinded when his headlamp slammed light against her bright pink cycling jersey. Facing him, the lip of the cliff to her left, she pulled her bike quickly in fornt of her. She stood rigidly, as if she was now part of the jagged rock below her feet.

"Todd. Please go. Please." She began to cry.

She rolled the bike forward until the front wheel rested over the edge of the cliff.

"Kira, what the hell are you doing?" He stepped towards her. "What's wrong? Let me help."

"I just want to be left alone." He saw her expression change, as if the hard rock inside her had suddenly become molten lava. She looked beyond him. "Leave him alone," she yelled.

He spun to see who was approaching and the log struck him full in the face. Pain stabbed from his eyes inward, reaching deeper into him than he'd ever felt it before. He could hear Kira screaming. He felt something warm running down his face. His feet fought for purchase but unlike the dirt, the rock was slick in the dampness. He stumbled and fell, but the ground didn't meet him. Kira's screams grew fainter as the wind picked up in his ears.

He felt nothing when he finally landed at the bottom of the cliff. The light of his headlamp tried desperately to break the darkness but the halo remained intact.

Chapter 1

"Just don't hurt yourself. I hate having to go the hospital to visit you. Too depressing and so inconvenient."

Keely laughed. Elise was always making him laugh. Part of why he married her. "Don't you trust me?"

"No. Nyet. Nein—"

"Okay, I'll be careful."

"That's all I'm asking," she said plainly. "I guess all the pros are there? The weekend warriors, too?"

"Yep. I don't have a hope in hell of winning. One guy has ten laps already," Keely said and watched a man wearing a bright red bodysuit and a Viking helmet ride by. "But I think I got the weekend warriors figured out."

"Well, at least you can beat someone."

"Why'd I marry you again?"

"For my money."

"You're broke."

"Then it must be because I'm great in the sack."

"Bingo."

"Gotta go, natives are restless. Have fun on your little bicycle and please don't hurt yourself," Elise said with a hint of pleading. "Keely, honey, you're not twenty anymore."

"Neither are you, but I still love ya. I'll call you again later."

"Love you, too. Bye."

* * * *

"You okay?"

Keely looked up and saw the young girl break the plane of light from his headlamp. He was doing so well until that damned tree.

"Sir, are you all right?"

Sir. I'm old enough to be your youngish father, he thought and rolled onto his side. "Yeah, I'm good. Bloody Ontario jumping pines will get you every time."

"The what?" she asked with a tilted head, more to keep the light from her headlamp out of his eyes, he knew. Still, he couldn't believe she didn't get the joke.

"You know. The Ontario jumping pine trees. Trees that jump right out—Never mind."

"Well, if you're okay," she said and pushed down on her pedal to roll out of his light's scope.

He was so sure he could make that last section of tight single track at a faster speed than on his last lap. He got to his feet and suddenly felt the cool of the night touch his skin. His sweat was doing its job. It helped cool him, but at this time of night, it *colded* him. He laughed to himself and the jumping pines around him. The night was always cool this far north, even in June. The ground was slightly soggy the farther you ventured from the trail. Keely had ventured about a dozen feet – his bike about six.

He walked back and eyed the trail he'd unsuccessfully negotiated. He picked up his bike and gave it a quick glance, running his hand over the seat, checking the handlebars and brakes – everything was in working order. Then he checked himself for any major cuts. Nothing was broken, of that he was certain. At night the temperature dropped enough to play with your senses at skin level. What you thought was a small nick could turn out to be a deep gash. The cold and the adrenalin were great pain inhibitors. He looked down his fairly thick arms. They were crusted with dirt, the dark hairs that usually scattered this way and that were matted and flat. He glanced at his thin wrists, he hated his damned tiny wrists, they made his arms look too Popeye-like. Elise thought he was nuts, since she never saw that at all. He checked his legs and not surprisingly found a few scrapes. He was much happier with his legs, good muscle tone if not a bit bowed. The rest of his 190-pound, six-foot-one frame was intact. His forty-five-year-old body would definitely complain to him at the end of the race and for about a week afterward.

He tucked a lock of more salt-than-pepper hair back up under his helmet and made a note to cut his mid-length mop before his next race. He had enough to worry about without hair obscuring his vision. He checked his watch. It was 12:11. Slightly less than twelve hours to go. This was lap four. How many more was he really capable of finishing in another twelve hours? Why the hell did he do this to himself?

"You okay?" a disembodied voice yelled from the woods back down the trail accompanied by a light zigging and zagging along the single track towards him.

"I'm good. Keep going. Thanks." Keely loved that part of his favourite sport — the moment you put your ass on a mountain bike seat, no matter your caste or station in life, regardless of gender, age or ability, you were in the club, no questions asked.

"Have a good one," said a young and muscled kid, no more than eighteen. He easily negotiated the tight stand of trees responsible for felling Keely. The boy whipped by causing a breeze and making Keely shiver. It was time to get moving. He threw his leg over the frame of the bike he loved so much that he kept it in his room. Elise called it Keely's two-wheeled whore. It was nothing like that at all. They were just very good friends.

He felt his feet sink into their pedals and heard the confirmatory click from each. He was back on the trail cruising up a slight rise through trees, rocks, roots and would soon meet up with a few logs if memory of his previous lap served him well.

The day Keely brought home his 'rally blue' full-suspension mountain bike was a happy one. Elise was thrilled for him and even took her for a spin down the driveway. Keely never said a word and kept the smile slapped to his face, but the whole time he was shitting bricks that she'd lose her balance and scrape the paint of his other love on the very first day she entered his life. As luck would shine on him, she was fine, and so was Elise.

She was a delight from the first time they'd been together, taking every bump with ease and elegance. The Fox front forks were supple but paled to the float of the rear shock. Both offered ten centimetres of travel and that clearance was a godsend at the moment – several nasty roots had spread like long fingers across the trail. When damp or wet, a root at an odd angle could bring down the most seasoned rider. Keely raised himself out of his seat, drove hard through several pedal strokes then bent at the knees and elbows, allowing the suspension to absorb the bulk of the shock, his body merely floating over his bike as it sailed through the obstacle. A few small logs, a few wide turns and a dip into a ninety-degree turn led Keely to the most boring part of the 25-kilometer course – the flats.

Though there was no moon, the forest reflected light from somewhere. It gave Keely pause to think of where the light might be coming from, then he simply stopped caring so he could turn his full attention to the experience of being on his bike, late at night, deep in a forest with no other living soul around him. And that solitude would last if he kept a fairly decent pace.

The smell was a mix of damp and dirt. He could taste it, too. Only a mountain biker would understand that, or a little kid eating mud pies. Another hearty internal laugh at his own joke, then a rustling to his left brought his head around. He scrutinized the woods where he knew the sound originated but the dark between the trees was more than a blanket, it was a wall easily stopping his light.

A branch snapped closer to him and Keely hammered the pedals with all his might. He squeezed his gear lever several times, the succinct clicking followed by a rattling of his chain through the rear cogs to climb gears and put more tension on the chain and pedals, and his legs. He pushed with all his energy to flee the scene of what could be his biggest fear of all, bears. Keely McAdam and bears did not get along.

Without warning, he felt the bike stop, his body continuing forward. He let go of the handlebars, having made the quick assessment that he was going end over end. His feet left the pedals without him even having to twist his ankle or manoeuvre them in any way – the joy of clipless pedals – an oxymoron of the highest degree, he thought, as he stretched out his arms and waited for impact. His forearms met soft ground off the trail, and he tucked in preparation for a roll, his chin touching his chest to protect his neck. His back slammed hard against a tree, and Keely felt the air leave his body.

He was now a heap of slightly older rider with a great sense of humour trying to breathe. He would eventually take a breath again, he knew that. What worried him was that he hadn't gotten very far from where that bear might be. Through watery eyes he saw his bike on its side off the trail, the front tire pointing at him from the other side of a log. He deserved this one. He wasn't paying attention, he'd turned his head left to check out the forest and the bike turned with him. Cold air seared hot in his lungs. *Was that another oxymoron?* He rolled over to rest on his hands and knees.

"You're not twenty anymore, honey," he said in his best imitation of his wife. He picked himself up and brushed off the dirt that magnetized to him on landing. He gave himself the once over again to discover not a scratch, thankfully. The tree he'd hit was a big one, so it acted more like a wall than a pole to separate his spine in some gruesome way. His hydration pack, half full of a mix of water and a Drink Pink sports drink, worn like a knapsack, also helped cushion the blow. He managed to get his lungs completely expanded and coughed a few times against the burn. He stuck the end of the plastic tube in his mouth and bit down to open the slit in its end. Then he sucked in warming liquid. Its temperature didn't matter, it was wet and cleansing.

He walked back to his bike measuring the distance by steps – ten, to be exact. Another successful launch but he didn't laugh. The trail was empty and he wondered why there were suddenly few riders. He answered his own question without much thought. There were two races going on, each with many different categories. There was the 12-hour race, with its solo riders, and various teams of varying classifications. And, there was the 24-hour race with its soloists and teams. The 12-hour race had finished, so there were far fewer riders on the course now.

He shouldered his bike and carried it over the Ontario 'hopping log,' laughed, then placed his bike back on the trail, mounted her and pushed off. He needed to slow down and enjoy the ride. The flats were the perfect place to take a break, especially if you were out to enjoy the race, not win it. In earlier laps he'd been passed by numerous riders cranking high gears but barely sweating. Most said, "On your left," or "On your right," like they were chatting rather than riding their bikes through some of the toughest trail Keely had ever attempted. They'd fly by and make him feel like he was standing still. His ego was only bruised for so long, then his body let him know that it was okay, he was out for the fun of it, there was no way he could ever keep up with those riders. After that, the race was just against himself, and to win, he simply had to finish with as many laps as possible.

The trail and everything around it took on a single colour, a dirty grey, yet its depth remained intact; shadows cast from the light of Keely's headlamp danced in rhythm to his pedal strokes. He tucked that loose tendril of hair back under his helmet again. He noticed steam rising from his body, the sweat leaving him in an odd way. Dust particles swam across his vision but never landed in his eyes, or at least they were so small that it didn't hinder his vision. His body ached badly where he'd just hit the tree. His muscles were loose but tired. He'd stopped after every lap to rest and eat. He loved this. Other than lying naked with his wife in his arms, there was no place he'd rather be.

Yeah, he was a city boy, but he loved the feel of riding his bike off road. His uneasiness with nature was squelched in comparison to what he was feeling this very moment. A coolness caressed him as he sliced through the air, and beyond the chain gently buzzing against the metal teeth of its ring and cogs, the tires humming their want to eat earth, and his own breathing, there was silence. There was nothing but he and his good friend painted 'rally blue.'

The most amazing part of his passion was that though Elise never shared in it, she always encouraged it. When he'd worked a tough case, seen terrible things, made tasteless jokes to pretend and deflect, she'd never scolded him. Instead, she would wrap her arms around his waist and rest her head in the nape of his neck. Her voice was always tinged with empathy and awareness.

"Hey, cops are people, too. Go ride your whore."

He smiled and felt dirt automatically stick to his teeth. He licked it away then reached for the 'hose' as Elise called it, placing the rubber tip of the plastic tube in his mouth. He rinsed and spit, then drank. He was at the end of the flats and the climb was going to be tough.

"Fifth time's a charm," he said, the words carrying no further than the distance of the light that ensconced him.

He saw the line of trees arching right before he spotted the yellow tape slaloming through them. He hated the tape they used to mark the course. It reminded him too much of his days as a homicide detective. Here, in his favourite place, he wanted to shed those memories most of all.

Keely made a mental decision regarding which of his twenty-seven gears was appropriate. Climbing was not exactly his specialty but it was the one part of his skill set he worked on most. That, and falling properly.

He shifted gears and they complained with a loud clang. He powered through it to quickly find his pace again then swung alongside the trees starting his slow ascent up the worst climb on the course.

The grade was slow at the bottom but Keely found himself dropping a gear in the first twenty yards. That was okay though, in fact, it was the plan. He'd learned long ago that cadence is one of the keys to climbing successfully, it didn't matter if you had to drop ten gears to your lowest, what mattered was that you kept the pedals stroking as piston-like as possible, not losing your rhythm or speed.

The trail wound through pines and Keely concentrated to make each tight turn. Ripples on the ground made maintaining speed nearly impossible, rocking him forward and backward, the stresses on his lower back beginning to tighten in his muscles. Standing was a short relief. He tried to keep his weight centred over the frame. He clicked down two more gears and knew he was going to have to shift next to his lowest front ring if he wanted to access his lowest gears.

Trees lined only the right side of the ever rising trail. He moved his ass up slightly on his seat, shifting his weight forward to give the rear tire more bite into the angled trail. A quick head flick and Keely saw the start of the long drop through brush on his left. During the day it was even more unnerving since he could see not only the distance he'd climbed thus far, but added to that was the cliff of eighty or so feet as well. He had to be 120 feet up now and still climbing. He thanked the darkness for hiding the truth.

The cliff ran through the park and was part of a fairly long escarpment. It ran about forty kilometres from south to north. Right now, Keely was only concerned about *this* kilometre.

As if the ever increasing slant of the trail wasn't enough, the erosion from water spilling across the single track caused it to slant with the hill face in several places. Keely leaned right slightly and prayed his tires would continue to grip. He clicked down another gear desperately attempting to maintain his cadence – it wasn't working. He was losing momentum and his legs were taking far greater strain. The front wheel was popping up and he was losing grip and balance.

The biggest problem with gear design was when you went from the middle ring to the lower ring – you didn't go from tenth gear to ninth gear. No, you went from tenth gear to first gear. Keely was ready for that and as he pulled the lever with his left index finger sending the chain down to the lowest ring in front, he rapidly fired the lever on his right with his index finger trying to get the chain onto the biggest cog in the set attached to his rear wheel. He could feel the chain move down in front and up in back, but it was too fast or there was too much dirt between cogs or the chain didn't have enough lube on it – for whatever reason, the chain got sucked between cogs and jammed.

The bike stopped.

His forward momentum swung sideways, to the right because of his lean to compensate for the wonky trail. The bike was sliding left, down the slope off the trail, pulling Keely with it. A quick twist of his ankle and his foot was free of the pedal searching for a hold on the slanted trail.

"Shit." He was on grass and it was wet and then the hill sloped even more and Keely tried to remove his left foot from his pedal but it was no use, he was going down with the bike. He reached up and tried to grab at shrubs now flying past him but he couldn't grasp one. All he managed to do was get cuts on his arms and legs, the harsh brush like wire against his skin.

He felt a jolt against his crotch, pain shot from his abdomen, and he was airborne, free form his bike. He landed farther down the steep hill and heard the crash of bushes and small saplings snapping under his weight. He had to slow down. The slope levelled to a ledge before the cliff but it was only about a dozen feet wide. If he hit that slope at this speed he was doomed.

He did the complete opposite to what he'd been taught – he spread out wide, stopped rolling and started sliding. He'd much rather have a broken limb than hit the bottom of that cliff. Tall grass ripped at his skin and caused a fire of pain. He could hear it whip and snap against his flesh and grimaced with every strike but happily so — he was slowing. But was it slow enough?

He looked down the length of his body as the ledge rushed up to meet the light from his lamp. His right leg buckled on impact and it was that more than anything that slowed him. Pain like lightning struck out from his ankle. He was flying again, but it was a short flight. His entire body crashed onto the moss-covered rock of the ledge and bounced once, flipping him onto his back.

He came to rest with his head leaning back over the edge of the cliff. He took stock of the multiple bumps, bruises and cuts, but nothing hurt as bad as his right ankle. He rolled slowly onto his stomach and let out his first moan. He deserved that much.

That's when he saw the light of a fallen rider at the bottom of the cliff.

"Beats my endo by eighty feet."

Chapter 2

Standing near the edge of the cliff, it was easy to see the source of the mysterious light Keely had noted earlier; everything was bathed in starlight. In the city he struggled to find stars, and only saw the brightest. Here he strained his eyes to see a patch of black devoid of twinkling brightness.

Brighter still was the dome of light surrounding the recently departed cyclist lying amongst fallen shards of rock at the bottom of the cliff. Like beacons from above, streams of light from flashlights struck the area from people Keely and his fellow officers used to call 'morbids,' more commonly known as onlookers.

The word had spread about the untimely demise of a fellow pedaler and the crowd at the edge of the cliff was growing, no doubt hoping for a glimpse of the corpse. If they were lucky they might see blood, or maybe he was decapitated, Keely thought. *Wow, what a treat.*

"Holy shit. That's Mr. Clean, man."

"No way."

"Way. That's Watkins, man. Number one on the bike plate. Look."

The tall guy in dark sweats with his hood up shone a light on the bike that had landed about fifty feet from the dead cyclist. Sure enough it revealed one on the number plate. Every competitor affixed a number plate to their bikes for the race.

A girl screamed then laughed when someone grabbed her, stopping her stumble at the edge of the cliff. Things were getting a bit out of hand. Keely wheeled his bike to the hooded cyclist, leaning on it for support so he could rest his sore ankle.

"Hey, Kid, can I borrow that for a second."

The guy handed the bulky flashlight over with a smile.

"Pretty gruesome, eh? What an endo."

Keely moved the light from Watkins' body to his bike and back again. Something didn't look right but he had more pressing matters to deal with. He flashed the light beam on a group of people, all wearing tan shirts and shorts, green caps hiding their faces. One broke from the circle and walked toward the body. Keely's senses went critical.

"Hey! Stop!"

The crowd of people at the cliff's edge froze. No one took a breath. The park warden looked up at Keely, shading his eyes against the beams of light from above. Then took several more steps towards the body.

Keely quickly removed his hydration pack and took out a small black wallet. He dropped the pack and his bike, then shone the light on the open wallet. Gleaming into the night was his detective's badge. They didn't need to know he was retired.

"Wait. Don't go any closer, please," Keely yelled.

Murmurs from the crowd got louder and the warden must have heard the several 'he's a cop' comments.

"I have the situation under control, officer."

"How do I get down there?"

A hand touched Keely's shoulder and he spun to see a short, happy man. The smile was too wide, too forced. His face looked like it was made up by a special-effects artist – deep grooves gave his skin a rubbery look.

"I'm Warden Stanski. What can I do ya for?"

"I'd advise you to set up some tape about twenty yards back from this cliff face so no one else falls over trying to get a good look at the guy who already fell over."

"Of course, officer."

"It's detective. And you can tell me how to get down there."

"The victim is dead, *detective*. We pronounced him so about—"

"I'm sorry, you can't pronounce him. Only a coroner can. But, I'm sure you knew that?"

"Of course. Right."

"Tape this area off and get me down there, *please*."

* * * *

After taping off a reasonably sized area and then walking a few hundred yards along the cliff to the left, Keely followed Stanski down a slim path to the ground below. It was rough going with a lot of loose rock and dirt, but Keely's headlamp made the difference.

Twenty yards from the body, Keely knew the area was a crime scene. In fact the edge of the cliff above could be included. He took in as much information as possible with a quick scan. He'd slipped into job-mode without even realizing it.

Todd Watkins, a.k.a. Mr. Clean, was on his back between two large boulders, as if reclining for a better view of the top of the cliff. His arms were folded neatly on his chest and his feet were pointed at the cliff face. Someone had made him comfortable, either before he died or after. Hopefully after, Keely thought.

"That's far enough, officer," a burly man said in a deep voice. He was one the hairiest people Keely had ever seen. "The victim has been identified, the coroner and chopper are on the way. The area is secure and—"

"My name is Keely McAdam and this area must be considered a crime scene. Has anyone called in the OPP?"

All that faced Keely was stunned looks from the four identically dressed people, three men and a woman. She spoke. "This man fell during a race. It was an accident. Surely there's no need to call the police?"

"I take it you're in charge here."

"I am," the burly man said. "I'm George Arnsberg, head park warden. This was obviously an accident."

Keely studied the furry man's face for a second. "Mr. Arnsberg, I'm sorry to disagree, but my fifteen years as a homicide detective tells me otherwise."

"I'm certainly not trying to say—"

"It's okay. This isn't a pissing contest. I just need to approach the body for a minute. May I do that, Mr. Arnsberg?"

"Yes, of course."

Keely reached out a hand and the woman automatically placed her flashlight in it. He clicked off his headlamp and immediately turned his attention to the ground.

"What direction am I facing?" he asked with his back to the foursome.

"North."

There were several sets of footprints, all with a hiking boot pattern.

"I guess four people have to feel for a pulse, eh?" He didn't have to turn around to know they looked guilty. He could sense it.

Keely moved to his right, closer to the cliff face. It was after one in the morning and he felt slightly chilled. The rock face was cold, only adding to the surrounding air's low temperature. The light beam reflected brightly from the rock of the cliff, but not so much from the large boulders on the ground – the rocks that had broken loose to find their stationary home. That rock was dirtier and Keely made a mental note to check the boulders for any prints, hand or foot.

He'd walked past Todd's body by about ten yards, then turned to his left, shining the light on the ground. He saw a few partial footprints in some exposed dirt and bent down for a closer look. Running shoes, not boots. They pointed north.

"I want you to tape off the area fifty paces north and west out from the body and fifty paces south out from the bike. Please start at the cliff face and work all the way around him. Mr. Arnsberg."

"Yes," he said and moved toward Keely.

"No. Stay there. I'll come to you." Keely took his time and when he arrived said, "I need all your hats please."

"Look, I'm sure you're very good at your job, detective, but isn't this obviously an accident. He took a wrong turn and fell. What else could it be?"

"Give me your hats and please don't move until I come back. Okay?"

Keely made his way back to the two footprints north of Todd's body and placed the four hats around them, then carefully scrutinized the ground on his way up the rocks to where the dead man lay. He found nothing. Not with the naked eye, but a crime scene analyst would have more luck. Once the OPP were called in they would notify Forensic Identification Services in Toronto. He just had to make sure to secure the scene until then.

He carefully climbed onto a boulder that gave him a better view of the rocks responsible for holding up Todd's body. There were no visible prints of any kind. No blood either. He traced the light from Todd's face to his feet, then slowly back again. Todd Watkins' face was covered in blood and his eyes were closed. He smelled of bug spray and another pungent odour Keely found vaguely familiar yet couldn't identify.

Todd's nose was broken, the bone jutting off at an odd angle under the skin. He had a gash on his forehead just under his helmet. It had stopped bleeding as far as Keely could tell. He hadn't bled out so it was probably the cold that helped stop it. There were bruises and cuts all over the body where skin was exposed. Todd's black cycling shorts were torn on the left leg where a cut could be seen. His bright Drink Pink cycling jersey was intact, though it had soaked up a fair amount of blood. Whether that was from Todd's face or cuts on his torso, the coroner would have to decide.

"What the hell are you looking for, the murder weapon?" Arnsberg asked.

Keely tilted his head back and pointed the flashlight beam up at the edge of the cliff. It was approximately eighty feet high along this stretch, at least that's what the race literature had stated. It looked a lot higher and he hoped that Todd Watkins didn't suffer. He was about ten yards from the face of the cliff on his back with his head pointing away from its face. His bike, both wheels mangled into taco shapes, lay fifty feet away to the north and was farther from the cliff face than Todd.

"Did you find the gun?"

Keely backtracked his route to Arnsberg and looked down at the stocky man. "He was murdered."

The four wardens chuckled.

"Come on. Look at him. He was in a race—"

"And was thrown off that cliff. Actually, I think someone took a swing at him and he fell."

Arnsberg pulled a radio from his belt. "Chris, come in Chris."

"Yeah. Has the helicopter arrived yet?"

"Chris, we have a problem. You'd better get down here."

"George, I've got the race organizer and sponsors all over my ass for shutting this thing down. I'm a bit on the busy side."

Keely reached out and put his palm up. He arched his eyebrows and cocked his head. It was enough. Arnsberg gave him the radio and Keely pushed the talk button. "This is Detective Keely McAdam, formerly of the Metro Police. I'm advising you to close the park immediately. No one in or out. Todd Watkins was murdered."

Keely threw the radio back to Arnsberg who promptly dropped it.

After a few seconds Chris' defeated voice crackled through the radio. "I'm on my way."

"Who's Chris?" Keely asked.

"Chris Nadal, park superintendent," the woman answered.

"Look, I don't know who you really are but are you absolutely sure about this?" Arnsberg's eyes were watery.

Keely put his arm around the beefy man's shoulders and turned him in the direction of the body on the rocks.

"See that guy lying back looking up at the stars with blood all over his face."

Arnsberg nodded.

"That is Todd 'Mr. Clean' Watkins. And do you know why they call him that?"

"He's one of those neat freaks?"

"Nope. They call him Mr. Clean because he can clean anything. In mountain biking that means he rides over anything and rarely takes his feet off his pedals to touch the ground. In fact, you'd be hard pressed to find anyone who could tell you the last time they saw Todd Watkins fall off his bike."

"I can," Arnsberg said and smiled. "A few hours ago."

"Mr. Arnsberg, that is incorrect. And I'll tell you why." Keely spun the man to face the cliff. "If you endo, that is, if you go end-over-end off your bike over this cliff, which way do you think your feet would point?"

It didn't take the park warden long to come up with the answer and it showed on his face.

"Exactly. Todd's head should be closer to the cliff and his feet should be pointing away from it."

"Not necessarily. It all depends on how fast he was travelling when he went over the edge." Arnsberg let another smile creep onto his face.

"Sorry, wrong again. No matter how fast he was travelling, he would land one of two ways – face up with his head closer to the cliff, or face down with his feet closer to the cliff. Pro cyclists know how to fall. He would prepare to land by instinct." Keely had a vision of himself flying off his bike, his back slamming against that tree. "In fact, I think someone positioned his body after the fall. His arms crossed on his chest like that is pretty convenient, don't you think?"

"I'm not really sure."

"Here's the kicker. I think he landed closer to where his bike is and someone moved him to make it look like he veered off the trail and over the cliff by accident."

"That is possible."

"I'll bet that somewhere between that bike and Todd's body, we'll find where he hit the ground. You a betting man, Mr. Arnsberg?"

"Oh no, I don't bet on anything—"

"I'm sorry to hear that. I could have used the money."

"George, come in, George."

Arnsberg clicked the button on the side of his radio. "I'm here, Chris."

"I'm shutting down the park."

"You don't think that cyclist was murdered do—"

"George, Kira Bremner is missing."

Chapter 3

Keely helped the wardens tape off the area around the body. He wasn't being entirely altruistic; he wanted to study the body a bit more. Just as he was tying one end to a particularly pointy rock a herd of people with radios, or maybe cell phones, descended on the area from the south.

"How the hell could you let this happen to my rider."

"I'm suing your ass."

"Look at him. He's fucking dead. You killed one of our best riders."

All of the accusations were being thrown at a woman at the head of the pack. Her stride was strong, as if every step was to stomp a bug. Yet as she closed in on the area covered by the work lights the wardens had set up, Keely could see her features were soft; large eyes, high cheekbones, full lips. Her long, blond hair heightened her attractiveness. Keely knew by her posture and movement that under her cargo pants and sweatshirt was a well-defined body.

She spun on the men tailing her.

"Gentlemen, please have some respect for Mr. Watkins. You lost property, but he lost his life tonight."

The men stopped as if lassoed, turning to face one another and mumbling. Keely smiled for the first time in an hour and that was saying something considering the pounding in his ever-swelling ankle.

"George," she said and Arnsberg trotted over to her. "Chris is at the park entrance coordinating the closure. The police will be here soon."

"They're already here, Amy," he said and nodded at Keely.

She changed in that instant. She was suddenly a hostess greeting a guest with her arm extended and the obligatory smile pasted on her face. "Amanda Zendastra, owner-operator of Day Long Racing. And you must be the detective."

"Keely McAdam."

They shook hands and Keely noted how sweaty Amy's was.

"Thank you for all your help. I don't know what we would have done without you. I was hoping you could help us find Kira."

Keely pulled his hand away. "I'll let the OPP take care of that."

"No. I'm sure it will be the RCMP that takes this on. This is a national park."

"On Ontario soil. Jurisdiction will go to the provincial police. Trust me, I've tussled over cases like this before. Best to let departments settle who gets dibs."

"Disappointing. I was looking forward to seeing a Mountie."

"Horses smell bad." Keely screwed up his face. "I'd settle for OPP."

"What can you do to help with Kira?"

"I think — Mr. Nadal, is it?" She nodded. "I think he's doing the right thing until the cops get here. Shut the park down and wait."

Amy squinted as if fighting a bout of gas.

"Look, I'm sorry about all of this. It can't be good for you. You're losing a lot of money I'm sure," Keely said.

Her gas fight heightened to what Keely suspected was nausea.

"I'm hoping insurance will take care of some of this. But, yeah, it could ruin me. I can keep rider registrations but the sponsors are another matter."

"You mean I don't get my money back?"

"A few other promoters would be very happy to see me go."

"That bad, eh?"

"The twenty-four-hour bug – I thought I had it licked."

"What?"

A voice crackled from Amy's radio. "George. Come in, George."

"Yeah, Chris, go ahead."

"Coroner's en route by chopper. Should be on-site inside a half hour."

Amy turned down the volume on her radio. "How do we find that girl and who the hell would hurt Todd?"

Keely put his hand gently on her shoulder and squeezed. "Since the park is shut down, I'm not going anywhere. This area's secure now so I'm going to my campsite to change into some warmer clothes. I'll catch up with you a little later. I'll do whatever I can to help."

"Thanks, Mr. McAdam—"

"Keely."

"Thank you, Keely."

* * * *

"It's been weird. No, make that bizarre."

"Just tell me you're okay."

"Honey, I'm fine. No one pushed *me* over a cliff."

"Keely, what happens now? Are you coming home?"

The cool air made his skin goosepimply and Keely picked up his pace. The park was filled with cyclists banned from cycling so there were more than a few pissed off faces amongst the rows of campsites. Still, most were just hanging out and drinking what they'd smuggled into the park. A smattering of a party atmosphere. Keely thought about putting all those cyclists to good use.

"Not right away. I want to help find the missing girl."

"I want you to come home. It could be dangerous."

"Elise, honey, relax. I'm not riding my bike. The danger's over."

"Good point."

* * * *

Keely put on a red hoody with the race organizer's logo on it, Day Long Racing in script across his chest. He wore olive-green hiking pants with zippers just above each knee to remove the lower pant leg when it got hot. His hiking boots replaced his cycling shoes and felt far more comfortable and warmer. He had a little bother getting his right foot into his boot and when it was laced his ankle felt better, more stable.

He'd heard the helicopter fly in a few minutes ago but wanted to finish his notes. Old habits definitely die hard because he couldn't leave home without a small note pad. Elise figured he'd filled enough of them over his career to write a dozen novels and even suggested he take up creative writing. It was the furthest thing from Keely's mind. In the year since his retirement he hadn't cracked a single one of his note pads and figured he'd never have the nerve to read them again. Though filled with more technical information about his cases, the memories were hard enough to erase and he didn't need the refresher. He made a note to destroy his note pads when he got home.

His tent was small and rated for low temperatures, which meant he was way too hot at the moment. He made a few more observations about the crime scene then flipped his pad closed, stuck it in one the many pockets on his pants and shimmied his way out of the tent. He glanced at his bike resting against a tree but decided to give her the rest of the night off.

He felt refreshed and ready to lend a hand, sore ankle or not. The whole area suddenly seemed juiced with energy. People were awake and sitting by fires, talking about the tragic events of the day. Yet there was an edge to it all. The voices drifting to him sounded optimistic and charged. Though separated by tents and riding ability, this was a riding community and they were ready to help one of their own.

But is one of them a murderer?

He was certain that Todd Watkins was murdered. He fell on his face and was turned over, either by someone who knew him or by someone who felt guilty about his death. They'd moved the body and positioned him in the coffin pose, hands crossed on his chest; all that was missing was the lily. Watkins was murdered. The only thing Keely forgot to check was the tape marking the course and he was going to do that now.

He patted his right rear pocket and felt the lump of his badge. He had to help. A girl was missing.

* * * *

By the sound of it, the helicopter had flown low, headed, Keely figured, for the main building complex of Algonquin Park. A contingent of OPP officers would be there by now. Keely figured they'd come from either Whitney, a satellite station of the host detachment in Killaloe to the east, or from Bancroft, a bit farther south but a detachment with a full complement of officers. Keely had worked several cases with OPP inspectors. They were excellent in their element and this was definitely *their* element.

Keely smelled plastic burning; someone disposing of garbage from their site. The smell was replaced with the pungency of bacon and the sound of it frying quickly followed. Keely turned to see a man in a white apron dancing around a grill sitting on a picnic bench. A woman played with eggs atop another grill on the same bench. Keely's stomach yelled at him, then begged him to stop and ask for a taste. His mouth watered its vote but Keely had one thing on his mind, the tape.

The lights up ahead meant he was getting close to the start/finish line. It was lined with sponsor banners and had a tower built from scaffolding, topped with bird's nest for an announcer. There were a few trucks for gear. There was the media tent, the mechanics tent, and what Keely thought was the most important tent of all, the medical tent. He'd entered several twenty-four-hour races but none seemed as organized as this one. To land an event in a park like Algonquin must have taken a lot of effort. After all, it was the crown jewel of the national park system. Either a lot of palms were a bit greasy or one was extremely slippery.

He moved along the gravel road leading from different camp areas, his flashlight catching sight of the occasional camper, rider, bat or raccoon. The music from the start/finish line had ceased hours ago but faint beats could be heard from distant sites. The night had activity and that was good, Keely thought, for no one else but him. He needed motion after seeing the motionless – he always did.

The cliff face was a kilometre or so if one walked straight to it. If you rode the course it would be about ten K. Keely smiled at the memory of being on his bike. This had been the toughest terrain he'd ever ridden and he'd have the scrapes and bruises to prove it. He was satisfied with his four and a half laps. They were killer laps.

The scaffolding of the start line appeared above the trees to Keely's right and the farther he walked the noisier things got. He got to the end of the stand of trees and heard Amanda Zendastra's quivering voice.

"We *are* legit. This race proves that pros should be earning points toward overall championships."

"It proves that it wasn't well organized and that the CCA cannot, given the circumstances, sanction any of your events."

"Mr. Adduce, please, you can't do that. There is evidence that Todd was murdered. How can I be held responsible for that?"

Silence, then Adduce took a deep breath. Keely held his.

"If that is what the police investigation reveals, then we'll attend your next event and try this again."

"Oh, thank you."

"Don't thank me yet. If you think we were hard to please this time, next time you had better be absolutely perfect."

"We will. I promise you that."

"I'll be watching for the police report. Good night."

Amy appeared from around the trees.

"Oh. Keely. Hi."

"Amanda. I'm on my way to the cliff. I just wanted to take a last look around. How is the hunt for ... What's the girl's name again?"

"Kira. Kira Bremner. She was Todd's teammate. Their sponsor is understandably upset. One rider dead and another missing. This has been such a nightmare."

"I heard. From where I'm standing this is definitely a homicide. At least where Todd Watkins is concerned. All we have to do now is find Kira and you're back in business."

"There are all kinds of policemen at the hut and they're making plans to search for her. They've already sent out some officers with dogs. I hope she's okay."

In the forty-five minutes they'd been apart, Keely thought Amy had aged ten years. Her face was hard and her eyes clouded.

"When was the last time you sat down?"

"I've been drinking that pink stuff. It definitely gives you a boost."

He gently grabbed her arm and they stopped on the gravel trail.

"I was a cop for a long time. I've seen very tough people crack under a lot less stress than you're going through right now. Go to the hut or main building or whatever the hell you want to call it, sit down and have a rest. Otherwise you're going to end up with an IV in your arm and then you're no good to anyone."

She lowered her head, revealing the dark roots of her hair in the glow of the lights from the circus that is the start line of the race. When she looked at him, her face was softer but stronger, as if she'd already received much-needed energy.

"Do you want one of my staff to drive you over on an ATV?"

"Nah. I need a little solitude."

"Don't we all."

* * * *

It took about a half hour but Keely finally found the trail markers he was looking for. They wound through a set of trees pointing in the direction of the cliff, then bent right and weaved through trees heading up the nasty climb that claimed him and caused the throbbing in his ankle.

Keely checked every stretch of yellow tape with its bold capitalized 'caution' printed on it every foot or so. The tape was intact. It was stretched slightly about twenty feet up the climb where someone might have leaned into it, but other than that, not a single tear.

Todd Watkins did not veer off the trail unless he was dragged off or rode off it before the caution tape began.

Keely skipped the short distance down the hill and then walked back along the tape, unconsciously checking it again to make sure he hadn't missed a break or two pieces tied together. When he got to the stand of trees where the tape started, he groaned. Dozens of bicycles and people had left the trail at this very spot to get a look at Todd Watkins' body.

He didn't even watch where he was walking as he headed to the cliff's edge. He knew that all the tracks or apparent evidence was caused be the morbids. "Shit."

He felt the hard rock of the top of the cliff under his feet and began to scan the ground in a wide arc with his flashlight. Never could tell what one might find. He was glad to see that the wardens had indeed placed tape well back from the cliff edge, but this tape was broken in spots. How people could be that desperate to see a dead body he just couldn't understand. *Work a case, then we'll see how you feel.*

He ducked under the tape and looked down to see that Todd's body had been shielded by a tarp held up with poles and ropes. The coroner would have pronounced Todd dead and had multiple photographs taken of the body and the area around it. The scene was guarded by two OPP officers. They would keep it secure until Forensic Identification Services flew in from Toronto. Which would be any time now.

Why don't they consider the cliff edge part of the crime scene?

"Hey! What the hell do you think you're doing?"

Chapter 4

"And you've been retired for how long?"

The French-Canadian's sarcasm wasn't lost on Keely; this man was well aware of the timeframe. Plus, in a year he'd gotten used to the barbs and coming from someone he already disliked, it was much easier to take.

"Must have been one hell of a good dirty cop to collect a nest egg big enough to retire at fifty, eh, McAdam?" Det. Sgt. Rene Robitaille was fifty if he was a day but his mid-length hair was jet black, as were his very bushy eyebrows and moustache. He wasn't too tall or too heavy, he was average. Probably made the height-weight restrictions on the nose, Keely thought. He'd been on the job long enough to recognize one thing in Robitaille: the man was mean. He didn't have battle scars or missing teeth or tattoos. There were no stereotypical, bullshit signs. It was in his eyes. Det. Sgt. Rene Robitaille and Keely had crossed paths before and their dislike and mistrust of each other showed like bright outerwear.

"Forty-four. I retired when I was forty-four last year."

"Maybe he's squeamish. Can't take the job anymore," an OPP officer with no neck said. "He wouldn't be the first to crack, won't be last."

They were in a small room in what Amy called the hut, the main buildings housing the park superintendent's office, quarters for the wardens, dining halls, some sleeping quarters, a nature centre and it was getting warm. The neckless constable was standing by an open window and Robitaille was sitting at a small table. The room reminded Keely of interview rooms at his old 52 Division.

"Constable Ferguson filled me in on everything you've done so far. And we appreciate it—"

"But..."

"*But*, it is time to let us do our jobs," Robitaille said. "You know the drill. Only civilians with a purpose are hired onto a case. And they're all from forensics."

"I can help you with interviews. I've got plenty of experience."

"Oh, I know you do. And, as I said, you've done us a great service controlling what was left of the scene. Your notes give us a great starting point. Thank you," Robitaille said, standing and extending his hand.

Keely gripped it, tightly, and pulled the other man closer. "I'll be in the park until Monday. I paid for my campsite," he said almost without moving his lips.

"One wrong move and you'll be spending the weekend in a holding cell in Whitney with the rest of the troublemakers," Robitaille said.

Keely held the other man's hand for a few more seconds. He wasn't sure why, but he wanted Robitaille to pull away first. He did, because the coroner walked into the room. Robitaille made sure to give Keely's hand one last hard squeeze.

"Am I interrupting something?" the skinny man in baggy shorts and a white T-shirt with Drink Pink on it said. Keely recognized him immediately. "I can come back."

"No need," said Robitaille, the bounce back in his voice.

"Keely McAdam, you old screw. How are you? I just worked a case with Elise. You are such a lucky man."

"And she never lets me forget it, John." Keely moved around the table and shook his hand. "How are you? It's been a year at least."

"I'm good. I hate helicopters though. Too small and noisy. Makes me nervous."

"You look good. You've put on weight."

Both men chuckled.

"Excuse me," Robitaille interrupted. "You have an initial report, yes?"

"Of course," John said. "Keely, you'll be here later?"

"He will but you are not to discuss this case with him under any circumstances," Robitaille said. "And if I discover that you have disclosed confidential information regarding this case I will see to it that disciplinary action is taken against you. Is that understood, Dr. Krull?"

Keely and John exchanged a glance that spoke volumes about Robitaille. Finally John answered, "Perfectly clear, Detective Sergeant."

Keely turned to leave.

"I'll be giving my best to Elise," John said and winked.

Keely left the drab, hot room and after a few turns down the just as drab hallways, he was outside. There were large numbers of people on the grounds around the hut sectioned off into groups. At the head of each group stood several OPP constables. Keely wanted to help, but it wasn't the right time. Todd Watkins was on the same team, Drink Pink, as Kira Bremner. If Robitaille wasn't going to make the leap, Keely was.

He walked in the direction of the start/finish area.

* * * *

Keely jumped over one of a row of four-foot-high barriers into the 'alley' – every lap finished down this twenty-foot-wide lane plastered with sponsor signage. Music from some unknown source blasted you across the line and made the announcer have to yell to be heard, even over a P.A. Now, all was quiet but the bright lights still gleamed down on Keely as he walked over to Amy, who was checking something off of papers on a clipboard.

"Do you ever take a break?"

She hadn't heard him coming and whipped her head up quickly, her hair covering her face. She wiped it away and smiled. "You stalking me?"

"If I was, you wouldn't know it." By the look on Amy's face, she thought he was being serious. "I'd probably hire someone else to do it for me. Who needs all that creeping around. Besides, my wife is the pro photographer – better trained in stalking."

"I'm just checking the list of riders. Everyone's been accounted for except Kira. You were first to get a little red checkmark by your name. Thanks again for all your help. I don't know how to repay you."

"Give me my entry fee back." This time she took it as a joke when he was being serious. He sighed. "Have they told you where Kira was last spotted? I've seen plenty of photos of her but has she changed her look recently?"

"She left for a lap and one of the other pros saw her just before Dead Man's Gulp."

Keely's skin tingled. Dead Man's Gulp was a monster descent at a radically steep angle. It was one of his favourite parts of the course. "That's halfway through a lap, right?"

"About that, yeah."

"Did this rider say she was okay? Did she look stressed or in trouble or hurt?"

"He said she passed him. She was flying, I think that was his exact phrasing."

"And that was the last person to see her?"

"Yeah. That's what I heard."

"She have any recent injuries?"

Amy dropped the clipboard to her side and leaned against a barrier. "If you want to know about Kira Bremner, you should go to her team's camp. The horse's mouth, so to speak."

"Good point. You'll be around, right?"

"Listen, there's something you should know before you head over there."

* * * *

Twenty-four-hour riders needed their campsite to be right off the course. When a rider approached their camp they could simply duck off the course, take on water and food, switch bikes, if they had more than one, or rest. When they accomplished any or all of that, they hopped back on the course and rode through the start/finish. There they would dismount their bike and walk it through the transition zone – a covered area that housed a small scanner. Each rider would pass a small, flat, laminated card over the scanner to record their lap time.

For Keely, it didn't really matter. His camp was a few hundred feet down from the alley. Between his site and the start of the alley resided all of the pro soloists' campsites. Even though Keely did these races for fun and never expected to win, he was always envious of the pros. Everything they wore, rode, drank, ate — it was all the best money could buy.

Body Fuel was a company that made energy drinks, supplements and bars. A very big sponsor of pro cycling, they'd recently made the jump to mountain biking. Everyone knows Lance Armstrong, but they might think that Tinker Jarez was a golfer. However, mountain biking revolutionized the cycling industry, allowing more people access to more comfortable bikes. Keely and every other mountain bike enthusiast cringed at the sight of an out of shape man or woman trudging a beautiful mountain bike up a road. Mountain bikes were meant to be off-road. But, more people were riding, more people paid attention to the sport since its inclusion in the '96 Olympics and, most importantly to Body Fuel, more people were buying energy drinks.

Body Fuel's new drink was lemon-flavoured, thus the team was currently known as Drink Pink. The twelve-foot-tall tent was pink, the chairs scattered in the vestibule were pink, pink bikes on work stands and more hanging on what looked like a clothesline. It was over the top. The jealousy and admiration Keely had felt for these pros evaporated when he got closer to the tent. There were lights on inside and it glowed pink in the dark.

"Hello. Is anyone home?"

"Go away," a woman said from inside the pink.

"I'm sorry to bother you. I'm Detective McAdam and I just have a few questions."

The tent flap opened and a young woman in a loose pink T-shirt and jeans stood there looking bewildered. Keely couldn't tell if she had hair, half because of the light and half because of the Drink Pink cap she wore. She was obviously upset. Her lips were pursed and her forehead was wrinkled as if she were in deep concentration.

"Come in."

Keely stopped the tent flap from slapping him when the woman let it go. He entered a spacious tent housing two cots, two chairs that still had room enough to move around without bending or walking into anything. The woman motioned to one of the folding chairs and Keely sat.

"I've already told you everything I know. I don't know what else I can do."

"Sarah Stokes, right?"

"Yes, that's me."

"I'm very sorry for your loss. I promise we'll get to the bottom of this."

She was suddenly irate. "There is no way Todd fell. No way in hell. He's the best. He's Mr. Clean. She killed him. I swear if you find her I'll kill her—"

Keely was standing before he even realized it and moved quickly to kneel in front of the distraught woman. Her hands were clenched together in her lap in some vicious prayer. He gently glided his hands over her forearms. "Easy, Sarah. Take a deep breath. Can I get you some water?"

Tears spilled down her cheeks, a few dropping onto Keely's wrists. "No. I'm fine. I'm sorry. I just can't believe he's gone."

"Is there anyone you can spend time with? A friend you can talk to, even on the phone. It might help."

She huffed. "I used to talk to Kira all the time. But now …"

Keely moved his hands up Sarah's arms to her shoulders and gave them a reassuring grip. "You okay?"

"Yeah. I'll be okay."

He moved back to his seat. "Sarah, can you answer a few questions for me, please? I promise, only a few."

She nodded.

"How long have you and Todd been together?"

She struggled to breathe let alone talk. Finally she said, "Just over a year."

"Why would you think Kira had something to do with his death?"

Sarah's voice rose to a high pitch. "She said I stole him from her. I didn't do that. They broke up months before me and Todd got together. I was on a different team back then. We were friends. We'd talk about all kinds of shit. She helped me out, you know."

"You were a rookie and she showed you the ropes?"

"Yeah. She was great. And so was Todd."

"Even though they were on a different team they still helped you out?"

"Sponsors are checkbooks. They throw money at you and figure if they spend enough you'll win and they get the big sales. They don't have a clue what we do when they're not around. Besides, we weren't hurting anyone. We raced hard. We raced even harder when I joined the team."

"What do you mean?"

For the first time Keely noticed a water bottle on the floor by Sarah's chair. She drank from it and put it back down.

"Kira is tough. Ask any of the girls, they'll tell you the same thing. Kira would do anything to win. She'd run you off a cliff—"

"You think she ran Todd off a cliff to beat him?"

"No. She ran him off the cliff because he loved me and not her. She hated us. She barely spoke to us once we got together. We tried to smooth things out with her but she would just yell and call us filthy names. I swear she killed Todd."

"So you don't think she's lost or hurt or worse. You think she's on the run."

"She killed Todd and now she's trying to get away," she said, her hands balling into fists. "You should be out there looking for her."

Chapter 5

He walked out on a waking world. The sun was coming up, the sky showed it. Keely headed toward the alley, churning everything through his mind that Sarah Stokes had just told him, and writing down as much of the information as he could in his little note pad. He banked a corner and entered the long row of bright signage.

"Dude. C'mere."

Dude?

Keely turned to see a thin man, skin stretched over sinewy muscle, covered in tattoos. His hair was, well, just there, jutting out wherever the hell it liked. As Keely got closer to where the guy was standing on the other side of one of the barriers, a Drink Pink sign hanging from it, he could see his hair was blue. Mostly blue, with black roots. More disturbing was the amount of metal in this guy's face. He had bolts in his lips, nose, eyelids, and some kind of metal rings that sat in his earlobes. Keely could see the forest through the holes they made in his ears.

"Did you call me dude?"

"Whatever, copper. I heard you flapping with Sarah. She's wrong, dude."

"First, my name is Keely. Second, who the hell are you and why were you eavesdropping?"

"Name's Pepe, pleased to meet you." He reached a hand over the barrier and Keely shook it. "I was breaking down the bikes, Keely-dude. That's when I heard you and Sarah. Kira wouldn't kill anyone, man."

"You must be the team wrench?"

"Fuck no! I'm the team god, man. I'm an artist. These spoiled jerks would be riding junk if it wasn't for my gifts."

"My apologies. I'm sure you're very good at what you do."

"Apology accepted. I make shit happen for them. I make choices that win them races, man."

"Again, I'm really sorry. I didn't mean to offend. So, you don't think Kira had anything to do with Todd going over that cliff?"

"Mr. Clean was a good guy. He was the only one who'd thank me. He understood the art. He even got his hands dirty once in a while. Very cool dude. And no way he fell. He was too good to go out like that. He had help but it wasn't Kira."

"Why do you say that?"

Pepe looked around as if he expected to be caught doing something he shouldn't be. "She was an amazing rider, Keely-dude. You don't win four championships and dozens of races because you suck, you know?"

"I hear ya."

"She took her riding seriously. Shit on me if she thought I got the bike set up wrong. I never did but she was too intense to argue with. I'd just pretend to do what she asked and do it my way. She kept winning so I kept doing my thing."

"Was she dirty?"

"No way, Keely-dude. She'd ride you hard, stay on your wheel until you made a mistake, but she'd never shove you. Not on purpose anyway."

"How do you know all this? You ride with her?"

"People talk and tents are thin. Anyway, there's more video on Kira than any other female rider since she's a champ and all. Shit, Athens Olympics had more cameras than Fort Knox, baby. Check the tapes, Keely-dude. She even helped other riders when they went down."

* * * *

The sun was cresting the tree line as Keely reached his tent. It was time to rise and he felt like it was midnight. He hadn't slept. He'd rested for a few minutes between laps, but he never slept. He must have unzipped his tent without realizing it because the next thing he knew he was zipping it back up from the inside. It smelled musty and everything felt damp, but once inside his sleeping bag, none of that mattered.

He pushed a few buttons on his watch, the beeps confirming his choices, then lay on his back looking up at the soft glow of blue nylon. He'd made a stop at the Body Fuel sponsor's booth. There was a huge area in a field near the hut that had been mowed specifically for all of the sponsors to set up tables or tents or whatever contraptions they could think of to sell their wares. Drink Pink was dead centre and the biggest tent. Though the colour alone made it the easiest to spot.

Keely had walked through four-wheel-drive vehicle areas where you could test drive the latest model. He negotiated a course of more bike dealers than he'd ever seen at a race before. Energy drinks and bars, clothing, bike accessories, and there was even a tent where you could get a shiatsu massage. It was tempting, but he was on a mission.

There were few people at their stations and many of the tent flaps were closed. Pink was no different, but as a former cop Keely figured he had an advantage. It wasn't breaking and entering, it was investigating.

He'd slipped under the tarp unnoticed, popped on his flashlight and the rosy glare nearly blinded him. Everything seemed to be pink; shirts, hats, sweaters, pants. Drink Pink cups, travel mugs, shot glasses, beer steins, coasters, playing cards — it was magnificently ridiculous.

Keely had moved from row to row of merchandise and never found what he was looking for – DVDs of Kira's races. There were no videos of any kind, so Keely left the way he came.

"Find what you were looking for?" A woman said from behind him.

"No, I didn't." Keely flashed his badge. "I'm Detective McAdam. I was hoping to get my hands on some video of Kira Bremner."

"Why do you want that?"

Keely'd retired, but he wasn't about to switch roles just yet. "Who are you?" He'd practiced a steely gaze he felt would unnerve people and it seemed to work on this girl.

"I'm a rider. Why you stealing stuff from that tent?"

Keely knew the girl was a rider by her physique – lean, muscular, long arms and legs. She had short spiky red hair and wore loose-fitting black pants and a grey sweatshirt with the logo *Kickers* on it. When he saw that, it could be only one person, Denise Helwig. She looked different on television and on her posters. More polished. In this light she looked like every other camper in the park, tired and dirty.

"Ms. Helwig, I was looking for video evidence of Kira Bremner. Anything I'd found I would have either purchased or returned. I found no such evidence and as you can see," Keely said, then lifted his arms. "I'm not concealing any stolen goods."

"Ms. Helwig? What're you, like, forty?"

Keely flipped over in his sleeping bag, that comment still stinging. He guessed after zinging him it must have put her in a talkative mood because she'd been pretty forthcoming after that. She spoke of her and Kira's battles on and off their bikes.

"Since the Olympics, she's been a real bitch."

"How so?"

"Like a bitch. Duh."

"Can you be specific?"

"Well, on the bike, she was meaner than ever. Shit, we used to pedal stroke for stroke and hammer the hell out of each other on the bike. Kira is the toughest rider I ever raced. After 2004, she got cranky. Hell, she cut me off once and I slammed into her rear wheel. I endoed and landed against a tree. A little piece of the branch left on the trunk, you know, like a spike, it stabbed me between my ribs. Hurt like hell."

Keely stirred in his sleeping bag again, an image of Denise Helwig squirting blood from her back making him queasy.

"Kira said sorry after the race, but I could tell she didn't mean it. Her face was deadpan, man. Nothing. No emotion. So I guess I'm the one responsible for us bitching off the bike, 'cause anytime I see her, I call her a bitch. She doesn't like that too much."

She'd shared more horror stories of Kira kicking riders and bumping them off their bikes. Still, Kira was apparently a bit of an enigma because on training rides, every so often she would stop and help riders who'd fallen, or give up her hydration pack to a rider who was out of water. Spur of the moment kindnesses out of a sea of bad blood.

"I still hate her though," Helwig had said. "You don't get over getting stabbed by a tree too easily."

Keely rolled onto his back, new questions floating through his head brought on by these early morning conversations. How old was Kira Bremner? How did she get along with Todd Watkins, her former lover and still teammate? Was Denise Helwig the only person who saw a change in Kira since the Olympics in 2004? Most importantly, where the hell was Kira Bremner now? Was she on the run because she had killed Todd or was she, too, the victim of foul play? Did a bear or some other wild animal just drag her body away?

Keely answered that one quickly. It was unlikely because wild animals would not have dragged away her bike, too. Kira did not fall off the cliff with Todd, of that he was certain.

His body sent a wave of aches from his calves to his stomach that Keely couldn't ignore. He rubbed his legs for a minute and felt his muscles relax. He curled into a ball and tugged his sleeping bag tight around his shoulders. One last deep breath and long exhale and he'd be nearing slumber. His head was full but floaty, as if air had somehow seeped in through his ears. It was a pleasant feeling, like the moment of a perfect buzz, just before you have one beer too many. His eyelids were so heavy and trying to open them just added to the serenity.

The trill was deafening in the quiet country morning and Keely desperately hit buttons on his watch to shut off the alarm. Then he got a good look at the time — he'd only been lying down for a few minutes. What the hell was so loud?

He grabbed at his shorts and found the little folded up metallic cell phone and flipped it open.

"Hello."

"Well, good morning to you, too, sunshine."

"Elise, honey, I'm tired. Call me later."

"Okay, but John wanted me to send you his regards."

Keely flashed back to the coroner's wink. "Good man that John Krull, don't you think?"

"He would grab my ass if this was nineteen-sixty and if he undresses me with his eyes one more time I'm making him a soprano, but other than that, yeah, good guy."

"He got to you pretty fast."

"I got a call about a half hour ago. He's on his way back to Toronto. He's waiting for the forensic boys to finish up with Todd Something."

"Watkins."

"That's him. John wants me there when the body arrives to document the autopsy. Could probably have called a few other guys but they're guys, ya know?"

"Elise, what did John tell you?"

"It doesn't bother you that he looks at my ass so much?"

"No. What did he say?"

"God, you need some sleep because you should be upset at his—"

"Elise, for fuck sake—"

"Okay. I was joking around. Remember, this is just from his initial look. He's gotta put the body on ice – bad weekend for deaths. He should have the autopsy done by Monday, Tuesday the latest. So Todd's major injuries were suffered in the fall. He broke his neck and his spine. He suffered several lacerations on his neck, shoulders, back and the backs of his legs. Definitely hit the ground back first."

"I knew it."

"Yeah, yeah. You're the best," she said flatly. "What he was most interested in was Todd's busted nose and a cut just above his brow. Bruising indicates a blow of some kind. John was leaving it to the forensic guys to collect, but he pulled a sliver out of the cut, so he's pretty sure it was a piece of wood, like something off a branch."

"He wasn't even riding when he got hit. It was a baseball bat kinda swing that sent him over the edge I'll bet."

"If you say so. Hey, that's about it. I gotta go get beautiful so I'll talk to you soon."

"Wait. John didn't say anything about evidence of a second body, did he?"

"Nope. I told ya what he told me. That's it. And you didn't hear it from me or him, right, copper?"

"I love you. Oh, and I need you to pick me up a few DVDs."

"Honey, aren't I good enough for you? You need porn now?"

"Not yet. Maybe in a few more years. No, I need any video you can find on Kira Bremner. See what you can do, please?"

"I must love you or something. I'll check our video store. Call ya later."

"Bye, honey."

* * * *

The little beeping was right next to his ear. *That* is my watch. He eventually hit the right button to shut off the alarm and propped himself up on an elbow. He checked his watch again to make sure of the time. It was seven a.m. The tent was hot like a mild sauna and Keely scrambled out of the sleeping bag. He lay there naked for a few minutes.

"A few hours of sleep and I feel as good as I did before I went to sleep."

People were moving around outside his tent. A lot of people. He quickly grabbed whatever clothes were handy and threw them on. He groaned on the way out of his tent, the entrance so low it made him crawl on his hands and knees. He spun back around and zipped up the mesh opening, his jealousy of the pro team's tents back full-force.

"They found her." Amy was trotting up to him, her face flushed and her eyes redder than her cheeks. "They found Kira's body."

She collapsed against him in a dead faint.

Chapter 6

He'd carried her, like a fireman carrying a victim from a burning building, over his shoulder, to the first aid tent. She'd wakened with a start as if the young medic had thrown water on her face rather than placing a cold cloth on her forehead.

Once Keely knew the medic would force Amy to rest, he ran back to his tent and put on his riding shoes. His hiking shorts and white T-shirt, though a blind grab, were just fine. The shoes were the only thing that would feel comfortable against his small pedals.

He quickly tied his laces and jumped to his feet, ran behind his tent and grabbed his bike from its resting place against a pine tree (apparently *not* a jumping pine). Snapping his shoes into his pedals reminded him of the pain in his right ankle. The swelling had subsided, so whatever had happened, it was deep. He'd ride by the first aid tent later and have it checked out. He swung onto the course and pedalled through the alley and timing tent, then made a sharp right heading south to the hut; if a body was found that is where he'd get the scoop on it.

A hint of red tinged everything and Keely heard his wife's excited voice from some past early morning excursion saying, "Sweet light." This, according to Elise, was a magical time for photographers because the light made everything warmer. Keely had no idea what she was talking about and her saying that a bag of nails would look great in the sweet light didn't help. He just didn't see things the same way. Bright, harsh light had been sweet to Keely because it helped reveal tiny little clues. Nothing was sweeter than to find some fiber or blood spot or minute traces of dirt, something that put a guilty person away for a while or, better, for good.

He pushed down on his handlebars and compressed the shocks of his bike then pulled up hard with his hands and feet; both of the bike's wheels left the ground simultaneously to sail over a small log. When the bike landed Keely pedalled hard to coast down a hill. He could see the complex of buildings a few hundred yards away. His thoughts drifted back to the guilty he'd been able to get off the streets. Too few by his calculations. Finding evidence didn't always result in the guilty going to jail. At least Harper wasn't going to see the light of day for a long time. Keely shivered at the memory of seeing Janet Harper's body crumpled at her father's feet. The back of her head a cavity. He'd had no choice. He'd had to go in that apartment.

His bike stopped dead, and he flew over the handlebars. Before he knew what he'd hit he was coming out of a roll on loose gravel. He stood up quickly and heard clapping from somewhere to his right. A pair of OPP cops were laughing and applauding him. Keely realized he'd hit a parking stave, the long cement blocks used to separate the lot into rows. Another rider, a complete stranger, rode up to him and skidded to a stop in the parking lot of the main complex.

"Shit, man. I thought you were going to bunny hop that thing, but you drove right into it. You okay?"

He looked at the girl and instead of seeing another anonymous rider, he saw Janet Harper's young, innocent face.

"Hey, you okay, mister?"

The girl's bright, red-tinged face looked concerned and Keely nodded.

"You sure?"

She was wearing too much makeup, he thought, especially at this time in the morning. "I'm good. I wasn't paying attention."

"You better get someone to pick the gravel out of your back. You're bleeding," she said and rode away.

He went back and picked up his bike. To his dismay, he'd tacoed the front wheel. It was severely bent out of shape. She had broken spokes and the tire was toast.

"Nice riding," one of the cops said.

"Yeah," the other added. "I wish I had a video camera. I might've won some cash for that crash."

Keely eyed the cops like they were about to jump him. Take off the uniform and they'd look like guys outside a bar. "Did you find Kira?"

"Nah. It was a hiker we've been looking for since January."

"Yeah, only found parts of him."

"The good parts though."

"The identifiable parts, anyway."

Keely wanted to punch them both. "Any word on Kira?"

The tougher-looking cop took a step closer. "You'll have to check at the shack. We're going home. Shift's over."

"Have fun riding your bicycle," the other one said and they both laughed.

Keely watched them walk away and knew he'd be a story in their squad room for months. It didn't matter. They were blowing off steam. He'd done it, too, when he was on the job. An image of Janet Harper's body flashed in his mind. He quickly shouldered his broken bike and walked to the hut.

He left it leaning against a wall just outside the front door. His ankle felt great, since the new pain all down the right side of his back was on fire. Road rash had that effect no matter where you got it – searing hot pain for days at a time. He didn't even want to think about the next time he showered.

The foyer of the main building, a large, open octagonal area well lit by a series of skylights, was obviously set up to handle the volunteers. Whiteboards on stands had names written in groups, with each group assigned an area identified by a letter and number. Keely knew that the simple letter and number system would correspond to a chart with exact coordinates of the area being searched by each team. It was efficient and organized. The two most important elements in finding the missing. Time was always a factor and though not an outdoorsy kind of guy, it didn't take a genius to figure out that the elements in the north didn't help the situation. Low temperatures at night, quickly changing weather, plus the added risk of animal interference were constant threats.

Keely was impressed with Robitaille's operation. He'd be more impressed if he could walk up and shake hands with Kira Bremner.

"Mr. McAdam?" asked a boy of a man. He had dimples and perfect teeth and did not suit his black OPP uniform.

Keely nodded.

"Right this way."

He followed the kid through the building into a room lit red by early morning sunshine.

"McAdam, sit," Robitaille said, indicating a chair in front of his temporary desk. "That will be all Berard."

"Sir. The gentleman is bleeding."

Keely swung to face Berard. "I know. I'm okay."

"Holy shit. What'd you do, fight a bear?" asked Robitaille.

"Nope. I lost my concentration and did an endo in the parking lot."

"What the hell is an endo?"

"End over end. Don't worry about it. What's the news on Kira Bremner?"

Robitaille shuffled a few papers on his flimsy desk and breathed heavily through his nose. "Heard we found a body, eh. It wasn't her. It was a—"

"Hiker you've been looking for since January. I know. What about the girl?"

"I knew you'd want to keep your nose in all this. Well, don't. We haven't found her and I don't want you doing anything stupid."

"What the hell are you talkin' about? I can look for her like any other volunteer can't I?"

Robitaille stood up quickly, his cheap metal-legged chair scraping the linoleum. "I don't want you anywhere around this investigation. You can't be a cop anymore, so why keep trying? Retired, bullshit."

"I am retired. No one forced me to quit."

"You were assigned to a desk for shit's sake," Robitaille said, spittle flying from his mouth. "You were not fit for duty. What makes you think I want you anyplace around these cases, huh?" His French-Canadian accent increased with his ire.

Keely lowered his head and took a few deep breaths, more to give the situation time to cool than to calm himself. He lifted his head slowly and made sure his face showed no sign of aggression.

"That was almost two years ago. I've dealt with it. I can help you find that girl and whoever killed Todd Watkins. I know I can help you."

Robitaille walked around the desk and sat on the front edge, looking down at Keely. "Protocol says that you stay put, everybody does, until this park is reopened. So we're stuck here. Listen very closely to what I am about to say because it could mean freedom or jail time. Are you listening carefully?"

Keely nodded.

"I don't care who asks you to help. Even if it is the goddamned prime minister himself. If I catch you investigating this case, I will have you arrested."

Keely left that little room knowing two things. Robitaille had eaten already — there were crumbs in his moustache — and Keely would be spending some time in jail in the next day or two.

* * * *

"How you feeling? Ow!"

"Better than you," Amy said from her cot, a cold compress resting on her head and one shoved behind her neck. "Where do you get road rash in the middle of the forest?"

"They don't call me Crash for nothing."

She laughed and looked much better to Keely.

"For an old guy, you got some muscle."

"What do you mean *some*? Ow!" Keely shot a look over his shoulder at the medic who was working on getting the gravel out of his hide. "What are you doing back there, taking out my spine?"

"Sorry, but there are a few deep ones," the medic said. "Almost done."

Amy sat up to the creaking of the cot.

"You look better," Keely said. "How do you feel?"

"To be honest, like hell."

"Listen, I had a conversation with my wife and I know for a fact that the report..." Keely turned to the medic. "Could you give us a few minutes please?"

The medic left the tent, glancing back at the door and then ducking through it.

"Todd Watkins was definitely murdered," Keely said, keeping his voice low. "Coroner's initial report to me was that he was hit in the head with something, a heavy stick or branch, and I'm sure that's what sent him over the cliff."

"That poor man. Why the hell would anyone want to hurt him? He was so nice, Keely. I mean it. A real gentleman, too. I feel terrible about it." Her hands shot up to cover her mouth, which apparently kept her from crying.

"I'm working up a few theories already. Don't worry, we'll find out who did it."

She nodded and dabbed under her eye with a bent knuckle. "Sorry."

"No need. Perfectly understandable. Hey, what was that whole CCA thing about?"

Keely heard the puff of air escape the orange juice bottle when Amy twisted the cap off. She held it out to him but he shook his head. She took a big gulp.

"Is this your first twenty-four-hour event?" she asked.

"Nah. I've been doing them for a few years now."

"I've been promoting these events for a dozen years and there are three other promoters in Canada doing similar events. Though I truly believe that All Day Long is the best-run 24-hour race in North America. Besides Ontario, I've got races in B.C., Alberta, California, Arizona and New York."

"I agree with you. I've entered a few others and this one is by far the most organized and best run."

"Thanks. I appreciate that," she said unscrewing the top on the bottle and taking another drink. "For a lot of years pro riders did these races for fun and training rather than to earn any money. Hell, sponsors wouldn't even pay them to be here and some told their riders to stay away because if they got hurt they wouldn't be covered for medical or get paid. We were just these fun events that mostly weekend warriors showed up to and that was okay. I had a bright idea about five years ago to offer up some decent prizes. I showed a few companies the enrolment numbers of previous events and they jumped on my wagon with both feet."

"I read the winning solo male and female riders this year were getting fifty-grand apiece. I was amazed. That's big money."

"My numbers have gone up steadily every year. I hire more staff, we put on a bigger and better event, I get more sponsors, everything is going great. You want to know how I got this park to open its doors to me?"

"Everybody does. This is Algonquin Park. A national treasure."

"I got wind they were putting in a series of looping hiking trails. It all started with that poor hiker that got lost in January. I feel so bad for him. Anyway, they wanted these trails put in and I said I'd pay for the creation of the trails and they could put in the signage. It cost me a fortune to get trail builders in here and we were watched every second by naturalists and biologists and wardens. It was a nightmare. But it was worth it, because once the trail was in I had exclusive rights to the races held here."

"Your competitors would have been pretty pissed about that, eh."

"Oh yeah. I've even gotten death threats. Two of the other promoters are on the verge of going out of business. One, Active Sports International, they're doing okay. They seem to be keeping pace with me."

"So what does all this have to do with the Canadian Cycling Association?"

She finished taking another gulp of juice and said, "Points. Sanctioning one of the promoter's events."

"Wow. That would bring in more pro cyclists and way more sponsors and way more—"

"Money!"

He dropped his head in his hands.

"What's wrong?"

"Money. The leading cause of death due to murder."

Chapter 7

His broken bike on his shoulder like a wounded soldier, Keely made the hike of shame back to his campsite. The few people he passed looked sympathetic to his plight and his bike's injuries and that made him feel a bit better. It was when he was passing the Drink Pink site that he suddenly felt a lot better.

"Keely, dude. I can fix that."

Pepe not only offered to fix his bike, but he gave Keely one of the pro's bikes as a loaner. The only downer was that it had "Mr. Clean" painted on the top tube near the seat. It was obviously Todd Watkins' ride, and what a ride it was. Keely was well aware of the top level bikes, had even touched a few at the last bike show in Toronto, but to be on one, it was exhilarating. His ass was on the seat of the very top of the Specialized mountain bike heap, a company renowned for its innovations.

The S-Works had a super-light carbon frame. Keely didn't even want to guess at the price tag. He could probably buy a good used car for the price of the bike he was riding. When he'd balked at taking the loaner, Pepe had read his mind.

"Don't worry about wrecking it, man. I can fix anything. If not, we got enough parts to build ten more bikes. Go rip up some shit."

It was a few hundred feet to his campsite and he felt as if he were gliding on air. He clicked down a few gears and barely heard a sound when the chain leapt from cog to cog. Keely clicked up several gears, stood and hammered hard on the pedals. The bike stayed as level as if he were sitting in the saddle and gently pedalling.

He deftly steered the bike around his tent, unclipped his feet and gently leaned the bike against the pine tree. He took a few steps back to admire the beauty of this machine. A high gloss black with red highlights, the silver and gold of the components were like added jewellery. Keely believed the bicycle was truly an ingenious invention. It was accessible to all, there's a bike to fit every budget. You don't need a license to ride a bike, all you have to do is practice. It truly changed the way people lived. It had changed the way he lived. It was his escape.

Heat touched the back of his neck from the rising sun and Keely felt his stomach grumble. People were milling about their camps, probably back from a shift of searching for Kira. Once his stomach was full, he'd ride out and check a few things that were on his mind.

He didn't feel like building a fire or starting his small, tabletop barbeque, so he settled for peanut butter and jelly sandwiches, a breakfast bar and some juice. After cleaning up he poured water onto a hand towel and gave himself a wipe where any skin was exposed. He could feel the gauze taped to his back and was pleasantly surprised at how little his road rash was bothering him. His ankle wasn't bothering him, either. Still, he'd get it checked out when he got a chance.

He climbed into his little tent and changed into his riding gear. He emerged after straightening things up inside only to do the same around the site. Hydration pack filled with water and ice, he popped his helmet on and felt the cold, wet strip of lining press against his forehead. The knowledge that cold sweat was now seeping back into his skin, even though it was his own, made his body tense. He donned his riding gloves, padded on the palms for extra comfort, and threw his leg over the bar of the S-Works. He pushed off and before he could even clip his left foot into his pedal, he gripped the brake lever and stopped.

A well-groomed man of no more than twenty-five was standing beside his tent, smiling. Keely instantly thought the guy was plastic – a Ken Doll.

"Well, how are you, Detective McAdam? It is a pleasure to meet you," the man said, his tone more like a sales pitch than a greeting. He walked over and placed a hand in Keely's, shook and released it. He took a step back and smiled too brightly, the glare from his teeth matching that of his yellow polo shirt. Keely wished he could keep his eyes on the guy's cream-coloured shorts – though cuffed and sharply pressed, they were easiest on his vision.

"I'm good. I was just—"

"My name is Steven Bishop, vice-president of promotions for Body Fuel, and I was hoping we could have a word?"

"Well, unless I run you over, I guess I don't have a choice. What can I do for you, kid?" Bull's-eye. The guy flinched for a millisecond.

"Detective, I know that you're aware we have one expired employee and another who is missing."

Expired? Employees?

"We are gravely concerned about our employee and wish to do everything in our power to ensure her safe return."

"I'm sure you do. I can feel the love."

"Yes, of course," Bishop said, tilting his head and raising an eyebrow. "Don't let my demeanour fool you, detective. I am, as is the rest of management, upset and worried about Kira. We want nothing less than her to be unharmed and safely returned to us."

Keely leaned forward, resting his forearms on his handlebars. "Can you get to the point, please?"

"Find Kira Bremner and we will pay you what the winners were to receive at this race."

Keely stopped breathing.

"She is an asset to our company. A champion. A winner. Our demographic of women from 35 to 50 are in love with her and tied to that is a love for her accomplishments. The more she wins the more they want to emulate her. If a thirty-five-year-old woman can be that good using Body Fuel products, then so can they. It is a costly but very effective connection for our company."

"Ah, yes, the product and sales and margins and shit I don't care anything about. What I care about is people, not bottom lines. And, as much as I'd love to pull in that kind of coin, I think I'll pass." Keely clipped a foot into his pedal and pushed forward, the bike held back by his pull on the brake levers.

"Kira is worth far more than we pay her. We've put millions of dollars into her and our business. To start over would be devastating to us. Our competitors would eat us alive. Please, detective. We need your help."

Keely huffed. "Next you're going to tell me you'll pay me whatever I want."

"Name your price."

Keely rolled his eyes and shook his head. "Kid, I mean this exactly the way it sounds. You are a heartless corporate drone who only sees dollar signs. Fuck off."

Unfortunately, Bishop managed to move out of the way when Keely let go of the brakes and rolled by him.

"Please come by our camper any time to discuss this, detective."

* * * *

The race course was still marked and Keely flew through the first few kilometres wishing he'd been wealthy enough to afford such an amazing bike. He always thought that proper fitting equipment was the most important, not how much you paid for it. He was wrong. You get what you pay for. He realized that high-end stuff enhanced one's abilities. If you were fast, a good bike made you faster. If you could climb, you climbed better on a high-end machine. Fit was probably the most important factor in choosing equipment, but higher quality was now on Keely's radar.

Elise was not going to like that. *"Honey, I found this amazing ten-thousand-dollar bike."* Keely flew around a tight bend in single track he'd been riding for a few minutes now. He knew Elise would kill him if he even suggested spending that kind of cash, but she'd let him push the budget a bit if it was important to him.

The old adage of drink before you're thirsty was appropriate since Keely felt his core temperature rising. He was easily a third of the way through the two litres of water in his pack. He slowed his pace until he recognized a dropoff he loved, then he hammered hard on the pedals; the S-Works seemed to be alive and as excited about the drop as he was.

Keely spied his line through some rock outcroppings then looked ahead on the trail for the launching point. A smattering of trees lined both sides of the trail right up to the edge of the dropoff. He used the trees to estimate where he'd be pulling up hard on the handlebars and quickly approached it. Cresting the rise through the rocks he spotted the edge of the drop and weighted the suspension. He pushed down on the handlebars to load the suspension and drove hard through the last pedal stroke then pulled back hard on the handlebars. He needn't have. The suspension was so tuned it snapped back and launched the front wheel sufficiently in the air so it stayed level with the back wheel, which was still on terra firma. Once the back wheel left the rocky ground both wheels descended simultaneously, the back wheel hitting the ground just before the front. Keely leaned slightly back to prevent any chance of going over the handlebars.

A six-foot drop and Keely barely felt the landing. He couldn't stop smiling. If he wasn't careful, someone might notice the tent in his shorts.

He had never ridden so fast in his life. The ten kilometres of trail to the cliff face went by too quickly. He approached the cliff from the long, flat section of the course, thankful that he could rest before attempting the climb that hours ago had sent him tumbling down the steep slope to eventually find Todd Watkins' body.

He felt a responsibility to him, a man he'd never met and only seen on television. Mr. Clean may very well have passed Keely on the trails, but Keely'd never be able to tell since he'd had a few things on his mind, like trying to stay upright. He was going to do what he could for Mr. Clean, but he also knew that by helping Todd, he'd be helping Kira. Keely felt that.

He stopped on the trail twenty feet from where the yellow tape wound through tree trunks, as if holding them together. He unclipped his shoes, hopped off the bike and walked toward the first tree. This was the jumping-off spot. If you wanted to get to the cliff face, this is where you'd leave the trail. He scanned the ground as he walked. He found nothing. Well, he found the footprints and tire tracks of the dozens of people who'd headed this way for the cliff and a look at Todd's body.

He picked up the pace slightly, jogging, and marvelled at how easy it felt to walk the S-Works. There were several people standing near the cliff, all in bike gear, bikes lying on their sides behind them. When Keely looked at the single- and double-digit numbers on their race plates, he knew these were all professional riders. He secretly thanked Pepe for removing Todd's number plate before lending him the dead man's machine. Keely lay his bike down amongst the rest and walked to the cliff's edge.

Looking over, he could see two officers in white coveralls taking samples from two different parts of the scene. These officers would be specially trained as crime scene investigators. Their responsibility was to collect physical evidence which would then be transported to Forensic Identification Services in Toronto, where a specialist would examine it. He knew Todd's body would have been removed by now, but the tarp had been left up to help protect any evidence that might be there. He watched a female officer grabbing rocks with a pair of tongs and carefully placing them in a plastic bag.

Keely recognized one of the cyclists standing beside him as Daniele Biatola, a man who'd ridden in several Tour de France races and other road events before being lured to mountain biking by a soft-drink sponsor. He was thick, all muscle and black hair. He was more like a European linebacker than a cyclist. The others looked familiar, but Keely couldn't put any names to faces.

"Hey, cop."

Keely turned to see Biatola looking right at him.

"Todd and me, we were not close, but I did not do this," he said then turned and walked to his bike. He mounted her and rode away.

The skinny man who'd been standing next to the big Italian chuckled. "Somebody got up on the guilty conscience side of the bed this morning."

Shit. Keely'd forgotten his note pad.

Chapter 8

"Mr. McAdam?"

Keely spun to see George Arnsberg trotting across the rock, most of which made up the top of the cliff. Keely thought the brawny man was wearing a dark cap until he realized it was his Moe-of-the-Three-Stooges hair.

"What're you doing here, Mr. McAdam?"

"What're *you* doing here, Mr. Arnsberg?"

"I work here."

"I *walk* here."

Arnsberg paused and furrowed his brow. "No, you crawl here. You're not supposed to be poking around."

Keely realized that being on his hands and knees crawling around the rock and dirt with his face a few inches from the ground might give one the impression that he was indeed "poking around."

"Who's poking around?"

"You are."

"I lost a contact."

"Oh. Let me help."

"No! If you come any closer you might step on it. Go away, I got it covered."

Arnsberg didn't move. He just stood there with his arms folded across his chest and resting on his bulge of a stomach.

"Tell Nadal that you checked up on me and that I'm not causing any trouble. That's why you're here, right?"

"Yeah, but somehow I don't trust you. I get the feeling that you're the type of guy who opens his Christmas presents and reseals them."

Keely scrunched his face and wondered what the hell the warden was talking about.

"Whatever. Have you found Kira yet?"

The warden's face softened and Keely swore the guy was ready to break down and cry.

"No. Not yet. All the cars are accounted for. You know, it would be useless to count the people in the park. They come and go from sites so often that we'd miscount for sure. Plus, we have interior campers that are a few days' hike from here."

"Could someone hike out of this park in a few hours?"

Arnsberg brightened. He must have felt good that Keely wanted his expert opinion.

"If they were already camping close to a border of the park, sure. But, from here, this cliff, no way. I know we're pretty close to Highway 60, but even if someone got to that road, they'd have to make it through the checkpoints and blockades on both ends where it meets the park."

"So someone couldn't have grabbed Kira and gotten to the highway before we noticed she was missing?"

Arnsberg sucked on his lower lip and blinked a few times. "No. Her last lap started at 11:12. Then it was about one in the morning when they made the call that she was missing. Hell, they got concerned about 12:30, 'cause this girl can do a quick lap. We had all-terrains out looking for her by then in case she was injured. There is no way anyone could have gotten her to the highway in an hour and half."

"It's rough terrain, no question about that." Keely's knees were hurting, so he stood up. Arnsberg remained about ten paces away, the forest behind him, cliff to Keely's left. The numerous possibilities flew through his head. "No one saw her after she left for that last lap?"

"Well, the last person to see her was a rider that said she passed him with ease. He couldn't say what time, but it was a few kilometres back in the course from here. They figure at her pace, that would have been about ten or five to midnight."

"So that would have been an hour to get her out of the park before it was shut down. Any way—"

"Not a chance. Just over five kilometres through thick forest to get to the highway."

The beefy warden seemed to realize the implication at the same time as Keely; they dropped their gaze to the ground.

"You think she's dead?" Keely asked.

Arnsberg took a long time to answer. "Yeah. I do. If she was kidnapped, we'd know about it." He looked off in the distance, across the valley. "One thing is bugging a lot of us, though."

"Where's her bike?"

"If she did get kidnapped, then they might have grabbed her bike, too. If she fell or was hurt and unconscious, an animal might have made her a meal, but not her bike. Her bike should be here."

"George," Keely said and walked over to put a hand on his shoulder. "You would have made an excellent detective."

Arnsberg beamed. "Thanks."

* * * *

"This has to be a record. You haven't called me this much since we were dating."

"Sure I have. Remember when you went away on the girls' weekend. I called you like every two hours."

"Keely, you called me because you couldn't find anything. I still can't believe you didn't know where the steak knives were."

"It was a new house. I can't be expected to keep track of everything. Hey, I knew where my tools were and where the lawnmower was. The important stuff."

"What do you want, Keely?"

"I've been having some very interesting conversations up here." Keely took a swig of his energy drink then put the bottle back in the little hole in the arm of his folding chair. "I need you to look into someone for me."

"Can't you get someone else to do it? I'm busy."

"No. You're it. The Body Fuel team has been full of drama for a few years, at least according to the pros I spoke with. They told me that a coach got fired shortly after the Olympics and it was pretty ugly. Guy went to the media and spouted off doping accusations until Body Fuel got an injunction gagging him."

"Remind me not to drink that pink stuff anymore."

"Elise, they didn't dope up all their products. The old coach, a guy named Galdeano, Roberto Galdeano, said they were doping the riders or at least they were going to. That's why he got shut up, because you can't accuse someone of something they haven't done yet. Still, the CCA checked into Body Fuel and found no evidence of any wrongdoing. Cleared them inside of a week. Tested their riders more than any other riders and they consistently peed clean."

"Nice image."

"You know what I mean. I need you to do a few things for me."

"A few?"

"See if you can locate the old coach. I'd love to talk to him. I'll bet he doesn't really give a shit about the gag order."

"Watch yourself, McAdam."

"And see what you can find out about the doping tests. Maybe get a list of the last several tests and the results? I'm betting they're public record."

"Anything else, Columbo?"

"A better attitude would be nice. Hello? Elise?" Keely laughed.

* * * *

Keely was back on his own bike. Pepe had treated her with the utmost respect and replaced both front and back wheels with better ones.

"It's not like I've got a shitload to do, Keely-dude. I should be thanking you for giving me something to do. Keeps my mind off Todd and Kira," he'd said after Keely apologized for adding to the wrench's workload. He felt happy and sad for Pepe but above all understood the need to keep busy. The mechanic was now on his way to joining the official search for Kira Bremner.

Keely had parked his bike against the tree behind his tent a few minutes ago and was now walking to the sponsor area. None of the retail displays had been packed away since the park closure gave people an opportunity to shop. And today they were. Keely had to squeeze by more than a few patrons before clearing the tents. He stood in front of a fair-sized camper, Drink Pink magnets of various sizes stuck all over its body. Some were the size of ads you see on the sides of buses, while others were more in keeping with the fridge variety.

Before his knuckles could rap the door, it flew open.

"It is a pleasure to see you, detective," said Steven Bishop from the shaded interior.

"Ah. Yeah. I was hoping you could tell me where to find Paulo."

"I'm so pleased you've agreed to help us. I can't tell you how thrilled we are. We must find Kira before it's too late."

Keely's glare was enough to change Bishop's sunny disposition. Keely asked, "What do you mean, before it's too late?"

The heat of summer was rising with the sun of the June morning and Keely's back was sweating. Not as much as the instant perspiration that appeared on Bishop's forehead.

"Detective. You and I both know that in missing persons' cases time is critical. We need to find Kira in the next fourteen to sixteen hours. We are petrified she might not be healthy."

"Good recovery."

"I don't know what you—"

"I need you to keep my involvement in this case very quiet. If certain individuals catch wind I'm nosing around, I'll be in deep shit. Hush hush, okay?"

Bishop straightened. "You may rest at ease, detective. My team and I will protect you at all costs."

"Let's not get all Patton on me. Just keep your mouth shut, okay?"

"No one will know. I assure you. We need you."

"I need to speak to Paulo. Where is he?"

"On the search I believe."

"I was afraid of that."

* * * *

The search command centre was fairly quiet since most of the individuals involved were out doing what they volunteered to do — search. A few stray officers were keeping track of the progress. The whiteboard had the names of search teams but not individuals.

Keely began checking clipboards on a table near the whiteboard and it didn't take long to find Paulo Chagas' name. He was on team H4. Keely went to the map of the park and searched H4.

"Can I help you?" a young, pretty female officer asked. Keely thought her exotic and very attractive. Too attractive to be a cop. Then he mentally berated himself for thinking in stereotypes.

"My friend Paulo is in H4. Where is H4?"

"Detective, you shouldn't be here. You should be riding or relaxing, not working."

Her eyes were shaped like the profile of a thick airplane wing, their colour seemed all black. She could stop traffic with those eyes, Keely thought.

"I'm sorry. What?"

She smiled and he felt his heart slap his ribcage. "Nice try, detective. Time for you to go. Detective Sergeant's orders."

"Officer—?"

She tilted her head and Keely watched black hair in a ponytail slide across her shoulder.

"Officer Ono."

"Officer Ono, when will that particular group be back?"

"They're a drive away from here, several kilometres outside the race course. It could be hours before they get back from their shift."

She put her hand on the small of Keely's back, her head coming to just above his shoulder, and gently nudged him in the direction of the door. She smelled fantastic.

"Let's get you outside, okay?"

The heat was getting unbearable but at least it kept a lot of the bugs away. Ono motioned for Keely to walk to the side of the building. "It's a small world, detective, so I'll help any way I can."

"A small world? I'm not sure I follow you?"

"We've never met but you helped my family out of a jam. About five years ago, the so-called Japanese mafia. My uncle Takata was accused of killing some people in Scarborough."

"I remember that. Shit, it didn't take much. I followed the evidence and it led way away from your uncle."

"I know. My uncle is a tailor, he's never fired a gun in his life. There were some people ready to lynch him. We'll never forget your help. You are well respected and people listened to you."

"I *was* well respected," Keely said quietly.

She grabbed his elbow. "My family will always respect you." She pulled him by the arm and guided him further behind the building, into a shadowy corner. "If I get caught it's my job. You know that, so we don't talk often, okay?"

"Sure. I just don't know how—"

"I didn't interview Chagas but heard all about it. Guy is freaking out about his riders and he's desperate, and I mean desperate, to find Kira. Like he knows something we don't."

"You know, I'm getting the feeling there's a few people around here holding back."

"I don't know much about this coach, but I do know that he's pissed at his bosses and has to find this girl. There's something really wrong about it, you know? Like he knows if he doesn't find her, she could be in big trouble."

"Or, maybe it's Mr. Chagas that could be in shit?"

"Ya ask me, Kira Bremner is alive and someone's got her."

"I didn't ask you, but thanks," Keely said lightly and turned to walk away.

"Hey," she said and grabbed his arm. She moved close to him, her scent sweet. "What if there's a ransom and we don't know it?"

"You think?"

She pressed herself against his arm. Keely was involuntarily aroused by the feel of her firm breasts and the sight of her cleavage. He missed Elise.

"If someone goes missing you get concerned, but some of these people, the ones from that team, they're frantic."

"Not unusual."

"But all the time? It's unnatural. They've been like that all night now. Eight hours of high tension."

"Doesn't prove there's been a ransom demand."

"Okay, call it a hunch then."

Keely leaned into her but avoided meeting her eyes. "Thanks for the information. You don't know how much help you've been."

She hooked her other hand around his arm and squeezed. "Maybe we can get together a little later?" She looked into his eyes and he felt his lips quiver. She was beautiful and sexy and most likely an excellent conversationalist. But...

"I'm flattered, believe me, but I'm in love with my wife."

She huffed. "Shit. That just makes me want to be with you even more."

As Keely walked back to the Body Fuel camper he kept telling himself that he'd never, ever be able to figure out women. Impossible.

* * * *

"I assure you, detective, we have had no ransom demand delivered to us."

Bishop didn't stand out as much as when Keely had first met him, since now he had a corporate twin. A woman who introduced herself as Leila Marques, marketing director for Body Fuel. Her tanned skin and lean, athletic body made her seem taller than her five-six. She sat rigidly on one side of a small table in the cool camper. Her tan shorts and pink shirt were, as far as Keely could tell, the uniform of the weekend for this team.

"Detective McAdam," she said softly, and Keely instantly warmed to her. "If we'd gotten a ransom note, don't you think it would make sense for us to tell the police?"

"A lot of people in this situation believe that when kidnappers say no police, they are somehow able to keep tabs and know if their mark has contacted the cops."

"That is not the case here I assure you, detective."

"Steve, please," she said and Keely knew he was wrong about his physical assesment of this woman. She was engaging and personable. She was real. "Detective—"

"Call me Keely."

She smiled and Keely felt good. "Okay, Keely. I'm telling you, we've had no contact from anyone about Kira or Todd for that matter."

"You think they're connected?"

"Of course."

"Leila, that's quite enough."

"No, Steve, it isn't enough. We want Kira back safe and sound. She's my friend and I'm sick about this. I can't sleep or eat. I've already been on two searches. What the hell have you done? Nothing. So either you want to help, or you can go back to Toronto."

"I am as concerned as anyone about our assets."

"Oh, for Chrissake, her name is Kira."

"You know, I'm really enjoying this, but I could come back later if you like," Keely offered.

"Keely, we have to find her, that is all I know. We really have to find her, okay?"

"I get that. She's worth a ton of dough to you."

"It's so much more—"

"Detective," Bishop said, in a raised voice. "Is there anything else we can do for you right now?"

"Yeah, you can tell me what the hell is really going on."

"Kira Bremner is missing and we want to find her," Bishop said, his face like stone. "That is what it is going on."

Keely swivelled his chair to look out the window at the retail area. People were milling in and out of tents, new purchases in their hands. He swung his chair back around to face Leila and Bishop, each taking a similar pose on either side of the little table.

"What was the team chemistry like?"

"How do you mean?" asked Bishop.

Leila didn't have to be told. "It was no secret that Sarah and Kira did not get along," she said. "Sarah was with Todd who used to be with Kira. It made for some very tense team meetings." Leila picked at the label on an unopened bottle of Body Fuel.

"I got that. What about other riders and team support staff?"

"As a company, we felt it prudent to sponsor only the best. Sarah was recruited to the team since she was consistently finishing in the top five and we thought she'd make an excellent addition." Bishop spoke as if going over box scores. "Todd and Kira are the two top riders on the circuit."

"Todd *was* a top rider and we're hoping that Kira is all right and will be back riding with us very soon," Leila said. "I can't tell you how much this hurts."

"What about support staff? Coach, mechanics, drivers, masseurs, dieticians?"

"Detective, we all get along famously. We are indeed a very tight group. Our bond has created a winning attitude and reflects—"

"Christ!"

Keely watched Leila roll her eyes and had some difficulty stifling a laugh.

"Keely, we did get along. Even Steve here can let his hair down and be a good guy. We had fun and we talked. We all travelled well together. We don't always attend races, but when we're a title sponsor and have riders in the race, we go no matter where it is. We were having a typical great race weekend. Pepe was doing his usual great job, Todd and Kira were first, Sarah was in second and even a prospect of ours was doing well."

"Prospect?"

"Daniele Biatola. He was second when the race was called," Leila said and raised a brow at Keely's wide eyes. "What?"

"Do you guys thrive on putting people together that don't like each other? Next you'll tell me he's sleeping with Kira."

Bishop tried to be professional looking when sliding from the little bench seat on his side of the table and instead looked awkward.

"Excuse me," he said. His footfalls were heavy and the door slammed loudly as he left the trailer.

"What's wrong with him?"

Leila sighed. "*He's* sleeping with Kira."

Keely shook his head. "Holy shit. You guys really keep it in the family, eh?"

Chapter 9

The flimsy, pale blue door opened slowly on an olive-skinned man whose age Numbers couldn't peg. He looked about mid-fifties, but was toned and muscular so maybe he was older and just looked damned good for his age.

"Mr. Galdeano? Once coached Kira Bremner?"

The man was eye level with Numbers and that disappointed him. If the guy was even a few inches shorter, despite the physique, he'd be able to intimidate him with his size. Numbers could never be accused of being small.

"Yes. Who are you? What do you want?"

"Mr. Galdeano, my name is Mick Moyer. I'm a private investigator. I've got a friend who is very anxious to talk to you."

* * * *

"Elise, I hate to do this to you, but I hope you're free around two this afternoon."

"John, you can't be serious. You told me Tuesday. I'm meeting Numbers for dinner."

"That old screw. I'm doing you a favour. Look, some big shit from a drink company has pull 'cause my boss just shuffled the cases. Watkins is up next."

Elise felt the phone slipping from between her shoulder and ear, readjusted it then continued applying her makeup. "What time again?"

"Two."

"How long will it take?"

"You should be free and clear by four the latest."

* * * *

"This won't take long. I promise," Numbers said and sank his big frame into the well-used motel chair. "I just want to know a few things about Kira Bremner."

"Why? You think she cheats?" Galdeano said, his accent flaring along with his nostrils.

Seeing a hook sink in that he hadn't meant to set, Numbers started reeling it in. "I hear things."

"She is the best. But she could be so much better. I think she doesn't know what they're up to." Galdeano sat on the edge of the bed. "She is so damned good. She is champion."

"Are you saying that you know for a fact that she's cheating?"

Galdeano stiffened. Whatever youth he held onto disappeared and he suddenly looked frail. "I tried to stop her from staying with this team. There are always rumours of doping and even though I did not know the truth, I suspect. That was not enough for her so we stayed."

"Why did you get fired?"

The old coach found strength again and leapt to his feet. "What the hell you ask these questions for? Who the fuck you are?"

Numbers stood slowly, letting his largeness sink in. "Easy, coach. I'm here because Todd Watkins was found dead at the bottom of a cliff and Kira Bremner is missing."

The seconds of silence had weight and it pressed down on Numbers. He struggled to hold his steely gaze on the coach whose expression was stone, unmoving. He glared at Numbers and held his mouth slightly open. The dam finally broke and took the big PI completely by surprise.

"Oh no!" Galdeano yelled as he threw his arms over Numbers' shoulders.

"Easy there, buddy."

Galdeano cried, sobbed, cried louder, controlled himself for a few seconds and then burst into tears yet again.

"The boy so good and now he gone. Oh no!"

"Get a grip, man, I need to ask you some questions about Kira," Numbers said and pushed the blubbering Italian away. "This could mean the difference between finding her alive or dead."

Galdeano stood with his shoulders slumped, head down. Then he slowly lifted his head to reveal a distraught face, his eyes puffy and red. His lip quivered slightly, then he threw his hands in the air. "Not my little bella. Oh no!"

"Oh, shit! Get it together for fuck sake."

* * * *

"Hi, sweetheart. Break anything yet?"

"Elise, I'm walking, I'm not riding."

"Good choice, much safer for you."

"Got news, honey?"

"Numbers found the old coach pretty fast. Never guess where he is."

Keely stopped just before the alley. A few cyclists glided past. "In Toronto."

"Close. Hamilton. World Championships and he's hoping for a new job."

"Wow. He was let go about what, a year and a half ago? Still doesn't have a job?"

"What the hell do I know? Numbers will tell me at dinner. Won't call you because it's long distance."

"Always playing the numbers, eh. Let me guess, you're paying for dinner."

"Pretty cheap for his services, you know," she said and laughed. "Hey, I'm shooting Watkins' autopsy at two this afternoon. Got moved up. Then I'm at dinner with Numbers. I'll call you later."

"Tell him no appetizers or dessert."

"Who, Watkins?"

"I love you, honey," Keely said and disconnected the phone to the sound of his wife's laughter then aimed himself at the alley.

"Detective! Wait, please?"

Keely turned to see Leila running up to him. When she spoke it was as if she'd just got up out of a chair rather than running a few hundred yards to catch him.

"We're not the horrible people you think we are."

"I didn't say you were."

She pressed her lips together in a mock smile and raised an eyebrow. "Your face said, 'Evil, heartless corporate drones who think about nothing but money.' "

"Where have I heard that before?"

She laughed. A good, honest laugh that made her look even more attractive. "You are a delight in the middle of this chaos." She reached out and slipped her arm around his. "Walk with me for a while. I think it will do us both some good."

Keely shrugged and let her tug him through the alley.

* * * *

It had to be approaching noon since the sun, when visible through the trees, was nearing its apogee. The heat was sauna-like in the woods, the trees acting as barriers against air currents. *Is she trying to get my temperature up?*

"Biatola is an excellent rider," Laila said. "We have the funds to hire him. We have a great team. He wins, we win. Simple as that."

They walked through a shard of light and couldn't dodge bugs dancing on dust clouds. The forest was dry and Keely wished he'd brought some water.

"He rides for a major competitor. They lose, you win. Simple as that."

She took a deep breath and Keely was amazed she didn't choke on the dust. "So what?" She pulled away from him, standing a few feet back on the trail. "My company sponsors riders so we can advertise our products. Why the hell is that such a bad thing, detective?"

Keely stalled for a moment, wanting her to think he was making up his mind. "I've never said what you do is wrong. What I object to is the bullshit you use to justify it all. You say one thing and it masks a reality. For who? The team, the company or the people buying your products?"

"I don't have to justify what I do to you, or to anyone for that matter."

"Then why not be honest? We want the number two rider because the number two team is getting too close. What's wrong with that?"

"Because I'd lose my job."

Keely smiled. "Now that is honesty. Thank you."

"Detective—"

"Time to call me Keely again, especially when we're taking a stroll arm-in-arm in the woods."

She huffed lightly. "Keely, everybody knows what's going on. The sponsors, the racers, hell, even the fans know exactly why we took Biatola away from Kickers. My superiors feel it unnecessary to extrapolate. Do *you* understand that?"

They were together again, her arm hooked in his, walking up a slight incline in the path. "I recognize it, but I don't have to understand it."

"You realize that we're not bad people. Steve is a great guy. He can be funny and thoughtful. You should see him with Kira."

She stopped, Keely's momentum swinging him around in front of her. Leila deftly wrapped her arms around his waist, lightly rubbing his back through his damp T-shirt.

"You have to find her, Keely. Please."

"I'll do everything I can," he said softly, lingering in her embrace, allowing her to feel the energy build between them.

"She's my friend. I want her back and I know that Steve would do anything to see her again."

"What do you think happened to her?" he said, and instantly realized he'd let the false airiness out of his voice. He'd asked the question with cool practicality.

She pulled away and began walking again. "I don't know. She fell, she hit her head and rode off the course…I don't know."

Keely grabbed her arm and she spun to face him. She made it look and feel as if he was in control of the distance between them. Her face was inches from his. He smelled her fragrance, sweet amidst the aridness. Her breath was tickling his upper lip. Her eyes were hungry, honest.

She moved to kiss him and he dodged his head to avoid her lips. Immediately she pulled away and brought a hand to her mouth.

"I'm sorry. I…I don't know what I was thinking."

"I know exactly what I was thinking."

He reached out and took her hand gently into his, then tugged her to keep walking.

"I'm sorry. I mean I'm sorry but I think you're an amazing man and I'd love to—"

"I was thinking of how much I love my wife with this head," he said and pointed to his temple. "And, I was thinking something completely different with this head." He pointed at his crotch.

"You'd like to…"

He stopped on the trail, light streaming through the trees, some of it touching them. Up ahead was a climb over some jagged rocks. He turned and faced her. "No. I'm sorry. You have no idea how sorry I am that I said that. But, no."

She smirked. "Thanks for that."

"Well, you're an amazing woman. Sorry, my wife is, well, incredible. I hope that you'll find someone you can love as much as I love her."

"I'm seriously jealous. She's lucky too, you know?"

"Oh, I try and tell her that, but all she does is change the subject, or tell me to clean the bathroom, or—"

Leila chuckled and hugged him. Then she headed for the rocks.

"Hey, wait up."

* * * *

Krull pushed the office door open with his elbows and simultaneously bit into his egg salad sandwich. His office was far more comfortable than the cafeteria and he could get a bit of paperwork done while he ate.

He plopped down in his leather chair and pushed his feet off the floor, the chair rolling to the other side of the desk. He put his sandwich down atop a manila folder, reached for the phone and hit a few numbers. He listened to the ringing on the other end of the line, then frowned and hung up the phone.

He eyed his sandwich and smiled. "Sorry, Jerry, I got the last one. Hope you like week-old salmon."

A loud clang travelled from somewhere and penetrated the door of his office.

"Hello," he said, his mouth filled with egg salad. "Jerry, that you?"

The door flew open and a large black man in scrubs, sporting a fair-sized afro, strolled to his desk. "You son of a bitch."

"Egg salad good. Salmon bad."

Both men laughed.

"Don't suppose you'd share?" Jerry said, his eyes round and watery for effect.

"Nope."

"Well, I'm prepping Watkins, then."

Jerry turned and walked to the door.

"I have some fruit if you want it."

Jerry thought for a second and headed back to the desk. "Watkins is dead. He can wait five more minutes."

* * * *

"Kickers has been breathing down our necks on the bike and in sales. It's amazing. The numbers show them up in the east and we're up in the west. It's pretty much for every category, too."

"Category?" asked Keely.

"Yeah, sports drinks, energy bars, water...categories."

Keely looked out over the top of a forest canopy from their high position on the trail. They were finally free of the forest and air swirled lightly around them.

"I guess the added pressure of having teammates that hate each other is giving the suits—sorry, no offence—"

"None taken."

"—Must have given you guys ulcers."

"It's not as bad as you think. To be honest, I think that Kira used her hurt feelings to outride Sarah. She turned all of her negative energy into strength and consistently beat her teammate."

"When did she start winning again?"

"It was after the Olympics. She pulled off two or three wins in a row. Drove Sarah crazy."

"And that was okay with you, because that made Sarah try harder to beat Kira and you guys got all this great exposure for the product. Right?"

Her cheeks expanded as she blew out a long stream of air. "I hate this tell-it-like-it-is stuff."

Keely threw a rock over the edge of the trail and listened to it tumble for a few seconds.

"Yes. It was a win all around for the sponsor. Again, why is that a bad thing?"

"It isn't. I just like to hear you say it."

"Don't get used to it."

A turkey vulture floated by a few hundred feet above them, its featherless, red head beaming against its black feathers.

"Since the Olympics, has Sarah beat Kira?"

"Nope. Not once. No matter how much she trains, how hard she tries, she just can't beat her."

"Huh."

"Was that the she-must-be-doping huh?"

"You gotta admit, unbeatable by a rider who up until the Olympics was beating Kira, not all the time, but sometimes. Plus, she's younger and probably just as strong."

"Kira Bremner has been tested as much, no, more than Lance Armstrong. She goes to dinner with friends, they show up and ask for pee. Out for a training ride, they show up and ask for pee or blood."

"Who shows up?"

"World Anti-Doping Agency for world-class events like the Olympics or World Championships, and local events like this one is Ontario Cycling Association."

"Can you blame them for wanting to keep the sport clean?"

"C'mon, Keely. How many times would you have to pee in a cup before your cop's union put a stop to it? Once, maybe twice. They're on a witch hunt. I've seen every single one of her results and they're all clean. No sign of anything."

"Why the hell does a world-class athlete at the top of her game go missing after another world-class athlete gets killed?"

"I told you, I don't know. You have to find her. I just know she's alive. She's tough, strong. She'll make it as long as we keep looking."

Keely threw an arm casually around her shoulders. "If you honestly want to find her, then let me talk to everyone on the team, starting with her coach."

Chapter 10

John twisted to put his back to the door then pushed it open with his butt. He slid inside and froze. The long autopsy room with its bright silver baffled lights, its six stations, gleaming silver tables with troughs to collect fluids, was spotless and empty. Watkins was still not prepped.

John growled, the echoing sound in the empty room feuling his anger further. He walked purposefully between the tables then took a sharp left and pounded open a pair of double doors.

Jerry lay on the floor, face down. The back of his head was crushed, probably from a blunt instrument. John admonished himself for slipping so easily into his role. He stepped farther into the room careful not to disturb any evidence. Jerry was in a kind of I'm-a-little-teapot pose with his left hand jutting out for the spout and his right arm bent, hand resting by his hip. Nothing in the room was disturbed. *It was quick and I hope it was painless.*

Something stabbed at John. Fear, he thought. Whoever did this could still be in the building. He chanced turning around slowly to take in the entire scene. The room consisted of a bank of body drawers, a slot in the front of each for labels, a handle just below that. At the far end was a sink and some cabinets. At the near end, just inside of the doors John had come through, was a desk with a computer and files. The wall behind him was empty but for a few photographs, and it ran the length of the room, flush at either end with the door frames. One empty stretcher beside Jerry. Nothing seemed out of the ordinary except for his dead assistant.

It was getting hotter. He was wearing his apron but not his gloves. His mask was dangling over his chest, having been only half tied on. Scrubs were always comfortable and the temperature was cool but not cold. He had to stay calm. He listened intently for any sound in his subterranean world. All he could hear was his heart punching his ribs.

He smelled the blood. Occupational hazard. Tinny. He could taste it, too. Sweat dripped from his forehead to his cheeks. *There's no one here. No sound. Can't smell any cologne or perfume. No detergents on clothes. I'm alone.*

He shuffled forward, staying to the left of Jerry's body and the cabinet doors hiding their dead contents. He approached the doors at the far end as if he were a cop, crouching slightly to stay clear of the small square windows at eye level. Once he made it to the door, he slowly stood and peaked out the window. He was greeted by an empty hallway. He listened closely for any movement.

He felt confident he could now call the police. He could walk up two flights of stairs, go out the back door and yell to them. They were a block away.

He spun and walked toward the desk but something caught his eye. One of the cabinet doors was open slightly. The latch hadn't been fully engaged. It was the locker for Todd Watkins. The empty stretcher was near it, Jerry was below it.

"Shit!"

John dashed forward and pulled open the door so fast it almost hit him in the chest. He grasped the handle of the tray and dragged it out. He unzipped the body bag inside and Todd Watkins' blueing face looked up at him.

"No."

He no longer cared about evidence, he wanted to live. He had to get out of that building alive. He pushed Watkins' body back into the drawer and swung the door closed. He jumped back, frightened by his reflection in one of the cabinets above the desk.

Stepping carefully over Jerry's body, John headed for the double doors that led to the hallway to his office. His gun was in there. His wife had begged him to get some kind of protection.

"You never know what some crazy will do," she'd said. It was easy enough to get the permit to carry a handgun considering his position. The application had been fast-tracked and he had a police issue Glock inside of a month. He'd fired it once and hoped it would stay that way.

Solitude never bothered John. Part of the reason he loved his job. This particular Sunday, he wished his regular staff was here, all making noise, bugging him for help, bitching about their hours or case loads. Jerry would still be here. *Oh, God. Elise.*

His office felt uncomfortable – like a dead end. He reached for the phone in his pocket. Why hadn't he thought of that before? Hell, the cops would be here by now.

That was when he smelled him. Pungent. Not cologne but human sweat.

He instinctively ducked, thinking the killer was aiming for his head. John was wrong. He felt a sharp pain in his side. His kidney. He fought to stay conscious. Intense pain burned through him. He couldn't speak let alone yell for help. He fell forward onto his desk, but there was no chance of reaching the drawer with the gun.

The pain went critical when his assailant twisted and shook the knife deep into his flesh. John felt shards of pain race down both legs and burning in his spine. He couldn't move. No matter how hard he tried his body would no longer listen to his brain. He lay over his desk and thought of his wife. He knew he was joining her and that comforted him. He hadn't seen her in over five years.

"Take care of him. I'll get the body."

Who will get my body? Better not be Velazquez. She couldn't find a clue if arrows were pointing at it.

John never felt the blunt object strike the back of his head.

* * * *

Keely thought that Babbette Boudreau was tough wrapped in a pretty package. Her slender frame was toned, but not overly muscled. Her pink tank top clung to her and accentuated the curves of her hips. The black tights grounded her but Keely thought they might have been chosen to help prying eyes see someone slimmer. Her red hair was pulled back in a bun and showed off her angular features. Her eyes were brown and empty. This woman had no secrets.

"I just want to get the fuck out of here. That's it."

She was feminine on the outside and trucker on the inside.

"I understand. So do I. My wife is pretty upset at me having to stay an extra day."

"My girlfriend gets upset at these long trips, ya know. Doesn't matter how many times I fuckin' tell her that it's part of the job. She doesn't fuckin' get it. Shit, what a pain."

"Why stay with her then?"

Babbette's wry smile was all the answer Keely needed and he laughed. "Congratulations to you."

"Thanks. Now you know why I gotta get outta here. How long you figure they'll keep this place shut down?" she asked and stubbed her cigarette out on the ground beside her folding chair.

"Your guess is as good as mine."

She pulled a small pack of smokes from the little hole in the arm of her chair meant for drinks, opened it, drew out another long cigarette and lit it. She took a deep drag off it then blew out foul air. There were easily a dozen butts crushed out on the ground beside the chair but the rest of her campsite was clean enough.

"They let you smoke? You're the masseuse, you're hands on and I thought—"

"Who gives a shit what you think, or what they think. I'm good. I'm the fucking best there is. So they can't say shit. As long as I smoke away from the athletes, their tents, the corporate area, the—"

"I get it."

She raised an eyebrow at him, took another drag of her cigarette and blew out smoke like a dragon. "So what the hell did you want anyway?"

"Just want to know what life is like in the Team Pink camp is all. Did everyone get along?"

"Yeah."

Keely waited but there wasn't more coming.

"How did Kira seem to you?"

"Good."

Again, he waited for her give more information, but she was done answering that question.

"Do you like Sarah?"

She sat up a little, more square. "What do you mean?"

"Does she bitch about anything, anyone?"

"You mean does she bitch about Kira?"

Keely nodded.

Another drag of her cigarette and another toxic cloud floated by Keely. "All the time."

"What does she talk about?"

"The fucking weather. What's it to you? You're not a cop anymore so why the fuck should I answer your shit?"

Keely slid forward in his chair and leaned closer to Babbette. He straightened so he could look down on her. "Because your boss hired me to find Kira." He paused for a few seconds to let it sink in. "Talk."

The smoke was disgusting but Keely held his ground.

"Working for the bad guys now, eh, detective?"

"Bad guys?"

"C'mon, sweetheart, you know all the rumours. Body Fuel cheats. They dope. They sure as hell do something. Ya had to've heard that rumour."

"Of course I have. As far as I can tell, there's no proof of any doping."

"I'm with you. I work those fuckers over after ever race. Hell, between laps in a twenty-four race. They're in amazing shape, eat better than any team on the circuit, train better, live better."

"You don't think they cheat?"

"No way. I'm as close as you can get to these guys and I can't smell anything rotten in this Denmark. They're legit. They work for it and they get it."

"What about injuries?"

"Yeah, couple muscle pulls and a few strains here and there. No track marks or anything like that. They take supplements like any other rider, some orally, some injected. But all of them are scrutinized, man. No hanky panky here."

"And they got along okay?"

"I didn't say that," she said, flicking ash from the end of her cigarette. "Every family has its problems."

"Sarah and Kira fought, didn't they?"

"They were more on the quiet side. It was Daniele and Todd that went at it. Threw a few punches once."

"The guys were fighting."

"Like brothers."

Keely sat back in his chair, more to get away from the smoke than to get more comfortable. The day was going by fast and he wondered how Elise was doing. He pictured her bored, or slapping John's hands away, or eating a salad. Yeah, she was having a salad just before the job.

"Am I disturbing you?"

"Oh, sorry. I was thinking of my wife."

"Don't suppose you could describe her for me?"

Keely laughed. "You *are* desperate to get outta here."

* * * *

The salad was awful, limp and tasteless. Sundays were a tough day to get anything downtown. She sipped her soda and stared at the parking lot. Three cars other than her own took up spots. She instantly recognized Jerry's old VW van; bright orange with a white V in front. All he needed was flowers painted on the side and he'd be a true hippie.

John's white, pristine Cadillac outshone the newly painted white lines of the lot. Actually, she thought, it sparkles more than anything in the neighbourhood. Which wasn't really saying much. She was sitting in her car at the back of the building which housed the coroner's office. Dull, lifeless buildings surrounded her and helped block out the sky. *That's what gives John's car a chance to shine.*

The other car she didn't recognize. A town car of some kind. Long and black. She was surprised that there were so few cars in the lot. Even on a Sunday she thought more people would be working in a five-story building in the middle of downtown Toronto. She sighed, tossed the plastic salad container in the back seat, gathered her gear and got out of the car.

The back door was always open, but inside she'd have to swipe a card to get into the office and its subsequent chambers of the dead. This was not her favourite work. Photographing families or CEOs or wildlife, pretty much anything else was a welcome job compared to documenting the dead.

She slid her card down the security device and heard the lock pop. She quickly pulled open the door and entered the hallway. She might complain about John Krull's roving hands and eyes, but he was good to her. He could photograph his autopsies himself, but gave as much work as he could to Elise and a few other fortunate photographers. "Good work is hard to find," he often said. She'd taken the compliment and the pay. Deep in thought, she entered the elevator and pushed the button for lower level two. In no time at all the door opened and she stepped out into an identical hallway two floors down.

She smiled at her reflection in the glass door she approached. Her black slacks and top were a conscious choice. Every time she shot an autopsy she wore black. Ritualistic, she knew, but it seemed appropriate. The glass door open, she stepped into the hospital-like hallway. John's office was to her right, the 'rooms of death' to her left. She was a few minutes early, so headed for the office.

Something caught her eye in the little square window in one of the doors to the autopsy room. A dark-haired head bobbed in and out of view. John must be prepping Watkins, she thought, and turned toward the door. Another head came into view and she saw the man's face. She didn't recognize him. The two men seemed to be struggling with something, like they were moving furniture.

She stood slightly on her toes and peered through the window. Two men in street clothes, no scrubs or surgical-like attire, were carrying a body bag awkwardly between them. The taller of the two men looked up and locked eyes with Elise.

"Get her!" the man yelled, and the shorter, stockier man dropped his end of the body bag and ran for the door.

Elise bolted and reached John's office before the man had emerged from the autopsy room. She shut the door behind her and turned to see John sprawled face down over his desk. Blood soaked his scrubs from a gaping hole in his head.

"Don't panic, honey. Never panic."

Keely was in her head, thank God. She slid her camera bag from her shoulder, wrapped her hand in the strap and waited beside the door. Unconsciously, she'd removed her heels.

It didn't take long for the short man to burst into the room. Elise swung the camera bag as hard as he could at the man's head. She connected, but it did little to stop him. He stumbled to the wall but blocked her exit. She swung the bag again and again, the whole time screaming at the stranger to leave her alone.

The man pushed off the wall and threw himself at her, his hands stretched out to grab. Deliberately, she collapsed, crumpling to the floor and the man tripped over her. He sailed over her, landing with a thud behind her. She quickly got to her feet, the smell of her own fear a motivator to move.

"Run. You always run from a fight until there's no place left to run."

She leapt for the door but her attacker managed to get hold of her foot. She struggled to get free and fell against a chair, then rolled to the floor.

"Drop onto your back and kick. Your legs are three or four times stronger than your arms. Kick as hard and as fast as you can."

Her legs were like pistons on their highest revs. Her feet glanced off her attacker's thick forearms. Elise knew if she stopped kicking this man would kill her. Her feet rained down blows and with each she drove herself closer to the wall next to the door. She felt her assailant's nose crack under her heel. A direct hit. He yelled and when his hands went to his face, she jumped to her feet and ran from the room.

The hallway was deserted. She ran to her left, away from the autopsy room and her attacker's friend. Where to? The floor had a hallway that ran around the outside edge of the building. Doors were all on her left at this point and led to rooms in the centre. Most of those rooms led further into the centre of the building. It was a unique design but probably the reason she was going to die.

She heard the swinging doors to the autopsy room thump together. Was one going in or the other coming out? Time to gamble.

"Never take unnecessary risks."

Shut up, Keely.

She ran as fast as she'd ever run in her life down the hallway and made three left turns. The doors to the autopsy prep area were closing up fast. She didn't have a choice. The front door was not operable on weekends — security had it locked up tight. She didn't want to set off any of the alarmed doors either. She'd be easy pickings if that happened.

The only escape was through the back door and the two men she'd seen carrying a dead body were headed in that direction. They may not have killed Todd Watkins, but they sure as hell had murdered John Krull.

She peeked through the small square window and saw Jerry lying face down on the floor, blood all around him. Her guts seized up and she doubled over. Her body was shutting down but her mind was still sharp. She could remember every detail of the two dead bodies in the morgue. She forced herself to listen and heard the attackers somewhere in the distance kicking at doors.

She eased into the pre-autopsy room, lingering for a second to say goodbye to Jerry. Then she picked a drawer and hoped it was empty.

Chapter 11

He knew where he was. That amazing place — or was that time? — between asleep and awake. His body was so relaxed and felt so light he was certain he could fly, or at least hover. He allowed himself to be taken by the feelings and permitted thoughts to come, recognizing them, dealing with them, and releasing them. *Am I drooling?*

He was on a street filled with police cars, the lights atop them intermittently flashing blue and red. Instantly he was in a house. He knew the house. The Harpers'. Could he save her this time?

"Don't come any closer."

Keely moved closer.

"I'll kill her."

Janet was twelve. She looked twelve, too. Her hair was a mop of brunette with clips sticking here and there to give a modicum of control. She had braces. She was gangly and awkward. Skinny as a post. Just what a kid should be on her way to being a teenager — all arms and legs.

"Please, Daddy. Don't!"

"She's dead if you don't back off."

Harper's mouth was moving but his eyes were doing the talking. Keely pulled his gun. It was smooth, quick. He fired.

"All done, sweet cheeks."

The slap on his ass brought him hurtling into the present. His butt was stinging thanks to Babbette's thoughtfulness.

"Get dressed and out you go or people might think I swing both fucking ways. Can't have that."

He heard her light up a smoke.

* * * *

"Mrs. Detective McAdam?"

One of the killers was close by. How close was difficult to tell through the partially closed door. The voice was lilty and mocking, which could mean only one thing. They'd found her camera bag and her wallet. She always put her wallet into her gear bag on shoots; no sense carrying two purses. They must have done some checking on Keely and made the obvious connection. Anyone with access to the internet would read stories about him. Janet Harper had been all over the news and Keely's name was right beside hers.

"Come out, come out wherever you are."

He was closer. In the room at the very least. Her legs were shaking. A combination of the cold and her fear.

"Maybe she went upstairs?"

Another voice, much deeper than the first. The pair of killers were together again.

"Maybe, but I didn't hear the elevator and no one's come down here after us."

"Building's empty then?"

"I doubt it." The man paused and Elise heard him walk closer. "I think she's here. Right in here."

A latch clicked then a door slammed against the wall as if the killer had tried to whip it off its hinges. Elise tensed so much her body jumped off its tray. Recovering, she concentrated all of her efforts on getting her breathing even and quiet, and on not shivering anymore. The tray was metal and the flimsy material of her slacks and blouse did nothing to hinder the transfer of the cold.

"Mrs. Detective. Your husband is being such a bad boy. How about you get him to help us? He really must take a more active role in finding Kira."

Another door slammed open. Closer this time. The blackness around her only heightened the fear. She urgently slid her hands across the walls beside her, the ceiling, too. She probed the back of her tiny prison with her feet. She needed purchase.

Desperation made her hands move faster, her brain process little bits of information at lightning speed. She touched a cross brace at the end of the drawer and her brain explained quickly that it was there to hold up the tray. There'd be one at the head end as well.

Slowly, soundlessly, she turned her body over so she was face down.
More doors were opened around her, their gunshot slams like slaps to her
face, awakening her mind to solutions and reminding her it was only a
matter of time before they opened her drawer. How closely would they be
looking? How fast could their minds process information?

Timing was the key. She placed her toes on either side of the tray, her
fingers on the cross beam and waited.

"Why the hell would she lock herself in one of these drawers? She'd
freeze to death."

"See this little lever here," the killer with the higher-pitched voice said.
"You get locked in here, you push this and the door pops open."

"What the hell for? So dead guys can get up and pee at night?" low-
voiced killer said and laughed.

"How the hell should I know? Maybe people were playing around too
much and somebody got stuck. College kids or something."

Another door slammed open.

"C'mon. We gotta go. The cops could be here anytime."

"They'd have been here already if she got out of here. Shut up and open
a fucking door."

Elise heard the latch of her drawer click and a blade of light cut the
darkness.

"Fine. But hurry up. Stop playing."

She was up on her fingers and toes as the door was opened all the way.
She could see his feet but not his face. He'd done exactly what she'd hoped.
He'd bent slightly and looked down into the space, only able to see about a
foot at the head of the tray. He'd missed seeing any part of her. If he'd bent
down even a few more inches he'd have seen her hands. The door slammed
shut and she collapsed onto her tray.

Doors were opening faster now.

"Nothing. Let's go."

"Fuck! She's gotta be here."

* * * *

Keely loped out of the masseuse's tent and nearly ran over Leila.
"Wow. You look rested."

"Thanks to the best massage I've ever had. Well, except for the huge stinging handprint on my ass. Not the best finish."

"I heard that," Babbette yelled from inside her tent.

Leila laughed then said, "She is the best."

"Is Paulo back yet?"

"No. Apparently he stayed out longer than expected. He didn't come back with his search team. An officer said he was hooking up with another team in the area next to his."

"Do you have any clue when he'll be back?"

She shrugged.

"Who else can I talk to?"

"How about Biatola?"

"Great. When?"

"I'll find him. Go to your tent and we'll come to you. Okay?"

With a nod Keely turned in the direction of his campsite. He walked along a well-used trail beside which were the sites of cyclists of all levels. The novelty of the weekend hadn't dissipated for any of them. Locked down in this remote park or having the race weekend in full swing didn't matter to them. They talked, played cards, cooked, ate, read books and magazines. They interacted with other campers and relaxed.

That was one of the main reasons Keely ventured to ride in these events. It was a drive and a half to get to most of the races but the distance it put between him and ordinary, worrisome, always busy regular life was well worth the effort. Elise often said that his whore was good for one thing, well, two things: riding and getting him to relax. He smiled at the thought of his wife and his two-wheeled whore.

His camping neighbours were both gone – riding or swimming or who knows what. Even with the park in lockdown he thought that Nadal was smart to keep the regular park attractions available. People could still swim and bike and barbeque. It kept sanity in the midst of an atrocity like murder. This was still a time to get away from their regular lives, at least for the moment. Keely wondered how long it would take before people complained to the park wardens about getting back to their lives, the everyday ones from which they had desperately escaped.

Keely reached for his cell phone and hit a well-used button. He put the little device to his ear and listened. Then he said, "Voice dial." After a few seconds he said, "Elise."

* * * *

Her cell phone rang, an annoying metallic shrill. She put one hand over her pocket to deaden the sound while her other hand plunged into her pocket.

The door flew open and she slid out on the tray. She couldn't look. Couldn't bring herself to turn over and stare at the faces of the two men who would end her life. She closed her eyes and thought of Keely. His rugged good looks. His crooked smile. His touch. He loved her. That was what mattered. She thought the phrase "I love you" and hoped that somehow her husband would receive the message.

"Mrs. Detective. Hello. We're up here."

"You know, it's very rude to ignore someone when they're talking to you."

"When you're backed into a corner, and you can't run, then, and only then do you fight."

She grabbed at a set of legs to her right, wrapping her arms around the ankles and squeezing them together. The killer fell backwards and screamed when he slammed against the stretcher, sending it rolling across the floor to ram the wall. Metal instruments clanged to the floor, sounding like wind chimes. She bit down hard on the man's shin, his screams making her bite harder. Her legs were already flailing, trying to kick at the other murderer but they couldn't connect.

She heard a slight click near her left ear then something hard pressed against her head.

"That was the safety coming off. Teeth off my brother's leg and hands behind your head."

She did as she was told. Her face resting on the cold floor, she looked right into the empty, dead eyes of her friend Jerry.

"Fucking bitch."

The man she'd bitten struggled to his feet and she heard him draw his gun.

"I'm going to enjoy this."

"No."

"Fuck you."

"No. We need her."

She heard a gun slide into a holster.

"Up you get, Elise McAdam."

She ducked her head down, chin to chest. She closed her eyes as they dragged her to her feet.

"Elise," the man with the high, smooth voice said. "You can look at us. We're not going to kill you."

"We're not?"

"Elise, open your eyes or I *will* kill you."

She felt the gun pushing against her temple and it acted as a button to open her eyes. A tall man with a pleasant face smiled back at her. His hair was mid-length but thinning giving him a high, wrinkleless forehead. He looked like anyone you'd see on the street. His jeans and T-shirt only helped to bolster that image.

"Thank you," he said. "I'm Sweet. And my associate is Sour."

"What the fuck are you talking about?"

Elise darted her eyes right and saw that Sour was dressed in grey sweats. He was shorter and stockier than Sweet.

"Let's get you home, Elise. You've had a rough day. Then we can call your husband and ask him to do something for us."

Sweet looked at Sour and waited. After a few seconds Sour's face flashed in recognition.

"I get it now."

"Go to the car and grab a zip tie for her hands. She's got some spunk this one. No sense taking any chances."

"Be right back."

Sour dashed from the room but it had little effect on Elise. Being alone with one killer instead of two did nothing to relieve her tension.

"Sit." Sweet manoeuvred Elise backwards until she found a desk chair and sat. "I hope you have coffee. I'm dying for a cup."

Elise's phone started ringing again and she wanted nothing more than to answer it in the hopes it would be Keely. If she could just hear his voice she knew she would be okay.

Sweet leaned down to face her. "I'll let you speak to him in due time. Gotta get you home first."

* * * *

Keely hung up the phone. She must be in the middle of the shoot. Never takes calls when she's working. He'd call again and if she was still busy, he'd leave a dirty message. The thought made him chuckle.

"What's so funny?"

He looked up from his comfy folding chair and squinted against the afternoon sunlight to see Leila, Daniele Biatola looming large by her side.

"We ride as team," the huge man said, "but I ride to win for me. So what?"

"Ah, it's nice to meet you, too," Keely said while standing, then he stuck out his hand. Biatola nearly crushed it as he shook it then abruptly dropped it.

"You'll have to forgive my straightforward friend. He doesn't believe in beating around the bush. Actually, he likes to pummel the bush and any living thing in it."

"I can see that," Keely said and smirked.

"Part of why we wanted him on our team. Killer instinct, ya know?"

"Please, pull up some chairs." He pointed to the folding chairs against a nearby tree. They set them up and sat in front of him. "Can I get anyone anything? A water, a cookie, raw meat?"

Leila grimaced and Keely wasn't sure if she was stifling a laugh or preparing for Biatola to lunge.

"Ask questions so I can go."

Keely thought for a few seconds, shrugged and dove right into the deep end. "What do you eat?"

Biatola crinkled his face as if he was struggling with constipation. "Food."

"You know, you may have your team fooled, but not me, pal. The 'I'm a dumb immigrant' act is so fucking lame a first-year detective could eat you alive in an interrogation. Accent, yes. Bullshit, no. Okay?"

"Okay. It's business. You understand."

Leila looked at Keely, amazed at what she'd heard. Biatola's accent had all but subsided.

"Why, Dan?" she asked, her mouth drooping.

"Allow me," Keely said and waited for Biatola to nod his approval before answering. "Because Danny here is playing a part. The strong, silent type. Or is that the loud, slow type?"

"Hey, don't make it personal."

Keely threw up his hands. "You're right. I'm sorry. It's entertainment, Leila. That's all. The man has a persona like a wrestler and he has to live with it until his career is over or he moves on to something else. My guess," Keely looked at Biatola like a designer would check out a model. "You took a shot with it and found it was working for you, then you were stuck with it."

"Pretty much. Though you're wrong about one thing. I like it. I may not sound smart, but my merchandise outsells every rider on the circuit."

"I don't bloody believe it. Daniele, how could you not tell me?"

"Sorry, Leila. Trade secret."

"Until Todd found out."

The weight of the outlandish possibilities in that statement hit Leila like a punch. Keely watched her face change, her body tense, as she weighed the facts in the sudden case against Daniele Biatola. "Did you—?"

"I'm a lot of things. But a murderer? Not a chance."

The man was at ease, almost lounging in his chair. He was a showman, an entertainer. Keely wondered, could he be playing the innocent man?

"What did you have to do for his silence?"

Now the muscular rider began to sweat – he fidgeted in his chair. "Can I get a bottle of water?"

Keely reached down and opened the cooler beside his chair. Pulled out a water and handed it to Biatola. He cracked the top and gulped half the bottle in seconds.

"Do I need a lawyer?"

"Do you think you need a lawyer?"

The other man stared at that open bottle in his hands like it was a crystal ball showing him the future. "I didn't do anything to Todd. Nothing. I swear."

Leila jumped in. "You threatened to, didn't you? That's why he wouldn't work out with you. He never wanted to ride with you."

"You're wrong, Leila. He threatened to expose me. To tell the world I was acting."

"So what?" she yelled. "You're one of the best riders in the world."

"That's not enough to make a living. I needed the persona to drive sales. It's a model. The detective is right, I picked it up from wrestling and it damn well worked. Nothing like this has been done in pro cycling but I knew it would work. I moved here, changed from road to mountain biking, it worked. If Todd had opened his big mouth I was finished."

"So you pushed him off the cliff."

"Look, detective, I liked Todd, but he didn't want to let it go. He was jealous. He didn't want to ruin me, he wanted—"

"A piece of the action."

"Extortion?" Leila said. "He was blackmailing you?"

"I made up my mind. I want a lawyer."

"Good call," Keely said. "Want to use my phone?"

* * * *

"Hey, Numbers. I'm surprised to hear from you, this call's going to cost you."

"Don't I know it."

"Elise said she'd be calling me after you guys spoke. Is she there? I've been trying to get hold of her all afternoon."

"That's just it. She didn't show for dinner. She's not one to skip a meeting, ya know?"

Keely turned the knob that cut the propane to the element of his small camping stove. The burgers were done. "Yeah, she's good about stuff like that. I bet she just got busy is all. Maybe she forgot."

"Oh, yeah. Like your wife ever forgets anything."

"Did you call her cell? Oh, wait. I've been calling it and no answer so never mind. Try calling Krull—"

"I did. No answer."

Keely cradled the phone with his shoulder and used a spatula to put the burgers on the buns. "Hey, Numbers, would you mind swinging by the morgue to check on her, please? I'll pay you gas money."

"And a dinner."

Keely listened to the line go dead. *She's just too damned committed to her work*, he thought, and squirted ketchup on a burger.

Chapter 12

"I'm at the door but you know this damned place. Fort Knox. Locked up tighter than a drum. Her car's here so I'll wait 'til they're done."

"Nah, you've told me all the information so I'll let Elise know we talked. No sense you hanging around."

"Keely, she's going to pay me gas money and buy me dinner, remember?"

"Oh, shit, Numbers. You never forget do you, ya cheap bastard."

"Frugal, my good man. Frugal."

They shared a laugh. "Thanks for talking to that coach. Good information that just makes this situation even more screwed up."

"Ah, then my job is done here."

* * * *

Of all the trails he'd ridden, Algonquin's was by far the hardest and most beautiful. He could perceive the latter now that the race was cancelled. During his four laps he was concentrating on the trail, his cadence, gear selection, body position. He didn't have time to soak up the pristine forest, the brightly coloured flowers, the flora and fauna of Northern Ontario.

Parts of the trail smelled as if the builder had sprayed them with a floral scent. Usually Keely had no clue as to its origin; he couldn't tell a daffodil from a pansy. On this particular section the trees backed away from the trail and allowed trilliums to hug its sides. Keely sniffed the air and enjoyed the mellow fragrance.

Elise would pull out a guide to flowers and name it – she wouldn't be able to pass it without knowing. Worse, she'd take photos of one flower for an hour, if he was lucky, longer if he wasn't. Part of the reason he rarely asked her to ride with him — it took way too long with all the stops for photos. Taking photographs wasn't his thing, and he sure as hell couldn't figure out the appeal for Elise, but there was no way he'd ever knock it. She loved it, so he bit his tongue and watched her enjoy her passion.

The wide trail narrowed slightly and ascended at a leisurely angle. Keely didn't even change gears. He put a bit more pressure on the down stroke and pulled up a wee bit harder on the upstroke which got him to the top of the short climb in a few seconds. The top levelled and the trees once again crowded around him. Some of them had the audacity to grow on the trail and he swerved around them. A few poked exposed roots across the barren dirt as if searching the opposite side or, Keely thought, to try and trip him up.

He'd seen no sign of bears and even felt his body loosen at the thought. He'd never encountered a bear near or far and was happy to keep it that way. He blamed his irrationality on nature programming. Elise was forever watching Animal Planet or Discovery or one of those stations that scared the crap out of you. He'd be sitting reading the latest Stephen King novel and his attention would be pulled to the screen where a narrator was telling of how someone had been killed by a bear, what they did wrong and what they could have done right to save themselves. He'd seen way too many of those programs for his liking and made a mental note to cancel those stations.

He clicked his gear lever and heard the chain engage a larger cog. Slightly more tension greeted his clipped in feet and he strained his legs for a few pedal strokes to increase his speed and level the tension. He settled into a rhythm and though conscious of all the hazards he approached like trees, roots, rocks and drops, he allowed his mind to drift, ruminating over the terrible situation in the park.

It wasn't even twenty-four hours since the body of Todd Watkins, number one rider in the mountain bike world, had been discovered at the base of a cliff. Shortly thereafter the best female mountain biker in the world goes missing. The odds of the two being separate, mutually exclusive incidents caused a gruff, "Ha!" to spring from Keely's throat. He slowed to a near crawl and threaded his bike through a pair of twin trees attempting to pinch off the trail. Both riders were on the same team and used to be lovers. Now, the second female rider in the world, Sarah Stokes, is with Todd, who is allegedly blackmailing the number two rider in the world, Daniele Biatola.

"One big, happily-dysfunctional family," Keely said to a squirrel on the trail, which flicked its tail and scurried into the underbrush. "You. I can take."

Was Kira pissed enough at Todd to kill him and then Sarah killed Kira? Stranger, far more perverse things had happened and Keely had worked the cases to prove it. Then there was Biatola. Keely couldn't blame him for wanting to hide his persona as long as he could. It was no secret that athletes' careers were short. Add an unforeseen injury and it was even shorter. Biatola needed to keep the cash flowing as freely as possible for as long as he could. Had he killed Todd to stop the outflow of cash and shut him up at the same time?

Keely rounded a sweeping bend that rose steeply for about twenty feet, and when he straightened the bike out of the turn, he'd forgotten the six-foot dropoff. His front wheel was over the edge before he could put is body in the proper position. His speed was wrong, his gear was too high, his bike was dropping front wheel first and there was nothing he could do about it.

He hammered the brakes but even that was the wrong thing to do. It slowed him even more to guarantee he'd be tangled with his bike when he hit the ground. He tried to correct by pushing hard on the handlebars to throw himself free of the bike. It didn't work. He tumbled upside-down and felt the full weight of his bike compress him into the hard ground. His body snapped open and the bike flew over him to land a few feet away. His head was next to the bottom of the six-foot cliff, his feet pointing down the trail. He caught his breath quickly, consciously slowing it. He mentally checked his body, waiting for pain that never came.

"This is how you should've landed," he said to Todd, knowing full well the man wouldn't hear him. "Someone hit you in the head and you fell off backwards. Tell me who it was."

A bike appeared over the lip, moving so fast that Keely couldn't even roll off the path to get out of the way. It landed with a clang not far from his feet then skidded to a stop.

Sarah Stokes dropped her bike and approached Keely. She smirked down at him. Her fresh, youthful face was still blotchy and puffy from crying.

"Having a bad day?"

Keely sat up and brushed dirt from his legs. "You have no idea."

"We better get you off the trail, 'cause not everyone can clear you."

Once they'd moved to sit a safe distance off the trail, their bikes resting on their sides behind them, Sarah asked about the case.

"I wish I had an answer for you. I just don't know what happened to him. Yet."

She instantly soured. "I know she had something to do with it. I just know it. Kira was so angry with him for choosing me."

"Look in your heart. Do you really believe that she would kill Todd?"

"Abso—"

Keely raised a hand. "I'm not looking for surface reactions. I want you to search your memories, to pull from all the experiences you've had with this woman, and tell me if you truly believe she killed Todd."

She squinted as if to suppress a sneeze, but Keely had seen enough people trying not to cry to know that Sarah was hurting. She propped her forehead onto her knees and wrapped her arms around her bent legs for cover.

"She helped you," he said and laid a hand lightly on her back. "She welcomed you to the team, helped you fit in, showed you the ropes. She stopped to help you at the Olympics. You'd fallen and she helped you up. She got your chain back on and push-started you."

Sarah's eyes crested the crook of her arm. "Yeah, she did all that."

"And you betrayed her."

Sarah squinted, forcing tears to spill on her eyelids. She hid her face and when she spoke her voice was muffled.

"It just happened. I didn't mean for it to happen. I loved her so much. She was so good to me. And then she just got so mean when Todd broke it off with her."

Keely rubbed the young woman's back and slid himself closer to her. "You hurt her. It was a betrayal that she obviously couldn't get over. Maybe she will in time. A long time."

Sarah stuck her head out of her shell. "You think she's alive, don't you?"

He eased away to put a foot between them. "I'd put money on it."

"Where? Do you think she killed Todd? Is she involved?"

"Easy," he cautioned. "I'm sure she's alive, but beyond that, I can't say much of anything."

Sarah wiped her face with the terrycloth side of her cycling gloves. The brightness of her pink shirt was darkened in a few places from spilled tears. She took a deep breath and looked at him as if preparing for a difficult race.

"Do you suspect her?"

Keely blew out a burst of air, like a whistle gone awry. "Kid, for now, even you're a suspect."

* * * *

She said she'd ride with him, but somewhere along the trail he figured that Sarah needed to search inside herself for the answer to that difficult question Keely had asked her.

He'd watched her manipulate her bike and body in such graceful harmony. She made riding a mountain bike look like a dance, the bike her well-tuned partner. After years of practice they were flawless together. When she'd catch air, Keely swore she floated – a ballerina tossed and twirling, defying gravity, then landing delicately on the ground.

She absorbed bumps with barely a motion in her body, her bike and hands and legs suddenly one – a machine designed for protection against whatever a trail could threaten. She did it all without a thought. He'd pulled up beside her and recognized every rider in her expression – gone, lost, in another place. She'd escaped with the rest of us, he'd thought.

Then she had lost track of her less-skilled riding partner. He didn't mind at all. It had been a pleasure watching a professional at her craft. She'd flawlessly geared up, hammered down, and left him behind, smiling.

She'd asked a very important question. Keely was certain Kira was alive, but where? The answer to that question lay in whether she had been involved in the murder of Todd Watkins, or whether she was running from Todd's murderer. The answer was not going to be easy to find.

One thing became clear as Keely successfully cleared a log. The search for Kira Bremner was a complete waste of time. You won't find someone who doesn't want to be found.

* * * *

He sat on a hill overlooking a beach. Which one of the dozens of lakes in the park he was looking at, he couldn't say, nor did he care. Keely watched swimmers enjoying themselves in the light of the late-day sun. He heard the occasional squeal from someone being splashed or splashing someone else. He'd go for a swim later tonight. He wasn't a strong swimmer and always felt embarrassed about it. That, and he hated his body. Elise said he was just showing his feminine side. He told her it was his forming man boobs, or 'moobs' as Elise called them. Either way, he was waiting until the beach was empty.

A light wind cooled him but also forced him to smell himself. He definitely needed a swim, better yet, a shower. He lay down to stay out of the breeze. The sky was a deep blue smattered with red-tinted clouds. If this had been a race weekend he'd have finished hours ago and would have been in the car on his way home to see Elise. It was far from a normal weekend.

Kira's old coach hadn't been fired. He'd quit. He didn't want to be part of a team so heavily suspected of cheating. Numbers had no idea what Galdeano was talking about, but Keely did. There was a cloud of suspicion over cyclists that did well, just look at Lance Armstrong. The fact that *some* riders were caught had to mean that *all* riders cheated, right? So a team that had the top four riders in the world had almost everyone scrutinizing them, including governing bodies like the International Olympic Committee, the World Anti-Doping Agency, Canadian and Ontario Cycling Associations.

Keely couldn't blame them, or the fans, for thinking that all cyclists were dirty. It was so prevalent in the sport that prior to the 2006 Tour de France, team managers got together and banned cyclists from competing who were named in a drug investigation. Just *named*. They'd never been charged with anything, but realizing that the sport had to be held accountable, managers were banning their *own* riders. Keely found it an incredibly bold move and a massive step forward in attempts to get cycling out from under the doping scandal spotlight.

Yet he was forced to face the fact that Todd's murder and Kira's disappearance may have something to do with doping. He'd be a fool to ignore Kira's amazing turnaround and Todd's incredible record. The cycling world was all over it. The old coach's suspicions had to be taken seriously. What if a rival team was responsible? Keely's senses tingled at a new thought. What if a rival team *sponsor* was responsible?

Kickers was hard on the heels of Body Fuel and what would put them over the top? Getting rid of the two best riders on their rival's team. It was definitely another possibility. As was Amanda's trouble with her competitors. What a better way to knock out your main rival in the race organizing business than by committing a murder and a nice kidnapping during Amanda's race.

Keely's head hurt and he didn't have a light for his bike – night riding in these woods without a light could get him killed and not by bears either. He climbed back on his bike and pedalled for his temporary home.

* * * *

"We tried to stop them."

"What the hell did you do?"

"Looks like you get to go home."

"Lucky bugger."

Keely was greeted by a score of comments he didn't understand until he spotted George Arnsberg and Carl Stanski kneeling on his tent bag so they could zip it up.

"Detective." Arnsberg practically fell backwards when he saw Keely ride up. "We had orders."

"Yeah," Stanski added, his plastic face sullen. "We had no choice."

Keely looked at his things neatly packed away. They'd even taken down his makeshift clothesline. There was a duffle bag he didn't recognize leaning against his favourite tree.

"That's not mine."

"Oh, yeah. Whatever we couldn't fit into your other bags, we put in there," Stanski said.

"Please," Arnsberg said, his voice quivering.

"Let me guess," Keely said and dismounted his bike. "Robitaille."

"I'm sorry, detective, but you are being dismissed from the park," Arnsberg said and took a wide route around Keely.

"George, it's okay. I'm not mad at you."

Arnsberg stopped by the tree. "I'm really sorry. He was so pissed it scared me. He was swearing and I really wanted to get out of there."

"It's okay. Where is he? The hut?"

"Yeah. You're not thinking of going over there, are you?"

Keely turned to one of his neighbours, a slight woman and her overweight husband from Michigan. "Watch my stuff for a few minutes would you?" They nodded and Keely had to concentrate not to fall off his bike. He was shaking more than Arnsberg, except his tremors weren't from anxiety.

* * * *

Numbers hung up the phone and tried to think of how many times he'd called Elise and John. No one had come in or out of the building for over an hour. It was wrong. From what he could recall of John Krull, the guy was busy but made time if you needed him. How many messages did Numbers leave? Five?

He climbed from his little Hyundai and walked through the parking lot toward the back door. He made sure to stop at Elise's car for one last look. Might see something to explain all this.

He leaned against the curved window and with a salute, shaded his eyes from glare. The car was lived in but there was no phone, no broken glass, nothing out of the ordinary. He reached the back door of the building and by sight came to the same conclusion about the morgue. By gut, it was time to call in the troops.

Chapter 13

"Keely McAdam?" a large officer in uniform said.

Keely nodded, stopped his bike and got off. Another officer reached for the bike.

"Step away from the bike please."

"What the hell is going on?" Keely suddenly realized that he was surrounded by officers. "Am I under arrest?"

"No sir, not yet. I've been asked to escort you to my superior officer. Right this way."

A young officer propped Keely's bike against the wall and a parade of cops escorted him into the hut, through the halls and ending at Robitaille's makeshift office.

"That will be all," he said to the dozen policemen. He looked at Keely and motioned for him to sit down.

"No thanks. Say what you gotta say. Or is that, threaten what you have to threaten?"

The heat of the room had taken its toll on the detective sergeant. His eyes were puffy and red, he looked sick. An obvious lack of sleep in a high-stress situation. He rounded the table and stood a few feet from Keely.

"I was going to be nice, but if you want to be a prick—"

"You started it."

Robitaille stepped closer and Keely desperately wanted to back away.

"No. You started it when you got that little girl killed."

His fist was deep in Robitaille's stomach before his brain could signal the off switch. The French Canadian was doubled over and gasping for air. Keely stepped back and surveyed the damage. He didn't like what he'd seen. His mind now back to full capacity he turned to leave, but several officers were pushing him back through the door. One of them skilfully twisted his arm behind his back and slammed his face into the floor. He felt the cuffs dig into his wrists.

"Now you're under arrest, asshole."

Hands lifted him upright and shoved him hard into a folding chair. Robitaille had straightened, apparently recovering from Keely's punch.

"That will be all."

"But sir, there should be—"

"Out. All of you. Now."

Keely heard the door slam.

"Handcuffed. Doesn't seem like a fair fight, Rene."

"It isn't," he said, and smashed his fist into Keely's stomach. "Now we're even."

Keely tasted bile, its bitterness making him gag and cough. The pain was burning worse than any indigestion he'd ever had. There was no way he was going to show any of it to a man like Robitaille.

"You punch like a girl," Keely said, straining to make his voice loud enough to be heard. Robitaille's scarred face was inches away from his and Keely had to hold his breath to avoid the smell and taste of garlic. "You need to use more mouthwash."

"I warned you. Keep clean or go to jail. You didn't listen."

"I haven't done—"

"Shut the fuck up. You lying sack of shit."

Keely bent his head back and glared at Robitaille. "How do you really feel?"

Robitaille backed up, leaning against the wobbly table. "This is not a fucking game, Keely. People can get hurt. You're not fit for this anymore. Leave the park or I arrest you. Your choice."

"What's behind door number three?"

"I've got a guy saying Todd Watkins was blackmailing him but he had nothing to do with his murder. All before we even know if Watkins was murdered or if his death was an accident."

"You know he was murdered," Keely said.

"Do you have the coroner's report? Do you have the findings of the crime scene investigators?"

It took a few seconds for Keely to recognize that Robitaille expected an answer. Keely shook his head.

"Exactly. We don't jump to conclusions. Not like you. Because when you do, people end up dead, Keely."

"He was going to shoot her. I had no choice."

"You had a choice. You could have stayed out of that house, you fuckin' idiot. Janet Harper would still be alive."

Keely ignored the taunt. "Todd Watkins was murdered. He was hit in the head by a piece of wood and sent over that cliff. He was too good to make a mistake that big. Not like you, though. You're making a monumental fucking mistake right now."

"My only mistake was letting you stay in this park. I should have known you couldn't follow orders. You are out of this park in the next hour or you are under arrest for hindering an investigation. Your choice."

The door opened. "Sir. A Steven Bishop insisting he see—"

Bishop burst into the room. "I told him to investigate this case, detective sergeant. I hired him for the job. Get him out of those cuffs."

"That will be all," Robitaille said to the officer at the door then he turned on Bishop. "I don't care what you did. He only has two choices. Now, out he must go, and you, too. Out of my office."

"You can't do this," Bishop said. His face was pink and his hands slowly turned into fists. His body was rigid. Keely thought the man was going to have a heart attack at any moment. "I need Detective McAdam's expertise in this matter and he must be allowed to continue his work. I demand it."

"You demand it." Robitaille motioned for Bishop to step closer to the table. "You do nothing. You have been questioned in the case and now you'll step aside and let the proper authorities, not some mentally handicapped ex-cop, handle this. And if you persist you'll find yourself in the same jail cell as him."

Bishop was breathing erratically, his eyes darting about the room, searching for something. Maybe the answer to his predicament, Keely thought.

"Bishop. Hey, Steven," Keely said and waited for the businessman to look down at him. "Thanks. I'll be leaving the park. That's all. I'm leaving the park."

It only took a moment for Bishop to comprehend Keely's meaning, only Robitaille caught on at the same time.

"McAdam, I will be getting a court order that legally prevents you from participating in the investigation of this case. It is already in the works. Sorry, Mr. Bishop."

"Why are you so desperate to keep this man from helping?"

Robitaille softened, as much as a hard-assed, unfeeling man can soften. He looked at Keely and huffed. "You should ask Mr. McAdam that question."

* * * *

Keely had taken two of his folding chairs out of their bags and leaned back. The cold bottle of water he got from the vending machine at the hut felt fantastic against his throbbing head.

"You had no choice. You had to shoot him, right?" Bishop sat on the edge of the other chair, wringing his hands together.

"That's right. Get anyone to believe me and I'll wave that fee you offered."

"Why did you go in that house? Why did you disobey his order?"

Keely sat up and took the bottle from his head. "I've been asked that question about a hundred times by lawyers, union reps, cops, even my wife. I went in because Robitaille was wrong. I'd dealt with Curt Harper before. He was diseased. Hit first and don't give a shit later. Killed his wife but we didn't have enough evidence to hold him. He got bail. His kid was safe until Robitaille led Curt right to her. I knew before I got there he'd ask for something. Money, a plane to Mexico, something ridiculous. But he only wanted one thing. He wanted to kill the person that saw him kill his wife."

"He was going to kill his daughter no matter what?"

"That's right. When he didn't show up for his hearing, we put all points out on him. Thing was, Robitaille let it slip to the media that his daughter was ready to testify. He said all they had to do was go back to her home and get a few of her belongings."

"Oh, God. You mean that Robitaille was using that girl as bait?"

"Yeah. He thought they'd show up and Robitaille would knock on the front door. Harper hid in the house and waited until they showed. He grabbed the girl and forced all the cops out of the house."

Bishop reached out and snatched the bottle of water from Keely, cracked the top and took a drink.

"Help yourself."

"That's when you decided to act. To go in the house and try to save the girl."

Keely grabbed the bottle back. "No communicable diseases I hope." He took a drink. "Yep. That's it. I saw it in his eyes. The girl first, then me. So I may not have been fast enough to save her, but I saved me. Can't begin to tell you how guilty I've felt ever since. Survivor's guilt, the pros call it."

"I've heard of it. People who survive plane crashes often suffer from that."

Keely stared at the ground and tried hard to shake the vision of Janet Harper. "Well, I hate to rush you out, but I want to lug this stuff to my car before it gets dark. Thanks for walking back."

"So you're really giving up?"

Keely laughed. It felt good, too. "What are you, crazy? Of course not."

* * * *

Two patrolmen stood by the back door of the morgue. They looked happy to have something to do on a Sunday afternoon. A man in his Sunday best was unlocking the inner door.

"Yeah, station called the building management and sent a guy to open her up," the slender cop said. "Bada-bing."

"Thanks. I'm a bit worried about my friend. Two hours late for dinner and no answer and—"

"Don't worry about it," said the second cop, who could be the first cop's twin in body type only. "We're happy to help."

"Okay." The man emerged from the door. "Nothing wrong with the door. Here's the keycard."

"Stick around. We might need you."

Numbers let the cops do their job. He watched them walk cautiously into the building, then disappear through a door marked "Stairs."

He looked at the other man. "Interrupted Sunday dinner did we?"

"Thanks. My in-laws were driving me nuts."

"Glad we could help."

One of the cops burst through the door, his partner close on his heels but staying in the door frame. "You two get back from this door right now. We have a situation."

He grabbed the little radio clipped to his shoulder and pressed the mike key. "Dispatch. Unit 54-10."

A tinny voice came from the radio, "Go ahead, 54-10."

"We're at the morgue. Two dead men inside, one I know is the coroner. Please send appropriate back up."

"What the fuck?" Numbers headed for the door, his own gun drawn.

"Sir, you can't go in there," the cop at the door said stepping to block the entrance. "We haven't secured the area."

"I have a friend in there. Did you see a woman inside?"

"No," said the officer, motionless in the doorway. "Two men. One back in autopsy room, the coroner is in his office. I haven't seen anyone else."

"Kid, I think whoever did this is gone. I've been in the parking lot for an hour and there's been no movement."

The second cop must have heard every word since he was back on his radio. "There may be a third victim. Advise."

There was a long silence broken with short spurts of static. Then, "54-10. Advise. Wait for backup."

Numbers pushed the young cop aside and stepped into the building.

"Sir, we have to wait for backup."

He spun on the officers, both took a step back. "What if she's alive and needs medical care? What if she's being held hostage? We're wasting time." Mick turned from them and hear words, but they didn't register. Elise was in there and he was going to find her. The stairs were right beside the door and he remembered the layout of the building though he hadn't been inside in over five years. He came out of the stairs two floors down. It was too quiet.

"Elise." Numbers yelled. "It's Mick. You can come out. You're safe now."

* * * *

The last piece of gear was his bike, which he elected to ride to the parking area. Leila was leaning on his truck waiting for him, and two OPP officers were standing on either side of her.

"Fancy meeting you here," he said.

"Where are you going?" she asked.

"These fine gentlemen didn't explain it to you?" The two cops could barely make eye contact with him.

"Keely, I need you to stay. Please."

"You don't get it. I stay and they drag my ass to the nearest holding cell. I gotta go."

She grabbed his arm and looked intently into his eyes. "I need you darling."

Before he could react to her odd statement, she grabbed his face with both hands and kissed him.

"You can't leave me, baby. I need to talk to you, now."

It was something in the way she looked at him that made Keely play along. "Uh, guys, could I have like a minute or two, alone with…"

The subtle laughter was all the answer Keely needed. He took Leila by the arm and led her a dozen yards away from his escort.

"What the fuck are you doing?"

"Paulo Chagas is missing."

He had to consciously fight against yelling. "Is there a fucking black hole in this park that I don't know about?"

"He went out with one of the search patrols, told someone he was going to join up with another search party. No one has seen him since."

"You know what? I don't think he exists, because I've never seen him. I think you're making him up."

"Keely, this is serious. Some sick bastard is picking off my team one by one, and I'm afraid that eventually he'll get to me. I'm scared."

She sounded scared, too. He couldn't help but hug her. In that moment he tried to make sense of it all. Why Chagas? What was his connection?

"Did Chagas get along with everyone? Was there even more tension on this team beyond love affairs and extortion?"

"See, that's just it. They all loved this guy. Regardless of how they felt about each other, they would have done anything for Paulo. That's what scares me."

Keely felt his phone vibrate against his leg. If he hadn't been waiting to hear from Elise, he would have ignored it, but he'd been getting worried. He glanced toward the cops to make sure they were still out of earshot. He pulled out the phone and hid it as best he could.

"Elise."

"Keely, it's Mick. We have a problem."

"Keely," Leila said, sounding desperate. "What do I do?"

"Mr. McAdam, time to go," one of the cops said now at Keely's side.

Chapter 14

The stretch of Route 60 inside the park is identified on most maps as the Algonquin Route. A short haul of about twenty-five kilometres, at this time of year it was fairly busy with people heading into the park to camp, fish or hike. There are the sightseers, though, people who drive the route in hopes of seeing a bear, moose or deer. A nice, relaxing drive regardless of how you looked at it. Keely was doing 160 kilometres an hour. The only thing he hoped was that if he saw a bear, moose or deer he wouldn't hit it. Well, maybe a bear.

Elise was missing. He had to get home.

His Explorer groaned when he pushed the pedal down for more speed. Despite the complaint, his Ford went faster. Sixty took him to 11 South through Huntsville. He could be home in about three hours if he maintained a decent pace. Two things were going to slow him down: traffic and the checkpoint out of the park. He'd take the damned shoulder if he had to. Retired or not, his badge was all he needed and mentioning the homicides of the coroner and his assistant would be enough to keep him moving.

There was no physical evidence that Elise had been hurt, let alone killed. She may very well have eluded her captors and was now on the run, or better, hiding somewhere in that building or in its vicinity. She was smart. She'd survive given even a minute chance. *She's alive.* He said it in his mind a thousand times as the roadblock loomed in the distance.

Numbers had assured him that he would insist on being part of the investigation, considering the circumstances. Keely knew better. In fact, if Keely were in charge of the case, he'd have to hold Mick Moyer for questioning. He was at the scene and was to meet one of the parties involved. Knowing Numbers, Keely had no doubt the man had nothing to do with it, but the incoming investigator had to do his job. Numbers had good intentions for which Keely thanked him, but he was in for a few uncomfortable interview sessions. Then again, Mick Moyer had been a cop for thirty years. He'd danced the steps before, only in the lead.

Keely swore to himself he'd spring Mick the moment he got to 54 Division. That was the closest station, and it housed the homicide squad. The Forensic Identification Unit was in a nearby facility. Keely knew without being told that there was still no apparent motive for the murders at the coroner's office.

Murders. Keely rolled the word around in his mind, searching for a logical place to put it. He wasn't close to John Krull, but he knew him, had worked very well with him on dozens of cases and now that man was dead. His children would be devastated. Krull had been a tireless advocate of perfection. He believed that even the slightest error in this, our advanced technological and information age, would be enough to convict innocent people. The responsibility to get the job done right had never been greater.

A true pine scent from the trees on either side of the highway filled Keely's nostrils as he breathed in deep to control his emotions. He made himself stop the running eulogy to his friend and concentrate on driving. The last thing he needed was to end up in a ditch. The last thing Elise needed was for him to be dead and unable to find her.

The roadblock was on the opposite side of the road to prevent traffic from entering the park. It must have been a major inconvenience for residents in nearby towns since it was often used as a regular thoroughfare. An officer stepped onto the road but Keely was already slowing. He stopped when his open window was beside the officer.

"Detective."

"Officer."

The OPP patrolman had the look of a newbie – fresh and raw. He leaned on the frame of the window and, after a glance into the back seat, said, "Have a safe trip home."

"Thanks."

Keely floored the gas pedal, squealing his tires and causing the cop to stumble when the car sped forward. The roadblock was a speck in his mirror in no time. He gave his route choice a second thought, since side roads may be clearer, but decided to stick to his original plan. If things got bad he'd bail for an alternate.

He saw his first car, a station wagon filled with camping gear, headed east toward the park. The driver probably hadn't been listening to the radio. He'd have no idea his vacation would be on hold for a few days more.

Keely's cell phone vibrated in the square space in the plastic compartment of the console beside the emergency brake. He snatched it up and flipped it deftly open with one hand.

"Elise?"

"Not yet," a calm male voice said.

Keely waited, hoping for more. "Where is my wife?"

"Right here. Safe and sound with Sweet. Oh, and my colleague, Sour."

"I don't care what you call yourself, you're a dead man."

"Careful," the man said with more bite. "I can kill her. I could cut her throat right now and you couldn't do a thing to stop me."

Keely slammed on the brakes and the heavy SUV fishtailed on the asphalt until he negotiated it onto the shoulder. The Explorer slid to a stop on the gravel on the side of the deserted highway. "If you touch her," he screamed into the phone. "I swear I won't stop until you're dead."

"Detective. Calm down."

"I will fucking make you suffer you sick—"

"Detective," Sweet yelled. His voice crackly but clear enough that Keely stopped his rant. "Better. Much better."

"Let me talk to her."

"Not yet. Listen first, then you can talk to her."

"Fuck you."

The phone went dead. "No. No. Wait." Keely fumbled with the phone, his fingers suddenlty feeling too thick to press single buttons. Finally, after several failed attempts, he hit the speed dial number he'd used so easily and so often. Elise's phone rang.

"I want to talk to her first," he said the moment Sweet answered.

"No. I am in charge here. You do what I say and she lives. Make me hang up this phone again and she's dead. Understood?"

Never panic. Keely knew he had no choice and, after a few seconds, said, "Yes."

"That's more like it. Now, we know that I have someone of yours. I'll trade you for someone I need."

Keely waited through the silence, listening intently for any sound that would give him a clue as to where his wife was being held. It was easy to see that Sweet wanted Keely to be more active in this little game. "I'll bite. Who do you need?"

"Kira Bremner."

The shock wore off fast.

"She's alive somewhere in that park, isn't she?" Keely asked.

"I don't know and I don't care. Bitch could be in Brazil for all I know. You need to find her and bring her to me so you can get your pretty little wife back in one piece."

"I just got kicked out of that park. There's no way I can—"

"No way," Sweet said, the words sounding like daggers. "Then she's dead."

"Wait. I'm one guy. There's a whole department of cops out looking for her, what makes you think I can find her?"

"Keely," Elise's voice shrilled through the little phone. "Oh, God, Keely. I'm sorry."

"Elise. Honey, are you okay?" Keely asked, on the verge of tears at hearing how terrible she sounded. "It's okay. I'm going to get you. I'll find you."

"Keely, I'm at—"

"I suggest you get started, detective," Sweet said, Elise's muffled voice crying out in the background. "Call this number when you have Kira."

The phone went dead. Keely threw it on the passenger seat, pushed the shifter to drive, then hammered the gas pedal. He swung the truck sharply left and gunned the engine, spraying gravel out behind him until the tires found purchase on the solid, smooth road. He headed back in the direction of the park.

* * * *

His mind couldn't process the information fast enough. Murders, Elise's abduction, his banishment from the park, Todd Watkins, extortion. He was dealing with so much but instantly, upon picturing his wife's smiling face, his focus was clear – save Elise. Nothing else mattered.

How? He'd meant what he'd said to the man calling himself Sweet. He was working alone and very much on the outside. Need he go it alone? Could he trust the cops? Most of them, yes. But whatever cop he confided in would eventually have to report to Robitaille. That was a man he couldn't trust. Or maybe it was Robitaille's lack of trust in Keely that made him speed up when the roadblock appeared in the road.

He glanced at the speedometer; the truck was approaching one-seventy. Rookie stepped out in front of his cruiser, his partner nowhere in sight. Keely wondered how long the man had been on the force as he watched him raise his hand as if holding some magical power that could stop speeding vehicles.

Keely jerked the wheel and the Explorer glided into the left lane. It was completely clear of traffic and the newbie was smart enough to jump in his vehicle instead of jumping in the middle of the road in an attempt to stop Keely. The cruiser's lights sparked to life as the car backed up then pulled onto the road in pursuit of Keely. He noticed the rookie's partner in the passenger seat.

The cruiser was well back but closing. What was the plan? Had Keely even considered a car chase? What did he expect was going to happen – a welcome banner? He pushed the four-year-old Explorer to its limit, checked the rear-view mirror and was shocked to see it filled by the big white car with its blue trim. The siren was wailing at full volume.

The rookie'd radio ahead for sure, Keely thought. He had to shake these two and get off Route 60.

"For you, honey," he said. He manoeuvred the truck as far right on the road as he could without touching the gravel. He watched his pursuer carefully until the centre of the cruiser was directly behind the left taillight of the SUV.

"I hope you're wearing seatbelts, boys," he said and smashed the brakes with both feet. The sound of thunder and a massive thrust forward indicated the cruiser had slammed into the left rear corner of the Ford. Keely had been ready and torqued the wheel left to compensate for the impact. The Explorer bucked and slid and rumbled, but stayed on the road. The cruiser's front and back ends swapped positions several times as it skidded by Keely. It was off the road and in the ditch in seconds.

He had no time to check to see if the officers were all right, or to check if his bike was still safely attached to the roof rack. He drove on knowing he'd be a target. His was the only car on the road, and it was bright red to boot.

He knew of only two roads off of 60, both dirt, once old logging roads he figured. The first was the parking area to the day-use site in Algonquin, the second was beyond the last lake along the route. It was on the north side, but that was all he could remember. It was his only chance to get back into the park. If that road still existed.

He'd seen it when dropping off Elise for a five-day photography workshop with some pro shooter Keely'd never heard of. Elise, on the other hand, was ecstatic to be going. She'd had a wonderful experience. The photographs she'd shared a week later were absolutely spectacular. She was very good at what she did. He needed to make sure she'd get a chance to keep doing it. One problem. Or was that six problems? The half-dozen cruisers blocking the road ahead. The rookie had done the right thing. He'd radioed for help.

Keely slowed the car and stopped in the middle of the road a hundred yards from the blockade. *I am driving a four-by-four; could it make it through the ditch? Then what?* Keely unfastened his seatbelt and grabbed the door handle — making a run for it in the woods was his best option. The door wouldn't open. It had somehow been damaged in his collision with the rookie. He began the awkward climb over the console onto the passenger seat. There was a tap on the backdoor window behind the driver's seat. He turned to see an officer with her gun drawn, then another appeared at the passenger window.

Keely raised his hands and said, "Sorry, but I forgot something at my campsite."

* * * *

"Are you almost here?" Numbers said, his pitch as high as his concern. "They grilled me for two fucking hours. I gave them a complete description of Elise. They found no evidence—"

"Mick. I'm not coming."

"What? Are you drunk?"

"No. Look, I'm in a jam," Keely said and glanced around at the few OPP officers watching him make his "one phone call." "I need you to bail me out."

"You're in jail!"

"I'll explain when you get here. I'm in the Whitney detachment. Get your ass up here as fast as you can and sorry, Numbers, I'm going to need your credit card. My limit is almost maxed out."

* * * *

The Whitney detachment of the OPP was like any other in Northern Ontario, a brick box on the edge of a small town. There was plenty to do on a Saturday night in Whitney, but this was Sunday night, so all of those charged with drunk and disorderly had been released hours ago. Keely was alone in his cell. A bench in a horseshoe around the cement wall ended at bars in front. There was no window and no other cells.

He was shaking but not from the chill in the cell. The thought of Elise tied up somewhere, helpless or worse, hurt, consumed him. They wouldn't dare lay a hand on her. They needed him obedient and he sure as hell made it clear he wouldn't be if anything happened to his wife.

When Numbers posted his bail he'd explain the situation. Mick would help him find Bremner. He may have to cover the miser's expenses, which Keely would gladly do. Yeah, Mick was a good guy. He'd help. And, more importantly, Keely could trust him.

The grey metal door opened at the far end of the room. Keely had been waiting for this since his failed attempt to re-enter the park. Robitaille was going to eat this up. He could charge Keely with all kinds of offences, not the least of which was assaulting an officer. That one carried a few years in the clink and people always got the max. Judges were very sympathetic to the hazards of police work.

Officer Ono, her uniform looking as pristine as the day she graduated, strolled to the front of Keely's cell. She removed her hat to show jet-black hair pulled back in a ponytail. Even in his dire situation he couldn't help but notice her beauty. She grabbed the bars and leaned her head against two of them. He heard her take a deep breath, then she lifted her face so her dark eyes could penetrate him.

"You will appear when called. Right?"

"Of course," he said from his bench against the back wall.

"My family wishes to repay the favour."

Keely rushed to the bars. "I don't even know your first name."

"It doesn't matter. We are honoured to help you."

Chapter 15

Margaret. That was the name of his saviour and she was someone whose life he'd affected by chance. He was only doing his job during the investigation and hadn't at all gone out on a limb to protect Margaret Ono's uncle. If the evidence had pointed *at* Mr. Takata, then Keely would have been in for a much longer stay in holding.

They hadn't even formally charged him with anything when several people offered to post his bail. Besides Ono, there was a call from Numbers letting the OPP know he was on his way. Leila and Steve also offered. Leila he could almost understand, but Bishop? Yeah, he'd practically hired Keely to find Bremner, but he was speaking for the company. He didn't seem the type to easily open his wallet – a guy like Numbers. Leila must have strong-armed him.

He shifted his body to reposition himself on the plank they called a bench. He checked his watch, again. It was just after three in the morning. It should have taken no more than a few hours to book him and he didn't have to be present in court for them to set bail. Keely gritted his teeth, knowing that Robitaille was behind the delay. There could be no other reason for it.

The chill of the cement walls and the dampness of being subterranean was taking its toll. Keely felt clammy and several times had to clamp his mouth shut and breath slowly through his nose to help ward off vomiting. He needed to find his wife but what he did today was stupid. It was knee jerk. Slow and steady would win this race, he just had to fight his instinct to charge ahead.

"Last warning."

Keely was so deep in thought he didn't even hear Robitaille approach. He wasn't wearing his uniform jacket and his light blue shirt was untucked, the underarms stained dark blue. His thick black hair was dull and matted. His shoulders sagged but not nearly as much as the bags under his eyes.

"If only you'd see the truth. What happened is done. I can't bring that girl back. I was cleared of any wrong doing, as were you. Why the hell can't you let it go?"

Robitaille stretched his back, adding a few inches back to his height. "I could ask you the same thing."

Keely spit out a laugh. "So that's it. You'll only back off if I forgive you?"

"You arrogant fuck," Robitaille said.

Keely jumped to his feet and met the other man at the bars.

"You just won't admit that you screwed up and killed that little girl. If you'd stayed out of that house she'd be alive."

"No. That's what gets me through the night. I know she'd be dead either way. My mistake was not shooting the second I saw that sick bastard. That was my mistake. I can see it clearly, almost every night, that half second of time. I know what my mistake was. Why can't you see yours?"

Not a huge or powerful man by any means, Robitaille could still intimidate with posture and a certain look. Right now, as he wrapped his fingers around the bars, Robitaille's eyes flared like someone flaring their nostrils. He truly believed that he'd done nothing wrong. Or, at the very least, he would never admit to any errors.

It was an epiphany for Keely, one that might save his wife's life. "I'm sorry."

Robitaille stepped back, off balance. "What?"

Keely bowed his head and spoke to the floor. "I'm sorry. I was wrong. I should have followed your orders. You were in charge."

The dishevelled detective sergeant stared at Keely. His jaw was slack but his eyes twinkled.

"Let me work with you. I'll do whatever you want me to do. I'll man a phone, join a search party, clean your fucking shoes. Anything. Just get me back in that park."

The twinkle didn't last. "You want glory? Do you want to show me up so you can prove some stupid idea you have that I was wrong?" He stepped back to the bars and spoke quietly. "Now you're a liar, too. You'll do anything to make me look a fool, won't you, McAdam? But I'm not going to let you. You've made bail. Set foot inside that park again, and I'll shoot you myself."

"I could have you charged with uttering a threat."

"I don't give a damn." Robitaille released the bars and turned to walk away. He stopped and looked back with hate in his eyes. "Your mistake. Your half a second cost me more than you'll ever know. You may as well have killed two people that day. I've had to work ten times harder to get two steps ahead. All because you wanted to be a hero."

* * * *

His car had been impounded but he was allowed to remove necessities like clothes and toiletries. They didn't count his bike as a necessity. He was still crying over that one. The motel room was almost as bad as the holding cell, except it had gaudy floral patterned bedding and matching curtains. It was one room housing one double bed. The walls were cement blocks painted white. Quaint in a horror movie kind of way. The smell of bleach was settling to Keely. At least someone had tried to clean the place.

Numbers plopped himself in the only chair. Leila and Steve leaned against the slim dresser and Margaret sat on the opposite edge of the bed from Keely. He looked them over and smiled.

"What's so funny?" Numbers asked.

Keely shook his head. "Nothing's funny. I'm just glad to see you all."

"The big house was rough, eh?" Margaret said, still in uniform. "Didn't have any smokes to bribe the screws?"

"Now that's funny," said Leila, too big a smile on her face.

"Listen. I have to start somewhere and you're it. I don't know most of you very well, but I need to trust you with something."

They all listened intently while Keely told them about the phone call he'd received and the threat against his wife.

"I'm sorry, but if we find our cyclist she is our property." Bishop's heartless, corporate response wasn't a surprise – it was all about money.

"What about his wife?" Numbers said, his voice taut.

"We'll cross that bridge when we come to it," Bishop said.

Numbers put his hands on the arms of his chair and leaned forward to stand but Keely raised a hand to stop him. The big man eased back down, the chair squeaking its complaint.

"Right now, I'm exhausted. I have no idea where Kira is. I need you all to help me. And if you help me, Steven, there's a great chance you'll get your rider back. Will you all help me?"

They agreed. Even Margaret, who stood to lose the most if discovered assisting Keely, agreed to do whatever she could. "Robitaille is not a bad guy and he's pretty much interviewing and following the same leads you are, only he's thinking that she's dead. I think she's alive, like you do," she said.

A bit more discussion followed, but it barely registered with Keely. Everyone cleared out and agreed to meet first thing in the morning. He'd asked them to bring George Arnsberg along. He needed to get back in that park and who better to guide him than one of its wardens.

* * * *

He walked by the police barricades and strolled into the house. All the curtains were drawn and there'd been no movement. He walked in the front door, which was unlocked. He checked for his gun in the waistband of his pants, at the base of his spine. He had a little hope of talking Harper out of it, and showing empty hands was the right step.

He walked quickly down the hall and edged right, peeking around a corner to see Harper holding a gun to Janet's head. Harper's eyes had those crow's feet people get when they smile or laugh. His finger slowly squeezed the trigger. Keely pulled his weapon and fired. The sound was too loud. Harper fell back against the wall, frozen, his eyes still laughing. Keely looked at the floor in front of Harper's feet. Elise lay there, blood trickling from a tiny hole in her temple, blood flooding the floor around her. She was dead.

* * * *

Continental breakfast was stale cereal, warm milk and a muffin. It tasted about as good as Keely felt. He managed a few bites. His nightmare left him tired, as if sleep had been exercise.

"She's okay. We'll find her."

"Mick. I can't tell you how much I appreciate you dropping everything."

"Everything is really not much right now. I got a cheating husband thing that can easily wait a few days." Numbers took a big bite of muffin but still spoke as if his mouth were empty. "Besides, you'd do the same."

He was right. Numbers had been Keely's mentor as a homicide detective though they had known each other as beat cops first. They'd been through "stuff," as Numbers had once put it. Enough stuff to make two men friends for life. Keely smirked and slapped his big friend on the shoulder. "Let's go."

The coffee shop was a five-minute drive but felt like a world away from his dingy motel room. The sun spread through the window and struck Formica, chrome and glass. The glare and warmth energized all it touched, including Keely. Monday morning was obviously not the busiest day for this establishment since there were few patrons. Keely greedily ate his toast with renewed hope that he'd find Kira and get his wife back.

"How do I get back into that park?" Keely asked.

George cleared cups and plates from the centre of the little table and unfolded a map of Algonquin. "This park is the size of ten Torontos or New Yorks or any big city. Detective, you could fit Manhattan in here half a dozen times. How are you going to find Kira Bremner in something that big?"

Leila looked hard at him, obviously wondering the same thing.

"Good, old-fashioned detective work," Numbers said and swigged coffee from an ancient mug.

"Let's look at just the facts in Kira's case." George and Leila leaned on the table as if to make sure they wouldn't miss anything. Numbers' phone rang and he was soon in a conversation. Keely continued his rundown in a businesslike tone. "She was involved with Todd, who broke it off to be with Sarah. Todd is dead, possible homicide. Kira goes missing at the same time or shortly thereafter. We have an old coach who quit and a new coach that's missing. Alleged doping—"

"We're not doping," Leila said.

Keely raised a hand then said, "*Allegedly* doping. Okay, there are teams closing in, some dropping back, and let's face it, a whole host of reasons why Todd could've been murdered and Kira kidnapped."

"This is detective work?" asked George, his face screwed up.

Numbers snapped his phone closed. "They have their motive for the morgue murders. Todd Watkins' body is missing. They figure Elise stumbled onto the crime in progress and might have been kidnapped."

"You haven't told them she's being held?" Leila said and straightened.

"No. And no one is going to tell them." Keely lowered his voice. "I can't take the chance that it gets back to Robitaille. So now we know who has Elise, and it guarantees that Kira is alive and in that park."

"But—"

"They lied to me. They didn't want me to know that there is a connection between Kira and Todd," Keely said.

"We know the connection," Leila said. "They were teammates and former lovers."

Numbers jumped in. "Yeah, but whatever made these guys take a dead body from the morgue and kill two people to do it has a shitload more meaning than a screwed-up relationship. Kira saw what happened to Todd. She's running."

"That's what I figured, too," Keely said. "She's a witness to a murder and they need her out of the way. Only thing that bothers me is if that's true then they'd want the same end for Elise. She saw those guys kill Krull and his assistant."

Numbers slapped Keely on the back then squeezed his shoulder, a little too painfully. "We'll work it out. Don't worry about that now. Let's get this Kira girl first."

If anyone had an inkling of how Keely felt, it was Mick. Not that he'd had anyone close to him kidnapped, but like any detective or cop who'd put away bad people, he was always prepared for retribution. Bad guys rarely took it out on the arresting officers. They went after their families.

"That's a theory. Nothing more," Leila said and wiped tea from the corner of her mouth with the back of her hand.

"Yeah, it is. And a damned good one," Numbers said, a challenge in his tone.

"Look, Leila, the guys that stole Todd's body did it to hide some physical evidence that points to them. They would have taken his body from the park—"

"Shit. She's right." Numbers sounded hurt. "They couldn't have been in the park since George says no one could have gotten out in time. They couldn't have killed Todd."

Leila looked satisfied, but only slightly seeing as she'd bumped them back to square one. They ordered another round of coffees and a tea for Leila. As they were all preparing them to their liking, spoons tinkling on ceramic, George surprised them.

"Hey, what if the guys that have your wife aren't working alone? What if they have someone in the park that did the hit on Todd? What if the inside guy is Kira?"

Leila slammed down her spoon. "Don't be ridiculous. She'd never hurt Todd."

"Maybe not," Keely said. "But there are a lot of people in that park who'd benefit if your team lost. Better, if your team didn't exist. And there's still one other possibility that I'd love to check. Amanda's company took a huge hit because of all the shit that went down this weekend. She was on the verge of having the Canadian Cycling Association sanction her races. What if all this is sabotage?"

"Okay, forget all that for now and let's focus on the fact that this rider of yours is alive and well and hiding in the park." Numbers turned to George and pointed at his map. "Where? You'd know better than anyone the likeliest places to hide."

George looked out the window and Keely sensed his apprehension. "George, we won't get angry if we search somewhere and she's not there. We need the most likely spots she might go to. It's a place to start."

"You know, I always wanted to do this. I love *Law & Order*," he said and beamed a huge smile at Keely.

"Which one?" Keely asked.

"All of them."

* * * *

They'd spent an hour going over the map and George had been amazingly helpful. His knowledge of the park would be essential in the search. They had to be very specific in their targets. Using what information

Margaret could provide of the search patterns, they could stay well out of the grid and out of sight.

They all agreed, under the assumption she was alive, that Kira was still moving through the park. Which meant she would head for the nearest road out. That meant it had to be visible on whatever map was commercially available – she wouldn't have George's expertise. They picked two roads that were north and east of where the murder occurred. She couldn't go to the southern roads since she'd have to cross Route 60 and that was chancy when you were being stalked by killers and a search party of a few hundred people.

"My bet is Long Road," George had said, pointing to the track that represented the longest fire road in the park. Keely couldn't help but feel as though he were on a similar path only he'd describe it more like the song – long and winding. He'd entered a race for fun but now he was in a race to save his wife'sw life. It was absurd.

Numbers pulled his little Hyundai onto Route 60 and headed east toward Pembroke. Somewhere up there was Sideroad 28, which eventually disappeared and became whatever clear, flat surface you could find to drive on.

Chapter 16

"George said there'd be what looks like a downed telephone pole on the left side of the fire road about five or so clicks in," Keely said, staring out the front window.

"That's where the ATV will be?"

"He said to follow a path just beyond the pole. It'll lead to a little shack. ATV will be around that."

They were heading east on 62 towards Pembroke, but according to the map they wouldn't be visiting that little town. They were going to take a left on 17 then find Side Road 26. That would lead them to 28 and the fire road.

"I'm sorry I got you into this," Keely said, giving Numbers a quick, guilty look.

"What are friends for? Besides, it'll give you a chance to see how we work together."

Keely felt the same old knot tighten in his stomach. "I don't want to be a private detective."

"Thirty bucks for a license. That's it. Hell, I'll even pay it."

"No thanks, Mick. Save your money."

He smiled so warmly that Keely almost changed his mind. It was Numbers that had come to his rescue after the shooting. Robitaille had spread the word like a viral video – Keely McAdam was responsible for Janet Harper's death. Keely could still hear Numbers' words the night they'd gone to the local pub, twenty cops staring at Keely like he had pulled the trigger on the gun that killed Janet. "You gave her a chance." It was true. Keely knew that but it was great to hear it from someone he respected. The blue wall, as Keely found out, can shrink to a thin line. Having big Mick Moyer in his corner made life better.

Numbers had one big paw on the wheel and he rested the elbow of his left arm on the open window frame. He was as relaxed and casual as if he was taking a drive in the country with his wife.

"You know Nancy is going to have a fit."

"Are you kidding me? The moment I said I was going to be gone for a few days she took off to New York with her friends. She doesn't give a shit anymore. Might be fucking some guy for all I know."

"You're a private detective. Pretty easy to find out."

"I don't want to know. I love her in a weird kind of way now. That means if she's doing someone, I hope they're happy. Just wish she'd have the balls to say she wants out."

Numbers pulled the car onto 17 and hit the gas, speeding up when passing the sign for Petawawa, the Canadian Forces Base and a local airport.

"Not everybody has the courage or strength to do that."

"Tell me about it. Why the hell do you think I don't investigate? If I find something I'll have to act on it and she wins. She keeps pulling away and not talking or having sex. I figure eventually she's going to want out. Then she'll have to muster some balls."

"What about you, Numbers? You deserve to be happy, too. Why not just tell her *you* want out?"

He was silent for a long time and Keely thought the conversation was over. That was fine with him. He didn't mean to get so personal. He glanced out his window and watched small houses pass by surrounded by more shades of green than he ever thought existed.

"Because I don't want out."

Keely barely heard his big friend's whispered words yet their meaning was loud and clear. A football player in college, a tough cop, a big, brawny detective with scars and a bent nose, but a person who loved his wife enough to forgive anything she might do. Keely felt a mix of respect and pity for Mick. He wanted to shake him and make him see the light. "She's not coming back," he'd scream, but somehow Keely knew that it would do no good.

Long moments passed and both men stared silently at scenery.

"How 'bout those Bears?" Keely said and after a few seconds the car was filled with laughter.

"I needed that," Numbers said. "Oh, hey, what side road we looking for?"

"Left on 26 then right on 28."

"Almost there."

Good, Keely thought, he needed to act, to do something to help Elise. Was she all right? If they hurt her in any way, he'd kill them, of that he was absolutely certain. He'd made a promise to her when they got married. He told her that he would never let anyone hurt her. Yesterday he'd broken that promise when she'd been kidnapped.

She'd made friends quickly in the police community, so much so that her photography was in demand. She'd been hired full-time to shoot crime scenes and it wasn't until Keely retired that she cut back her hours. She eventually quit and took on the occasional job for John Krull.

Keely winced at the thought. Krull was dead and Elise was being held by God knew who. He couldn't do anything for the coroner, but he was going make sure his wife got home safely. Even if it meant killing to do it.

"Are you sure it was a right on 28?"

Numbers' question pulled Keely from his thoughts. "Yeah. No other road it could be. You go right to the end and it turns into—"

"New houses."

They sat there looking at the enclave of homes. "Should have known when we passed so many new houses on this side road. Must be a summer community or something," Numbers said.

"Maybe a retirement community. Right on the edge of Algonquin, close to Allumette Lake, Petawawa and Pembroke, too."

Keely watched a curtain of one of the houses pull back, a head appear and quickly disappear. In a few more seconds the front door of the two-story home, its white vinyl siding still glowing new, opened and a short man in shorts, a blue T-shirt and sandals sauntered down his walkway toward them.

"Morning, gentlemen."

"Morning," they said simultaneously.

"I suppose you're lost?" He was mid-fifties with a horseshoe of trimmed, grey hair. He was overly tanned and leathery. The man was a smoker and Keely tried not to breathe in through his nose.

"We're looking for the fire road that comes out of the park. It's supposed to be here."

"Behind my house. Developer is in talks with the province about making hiking trails but the fire road is right at the back of my yard. I'll let you pass for say…fifty."

"What the fuck are you on about?"

Keely stifled a laugh and jumped in quickly. "Excuse my friend. His wallet is sewn shut."

"Apiece. That's fifty apiece."

Numbers leaned over Keely, who couldn't do a thing to stop him. "Are you fucking crazy? We're detectives working a homicide investigation—"

Numbers leaned back to his side of the car and popped his door open but Keely got a hand on his golf shirt and held him back. He threw Numbers a look that was good enough to calm him down. He looked up at the tanned man and said, "How much for the car?"

* * * *

"Two hundred bucks to go up this guy's driveway, put a few tracks on his back lawn and drive between trees a truck could get though. Fuck, Keely, you gotta be crazy."

"Like a fox. We're here, aren't we? And we didn't have to wait until tonight. Just stay here and keep her running. A deal's a deal."

Keely leapt from the car and trotted up the back lawn to the tanned man, who was sitting in a lawn chair on a half-finished deck. He pulled the money from his wallet and the man snatched it with a grin.

"I hope you find that guy."

"Actually," Keely said, "we're looking for a woman."

"Oh, that must've been her husband came out of there last night then."

"Husband?"

"I was eating dinner on the deck with the missus when this guy, dressed like he's goin' in the jungle, all that khaki shit, ya know, he comes meandering out and just walks on by, doesn't say a howdy-do."

"Where'd he go? After he left your yard."

"Don't know. Didn't see him come back either. If I do, he'll be paying for access just like you two fellows."

"What did he look like, aside from what he was wearing?"

"He had sorta long brown hair and he was a white guy. Uh, he wasn't tall like you, but he wasn't short like me, ya know? Beyond that I couldn't say much else. All I know is he owes me fifty bucks."

"Right. Thanks," Keely said. He ran down the lawn and jumped back in the car. "Let's go."

The car lurched forward and Keely felt every bump. The old fire road hadn't been used much, so the foliage had closed in all around it. Numbers had to stay alert to steer clear of low and fallen branches. He flipped on his lights occasionally when the forest blocked out the midday sun. It was the jungle adventure Keely'd missed as a kid, including rescuing the girl.

The heat caused their body odours to mingle with the aromas of the forest. Keely chanced branch impalement by sticking his head a little out the window every few minutes for relief. Numbers didn't seem to notice it. "Smelt it, you dealt it."

"What's that?" Numbers asked, then yelled when the car's front end dipped drastically. A loud crunching sound hurt Keely's ears. Pain shot through his shoulder when he flew forward against his belt. A popping sound like fireworks accompanied the smell of chalk. Keely felt pressure on his body holding him up. Then silence for a brief moment until both he and Numbers began voicing their displeasure.

Keely knocked the deflating white airbag away from his face and turned to see Numbers swatting at his air bag like he was fluffing a pillow, his beefy arms flapping and causing a similar sound.

"What the hell was that?" Keely said then grabbed at his shoulder where the belt cut deep.

"I think we hit a hole. A very big, deep hole in the middle of fucking nowhere."

"Anything broken, big guy?"

"I don't think so, but I want outta here. Best way to tell if I'm in one piece is to see all the pieces," Numbers said and winked.

They fought their way from the nylon of the now fully deflated bags, struggled with their seatbelts, wrestled with the doors and won. They were soon walking around the car surveying the damage.

"I cannot believe there is a bloody hole in the middle of nowhere."

"Looks like a rain out," Keely said. "Runs off at the same angle long enough and you get, well, a chasm the size of a small Hyundai."

"That's got to be two feet deep."

"Blends perfectly with the rest of the dirt around it at the right angle. Nothing you could've done about it, Numbers. Not a damn thing."

"Look what you've gotten us into this time, Stan," Numbers said in his best Oliver Hardy. He even added the hand and facial gestures.

"Me? I told you we should have hoofed it, but no, you had to drive."

"I could have left you on your own. Let you walk the five-K by yourself you know."

Keely was amazed at how much damage a two-foot drop could do to the front end of a car travelling at around thirty kilometres an hour. The front bumper was mashed in and the grill was now part of the radiator. The car would probably run but not well and not for long.

He glanced at his surroundings, which were the same dense forest they'd been driving through for the last two kilometres. There were no discernable landmarks of any kind.

Keely walked over to his friend and put an arm around his shoulder. "You can go back and grab a ride from someone back to the motel. You can't send anyone in for the car. You know that?"

Numbers blew out air and nodded his head. "I know, it would attract too much attention. Can't chance it."

"You can go back or you can come with me and we'll share the ATV. Up to you."

The humidity was reaching the highest level of the weekend and Numbers plucked at his golf shirt to give his chest some relief from the sticky material. He ran his forearm across his head and considered the question.

"Either way I go, I gotta walk, so I may as well keep going forward with you." He shook his head. "You owe me big time."

"No I don't. You're doing this for Elise."

The big man flared his nostrils and squinted. "Yeah, I am. So *she* doesn't owe me anything. *You* owe me big time."

They shared a laugh.

"Well, I got my pack in there with a few bed rolls, a change of clothes and some food. I think I might have packed you a change of clothes, too." Keely made for the back of the car.

"I'm impressed. Thinking ahead. Nice going."

After retrieving his pack from the trunk. the pair changed their shirts; race tees Keely had bought with Day Long Racing logos on them. Keely changed his socks and Numbers strapped on a shoulder holster, his Glock sticking out from under his left arm. Keely wanted to caution his friend, but after a few seconds decided it was best to carry the piece instead of leaving it in the trunk for someone to find.

They hiked the long road and didn't see a soul. Nor did they hear much of anything — animals scurrying through the forest or foraging for food and a few birds. The sun pierced the canopy far too frequently for Numbers' liking. He kept complaining about the heat and drinking too much water.

Keely wasn't concerned since the map in his pack showed old hunting shacks, old and new logging shelters, and a few sugar shacks. All of them were good enough to sleep in and, if luck was on their side, they'd find Kira in one of them. Keely was certain that the man the tanned guy'd seen the day before was Paulo Chagas, the missing coach. It was starting to fit together. The main problem was that they were too few and the missing pair could remain that way by easily slipping by.

"Hey, is that the pole George was talking about?"

Keely jogged forward and saw a thirty-foot tree lying on the left side of the fire road. It had been stripped of bark and its branches as if prepared for life as a telephone pole. Not entirely sure what it was intended to be, Keely was just glad to see it. He effortlessly found the trail George had mentioned and walked about five minutes, Numbers close behind, before coming to the shack.

It had definitely seen better days, having been fully exposed to the elements. The wood was grey and dirty and several boards were missing. It stood no more than seven-feet high and was big enough to house a small car, and not by much.

Keely went left and Numbers headed right. They met behind the shack.

"Where is it? Where's the ATV?" Numbers asked.

"Your guess is as good as mine."

"Maybe it's farther back, over there?" Numbers pointed to overgrown grass and weeds covering a football field-sized clearing beyond a stand of bulbous bushes that surrounded the shack.

Keely moved slowly keeping an eye for cleared brush where an all-terrain vehicle may have passed. For once he was happy he'd spent time hiking with Elise – he'd learned a few things. He walked the area for ten minutes, careful not to run into the large argiope spiders that slung webs across the tall grass chest high. Their bright yellow stripes simulated bees and predators left them alone. Keely thought the webs were big enough to catch small birds, but Elise had assured him that couldn't happen.

He thought he heard something. A growling far in the distance. A motor. The ATV.

He ran toward the shack, bounding through the grass, no longer concerned about spiders, knocking the long stalks out of the way to get a quick glimpse of his friend. Something caught his eye through the long grass. It grunted and Keely froze.

He carefully split the growth in front of him and sliced off his breathing at the sight of a large black bear swaying from side to side over Numbers' prone body. It sniffed at him, pushing its massive snout into his back to easily move him a few feet. Keely hoped his friend was just *playing* dead.

Chapter 17

Trembling, Keely fought to keep silent. He had to stop himself from yelling and screaming, hoping to distract his living nightmare from Numbers. Of all the times to draw a blank on wilderness survival, this was the worst. Fear took the form of bile that stung his tongue and sweat dripped into his eyes blurring his vision. He suddenly realized he hadn't taken a breath and made sure to make it very slow and quiet.

He closed his eyes, half to try and remember what to do when encountering a bear and half to shield himself from what might happen to Numbers at any second. He wiped sweat from his face and opened his eyes, now able to see more clearly. There was no blood on Numbers or on the ground around him, so he must be alive and indeed *playing* dead.

You played dead when a bear attacked. Had Numbers done something to provoke the bear or had the bear provoked Numbers? It must have been Numbers' fault or else Keely would have heard gunshots. Numbers didn't have time to reach for his weapon.

The bear nudged Numbers over, sliding his body over the ground another few feet. Keely saw his eyes pop open for a second and noticed the empty holster. This was going from bad to worse. Mick was alive, but had no way to protect himself. Keely felt energy surge through him, bringing with it resolve. He needed to find the gun. Only problem was it would be like looking for a needle in a haystack with a bear chasing you around it. If he couldn't see the gun there was no way he'd get close enough to search for it.

The bear grunted and sprayed mucus on Numbers' face. Keely couldn't believe that he had to put a hand to his mouth to stop himself from laughing. He chalked it up to nerves. Now it pawed at its potential meal and Keely saw Numbers grimace in pain. The claws were big and they weren't just moving clothes around, they were digging into flesh.

Even though it was a black bear and relatively small in the ursine hierarchy, Keely thought it was at least three and half feet at the shoulders and a good four hundred pounds. He'd never wrestled a bear before and didn't want to start now, so he had to think fast. How could he get the bear away from Numbers and not get himself killed in the process?

He looked around and found a rock but it was too small to make any kind of loud noise. He searched the ground nearby for a few seconds, careful not to make too much noise and finally found a fist-sized rock. He whipped the rock as far to his left as he could. It hit the ground with a thud. Either the bear didn't hear it or it was just too interested in its quarry to care.

He decided to give it one more try and found another rock big enough to do the job. He launched it in the same direction. Unfortunately, the bear didn't pay attention to where the rock was headed, it paid attention to where it came from. Keely's arm had risen above the grass and the bear must have caught sight of it. He crouched as it turned towards him. Its head lumbered from side to side as if trying to shake off dizziness, grunting the entire time. As if coming to a decision, it launched itself in Keely's direction.

He ran as fast as he could under the circumstances, the tall grass impeding his speed. The bear seemed to be at a disadvantage since it had lost sight of him. He could hear it a few yards behind but it was not closing the distance. It might even be hurt, Keely thought, then the old saying of a wounded animal being more dangerous careened into his mind.

"Play dead. Fall down and play dead," Numbers yelled from somewhere.

"Get the fucking gun," Keely screamed.

"I'm looking."

"Look harder!"

Grass crunched closer behind him and Keely knew it would only be a matter of seconds before he was bear dinner.

"Play dead!" Numbers kept calling.

It was the most difficult decision of Keely's life and the dilemma played out quickly in his mind. Play dead but if the bear didn't fall for it he'd experience a slow, excruciating death. If he kept running he'd have a fighting chance. Playing dead *is* what the experts say to do when attacked. Then again, experts can be wrong.

"Have you found the damn gun yet?"

"Play—"

Keely nearly ran over Numbers, whose face went white at the sight of him and the big black bear close on his heels. Numbers took off to Keely's left and disappeared into the long grass, taking the bear with him.

"Find the gun, find the gun!" he screamed.

Keely couldn't help but laugh as he ripped through the brush in search of the weapon. "Where'd you drop it?"

"How the hell should I know?"

An unmistakable smell instantly had Keely on the verge of vomiting. He crawled forward and on the edge of the tall grass, between berry bushes, was a large pile of steaming bear dung. The Glock gleamed in the centre of it.

"You gotta be kidding me," Keely yelled just as Numbers ran past, knocking him down with a splat. The bear shit seeping through his T-shirt, felt hot against his skin. The gun dug into the centre of his chest. Keely gagged and did a quick push up.

Numbers' curdling scream meant only one thing — he'd been caught. Keely was out of time. He plunged his hand into the pile of fresh bear manure, digging for the now submerged gun. He got his hand around the barrel and pulled it out hard, spraying his face with feces. Momentarily blind as he wiped shit from his eyes, Keely heard Numbers call out again in pain.

"Shoot. For Chrissake, shoot—"

Keely ran toward the sound of his friend's shout and saw the bear on top of him. Numbers was holding his own. He had the bear's jaw clasped in his left hand, his arm straight, while his right hand was searching for the animal's eyes. The bear was swinging one big paw after another at Numbers' shoulders and it was taking a toll on him. Blood stained his T-shirt.

The gun had been aimed, the trigger squeezed and Keely couldn't remember doing it. He felt the recoil, smelled the explosion and heard the loud bang. The bear bucked sideways away from him, landing on all fours to Numbers' left. It backed up, reaching its big head around to survey the damage in its shoulder. Numbers scrambled on all fours towards Keely and the bear watched, Keely swearing to himself that the bear had a look of curiosity on its face.

The bear lowered its head, a low, steady growl emanating from its throat, its tiny black eyes boring into Keely. He heard a louder growl almost on top of him. The ATV was returning. Or was his gunshot enough to call unwanted attention?

The bear was confused by the sound of the engine and stood swaying back and forth as if drunk. The ATV crashed though the brush, narrowly missing Keely and stopping just short of the sprawled Numbers. The driver wore a helmet and goggles but the uniform was unmistakable.

The man pulled a canister from his belt and yelled for both of them to back away and cover their mouths. He pulled a pin on what looked like a small fire extinguisher and aimed it at the bear. He squeezed the lever and a long stream of white foam shot from the nozzle. Keely felt a stinging in his eyes even from his position behind the shooter.

The bear thundered away yelping and crying. It was a sound as unnerving as the big animal's snarl.

The driver pulled the goggles from his face and removed his helmet. George's forehead was crinkled and his mouth snarled at them. "What the fuck are you two doing here?"

"This is where we supposed to get the ATV, remember?" Keely said already having removed his shit-soaked T-shirt.

"I don't believe a pair of old cops can't get a time right. I said tonight. Not this afternoon."

"Bullshit!" Numbers was charging as hard as the bear did. "You said today."

"It doesn't matter." George threw a leg over the ATV to sit side-saddle, facing both men. "If we're right and she's still alive, she's probably long gone."

"What do you mean?" Keely asked.

"There are caves about a kilometre from the cliff where Todd was found."

"So? How far in do they go?" Keely was amazed at how George lost his child-like innocence of investigating when it came to his job and the knowledge of the park.

George reached around to the back of the ATV and lifted a small door. He pulled out a map, turned and unfolded it across the seat of the four-wheeler. "If you get your hands on the right map, you can switch from below and above ground and be out of this park in a day."

He pointed to the cave entrance he suspected Kira had used then traced his hand along a route he felt she'd most likely take.

"If she wanted out, she'd get out that way. It's the fastest way in her situation. Add travelling by boat and she could get out even faster."

"Why the hell didn't someone mention these caves before?" Numbers asked. "Does Robitaille know about this?"

"Detectives, I'm really sorry," George said, his voice trembling slightly. "I just found out that Robitaille had the caves searched last night. They were clean. I'm so sorry that I didn't know sooner. I just forget the caves are even there 'cause spelunkers say they're really boring and no one uses them and we monitor the ones that are used by animals and they're well signed—"

"Fuck!"

"Detective, I'm sorry. I don't know what else to say." George's whole body was juddering now.

"The World Championships. You said he was here for the World Championships," Keely said turning to his friend.

"What?"

"Roberto Galdeano said he was in Hamilton for the World Championships in cycling, right?"

Numbers nodded.

"Shit. They're not for another month," Keely said banging the Glock against his forehead. He turned to George. "What about if you add a plane?"

"Excuse me?" George said his voice still thick with nerves, his eyes glued to the gun in Keely's hand.

"How fast could she get out of here if she had access to a seaplane?"

"I thought the same thing."

Keely spun toward a man emerging from the tall grass and levelled the gun on his chest. "Freeze."

The man stopped ten yards away and threw his hands in the air. He was dressed in brown hiking shorts with lots of pockets, while a few small pouches attached to his belt held some helpful items like a flashlight and a knife. His khaki shirt was drenched with sweat and looked more green than it actually was. His light brown, mid-length hair was held off his face by a bandana tied around his forehead. This was who the tanned man had seen last night, of that Keely was sure.

"Paulo Chagas, I presume," Keely said and lowered the gun. "There're some people worried about you."

"Worried about me, no," he said with a slight accent that Keely didn't recognize. "Worried that I don't bring Kira back, yes."

"What do you mean?" Numbers asked.

"If I don't find Kira, they're going to kill me."

* * * *

Her own home had never felt foreign to her, until now. It was Elise's prison. She was in the basement, in the laundry room, bound to one of her dining room chairs, each ankle to a leg, her hands tied together at the wrists with each elbow tied to a piece of the chair backing. Her gag was one of her own good scarves that tasted bitter and cut uncomfortably into the corners of her mouth. She'd tried countless times to free herself but all she did was use up energy she knew she was going to need later. Keely would come for her, she had no doubt. It was simply a matter of staying calm and alive until he got there.

Every muscle ached. She'd only only been allowed out of the chair twice since arriving home. They let her go to the bathroom but it wasn't easy. They'd taken turns watching her. They were perverted and both wiped her clean after she'd finished her business. It was the most degrading thing that had ever happened to her. She hated both of them, but the one calling himself Sweet was the real threat. He was in charge of the other man and his tone, both spoken and physical, was dangerous.

He carried himself like a mobster in the *Sopranos* but at his core, his demeanour said street thug. Dark hair, dark eyes and olive skinned, Sweet could be Italian or Greek or from anywhere in the Mediterranean. He did have a hint of a New York accent. The only difference between Sweet and Sour was size and stature. Sour was a few inches shorter and he was bigger, stronger, yet he walked behind Sweet. Somehow, physical strength did not amount to power and control in this pair's world; Sour was obviously bigger but subordinate. He had dirty blond hair and his accent was a bit thicker.

Who were they and why did they steal a dead body? Elise had nothing but time on her hands and gave the question some serious thought. The most likely scenario she could come up with was that they had killed this Todd Watkins fellow but made a bad job of it by leaving behind physical evidence on the body. They took him to destroy the body and the evidence, leaving two more dead bodies behind.

How did all of that tie in to forcing her husband to find some woman cyclist? She hadn't a clue. She did know that unless she could escape or someone could get her out, Sweet and Sour were going to kill her. She could do more than pick them out of a lineup. She could paint a perfect picture of both of them, right down to the way they smelled. She'd seen far too much of them and her end would be a logical conclusion from their part. The thought made her try loosening her bonds again.

The laundry room doors opened and Sweet strolled in like it was his house.

* * * *

"Right now, I suggest we move away from this mustard gas," George said just as Keely's phone rang.

"Yeah."

"That's no way to answer a phone, detective," Sweet said.

"Put my wife on the phone."

"How is the investigation going?"

"I've got a few leads. Now let me talk to my wife."

"Keely, help me," Elise said, crying. "Please come and get me."

"I will, sweetheart, I swear I will. Where are you?"

"I can smell you— No!" she screamed and her voice faded into the background.

"Now now, detective, that isn't part of the game."

Keely could hear Elise's muffled cries in the background. "I'll get you Kira. No problem. Because that puts me in the same room as you."

"Get her. That's all you have to think about," Sweet said, his voice growing colder. "If you don't, I'm going to kill your wife slowly. Very slowly."

The line went dead. Keely gradually put the phone in his pocket then launched himself at Chagas. His hands wrapped tightly around the coach's throat and drove him to the ground. Numbers put a hand out to stop George from getting involved, but Keely knew George wouldn't intervene.

"You are going to tell me every fucking detail. Blink once for yes, twice to get strangled."

Chapter 18

Keely practically had to force Numbers to get on the back of the ATV. He'd been in rough shape on the way to the rendezvous and would be in far worse shape on the way back to his car. Still, he wanted to help. George insisted that they all stay together and Keely could tell by the park warden's look that he was terrified about what Keely would do to Paulo Chagas. Eventually Numbers convinced the warden to leave a bear repellent with Keely and for them to get going. They'd all meet up at the abandoned car.

Keely had changed his shirt to a plain white tee and tossed his bear shit-ridden shirt into the woods. He was hoping that tanned man would be home. Maybe he could pay him to use his shower. Guy's gotta make a living somehow.

"Who contacted you to find Kira?" Keely asked and swatted at an unseen buzzing insect.

"I don't know. He never gave his name."

"What did he sound like?"

"Serious."

Keely stopped in the middle of the old road, branches and stones scattered all about him. He took a deep breath and pulled the gun from his waistband. "I'm serious."

"You. He sounded like you and your friend," Chagas said, his hands and arms flying around to add punch to the words. "And like a guy I know in Atlanta. He sounded like everyone."

Even Keely jumped at the sound of the gun firing. Its loud boom sent birds flying from their perches and forced silence from everything else the forest. Chagas' hands covered his face but Keely could hear the man panting. He strolled purposefully up to him, pulled a hand from his face and pointed the gun at his head.

"You don't understand. *I'm* serious. You are going to answer every question and the moment you fuck around, I shoot. I have no time for your life. I don't care about you. I don't care about Kira Bremner. I care about Elise McAdam. Take me seriously because I have everything to lose."

"They'll kill me," Chagas said and doubled over, crying.

Keely tapped the man's head with the barrel of his gun. "I'll kill you first."

Chagas unwrapped himself and stood up straight to look Keely directly in the eyes as if he was given an injection of resolve. "If I talk to you, if I get out of here alive, I'll be on the run for the rest of my life. They will never stop until I'm dead. Until I'm silent."

Keely lowered the gun. "Now we're getting somewhere. It's that big, eh?"

"I don't know how far it goes, but big isn't big enough."

"What did he sound like?"

Chagas scratched his head. "He was American. Smooth. He had a bit of an accent. It could be Boston or New York."

"He didn't give any kind of name?"

"No." Chagas resumed their walk and Keely sped up slightly to catch him.

"You know that she's alive and you know where she's going, don't you?"

"I think so. But I'm...troubled. Why she killed Todd? And I'm amazed at how easy it was for her to leave."

"You think she killed Todd."

"Who else could it have been?"

Keely shook his head and sighed. "Stick to coaching, Sherlock."

"As I remember they were on the course at the same time. He is dead and she is gone. What more is there?"

"Oh, about four or five other people who had a reason to kill Todd. A jilted lover, competitors, the guy he was blackmailing. Like I said, stick to coaching."

They walked on with the sounds of the forest having resumed around them. Keely patted the canister hooked to his pocket and gagged at the memory of bear feces.

"If we find Kira, we cannot let anyone hurt her."

"Why does someone want Kira so bad? What is it about her?"

"She's a champion."

"There are champions in every sport, pal, but they don't run and hide from killers. What the hell is going on?"

Chagas stopped and bowed his head. Then he looked up through watery eyes at Keely. "I was so happy to get the job because I could live in the United States. I loved my home in Brazil, but it was a fresh start for me. Now, it is a nightmare."

Keely reached for the gun.

"Stop it. I know what you mean to do if I don't cooperate and it is wearing thin. I think you can find Kira but you must listen first. It is very important that you understand the size of this."

"I'm listening."

Chagas' head swivelled in search of something and it was only when he walked over to a stump and sat down that Keely understood what he'd been looking for. Keely strolled over and stood a few feet away.

"Like I said, I'm listening."

Chagas took a deep breath then squared his shoulders. "I cheated. I helped my team in Brazil cheat. I gave them steroids. It was new and supposedly undetectable but the agency catches up so fast."

"World Anti-Doping Agency?"

"Yes. They are as diligent about finding ways to cheat as the cheaters are. That way they can find ways to detect it before an athlete even starts using it. I was convinced that this new drug was ahead of them."

The moment he'd seen Keely open is mouth he read his mind and cut him off. "We needed to show better results or our funding was going to be cut and at the time it was already so small. We didn't have big corporate sponsors like in America. It was good for a few months, but one athlete was caught and then the whole team. I was fired and banned from competition for two years."

"So, Body Fuel is cheating."

Chagas closed his eyes, his shoulders slumping. "Yes."

"Kira knows all about it, right? That's why they have to shut her up. Big money from corporate sponsors will dry up if she gets caught."

"I'm afraid for her and me. I thought she may have panicked and killed Todd because he wanted her to go to the agency. I'd heard them talking a few times about it. She wanted to stop but not tell anyone because she knew it would be dangerous."

Keely began to pace, his thoughts turning to Leila. The lies slid from her tongue so silkily. "Todd and Kira were both on steroids or was it EPO?"

"None of those. EPO is so easily detected now. They can test your blood and there are markers, indicators of its use. No, they were cheating in a way that could not be detected, by anyone. Unless you tell someone what you're doing and where to look."

"What were they doing and where should I look?"

"I had to do this. You must understand. I needed to work and they said I would be deported if I didn't do it."

Keely stopped in front of the pleading coach. "I don't care about you, remember? I could give a shit why you did this. I need to know what's going on to help my wife."

Chagas softened and said, "Gene doping."

Keely backpedalled as if the words were hands on his chest, pushing him. "It's real? It's happening?"

Chagas nodded.

"I've read about it but the experts said it wouldn't even be ready for use for another decade."

"I got a phone call right after the Olympics," Chagas said, standing up. "I'm told to cooperate or I'm deported. I agree and they start to deliver the chemicals to my home once a month."

"How?"

"It is a small box wrapped in a newspaper, delivered the first Monday of every month."

"The whole team used it?"

"No. Kira and Todd only."

Keely turned his back on the coach and walked toward the opposite edge of the worn road. Why would they only use it on two of their athletes? A test. Make sure it worked before spreading the joy. Body Fuel had hired the two number two riders in the world to join their team. Why, especially if you knew you could win against them every time? And why bring them on board and not dope them? Or dope them, just not the same way?

Keely spun back to face the coach and said, "You're sure the gene doping couldn't be detected?"

"It's simple enough," Chagas said. "I inject their body with a synthetic gene that simulates an injury. That triggers stem cells to repair the non-existent damage, leaving their muscles bigger and stronger. Unless the athlete undergoes extensive imaging like an MRI before the drugs are administered, then the process looks natural. There are no foreign substances in the body to detect."

"Holy shit. Only way to know now is if the athlete or coach or the one supplying the synthetic drug comes forward."

"I told you this already."

"You're in deep shit, my friend."

"Why did you think I didn't want to talk to you," Chagas said, his hands flying around again, his accent more prevalent. "They find out and I'm dead."

Keely put his hands firmly but gently on the man's shoulders. "I hate to tell you this, Paulo, but they planned to kill you the moment Todd died and Kira disappeared."

* * * *

The car was out of the hole and by the smile on Numbers' face, it made him very happy. Keely, Chagas dragging his heels beside him, joined his big friend as he was climbing into his car.

"Check it out, McAdam, it even runs okay." He turned over the engine and it sounded good, a stark contrast to the car's new snub nose. Numbers climbed from the car and thumped its roof. "She's a four-by-four at heart."

"Where's George?"

"After he got a few of the other rangers out here to pull the car out, he said he had to get back to take care of a few things. One of them was an injured bear. He left the map and his cell number."

"Good. Paulo here's been telling me quite a tale."

"You don't say," Numbers said and gave the smaller man the once over. "He doesn't have any holes in him, so that's good."

"Okay, grab that map and let's see if we can't figure out where Kira is heading. You said," Keely turned to Chagas, "that you thought Kira might be heading for a seaplane."

Numbers unfolded the map on the trunk of the car and Chagas pointed to a lake.

"I think this is where she is headed. She'd have been there inside of a few hours using the caves. I hitched a ride on a canoe with some interior campers and that got me here," he said, pointing to the east side of a small lake. "A few more trails, a tough go in here until I got to caves here, then I came out a few kilometres from the old fire road where I met you."

"You basically took the route that we think Kira took," said Keely. "Any sign of her?"

"Not one. But she could still have gone that way and been very careful."

Keely turned to Numbers and shook his head. "I'm feeling overwhelmed, man. She could be anywhere and I still think she's meeting Galdeano."

"Roberto? He's here?" asked Chagas.

"Yeah. In Hamilton, about a five- or six-hour drive from the park entrance," said Numbers. "Said he was here for the World Championships."

"He is very fond of Kira and was of Todd as well. He would do anything to help her. I'm sure of it."

"Mick," Keely said and tried to hide the desperation in his voice. "There's too many possibilities. He could be meeting her at any airport surrounding the park."

"Not any airport, Keely," Numbers said. "There's two she could have gone to—"

"Wait a second," Keely said, turning his attention to the map. "We assumed she'd never head south since that lead to cops, and north was just filled with too much forest to get anywhere. What if she decided to risk going west? What if she had a canoe waiting for her at any one of these lakes near the cliff? It's a decent hike but I'd bet there's trail enough for a pro cyclist to ride it in half the time."

"She'd really have to push it to get ahead of any search party that went out after her. But yeah, that's a possibility."

"And look what airport is closest to the park." Keely put his finger beside a small green square with a white airplane in it. "Katrine, right beside Highway 11."

"Shit, she didn't need an airport if she went that way," Numbers said and stressed his point by indicating a few routes out of the park with a tap his finger. "All these side roads stop right at the west boundary of the park. She makes any of them and she's riding her bike all the way to civilization."

Keely, his arms outstretched, palms down on the car's trunk, surveyed the multitude of choices Kira had for escape from the park. She wanted to stop taking the drug. She wanted to come clean about it. For whatever reason she was running, Keely was certain Roberto Galdeano would be waiting for her when she arrived.

"Find Galdeano, find Kira."

Numbers squinted, thinking of the comment, then his face relaxed and grew a broad smile. "He rented a van. There was a van parked in front of his motel room. They track those now."

"Let's go. You drive and I'll call Ono."

* * * *

They were at a coffee shop in Pembroke when Margaret Ono called them back. It had only taken an hour and a half to find the van. Galdeano had flown into Toronto's International Airport, rented the van there and was now headed north on Highway 11 just south of a little town called Sundridge.

Keely McAdam silently praised and gave thanks to the inventors of GPS.

"Keely, we have to tell Robitaille," Margaret said with some urgency. "We can't be responsible for letting this woman go. She could be a murderer."

"Margaret, you've done a wonderful thing for me and I just need you to keep this quiet until I speak with Kira. Once that happens, I'll take her to Robitaille myself."

They said their goodbyes and Keely hoped he hadn't misplaced his trust and that Officer Margaret Ono hadn't grown out of hers. He quickly dialed Arnsberg's cell. "George, I need the closest seaplane and pilot in Pembroke."

Keely jotted down the directions on the back of the receipt for their coffee and donuts. When he was done he thanked George and hung up.

"A seaplane?" asked Numbers.

"Yep," said Keely. "I'm going to the bank. We're going to need cash for this one."

* * * *

The pilot was in his seventies, even said so quite proudly, Keely thought. He was tall and robust, a man who had spent a lifetime using his body. Scars and lines mapped his face and one of his fingers was so crooked it looked like he was permanently crossing two fingers. His name was Edgar but he wanted to be called Captain. Keely didn't care if he wanted to be called Kathy, so long as he got him to the South River airport before Galdeano's van.

He'd decided to go it alone and sent Numbers back to the motel to clean things up and wait for word from Keely. Chagas was more than happy to stick close to Numbers. His size could make anyone feel more protected.

The plane dipped slightly and Keely felt a shudder beside him. His concerned look prompted Edgar to give him a thumbs-up. It was not reassuring. Keely knew nothing about planes except, like John Krull had said, small ones made him nervous. They dipped and dropped and jostled far more than any large commercial jet ever would.

His seat was comfortable enough, but being so close to the controls and all the dials and buttons on the panel made the flight even more unsettling. Edgar tapped him on the shoulder then reached down and handed him a headset. Keely put it on and instantly heard the old pilot's crusty voice.

"Easier than yelling over the engine noise and wind, eh?"

Keely nodded but his face still felt tight.

"We're about a third the way over the park. Should be about an hour before we land at South River. Sit back and enjoy the view. Sure has hell paid for it."

Watching the foliage slip beneath them did help him relax and he couldn't help but think how much Elise would have loved being in that little plane. She'd have been giggling and taking a thousand photos. She said that she could smell him. Well, he understood because he could feel her skin on his. It was indelible, a feeling he drew upon whenever they were apart.

"Shame she's not going to look like that forever."

Keely struggled to separate his thoughts from Edgar's words. "How do you mean?" he asked, his voice sounding tinny in his ears.

"She's a jewel, that's for sure, but seventy-five percent of her is marked for logging. Doesn't have to happen all at once. In fact, they do it a little at a time so the public don't catch wind, you know."

"That can't be right," Keely said, then looked down at a forest brimming with trees.

"C'mon now. You can't be that naïve, sonny boy. The damn government can do whatever the hell they want."

Keely spotted a blurry dot in the distance that glinted harsh afternoon light, and grew rapidly larger in the front window. "What's that?"

"Oh, looks like a helicopter to me."

"DT-RAM, this is OPP-22. Please respond."

The helicopter pilot's request came clearly through Keely's headset. "What do they want?"

"DT-RAM, this OPP-22. You are flying over restricted airspace without clearance. Please respond."

"Well, that answers your question," Edgar said and laughed.

Chapter 19

"Hey, Kelly—"

"Keely. Keely McAdam."

"Whatever. Did I tell you about my wife, Stella?"

The white helicopter with its blue and red stripes hovered a few hundred yards away now and Keely felt his entire body stiffen, readying for the inevitable impact.

"Edgar."

"Captain."

"Whatever! We're going to hit them."

"She was something that woman. Rita Hayworth type, you know. Shapely. Long blonde hair, thick lips. A pinup if there ever was one. Did a bit of catalogue modelling for the Eaton's. A real firecracker, too, if you know what I mean?"

"DT-RAM, drop speed to one hundred and altitude to eight hundred and set a course for CFB. North Bay. This is not a request."

"I'm a structural engineer. I got my degree from the University of Toronto. Stella was there but we didn't meet until years later."

"For fuck sake, man, we're going to hit him." The helicopter was a few hundred feet away and they were closing on it fast. Keely raised his hands instinctively for protection but it seemed useless. He didn't know what else to do so he bent down in the traditional crash position, head in his lap.

"He'll move. He can go up or down for all I care. But, he'll move."

"Pilot! Change your course."

"OPP-22. Sorry, I'm having some bother with my ailerons. You might want to get clear or we're barbecued bear food."

They were so close now that Keely could see the panicked face of the helicopter pilot, then he was gone. The helicopter moved as if on a string, pulled swiftly upward out of their path. Keely heard its blades slicing through the air, and its pilot taking a chunk out of Edgar.

"What the hell is wrong with you, pilot? DT-RAM, acknowledge immediately or be treated as hostile. Acknowledge!"

"She was the hot and spicy to my boring and humdrum, ya know? Used to make me go places I didn't want to go. Drag me to the movies, shopping, dinner, shit like that. But, she'd do things to spice it up, ya know what I mean?" Edgar said and winked at Keely.

"What the hell are you trying to do?"

"I worked at a job that paid the bills but it was as boring as watching water evaporate. Stella made my life better. She was beautiful, funny, smart as all hell and I loved her."

The helicopter was hovering only yards above them, the long, black rails below its body ready to bash down on them. The plane shuddered, rattling so loudly Keely had to struggle to hear the words coming through his headset.

"DT-RAM. I'm sure your wife was a wonderful woman, but you will land or I'll be forced to change your course. Acknowledge."

"I got a problem with my aircraft and I'll take care of it when I land. This conversation does not concern you."

Edgar grabbed a dial on the control panel and turned it. Keely heard static then Edgar's calm voice.

"That's enough of that guy. He's starting to get on my nerves."

The helicopter was dropping closer to them but at an angle, aiming its skids at the plane's wing tip. The chopper blades whooshed through the air and caused the plane to shudder even more. It bounced so hard at the added turbulence that Keely had to tighten his seatbelt.

"Captain. You gotta move."

Edgar turned to see the helicopter dropping gently toward the wing as if it was going to land in a spectacular stunt. He looked forward and gripped the stick tightly with his left hand and grabbed a thick horizontal lever with his right.

"Hang on, Adam."

"McAdam."

"Whatever. Just hang on."

Keely heard the engines' revs drop, the noise level along with it. The helicopter shot forward, the propeller on its tail missing the wing by a few feet. Then the revs rose and Keely was looking at blue sky. His body was being shoved into his seat. He was surprised by the g-forces this old seaplane could generate. He felt the muscles in his neck relax and soon the horizon, its blue on top and green below, levelled in the window. He couldn't see or hear the helicopter.

Edgar turned to look at Keely, the old man's eyes watery, but energized.

"I lost Stella over ten years ago to cancer. My life has been one boring goddamned day after another since then. Not one day goes by when I wouldn't give my left nut to be dragged to some bad movie where we could cause some shit and have some fun. Hell, I'd settle for going shopping for crap we don't even need. Anything is better than nothing."

"I'm sorry."

Edgar smiled and turned his attention to the front window. "No need, Kevin. This is the most fun I've had in a long time. Besides," he said and turned to give Keely a thoughtful stare, "if what you tell me is true, then maybe I can help you stave off the nothing."

Keely reached out and gripped Edgar's shoulder. "You're a good man, Edgar. I bet Stella would have loved this."

"Are you kidding me? She would have hated this. She was terrified of flying."

The absurdity of it overshadowed his shock and fear and Keely joined Edgar in a hearty laugh. But, it was cut short by the sight of the helicopter, its very persistent pilot behind the stick, flying along Edgar's side of the plane.

"I get you to South River, you save your wife, right?"

"Yeah. That's about it."

"You a hitman or something like that?"

"No, of course not. I'm a detective."

"You're a retired detective with a gun stuck in your belt. Tell me the truth or I follow the cops."

"I did tell the truth," Keely said and twisted in his seat to try and face Edgar. "My wife isn't at the airport though."

"I didn't think so."

"She's being held somewhere else. I have to talk to a woman that might know where she is."

"Why the gun?"

The plane dipped sharply left and Keely's seatbelt tried to sever him in two. His lungs pushed up higher into his chest and made breathing impossible. He watched Edgar struggle with the controls, the old pilot's face red and contorted from the effort. The engine was screaming and Keely thought he smelled gas.

Keely grabbed at his door handle, pulling on it to right himself, then pushing on the centre console with the outside of his left knee to help him stay that way. He reached out and took the co-pilot's stick, careful not to push or pull on it, but to turn it right. The plane gradually levelled off and both men breathed a long sigh of relief.

"Thanks," Edgar said. "Nice work."

"No problem. It's my ass, too."

"Why the gun?"

"I swear to you, Edgar, I'm the good guy in all this. The men that were with me are helping me get my wife back. That's the goal here, nothing else."

"Why the—"

Keely felt a laugh brewing in his chest. "I don't know who's more persistent, you or helicopter guy?" He looked out the side window and saw the chopper pilot motioning to his headset. "I have the gun because the men who have my wife are also trying to find the woman I'm looking for. I need it to protect me and her."

Edgar considered this for a moment and with a wink, reached down and turned a dial causing static in a Keely's headset. Then the chopper pilot's voice boomed through his head.

"I didn't mean to hit you, DT-RAM. That was a mistake on my part. But, I will call for reinforcements who will likely take great pleasure in shooting you out of the sky unless you follow me to CFB North Bay."

Keely covered the microphone hooked around his face and said, "I knew things changed after 9/11, but I didn't think they were this bad."

Edgar hit a red button on the console then said, "You really need to get to South River Airport?"

"Yeah. I do."

Edgar removed his finger from the button. "Negative, OPP-22. I have little fuel left and more damage thanks to your stupid mistake. I'm going to South River. Confirm."

Keely watched the anxious chopper pilot convey the message to whoever was directing his flight operation. Then the man's voice crackled over his headset.

"You *will* follow me to South River?"

"Acknowledged."

The OPP pilot gave Edgar instructions on what speed and altitude was required for the trip and when the two had finished their discussion, Edgar turned to Keely, showing him flushed cheeks. "I guess I should've worked that out earlier. Then again, would've missed all that fun."

Keely wanted nothing more than to feel terra firma beneath his quaking legs.

* * * *

The flight had taken about forty-five minutes and after succumbing to the desires of the daredevil OPP pilot, it was almost pleasant. Keely had watched the park peacefully slide under him and even got to see a few moose grazing near a river. Thankfully he hadn't spied any bears. After his close-up view, he'd be happy if he never saw one again.

They'd flown high enough to stay clear of the occasional bird that Keely had spotted under their wings. Mostly geese, but he was also certain of a few hawks and a blue heron. He was surprised that he could even name the species but realized it was his wife's influence. When they'd hike she'd inevitably choose one field guide out of a dozen she owned to take with them. Her excitement around nature had obviously rubbed off.

Keely was aware that the plane had journeyed outside of Algonquin when he saw dirt sideroads in grids around the forest. Then houses and farms started to appear and here they were just a kilometre from the little airport, its two runways creating a giant X that couldn't be missed at any height or speed.

"We'll be on the ground in a few minutes. You know they're going to want to question you, too," Edgar said, his face tired but content.

"Actually, can you do me one last favour? Just make a pass of the parking lot? I want to see if a black Caravan is here. That'll seal the deal."

"Now that's an easy one," Edgar said and let go of the little red button. "Tower this is DT-RAM requesting a visual safety confirmation of my aircraft. Seems chopper boy wanted to put a hole in my wing. Over."

"Tower, this is OPP-22. Negative on that request. I've flown around the aircraft and there is no visual damage. Over."

"You'll pardon me if I don't trust your judgment, asshole. You tried to crash my plane. I think you just might want me to crash on landing. Please advise, *tower,* on that fly-by. Thank you. Over."

"DT-RAM, this is South River Tower. You are clear for fly-by. All eyes at maximum, over."

"Thank you, tower. Commencing fly-by. Please pay close attention to left wing. Over."

Edgar gave Keely a wink and proceeded to turn the airplane to the right, then just outside the airfield, swung it left in a slow arch. The parking lot passed under them and Keely not only saw the black van, but a man and woman running toward it. They climbed inside and in seconds, the van was backing out of its spot, swinging around and peeling out of the parking lot.

"Shit. Captain, we have to follow that van," Keely pleaded.

The moment the plane completed its circuit over the airport the radio sparked to life. "DT-RAM, this is tower. No visual damage on any part of the aircraft. Over."

"Tower, I'm having difficulty with my rudder. I'm just going to give her some juice and try a slide. Over."

The tower confirmed and the chopper got right onto the tail of the plane. Keely didn't want to know what a 'slide' was and just concentrated on watching the van move quickly up the dirt road leading into the airport.

"I'm going to have to slide her but it'll only last a few seconds. Gotta let them think we're in trouble, right?"

"What exactly is—? Never mind."

"I drop the flap on this side and raise it on that side. I lock the tail flaps and rudder in position and we slide sideways. Gets copper to back off a bit. Ready?"

Before Keely could answer, Edgar pulled and pushed several levers and switches. The plane's engine gunned and the body seemed to twist to the

left, temporarily tearing Keely's view away from the speeding van. Before
he registered the new view out the front window, the plane had snapped
back to its original flying position.

"DT-RAM, this is tower. Nicely done."

"Okay. So, what now?"

Keely hadn't thought of that. He had to follow the van, but the chopper
wasn't going away, and by the sounds of it, other choppers were moments
away if needed.

"Tower, this OPP-22. Intercepting DT-RAM."

"C'mon. What now?" Edgar yelled.

"I don't know?" Keely said shaking his head more to try and clear it
rather than to admit defeat. "I gotta talk to the woman in that van. I have to
stop that van. I have to—"

"Get in that van?"

"Oh, shit, Captain. I don't think so. The cops would easily follow us.
They'd arrest me in seconds flat."

"Damn, and you call yourself a detective," Edgar said, shaking his head
and making a tisking sound. "You never bluffed before?"

Keely rubbed his forehead. "What do you mean?"

"You said you weren't going to hurt anybody, right?"

Keely stared at the beaming face of the old pilot. After a few moments
he returned the smile. "You old son-of-a-gun. That's right. They don't know
that."

"Man, this day gets better and better."

Keely grabbed the sides of his seat so hard he was sure he'd punctured
the rough material with his nails. His head slammed back into the headrest
and his body was compressed as the plane dove for the van.

"When I get her close, you gotta tell them to stay at a hundred or we got
no chance. Okay?"

The plane levelled and Keely was able to sit forward and nod his
agreement of the plan. He took deep, calming breaths that didn't calm him at
all; they overloaded him with oxygen and he felt light-headed. He changed
strategy and visualized his task – sort of like a golfer visualizing the shot
before he takes the swing. His heart-rate slowed enough to stop his head
from spinning and he opened his eyes to see the road in front of him as if he
were no longer in a plane, but in a fast-moving car.

"Tell them to drop down to a hundred. Go on. Tell them."

Keely looked for a way to open the window but couldn't find a handle. "How do I open the window?"

"You don't. Take off your headset and get out there. The pontoon'll hold you no problem. Go on."

Keely stared at Edgar in bewilderment. "You're not doing this 'cause you're bored."

Edgar smirked and a sadness filled his eyes. "Smarter than I thought, gumshoe. I got another six months before I see her again. I have to have something to talk about."

Keely drew energy from Edgar who looked so damned happy. He pulled off his headset and threw open the little door. He stepped into gusting wind, constantly adjusting his stance to stay attached to the plane. He reached out and clutched a bar attached to the body of the plane that slanted up to attach under the wing. He balanced on the pontoon and heard every sound — the roar of wind, the engine growling, a helicopter's chopping blades and, most of all, his hammering heart.

He looked behind him to see the van slowing and chanced letting go of the crossbeam to wave the driver forward. He felt the plane decelerate but it was too rapid, the van charging up too fast, missing Keely, and the plane, by inches.

Keely awkwardly turned to yell at Edgar.

"Speed up. Go faster. We have to catch them."

The van was slowly being reeled in even though Keely could hear by the rev of its engine that it was speeding up. Galdeano was obviously unsure of who Keely was and, more importantly, he didn't know what Keely intended to do. So, how do you get someone to trust you when you're hanging off the side of an airplane that's chasing his van? All Keely had to do was talk to Galdeano and he was sure the man would understand.

The side of the van moved past slow enough for Keely to see inside its tinted window. He could make out the shape of a woman in the passenger seat. She was motioning to the side window and yelling something. The van was under the wing as if the plane was going to rest on it a while. The two vehicles were now in harmony, flying down the highway, one in the air, the other on the pavement.

The driver's-side window approached and Keely caught a glimpse of the old coach in the mirror. The man was obviously rattled. He darted his head out the window for a better look and the wind tousled his red hair. Keely's heart sank. Suddenly, the last thing he wanted to do was look inside that van.

The plane and van were now door to door and Keely's suspicion was confirmed. Numbers had described Galdeano as an older man with olive skin and greying hair. The man behind the wheel was not Roberto Galdeano, unless he'd gotten a hair and skin transplant. He'd seen enough photos of Kira Bremner to know she was not as dark-skinned as the woman in the passenger seat.

Keely yelled, "This is not your van."

"He paid me. I needed the money. Please don't hurt us."

Keely climbed back into his seat and strapped in.

"What the hell you doing?" Edgar asked.

"Right van. Wrong people."

Chapter 20

"I never thought my final days would be spent in jail," Edgar said, his voice somber. "It's been fun up 'til now, but I'm pretty sure we've broken more laws than I even know. I hope I get a cell with a good view."

Keely pulled the gun from his belt.

"What're you planning on doing? Shooting your way out?"

Keely shook his head. "Tsk, tsk. And you want to think of yourself as a detective."

Realization flooded Edgar's face.

Keely continued. "You're not going to jail. If anyone's going to jail, it's me."

In that moment, he felt oddly at peace. He had always said he would do anything to protect his wife and here he was, a man of his word. The engine hummed as the plane banked on its familiar course to the little airport. Keely could hear the tower and other voices screaming from the headset he now refused to wear. He wished he could smell his wife the way she was able to conjure his familiar scent – whatever that was. Gasoline was still the pervasive odour in the plane, though he did catch a whiff of leather from the seat.

"Where do you want me to park?"

"I have to use the bathroom, so I'd appreciate it if you could get to the main building or barn or whatever the hell they're using as the terminal."

Edgar chuckled. "Relax, would you? You're going to find your wife. I know you are."

He felt like he'd been swimming in water with his clothes on, the added weight a strain on every move. He chided himself because the journey was just getting started.

"I gotta take this one step at a time. Just get this thing close to the main building. Please."

The ground was coming up fast and Keely prepared for a bumpy landing. It turned out to be the smoothest landing he'd ever experienced. Once Edgar swung the seaplane to the right, off the paved runway, only then was Keely jostled mercilessly. He was sure he was going to lose a few fillings as the plane bounced its way towards the simple brick structure. If it had a second floor, it could have passed for the Whitney OPP station.

"Tell them I've got a gun on you and I want them to stay clear of the plane."

The few cruisers on the scene stayed well back of the aircraft as it taxied to its unusual parking spot. Keely was most relieved that the chopper had finally disappeared. When Edgar lined up his door on the plane with the glass double doors of the airport building, he cut the engine, which gave a few final belches before the prop came to rest.

Keely spotted an officer leading a line of people out of the terminal from the far end heading for the parking lot. He looked carefully for any sign of Kira or her old coach but realized that they would do anything to stay clear of the police. They were passengers on the same boat as Keely – not knowing who to trust. If she was involved with the doping then someone wanted her dead. They could very well have sent someone who was a bad cop or just dressed like one. Hell, they could send a guy in a seaplane with a big Glock smelling of bear shit to do the job.

"They're hiding somewhere in that the building," Keely said, more to himself than Edgar.

"Or maybe they're hidin' out in a hangar. Or they might've got away before we got here."

"Nope. It's their turn to bluff. I think they saw an OPP chopper, heard the radio chatter and decided to send us on a goose chase. They're here. Somewhere."

Edgar popped his seatbelt and pulled the handle on his door, making ready to get out of the plane. Keely stopped him.

"Wait. You gotta make it look good. Put your hands up and go slow. Please."

"Sure, kid. Just don't get all trigger happy on me. *Please.*"

Keely tilted his head and gave him a sideways smile. He flopped the gun on its side and said, "The safety's on." Then he popped his own seatbelt. He followed Edgar out of the plane and looked cautiously around. He didn't have to pretend to be nervous. Though he was sure it would take some time to get a tactical team to the airport, every cop in the north with a working radio was going to be begging their superiors to make for the airport.

He scanned the length of the short building in both directions. He'd already checked the roof when they landed and it was clear. He poked Edgar in the back and the older man began to walk clumsily to the doors.

"How am I doing?"

"Fine. Just don't talk to me like this is fun, okay?"

"Right. Sorry."

"Open the door slowly and step inside."

The setting sun did little to lower the temperature and Keely became keenly aware of his body. He was sweating and felt tense enough that all of his muscles ached. He was definitely afraid but his bladder told him to move faster, so he stepped quickly through the door.

The terminal was a single room with two ceiling fans, only one of which was working. It was a bus terminal without the vagrants and lockers. Around the room were what looked like four workstations. Directly beside him inside the double doors was a small coffee shop. Beside that was an information office of sorts with a spinning rack filled with pamphlets, a desk and phone. The opposite wall was where one bought tickets and checked luggage – it was split by a door that Keely knew led up to the tower at the end of the building.

Benches, facing in and out, were positioned in a square but not butted up at the ends so people could access the centre of the square – a garbage can. Keely moved a few steps past Edgar and spotted a little sign jutting out above a short hallway between the coffee shop and info centre. It had an outline of a man, a woman and a phone.

He gave out a huge sigh then asked Edgar to join him.

"I don't have to go," Edgar said with a bit of a whine.

"Wouldn't look good if I left my hostage out here all by himself now would it?"

Once Keely had finished his business they returned to the benches. Keely sat while Edgar poured them coffee.

"I know you're here somewhere but I'm too damned tired to look right now. I'm going to have a donut and a cup of coffee." Though Keely spoke loud enough for someone to hear him in other rooms, he kept his voice light and friendly. "We'd like very much for you both to join us. Please."

He was met with silence except for the occasional radio chatter coming from, he assumed, the tower. Edgar joined him on the bench and carefully passed him the coffee.

"I'm retired detective Keely McAdam and this is my friend Edgar... What's your last name?"

"Hodges," Edgar whispered.

"This is my friend, Edgar Hodges. He's a hell of a pilot."

"You think so?"

"Oh yeah. That was amazing flying. Not everyone can do stunts, you know?"

"Thanks."

He raised his voice again, looking around the empty room for some sign of listeners. "I really don't care what you've done or where you're going. All I want to do is get my wife back. So, what do you guys say, eh?"

Keely's phone rang so he handed Edgar the gun and dug it from his pocket. "What?"

"Nice to hear from you, too," Numbers said. "I'm about a half hour from the airport, what's happening?"

"Oh, nothing much. Almost rammed an OPP helicopter, which returned the favour and nearly knocked us out of the sky. I tried to jump from a moving airplane onto a moving van."

"Is that all?"

"No, actually, it isn't," Keely said, laying it on thick. "I kidnapped my pilot using your gun, which makes you an accessory. Congratulations."

There was a long pause before Numbers spoke. "Keely, I think it's time we called in the cops. We're way the hell over our heads, man."

Keely felt the huge weight of tiredness return and he slumped forward almost spilling his coffee. "I don't trust Robitaille. He'll fuck up for sure. God knows he may even be in on it."

"What the hell are you on about? The guy made a mistake but that doesn't make him dirty. You disobeyed an order, so I guess you're on the take, right?"

"Okay, okay. I get your point. Mick, this isn't a stranger we're talking about. It's Elise. And worse, I don't have a clue where she is. How the hell would the cops help now? They'd tie everyone up in interviews for the next fucking week and by the time they got around to doing anything Elise could be..."

Keely watched a pair of feet in hiking boots stop in front of him. He followed the feet up hairy legs to a pair of tan shorts and a light blue T-shirt. Then the olive-skinned, wrinkled-from-sun-exposure face of Roberto Galdeano looked suspiciously down at him.

"You talk to me. Then you talk to her."

"Ah, Numbers, stay a few klicks back of the airport until you hear from me, okay?" Keely said and hit the end button on his phone. "Mr. Galdeano, it's nice to meet you." Keely put out his hand but the muscular man ignored it. "Where's Kira?"

"I came out because you gave this hostage your gun. That makes him not a hostage. You are telling the truth, yes?"

"Yes. I am. My wife's name is Elise and men calling themselves Sweet and Sour are holding her."

Galdeano looked out the glass doors as if expecting to see a familiar face. He sat down beside Keely and continued to stare out the windows. "They mean to kill her because she does not want to take this drug anymore."

Keely slipped to the edge of the bench and angled himself so he could look into man's weather-beaten face. "Who? Who murdered Todd and wants to kill Kira? Who?"

Without moving his head or eyes, Galdeano answered. "I don't know what happened to Todd. And the people who want to kill Kira are very high up. They are faceless, nameless. They may not be after her but they send people to do it."

"People like the men holding my wife?"

"Yes."

"Why did you get fired from Body Fuel?"

He sat up rigidly. "I did not get fired. I quit."

"Okay. But, why?"

"I tried to talk to her. To tell her she was only going through a bad time and it would get better. She was the best in the world and because she gets older she has to work a bit harder. But she don't want that. She wants to cheat."

"You knew what they were doing?"

"No. Only that they were going to try something new and Kira wanted to do it. I tried to stop her, but it was no good. They come to me and threaten me and when I say I don't care – they can kill me if they want — they offer me money. That is when I quit."

"Why didn't you tell anyone what they were doing?" Keely regretted the words the moment he saw the coach's face turn a deep red and a huge vein bulge on the side of his forehead. "I didn't mean to insult you," Keely hastily said. "I thought that maybe if you—"

"If your friend was sitting beside me I would have taken that gun and shoot you already, you stupid man." Galdeano shot to his feet and paced the length of the benches.

"I'm sorry. I don't understand."

"I tell everyone. I love Kira like she is my own and I want to protect her so I tell the Olympic committee, the anti-doping agency, U.S. cycling association and Canada, too."

"And they did nothing."

Galdeano flinched then gave a pleading look to Edgar. "He is really this stupid?"

Edgar shrugged.

"They did nothing? They did everything," he said, his hands suddenly becoming erratic. "They tested them so much and over and over but nothing. They find nothing wrong, nothing abnormal." He looked as if he'd just been hit in the stomach and sat back down. "Poor Kira is tested so much because I, Roberto Galdeano, her coach, tells on her. She suffers from me."

"Coach. It was gene doping. I found out from Paulo Chagas."

Galdeano spit on the floor. "He is cursed. He does not care about Kira. He is a pig."

"He's a pig whose life has been threatened, just like my wife's."

A phone rang somewhere in the room. Keely stood and listened. It was the phone on the ticket desk. He sat back down.

"Aren't you going to answer it?" Edgar asked.

"Nah. Hostage negotiator. I'm not ready to talk to them yet. But I am ready to talk to Kira." Keely glanced out the glass doors at the reddening sky. This was too much like a chess game and not enough like an action movie. He needed to be moving. "Where is Kira?"

Galdeano's hard stare eased, his body relaxing. "Gone."

"What do you mean, gone?" Keely said in a way that made the old coach answer quickly.

"When we hear the police on the radio, we thought it was bad people coming to get us. I pay these people to drive my van and I give Kira their car." Galdeano smiled viciously. "I outsmart everybody. Yes?"

The room lost its supply of oxygen and Keely closed his eyes against the pain in his chest. He reached behind him and, without looking, grabbed the gun from Edgar. "What kind of car?"

"I don't know?"

The gun made little rattling sounds as Keely played with it, turning it over in his hands. The safety made a slight snap when he pulled on it. He glanced at Galdeano who immediately read Keely's malicious intent.

"It was blue. It was small, with two doors. I think it was a Toyota. She's going north in the direction of—"

"I get it." Keely flipped the safety back on the gun.

"Now what're you going to do, Kelly?"

He tapped the tip of the barrel against is forehead, ignoring Edgar's obvious mistake. He was deep in thought for almost a full minute. Eventually a tactical team was going to do something. It would be easy for them, he was out in the open. One flashbang grenade and he'd be dead. There were more cars out there and men were surely surrounding the building.

"Where is Kira going?"

He crossed his arms and tightened his jaw.

"Roberto, I don't want to hurt anyone. I swear to you. I just want my wife back. I only need Kira's voice, nothing else." Keely bent down in front of the coach, making sure to put the gun behind his back and to relax his face. "Please tell me where she was going? My wife's life depends on it."

"You swear on the life of your wife that you will not hurt my Kira."

"I swear."

He looked at Edgar, who gave a slight nod. "North Bay. A plane to nowhere from there. Okay."

"Okay." Keely felt rejuvenated. "Where did you hide from us, Roberto?"

"Why?"

"Oh, the detective has a plan." Edgar rubbed his hands together. "What do I get to do?"

"Who says you're in on it?" Keely said, teasing.

"C'mon. You need a pilot, right?"

"Can you fly any kind of plane?"

"Any small aircraft. I'm your man." Edgar was beaming with excitement.

"Okay, then you're my man. Here's what we're going do."

Chapter 21

It was a shambles. She'd clean it, organize it and that would lead to ease of use which would make her feel better not only about the space, but also about herself. The shelves in the laundry room were supposed to be for cleaning paraphernalia but somehow old paint cans, jars of nails and stacks of old magazines popped up between boxes of laundry detergent and fabric softener. The floor space of the cramped room was just as bad as the shelving. Unmarked boxes of various sizes, containing God knew what, were stacked against the back wall almost high enough to block the room's only window.

"Those will definitely have to go," she said. "Better hamper, new paint, more shelving. Yep, gotta get this room useable again."

The water heater was to her right, the furnace behind her, the new washer and dryer they'd paid too much for sat quietly in front of her. The shelves were above the machines. *Are they slanted? Damn.* She made a mental note to check them with a level when she got out of there. The swinging saloon doors were definitely on their way out, she thought. It is no longer the Seventies. Funny how she gave little thought to this room when decorating the house only to find out that it was as important as a kitchen.

She tried to squirm free of her bonds but it was far too painful and the cumulative effort had cut blood flow to her hands, numbing them. She'd turned her attention to the room in hopes of staving off panic. There was no way to loosen the zipties and that meant the only way out was rescue, murder or if her captors suddenly saw the error of their ways. *Why don't criminals find Jesus* before *they commit their crimes?*

She'd made mental notes about more than just her bad organizational skills. The more she thought about them the less important certain items seemed to be. Sweet had a smaller bladder and went to the bathroom more often than Sour. This was not going to lead to a master plan of escape. Even with Sour snoozing on the sofa outside the laundry room, there was little she could do to free herself and take advantage of his total lack of awareness.

They'd started out doing everything together — eating, watching her, watching television. Then they switched to guarding her in two-hour shifts. Recently, Sweet had missed a few shifts, prompting Sour to mumble and curse. She'd heard them each make phone calls, but every time Sour used the phone she heard Sweet rush him off the line. She wasn't positive that Sweet had referred to Sour as his brother, and by their looks it was certainly a possibility. Either way, Sweet was definitely in charge.

She'd have to change the curtains, too. The drab brown material killed any light in the room. She'd give more thought to paint colours, something to make the room brighter, cheerier and maybe help it look bigger.

Pain, hot and fresh, travelled from her wrist up her arm to stop at her shoulder. She grimaced until it subsided a few seconds later. They'd left her for what had to be six or seven hours now, the longest stretch without letting her relieve herself. Sweet loved watching her. She'd stared right back him, defiant, telling him he was not embarrassing her or in control. His arrogant expression frightened her and now she avoided looking at him altogether.

There were wraps you could buy for water heaters to make them look cleaner and match the colour of their surroundings. Keely would laugh at that for sure. "A sweater for a water heater," he'd say and she'd laugh knowing he was only teasing. He'd do anything for her. Even risk his life? Would she for him?

She was positive he was looking for her and hoped that her clue was enough to help him. She wasn't good at the cloak and dagger stuff. She concentrated for the next half hour on what she'd say to him if given the chance to talk to him on the phone again. Having decided, she considered the furnace. Only way to hide it is to box it in, she thought. Why do that if only she and Keely would ever see the room? It wasn't like they'd be throwing parties in the laundry room. Though there was that time Keely had wanted to know what all the sex-on-a-dryer fuss was about.

"What the fuck you smiling at?"

Sweet stared at her as if aiming down the sight of a gun barrel. He clicked a switch on the wall and the bare bulb spewed harsh light. She'd definitely do something about that damn light.

"I asked you a question."

He looked tired even though it was just getting dark. His slick hair was ruffled as much as his clothes.

"Fond memories," Elise said. "All I have right now. No TV, no music, just the guy in there bitching about the fact his brother is an asshole. A girl needs more entertainment than that."

Sweet ran his hand through his thick hair. "Nice try, Mrs. Detective."

"Can I at least go to the bathroom?"

His demeanour changed – Jekyll was Hyde in an instant. Sweet spun from the doors and they made a clunking sound as they swung past each other before coming to a rest closed. *Those doors are going for sure.*

"Hey, wake the fuck up."

She heard Sour moan and clear his throat, then with a thick voice he said, "What? What's the matter?"

"I'll tell you what's the matter. She's going to shit herself and I'm not the one going to clean her up."

"It's your turn to take her to the bathroom. Fuck, it's your turn to watch her. I've been down here all fucking night."

Elise couldn't help but tense at the raised voices of her captors since the fight was ultimately about her. Hopefully they needed her because the best way to solve this fight would be get rid of the cause. She breathed as slowly and deeply as possible, letting her body relax during the long exhales.

"I've been thinking about the job. That's my concern right now. Getting the job done. You watch her."

"We're in this together," Sour said. "We take turns watching her. Equal turns."

"You watch her."

There was a long pause and Elise continued her relaxation exercises. There was no need to panic, yet. Finally, Sour spoke in a low, threatening tone. "Who died and made you boss?"

"Dad," Sweet said matter-of-factly, then paused before saying, "Take her to the bathroom then give her dinner."

Elise heard Sweet pound up the stairs to the main floor followed by several minutes of Sour cursing and mumbling. *Round one, Sweet.*

* * * *

Keely stayed very close to his 'hostages,' not wanting to take any chances the cops would shoot first and ask questions later. He moved toward the door at the entrance to the hangar – a sliding metal door for giants, he thought, and hoped it wouldn't be too heavy to move. It wasn't. Staying behind the wall for cover, Roberto and Edgar pushed the door closed. Once secured, the two men climbed into the plane, Edgar turning back to say goodbye.

"It's been a real pleasure. Thanks for the adventure."

"I'm the one that has to thank you," Keely said, shaking the old pilot's strong hand. "Without your help, my wife would already be dead."

"Good luck."

"You too. Remember, fly south. Roberto," Keely said tilting his head to look past Edgar. "Wave the gun around a bit once in a while, okay? Give the impression I mean business."

"I understand," Roberto said. "Please take care of my bella Kira. Please. She so frightened."

"No worries. I'll explain everything to the cops when I get my wife back. Okay. Get going."

With that Edgar pulled up on a set of stairs that doubled for the door of the private jet. Before the engines could fire, Keely jumped onto the baggage claim conveyor belt and crawled through the rubber flaps, emerging between the hangar and the ticket desk. Roberto had been hiding up in the tower, but he'd seen this spot and thought it best for Keely's needs.

The conveyor was a solid black rubbery material stretched over runners and when switched on would move luggage from the ticket counter to the hangar where handlers would put it on board whatever plane was waiting. The conveyor was held up by metal framing covered on both sides by black metal panels. Keely searched for the removable panel Roberto had mentioned. He found it and easily jimmied the lock with a screwdriver from a toolkit he found in storage room.

It took less than two minutes to hide in the space. Moments later Keely heard the hangar door sliding open. Edgar had told the cops by radio to open the hangar door because his kidnapper wanted to leave. The last Keely heard the plane was it taxiing out of the hangar. After that, the airport was overrun with policeman.

* * * *

Sour's mood quickly began to match his name. He mumbled and paced not even glancing at Elise as she dropped her slacks and relieved herself. Then he escorted her to the kitchen and demanded that she make dinner.

"What would you like?" she said sounding like a polite hostess.

"Whatever."

She opened the fridge and wondered what was best for kidnappers. She gathered up leftover vegetables and half a roast from Thursday's dinner. She started some white rice and automatically reached for a carving knife among other knives stuck to a magnetic strip under the cabinet by the stove. Dare she glance at his position? Was he even paying attention to her? She could grab the knife and stab him before he realized what had happened.

"Stabbing someone is not as easy as they make it out in the movies," Keely had told her. "There's bone and muscle and fat to get through. Slicing is better than stabbing."

He'd shown her how to grip the handle, the back of the blade toward her forearm, the point at her elbow, sharp part of the blade out. The idea was to throw a punch like a hook, guiding the blade across the target. "The throat is great if you can get it, but any part where there are major arteries or veins," he'd said and showed her, the soft side of the forearm, the wrists, and the inner thigh among the vulnerable areas.

She stared at the biggest blade, its black handle above the magnetic strip an inch from the wall, the blade gleaming in the kitchen light. She pictured it in her hand, spinning, slashing Sour's neck open to the sound of air escaping from the hole.

Sweet would come. Even if he didn't hear his brother dying, he'd eventually come to the kitchen. What then? He had a gun.

She glanced to her left and watched the occasional grain of white rice float to the surface of the boiling water. Her mind was made up. She reached for the knife and heard metal scrape metal. She made sure the sharp side of the blade faced out and spun. Her wrist slapped into Sweet's hand and he ground his teeth together, the muscles in his jaw rippling. Two pale blue eyes bore into hers with such intensity that Elise was sure she could feel them on her skin.

She felt his big hand slap her hard, pain stinging her cheek and ear. She couldn't breath. Sweet was choking her. Panic stung worse than the slap and she struggled to breath. The knife clattered to the floor and Sweet's contorted red face began to fade as blotches of blackness danced across her vision. She thought of Keely. Saw his handsome, rugged face. She felt his touch. Then she gulped air, dry and hot. She tasted her tears.

She slid down the cabinet to the floor. The coolness felt wonderful but she wished it was on her burning cheek.

"What the fuck are you doing?" Sour said sternly.

"Are you stupid? What do you think she was going to do with that knife? You're lucky I stopped her."

"Bullshit. She was cutting the meat, you asshole. Right, Mrs. Detective?"

Elise managed a nod and rubbed at her tender neck.

"You're an idiot."

"You're an asshole," Sour said and stood up to face his brother. "I'm not babysitting her anymore. You got that? It's your turn."

Sweet was forced to back up a step. Water sizzled as it boiled over onto the burner. Elise pulled her legs under herself and waited for either man to move. Sweet reached behind himself and slowly wrapped his hand around the handle of a gun in his waistband.

Quicker than she'd seen the larger man move before, Sour grabbed at a gun in his belt and drew it on his brother.

"I got one of those, too," he said and stepped so close to his brother that from her position on the floor looking up, she thought they were kissing.

"Get her back downstairs, tie her up, gag her and then finish cooking. I gotta make a call." Sweet casually stepped around Sour and went through a door into the living room.

"Fuck you." Sour reached down and yanked Elise to her feet as if she weighed no more than a small child. He roughly shoved her in the direction of the basement stairs. "You weren't going to do anything with that knife, were you, Mrs. Detective?"

"My name is Elise," she said seizing the moment to rub and flex her wrists and elbows before they were once again locked down. "Of course not. I'm not stupid and neither are you."

"He's not my brother. Not my *real* brother anyway."

"Oh," she said rounding the corner at the bottom of the stairs and walking straight to the laundry room. "What do you mean?"

"You know, same dad, different moms."

"Oh. Yeah, I see." She looked directly at Sour, smiling, and gesticulating in some small way to emphasize her interest in everything he was saying. "You're still lucky, though, because I was an only child. I wished I could have had a sister or brother to play with."

"You're the lucky one," he said and his eyes went wide. They shared a small laugh as Sour tied her left leg to the chair. "He's always been pushy. Thinks he's better than me. His mom was, well, normal, if you know what I mean?" She felt her right leg being pressed into the chair leg. "She was like this perfect woman who worked with all these charities. My mom was someone dad needed to get away from perfect woman with, you know?"

She nodded and after a moment said, "How did you come to meet your half-brother?"

"Oh, he killed my mom."

* * * *

Hours. He'd been cooped up in a metal box with no light and very little fresh air getting in for at least three hours. Night would be in full swing and he hoped that Kira hadn't met up with her plane yet, and that Edgar was still flying south. The one thing of which he was positive was that Numbers would be waiting for him. He'd called and told him where to wait. Numbers would wait all night if he had to. He'd done it before, or so he'd said.

Numbers loved stakeouts. He'd sit at a good vantage point – by that, he meant any place he could get off a clean shot with his camera. He'd eat, drink, listen to music. It was, in his humble opinion, a great getaway. Probably why he'd been after Keely to join him. Keely had his reservations about being a private investigator. He didn't need to 'get away.'

The conveyor belt motor droned awake and Keely heard several voices all iterating the same sentiment. The airport was operational. He'd had a few close calls, hearing voices right above his position several times, but the police were now convinced that the airport was clean, that the kidnapper had indeed gotten on the plane with his hostages.

The panel was easier to remove from the inside. A simple twist on a flat metal strip released the tension and popped it free. He gently extricated himself from under the conveyor, replaced the panel, then cautiously stuck his head through the rubber strips to get a look around the hangar.

An average-sized man in overalls was at the far end of the room, which was the size of a small warehouse. A mechanic, Keely thought. He squeezed through the opening for luggage and dropped silently to the cold concrete floor making sure not to disturb the worker. He inched along the wall and glanced out the small, square window set in it at eye level. The night had encroached and made the river run with black water. At a dead run, Keely could be wet in twenty seconds.

He carefully opened the door and slid outside. The coolness shocked him but felt refreshing after being housed in a metal box for so long. He stood with his back against the hangar wall and counted to three.

"Go," he said to urge himself on and lunged forward. He took a dozen steps and heard the bark of a dog. Out of the corner of his eye he saw a large dog bounding towards him.

"On, on, on," a male voice screamed from Keely's right.

Keely felt his lungs burning and his legs cramping. He swung his arms harder to help propel his legs forward and with each step his heart would bump his chest in rhythm. He could feel the shimmering black water in the air and hear its gentle, lapping call.

Fifty yards to go and the dog was closing fast, its barks interrupted by long snarls as if it were slurping up a loved liquid.

Thirty yards and he could hear the dog's paws digging into dirt.

He could dive from ten yards. Twenty to go. Fifteen. The dog's teeth were on his ankle. He lost his balance and felt hard, dirt scraping his hands and knees. The dog growled and sank its teeth deep into Keely's left ankle. He screamed into the dark and kicked as hard as he could with his right foot. The water was ten steps away. All he needed was a few seconds.

Chapter 22

The German shepherd's head was bigger than a football. Keely felt the pull on his leg but his adrenaline killed the pain. He kicked furiously at the animal's massive head and every time he connected the dog would buck, sinking its teeth even deeper into Keely's flesh. He didn't want to hurt this magnificent animal but he had no choice.

He dug the screwdriver from his pocket, grabbing the handle so his thumb rested on the rounded end, the blade sticking down. He stopped kicking and lay as flat and still as possible. The pain in his ankle went on as if he'd flipped a switch, flashing up his leg into his groin. The ground was hard but damp; probably a layer of mist from the river, he thought.

"Hold, hold!" the handler yelled from nearby and the dog obeyed. It dropped its stomach to the ground, all four paws pointing at Keely, its teeth no longer in him, but ready to reattach at its owner's command.

Keely tightened his grip on the screwdriver and tried to ignore the pain in his ankle. He would only get one shot at this and he knew he had to get it right. The moment the dog was down, he had to flip over and scramble for the river. The handler was probably armed and Keely had no weapon against that other than the cover of darkness.

He sat up quickly and raised his arm, the screwdriver blade poised above his head. The dog jumped to its feet and Keely prepared to strike.

"Out. Out, Daisy, out."

Daisy? Out?

The dog obeyed, though voiced its opinion with long growls and a few barks as it backed away. It stayed low to the ground and Keely could see by the light spilling from the airport the animal's slender but powerful body moving fluidly backward all highlighted by a sinister smile of bared, sparkling white teeth.

"Keely. Get over here."

"Numbers? What the hell?"

"Shut up and get your ass over here."

Keely tossed the screwdriver aside, got to his feet and knew the night was going to be a long one. His ankle was throbbing loudly making every step a difficult journey. It made him realize that his big friend had never once complained about the gashes he'd received from the bear. He felt suddenly weaker. He hobbled the twenty yards towards Numbers' voice and saw him outlined by the lights from the hangar. He was much bigger than the dog handler, a black guy in his mid-thirties who looked more than a little pissed off. The man's uniform said he was not with the OPP and Keely stepped close enough to see the Sturn's Security patch on his shoulder.

"Looks like they left a pretender to guard things just in case you forgot something and came back," Numbers said holding a small, black handgun to the man's temple. "Seems he was distracted and didn't hear me walk right up behind him. Terrible job, don't you think?"

"Oh, I don't know. My ankle says he did just what he," Keely turned to look at the downed dog, "and she, were hired to do."

The dog growled and inched forward in the dim light.

"Settle her down, now," Numbers said and pressed the gun deeper into the man's temple.

"Down. Down, Daisy."

"Daisy?" asked Keely.

The guard shrugged, obviously embarrassed. The dog lay still, its head held high, alert and ready. Even in the drabs of light, Keely could see how beautiful the dog was and he sighed, relieved that he hadn't had to use the screwdriver in an escape attempt. Seeing Daisy now, he probably wouldn't have gotten far.

"What's your name?" Numbers asked the guard.

"Carl."

"Okay, Carl. You heel Daisy and we walk behind you along the river here until it meets up with the road. Don't make me shoot the dog. You I wouldn't lose sleep over, but her…"

"Nobody is shooting anybody," Keely said. "Carl, my wife is being held hostage and I have to get out of here or they're going to kill her. Please help me. Please."

Keely could see the confusion roll across the guard's face. "Help? I don't understand."

"If we can get to my friend's car, we can save my wife's life. Help me do that, please?"

"Don't stop you? Is that it?" Carl asked, his light-blue shirt growing dark, sweaty spots forming from the heat of the night and the situation.

"That's it. Walk ahead, lead us to the car, then stay quiet and we're all winners. Please."

"Sure. Nobody gets hurt, right?"

Keely asked the same question to Numbers using his eyes and body language. Numbers' mouth became a slit as he pressed his lips hard together.

"Heel the dog. Let her know we're okay now."

"Daisy, come."

The dog leapt to her feet and trotted to her handler. She remained rigid and on guard until he said, "Okay. Good girl. Okay." She settled down and actual licked Keely's hand, her tail wagging the whole time.

"She's beautiful," Keely said. "Can I pet her?"

"Can we go please? Wife, held hostage, get bicycle girl, release wife — remember?"

Numbers was right, Keely thought. His momentary escape from the insanity was distracting him from the prize – his wife. They moved along the river, Carl and Daisy walking a few feet ahead of Keely and Numbers, who held the gun on the guard the whole way. It took ten minutes to reach the road and another ten to find the car parked on the shoulder.

Just before Keely got in the car he turned to Carl. "After this is all over you're going to understand. One way or another you're going to find out that we're the good guys."

Carl chuckled nervously and watched uneasily as Keely climbed into the car and closed the door. Before he could say anything to Numbers, the big man was out of the car again and stepping in front of the bright headlights. He said something to the bewildered guard, whose face went rigid. Carl reached behind his back and handed a radio to Numbers. Then he dug into a pocket and gave the big P.I. his cell phone.

Numbers was back in the car in seconds. He tossed the phone and radio to Keely, then stepped on the accelerator. The car shot forward spraying gravel at the solo figure on the side of the road, his dog sitting calmly beside him.

"Couldn't take a chance he'd call someone."

"Good idea, Mick," Keely said, taunting his big friend. "There's no way that airport has a phone."

Numbers gave Keely a stern look but couldn't hold it for long and a smile appeared on his face. "I know, but this gives us maybe ten or fifteen minutes to find new wheels."

"I'd rather find a new foot."

"Bad?"

"Bad enough," Keely said and turned on the little interior light to have a look. There were several deep punctures in the skin around his ankle. He touched them gently and realized those closest to bone hurt the most. He applied a few layers of napkins from the glove box, pressing them against the wounds in hopes of stopping the bleeding. He pulled up his sock to hold the napkins in place. "Hurts like a bitch but nothing major looks to be punctured."

They drove in silence for several minutes. All Keely wanted to do was curl up in a ball and sleep. His entire body was aching, his ankle throbbing, and he was tired. It was natural — going with little sleep since Friday night was finally catching up with him. A stab of adrenaline shocked him awake at the thought of his wife in danger. He forced himself to sit more upright in the passenger seat and stuck his hand out the window, the cool air rushing past feeling good against his clammy skin.

"We're going to add car-jacking to the list, eh?" Keely asked. "What's next?"

"Not a good question, McAdam. 'Cause I know you'd do anything to get her back."

Keely watched the road roll under them in the skewed headlights of the little car and knew his friend was right. He'd kill to get her back. Keely reached for his cell phone.

* * * *

"I thought I told you to gag her." Sweet stood holding one of the swinging doors open, Elise's cell phone in his hand.

"Please don't. I have a bad gag reflex."

"How sad for Mr. Detective," Sweet said.

"She's fine without a gag. She's been good so far and even if she starts yelling the neighbours are too far away to hear anything."

Sweet considered what his brother said and huffed. "If she gives me any problems, I'll kill her without asking any more questions," he said and stared over at Elise to make sure she knew he was really speaking to her.

"Thank you," she said and nearly choked on the words. Thanking someone who had kidnapped her, tied her up and taken away any of her privacy to humiliate her. It was absurd, though Stockholm Syndrome was real. She had to consider that for a moment. Was she somehow, after only twenty-four hours, connecting with her captors?

Her answer was swift. No. She only wanted to gain any advantage in her fight for survival. If that meant befriending one and flaming fires of resentment between them, so be it.

"You're going to be good, right?" Sour said, and Elise knew by his affectionate tone that it was the captor falling for his captive. "He'll kill you if you're not."

"I will. Thank you for sticking up for me. I really appreciate you."

Sour backed up a little and crinkled his brow.

"Oh. Freudian slip I guess," she said and tittered lightly. "I appreciate *it*. Thanks."

Sour's wide smile made him look garish, almost fake. His skin was oily but when he was motionless she could swear he was a wax figure. She made note of a few scars around his otherwise smooth, round face.

"I have to go finish cooking dinner. Though it's pretty late for dinner." He laughed and winked at her.

"What time is it?"

"Late. Almost midnight," he said and walked casually through the swinging doors looking too comfortable in her very personal space.

"Get up there. Something's burning," Sweet called after him, then Elise heard the beeps of him dialling the phone. It was a one-sided conversation.

"Yeah. It's me. She's snug as a bug in a…Don't worry, she's not going anywhere." There was a long pause, then he said, "Okay, I'll give a bit more incentive. Any way I can help him get it done? Maybe throw the cops off his trail or something?"

He went out of earshot and everything else was mumbles. Elise was certain she'd heard him say her husband's name.

* * * *

Keely snapped the little phone closed and grumbled.

"No answer?"

"Busy." He rubbed his face with both hands then stretched. "How far to North Bay?"

"Two hours, tops."

"How long we been driving? Ten, fifteen minutes?"

Numbers screwed up his face and shrugged. "About that. Why?"

"Why don't we hear a helicopter? Should've heard that by now. Might take cars a while to catch us, but Carl would've called it in—"

"It would have taken him at least ten minutes to get back to the hangar."

"Something just feels wrong. I can't put my finger on it."

"Well, I think we just found a place to get a new car if that makes you feel any better."

Keely wondered if stealing a car was the right thing to do. The authorities would know they were heading north so any suspicious act would be flagged and that meant their new car would glow in the dark. Only problem was that the car they were in was slow and just as easily identifiable as any car they could acquire. The car was an issue and regardless of what they drove the best thing was to get off Highway 11 altogether.

Keely grabbed a map from the glove box.

* * * *

A few minutes passed since Sweet had made his call and Elise was keenly aware of him standing just out of sight beyond the shutters. She had to remain calm and be a good girl. The last thing she wanted was to piss off the man who had killed his half-brother's mother. Cold would be a great word to describe Sweet, but calculating didn't seem to fit. Elise was sure this man in his stylish clothes who played the mobster would be more likely to fly into a rage and kill rather than actually plan a murder.

"I gave you a bit of everything," Sour said as he entered the room carefully carrying a tray with a plate of food and an unopened can of soda on it. "I hope diet cola is okay?"

"That's fine. Thank you."

Sweet entered before the doors could stop swinging. He dialled a number on her cell phone. "Wait to untie her."

Sour backed away, almost hitting the water heater. He decided to lean against it as casually as he'd been walking around the house. She noticed for the first time that not only had Sweet changed clothes, silk shirt and black slacks, but Sour had donned jeans and a T-shirt.

"Hello, Mr. Detective. You've been a very busy little boy, haven't you?" Sweet smirked into the phone at Keely's answer as if he were standing right in front of him. At the thought, Elise ached to see her husband. "You can talk to her in a second. First, you listen. Our plan has changed. If you want to see your beautiful Mrs. Detective again, you'll find Kira Bremner and kill her."

* * * *

"What? Are you fucking crazy?" Keely gripped his forehead with his free hand, squeezing to help release tension. "I can't kill anyone."

"What? Kill her?" Numbers asked and Keely raised a hand to stop him from saying anything else.

The kidnapper's voice was emotionless. "If you don't, your wife is dead."

Keely tried to control his breathing. He gripped the edge of the dashboard to help him focus. "Fine. Let me speak to my wife."

"Keely. You can't do that," Elise pleaded. "You're not a killer."

"If it saves you, then I have no choice. Are you okay? Have they hurt you?"

"Keely, please listen to me. I keep thinking of Janet. I don't want to end up like—"

"You won't."

"McAdam. Find that bitch and kill her. I'll get a confirmation call, then I'll let your pretty lady go."

The line went dead. Keely snapped the phone closed and tossed it onto the dashboard. Numbers couldn't wait any longer and leaned closer to him.

"We can't kill her. What the hell are we going to do?"

"Something's going on, Mick." Keely turned to look at his friend. "Pull into the rest stop. I need to think."

* * * *

Elise couldn't stop her tears. Her body convulsed as she fought for control. Sour rushed to her, putting a hand gently on her shoulder. She shrugged him away. Sour recoiled and tensed then pulled out a thick-bladed knife. He walked behind her and cut the zipties binding her arms to the chair, then cut the tie around her wrists.

"That's not the plan," Sour said.

"It is now."

"Me for her," Elise yelled. "You're making my husband into something he isn't. You're making him into you."

Sweet stepped to her in one lunge, his face contorted with anger, eyes more white than their usual pale blue. He slapped her before she could protect herself. She immediately ducked to bury her head in her hands. For this she would not cry. She wasn't going to give that sick bastard any cause for celebration.

Sour stepped around her and grabbed at his brother's shirt. Sweet tried to knock his older and larger brother's hands away, but they curled around the material and the two trotted, quick step, out the laundry room door.

"Get the fuck off me," Sweet yelled and Elise heard an oath before a loud thud trembled back to her ears.

Her hands were free. All she needed was something with a sharp edge and she could be totally free. The only thing handy was the butter knife on her tray. She grabbed it and started to saw at the ziptie around her left ankle. This could be her only chance of escape. More thuds and yells travelled from beyond the saloon doors. The plastic tie snapped free and she wasted little time starting on the other.

She jumped at the thunderous bang and flash from beyond the doors. Someone had fired a gun.

Chapter 23

Elise heard a long, low, painful growl emanate from one of the brothers and it ended as she snapped the last of her binds. There was no time to think. She grabbed the half-full bottle of bleach from the shelf and darted to her right, hiding behind the water heater. She unscrewed the cap and waited.

Breathing wasn't an option since there were only two scenarios facing whichever brother entered the laundry room. She had either slipped past them in the commotion of their fight, or she was hiding behind the water heater. Sweat traced a tickly line down her neck and disappeared in her cleavage. She wished they'd let her change from her black slacks and blouse. Killing kidnappers was more of a casual wear event.

She heard a moan from the other room just as the doors to the laundry room swung in. The tray and its contents flew to the back of the room, where it slammed against the cement wall with a loud clatter, making Elise jump again.

"Come out, come out, wherever you are."

Elise thought small, trying desperately to shrink behind the big tank. She pulled her arms in and the weight of the jug of liquid dangling from her hands rested against her knees. She slid one hand carefully down the side of the bottle and hooked it at the bottom, tilting it slightly as if to pour it on clothes at her feet.

"I wonder where she could be?"

That's right, keep talking, she thought. His arrogance would blind him. If not, she'd do it with the bleach.

She felt a light touch on her shoulder and it was fear that held her hostage. She couldn't move.

"Let's get back in that chair, shall we?"

The doors burst open, hitting both walls with a loud slap. Sour tackled Sweet into the water heater so hard that Elise felt it move. The men collapsed to the floor, yelling and cursing at each other. They struggled for possession of the gun. Sour had a grip on his brother's forearm and held it high to keep him from pointing the gun at him.

Elise dropped the bottle of bleach and barely noticed it start to gulp out onto the cement floor. She ran to her right keeping the heater between herself and her fighting kidnappers. Ugly sounds followed her out into the basement as she headed for the stairs. Sickening moans of pain from strikes she didn't witness but could easily imagine floated to her ears and tightened her stomach.

"No!" one of the brothers yelled. She couldn't tell which in her urgency to escape.

She shot from the door and bounded right, reached out and grabbed the newel, swinging herself onto the stairs when she heard a bone-crunching thud followed by a gasp and then silence.

She stood on the first step wondering why she was lingering when freedom was only a few feet in front of her. She needed to know who won the fight and quickly decided she'd do it from a distance. She bolted up the stairs and reached the first landing at the side door. She fumbled with the locks because she kept looking down the stairs to make sure Sweet or Sour wasn't going to slide around the corner and shoot her.

The deadbolt was open and between the jangles of the chain lock she thought she heard something. She stopped, standing motionless with her hand gripping the slide at the end of the chain. She'd managed to get it half-way down the groove toward the goal of unlocking the door. Her hand moved purposefully but slowly right, making sure to keep her fingers tight on the slide.

"Help me."

She looked to the bottom of the stairs to see Sour, his face covered in blood. She froze, staring at him. There was so much blood she couldn't tell where it was coming from. She trembled with anger. Yes, he had been nicer to her, but he was just as responsible for her captivity as his brother. He'd tied her up, degraded her and threatened her. He was the reason her husband was out there somewhere trying to find and kill a woman.

"Please." He breathed the word more than speaking it. His hand was on the bottom step, the knuckles looked scraped. He pulled himself forward by gripping the back end of the open stair. His left hand was under his body, surely a hindrance to his progress. It was then she noticed the blood on his back near his left hip. He had lost the gun fight but won the deadly wrestling match.

He was kinder to her and tried hard to make her comfortable. He fed her and let her out anytime she wanted. He argued with his brother and got shot trying to help her. Or did he? Was this kidnapper really the good guy or just angered enough to want to kill the man who'd killed his mother?

The lock slipped out the wide end of the groove and she dropped the slide, hearing the chain jangle against the door. She glanced again at Sour then pulled open the door to a rush of cool night air.

* * * *

Keely sat in the car and stayed low, trying his best to bury his face in the map. Even though they'd parked directly behind the gas station out of sight of the road, he didn't want to take a chance of being seen by an employee or a car that happened by. It was a tiring task, he'd thought, trying to stay hidden. He'd chased dozens of criminals over the years but was always the hunter. Adrenaline of a different kind fuelled him then. He was unaware of the draining emotional toll that running had on the mind and body.

Sure, he had his white whale cold cases like any detective, but once he had a name he'd always get a face to go with it. After that, Keely had stopped at nothing to find and apprehend his target. He'd caught all of those criminals and the system had worked to put them behind bars. The only killer that got away took something with him, his own daughter.

The back side of the station was poorly lit helping to hide garbage spilling from a green Dumpster near the rear door. The empty parking lot spread out beside the station for a hundred yards but Keely was sure that travelers would fill this lot stopping on the way to and from their cottages. The rest stop had a coffee shop, burger joint, gift shop and of course the gas station. It had what every weary car traveler needed and it was the last stop before North Bay. He was suddenly pleased that it was nearing one in the morning and that they were alone.

He turned his attention back to the map. Numbers had been off on his estimate of two hours to reach North Bay. They'd be there in little over an hour, which triggered his restless feeling. As far as the authorities were concerned, they'd kidnapped two men and held a third at gunpoint while they made their escape. Why weren't there choppers searching the highway? It wasn't like there were thousands of cars on the road to sift through. It also bothered Keely that there'd been no road blocks anywhere.

A large figure appeared from the shadows and trotted around to the driver's side door. Numbers dropped into his seat and Keely felt the car rise a few inches on his side. Numbers passed a plastic bag over the console that Keely grabbed and dug through. He found a sandwich and struggled with plastic wrap.

"It's too easy," Keely said.

"What's too easy?"

"Our miraculous getaway."

Numbers grabbed the bag off Keely's lap and pulled out a sandwich for himself. He got the wrap off and was eating before Keely had found a corner of plastic to pry up on his own sandwich. In two bites half the triangle of roast beef and bread was in Numbers' mouth and he still managed to speak clearly.

"Nothing about us on the news, radio or television."

"See what I mean? We left that guard forty-five minutes ago and there isn't a copper in sight. No choppers, no cars, no nothing." Keely finally got the wrapping off his egg salad sandwich and took a healthy bite. It was bland, but delicious.

"If it was me, I'd have alerted the media by now, had a chopper light up the highway with a spot and probably alert Powassan to send cars south to set up a checkpoint between them and Trout Creek."

Keely wiped his mouth with the back of his hand. "All that is ten minutes and three phone calls. Not like there's much else going on. Or is there?"

It took Numbers a minute to realize what Keely was asking. "Nope. Nothing crazy going on as far as the news goes. The late edition of the paper was out a few hours ago and the early isn't due up 'til five a.m., so we should be the sensational story."

They sat in silence for several minutes, each trying to make sense of their situation. Why wouldn't someone put out a bulletin on them? At the very least there should be a helicopter checking the road. Was someone helping them escape? It seemed so unlikely especially since the cops had stayed in the airport for hours to make sure it was clear. If they had a guardian angel, the cops would've cleared out in half an hour.

"This is crazy." Keely felt a bubble of pain in his abdomen and rubbed it, producing a burp.

"We have a dead guy at the bottom of a cliff. We got a missing girl who was helped by her old coach. We have two shits holding your wife who were also responsible for killing two other people, that we know of."

Keely sucked air sharply through his teeth and turned a desperate gaze on his friend.

"Sorry, but we have to look at all this."

Keely nodded his weary head.

"We got a drug scandal. We got you kidnapping a pilot and then the coach. We got us both holding a security guard and his dog at gunpoint. How the fuck does all this tie in?"

"The dead guy, Todd, and Kira, are the ties here. I think someone is trying to silence Kira about the gene doping. To do that, they'll go to great lengths, like kidnap the wife of a cop and use her as leverage to—"

"Hey, how did they know you were in the park?" Numbers pinched his T-shirt, pulling it away from his chest, then ran a hand through his mussed hair.

"How did they know I was involved? I asked but they didn't tell."

"I can tell you. They got someone in the park who was watching you."

"Fuck! They told me that after I kill Kira they'd be getting a confirmation call then they'd let Elise go."

"Whoever's going to make that call is working for the bad guys," Numbers said and started the car.

"Whoever's going to make that call could *be* the bad guy."

* * * *

Sweat had dampened her shirt and made the night feel colder than it really was. Elise raced down the driveway and took a sharp right to cross the large front lawn, her bare feet feeling good in the grass. She'd have to go to the Calabresses' since the Nashes were on vacation. It was June, they always took a trip in June, so their house would be locked up tight.

She rammed through the waist-high bush separating their lawn from the Calabresses' property, the branches painfully poking through the nylon material of her slacks. She narrowly missed tripping on a tricycle beyond the bush on a wide section of grass edging the neighbours' driveway. She regained her balance and padded up the cool asphalt to the walkway. They were right about not gagging her. No one would have heard her scream unless they were ten feet from the window of the laundry room, which was on the other side of the house. She climbed the stairs by two and slammed her whole body into the door, tugging vigorously at the handle but it was locked.

Slapping her hand on the door and ringing the bell simultaneously, she yelled, "Maria, open up! Please!" She continued to assault the door until finally she could see a light go on somewhere on the upstairs floor. A short man in pyjamas and a striped robe clambered down the stairs nearly falling several times. After unfastening several locks he pulled open the door.

"Elise, what are you doing? It's after one," he said, the whites of his eyes glowing against his deeply tanned skin.

She saw the movement out of the corner of her eye and turned to see Sour finish raising his gun, pointing it at her and shaking his head. She could dive inside the door, but could they lock it in time? Even if they could, that wouldn't stop him from breaking in faster than they could call the police.

"I'm sorry to bother, Frank. I was sleepwalking and I just woke up."

Frank screwed up his face and leaned forward, but Elise put her hand in his chest and gently pushed him back inside his house.

"I'm so sorry to scare you like that. I'll let you get back to bed," she said and backed away from the door. Sour had ducked down behind the railing and even knowing he was there Elise had a hard time seeing him. Frank stepped out and tried to take in the whole street at once, his head darting quickly from side to side.

"Elise. You're sure everything is okay?"

"Yes," she said from her side of the hedge, and continued to back across her lawn.

"Well, goodnight then," he said and with one last look around, stepped inside his house and closed the door.

Sour stood and aimed the gun at her. Even in the dim light of the street lamps she could see the blood covering him. His light shirt was soaked with it, darkened all around the left side. He coughed and Elise heard a gurgling sound from his throat.

"Get up here, now," he said and flicked the gun at where he wanted her to go. She obeyed and climbed her stairs to stand at the front door. "You left me there."

"You kidnapped me."

"I was nice to you. *Was* nice to you." He pushed open the front door and shoved her inside. She turned to face him.

"I can't let you turn Keely into a murderer."

"Why not? He's killed before."

* * * *

Their hunches were right. No one impeded their progress through Powasson or North Bay. They sat in the car on the edge of another airport, only this one was bigger with a longer runway and more taxiways. All of the lights were out barring a series of red emergency lights that the government legislated be kept lit in case any aircraft needs to make an emergency landing at an unmanned airstrip.

"Someone has to be home," Numbers said, sounding unconvinced.

Keely shifted in his seat and tried to catch any sign of movement anywhere in the vicinity of the airport. "I see a wild goose."

"Maybe. But we gotta see if Kira at least passed through here."

Keely took a long breath, then exhaled slowly and loudly. "You only have one gun left, don't ya?"

"Yeah, but don't worry. I got your back."

Keely let out a light laugh. "Great. Who's got yours?"

Chapter 24

Numbers chanced turning out the headlights and Keely was amazed at how well he negotiated the roads leading to the half dozen buildings that made up the bulk of the airport. In the dim light Keely made out light-coloured metal roofs atop brick boxes. This airport was definitely bigger than the last one they'd visited, but the designer must have been the same.

Having pulled the car to a stop at the end of what they both thought must be the main terminal, Numbers turned off the engine. Light spilled from every window helping them see their way to the double glass doors at the front of the building. Keely tugged on them but knew before trying they'd be locked. A deep hammering of metal on metal confirmed his suspicion.

He noticed that several other buildings were minimally lit and wondered why he couldn't see a single person anywhere. There'd be cleaning staff and maybe even a single security guard. There should be people here. When they'd pulled onto the main road, Keely saw that the runway was of asphalt and twice the length of South Rivers'. It had several shorter runways angling across the long main runway, for smaller aircraft, Keely thought. This airport could easily handle larger aircraft, like the planes he'd see taking off from the island airport in Toronto, twin-engine props that held a hundred passengers.

"Bigger airport. Bigger planes. More buildings. This place should be busier, even at two a.m.," Keely said.

Numbers held his hands out palms up and shrugged. "You got me. Lights are on but nobody's home."

They split up to check the other buildings and agreed to meet back in front of the main terminal. His senses on high alert, Keely walked along the wall to his left, the brick pattern broken by intermittent slim, ground-to-roof windows that looked out onto the airfield. At the end of the main building he walked across a wide path or slender road, he couldn't decide which, to a smaller, similarly-styled building. Its lights were dimmer but still helped Keely see his way to its front doors. He yanked on the metal handle and the glass doors shuddered but remained closed.

Keely leaned against the window for a better look, trying discern dull images in the dim interior. All the doors were closed to the offices on the left and there was no movement from in or around the workstations on the right. He focused his attention on something in the middle of the room then forced his vision to blur. He waited several seconds to see if anything moved anywhere across his vision. Nothing. As he refocused, he noticed a chair back on the floor sticking out of one of the cubicles. *Knocked over by the cleaning staff maybe. What cleaning staff?*

He moved on to check the last building on his end of the main terminal and with the same results turned back to meet up with Numbers who was waiting for his return.

"It's weird," Numbers said. "You never think of an airport closing. You know?"

"Yeah. It's like a Seven-Eleven. They have locks but they never use them. Only thing is, we know that an airport can shut down, we've just never seen it."

Numbers rubbed his head and said, "Even if the place is closed there should be someone here. Right?"

"Cleaning staff at least."

"Well, not necessarily."

"What do you mean?" Keely said and yawned.

"They work at a certain time and then they leave. Maybe their shift is over."

"Should be a security guard here at least—"

"Keely."

"—Like our guy Carl back at South River."

"Keely."

"Do airports shut down completely without leaving anyone—"

"Keely," Numbers said and grabbed him by the shoulders spinning him in the direction of the runways. "That's a flashlight."

A small dot of light swung from side to side as if the person was on a nice evening walk and didn't have a care in the world. They were heading towards the north end of the runway and certainly weren't in a hurry.

"Get the car. Keep the lights out," Keely said and before he could leave Numbers tossed him the gun.

"You might need this." Numbers trotted in the direction of the car and Keely took off on foot for the light source.

In a situation like this there was no time for subtleties or explanations. Keely was younger and faster, both men knew that. He'd go on foot and Numbers would drive up behind their target, taking an alternate route. The gun was a precaution and nothing else. This was most likely a security guard on rounds, but there was no sense taking a chance and yelling out to them. May as well put a target on your back, even in the dark.

The grass was soggy with dew from the dropping temperature. Keely still hadn't felt the coolness since he was too busy with thoughts of Elise and finding a cyclist that just seemed one step ahead of them. Maybe whoever was out there saw something or someone, maybe they had a clue, because Keely was out of them.

The asphalt took Keely by surprise, jarring his leg and hip. His left ankle complained a little and that surprised him considering the small holes in it. He negotiated his cadence and regained his rhythm. Roberto had said that Kira was on her way to this airport, but there was no car in sight. Keely was no fool and knew the old coach could very well be lying to protect his former charge. It was obvious she'd had an impact on him by the way his face softened, tears forming on the rim of his eyelids at the mention of her name. She was important to him and that meant he'd do whatever it took to keep her safe.

He heard an engine rev and turned in the direction of the main buildings where Numbers should be emerging. He wasn't there. At least, it was difficult to see the car without its headlights. The echo made it impossible to tell from which direction the sound was traveling, but one thing was clear, the car was not Numbers'. He wouldn't be gunning the engine. Stealth was his aim.

Headlights blinked on to Keely's right and he squinted against their brightness. He raised a hand to shield his eyes from the glare and tripped where the runway's asphalt lip dropped down to meet grass. He slid head first with his hands outstretched like he was on one of those water slides he saw kids use in the neighbourhood. The car was closing in, its engine louder and headlights brighter. Keely scrambled to his feet, desperately seeking purchase in the dewy grass. He slipped and used his arms to stop from falling again. He finally found his balance and grip and ran to his right for a dozen yards, the lights of the car swinging to bear down on him. He changed his direction, darting left, only to find the lights altering their course to find and follow him.

He glanced at the figure carrying the flashlight to see if help was a possibility. Whoever it was had moved farther down the runway. The rev of the car engine was usurped by the reversing squeal of turbine engines overhead. Keely jerked his head up. A plane was coming in right on top of him, about a hundred feet up, landing gear down. He swung right again and heard the car slide in the grass, its light shining too far to his right. He wasn't the only one struggling for grip in the wetness. He was in the dark and knew he needed to stay that way.

His decision made he turned to face the car now searching the night for him, pulled the gun from his waistband and aimed it at the driver. When the headlights swung around to hit him with their full force, Keely lost sight of the driver and fired on instinct at the lights. He missed. Both headlights continued to blind him.

He dove right and the car missed him by a foot, sliding yards past him. Without thinking, he was up and running. He watched the figure with the flashlight charge toward the plane that was now taxiing up the runway.

Kira. It had to be Kira Bremner carrying that flashlight. This was the flight she was going to catch. Roberto had told the truth.

Keely heard earth being torn apart by tires spinning out of control. If the plane continued to taxi south he would meet it in a few hundred yards. His lungs seared with the strain of providing his thudding heart with enough oxygen to make the few hundred yard run a reality. His vision was blurred with the effort and his muscles cramped in defiance of moving one more stride.

Elise. It was a password that let him tap extra stores of energy because once he'd thought her name his body ceased to complain. His legs pumped in unison with his swinging arms. His lungs filled and refilled, fueling his body's needs. The plane was slowing and Keely was as far from it on his side of the runway as Kira was from her side.

In his excitement to get to the plane, Keely ran in a straight line and now the lights of the chasing car flooded the field for a hundred feet in front of him. He careened left but only for a few steps, then lurched right in hopes of throwing the driver off his trail.

The crash was thunderous knocking Keely to the ground. He had no idea what caused it and wasn't sure he wanted to look. He rolled over and turned back to see Numbers' little car embedded in the side of a sedan, the noise of their collision still reverberating though the dead night. Pebbles of glass were scattered about both cars and steam hissed from some unknown puncture. Keely smelled gas and oil and heat. He stood and darted toward his friend.

Numbers leaned from his window, his head bleeding from the impact with the airbagless steering wheel and motioned to Keely.

"Go. Get her. I'm fine."

Keely nodded and before he turned to finish his leg to the airplane, he hoped to catch a glimpse of the person who tried to run him over. It was a man but he was slumped over the steering wheel, hiding his face. Keely hoped that if whoever he was wasn't dead already, that Numbers wouldn't kill him.

The plane was stopping almost directly in front of Keely a few hundred feet away. It was a jet. One of those planes that stars use and the rich own. It had a double stripe down the side of its white body, ending in a series of numbers at the tail Keely didn't take the time to register. His body was fighting him again but he fought back and ran as fast his forty-five-year-old frame allowed.

Kira disappeared behind the plane as he rounded the nose. The sound of the engines wheezing to life pierced his ears. Now she was on steps hung from the body of the plane in front of the wing but no hands reached out to pull her in as the plane inched forward. Keely grabbed at the steps before Kira could pull them up and secure the door.

The plane was speeding up and Keely couldn't keep pace, grabbing the railing and hanging on as his feet slipped out from under him. The asphalt scraped his knees as he struggled to push up onto the stairs.

"I'm here to help," he yelled but she either didn't hear him or she believe him and began kicking at his hand. The plane's engines reached a fever pitch and Keely felt his legs lift from the ground as the nose of the plane went airborne. His heart was a fist pounding the inside of his chest, his eyes were wide and his breathing stopped. Kira connected with his hand several times but Keely refused to let go despite the agony.

He refused to fall to his death under any circumstances but knew only one way to prevent that from happening. As the plane lifted off the ground, cool air flowing over his body, he swung the gun around and aimed it at what he hoped was Kira's arm. He pulled the trigger.

She leaned back as if to slip the bullet like Reeves in *The Matrix*, but her squeal told a different story. She grabbed at her left arm and twisted out of sight. Keely fought the strong wind to get his legs on the stairs then his body into the plane. He dropped onto the soft carpeted floor and rolled onto his back. It was cool and quiet inside the plane despite the door being open. A panelled door edged with metal was to his left, no doubt housing the cockpit and pilots. To his right was a luxurious cabin with several leather chairs. Most important to Keely was the emptiness. He was alone with Kira unless the pilot decided to join them.

She was huddled against the wall beside the open door, gripping her wounded arm and crying.

Keely sat up and immediately shoved the gun in his waistband at the base of his spine.

"I'm sorry I shot you."

"Finish me. Go ahead. You've earned it," she said and oddly was able to stop crying. "I wasn't going to tell anyone. I just wanted out."

"You think I was sent to silence you?"

She said nothing. Instead her gaze was filled with resentment. If looks could kill, Keely thought. He swung his legs under him, knelt, then got to his feet grimacing the whole way. He was surprised that he could stand without crouching. His head had several inches of clearance.

He approached the open door cautiously, putting his right hand against the inside of the plane as leverage and used his left hand to pull the stairs up. They swung easily up and with a bump they slid into place. Keely turned a dial at their centre to lock them closed.

"I want to take a look at your shoulder," he said, "but first I need to speak with your pilot. Okay?"

Her look said she couldn't care less about what he wanted. He knocked on the door. "Mr. Pilot. Open up, please."

No response and Keely realized that the plane continued to climb. He huffed and grabbed his gun. "Either you open the fucking door, or I'll shoot it open." He waited a few seconds then tapped the door with the gun. "There's a peephole, so I'd suggest you take a look. I'm not fucking around."

Keely heard the latch release and the door opened a crack. Then it flew back and a hand appeared holding a black object. He didn't have time to figure out what it was and stepped left, letting the hand travel to his side before grabbing at the wrist. Then in a smooth motion, Keely twisted his body right, planted his feet firmly and brought up his right knee into the arm's elbow. He didn't break the arm but he did hit it with enough force to make it release the object. It thudded to the floor and Kira lunged forward. Before Keely's foot was back on the floor he used it like a hand, pushing Kira back into her corner.

He pulled on the pilot's hand, dragging him from the cockpit. The man stumbled toward the back of a leather chair and gripped it to remain standing. Then he spun back to look at Keely who was picking up the gun.

"What the fuck is wrong with you people?" Keely demanded. "Are you trying to get yourselves killed?" They were mute with fear. "You got a co-pilot?" They remained silent. Keely backed his way into the cockpit to see a man in his thirties, blond, blue-eyed, the poster boy for pilot recruitment. The man gave Keely a nervous half smile.

"Stay put, okay? And I need you to circle the airfield."

The man's face went pale and he swallowed hard, the gulp and bob of his Adam's apple almost cartoon-like. "Captain," he said in a fluttery voice.

"Do as he says."

"Thank you," Keely said and gave a slight bow. "Now, can we all sit down and talk this over, please?"

Chapter 25

She never thought her home would ever feel abhorrent. Sweet and Sour made themselves comfortable and at the same time desecrated any feeling of safety and security her home had ever offered. She'd be able to smell them even after lengthy cleansing sessions with the harshest detergents. How could she ever feel comfortable in that home again? If she survived this ordeal, she and Keely were moving.

They'd left her tied to her chair for over an hour now. She thought at one point her captors had decided to take Sour to the hospital since there hadn't been so much as the sound of a squeaky floor board. Then came the yell from what she guessed was the second floor. They'd found the first aid kit and no doubt were trying to patch up the damage they caused to each other. It was incredibly absurd. She was convinced that the brothers simply tolerated each other, most likely at the behest of their dead father, whoever that gem of a human being was.

She had been very careful in her choice of men. Her father was an alcoholic and even though he never once raised a hand to her, he was verbally abusive. He played head games with his children and she was never very good at it. He'd convinced her that she would amount to nothing. Oh, he'd never said it, but somehow it stuck and for a very long time. She'd had no choice and sought counseling, which turned out to be the best thing she could ever have done. She occasionally saw her therapist for a tune-up. Not to find some deep, dark psychoses, but rather to ensure she was keeping herself mentally fit.

Keely was a big part of that fitness. His honesty and gentleness were two of a multitude of attractors, including his rugged good looks, strength, intellect and, of course, his sense of humour. They had so much in common not the least of which was a love of life, yet they celebrated that in different ways. Yes, they'd share each other's passions for life, he going on outings with her and she with him, but it was great that they could be together and apart at the same time. She wanted to be independent but still know that at the end of the day Keely would be there. He gave her no reason to ever doubt that. Until now.

It was certainly not his fault. He'd had no clue that those men were going to kill the coroner and take her hostage. If he did, knowing her husband, he'd have put himself in harm's way to stop it. No, it wasn't that she blamed him for failing to be with her, it was that she understood the difficulties he faced in finding her. She knew her clues to him were far too circuitous. She was on her own.

The fact was brought painfully home when she tried to move her hands. They'd attached the zipties tighter than before and every scintilla of motion caused sharp-edged plastic to cut into her flesh. The warm trickle of blood traced a path down her palm and middle finger to drip into a pool on the floor.

She'd waited for the police. Frank would have called the police. Not because he suspected her of any wrongdoing, but because she'd always known him to be a practical man. When something didn't make sense, he needed to find a way to clarify it. What better way than to send a cop to her door to ensure, beyond reason, that she was all right?

The cops would drive by the house a few times then call in that nothing was out of the ordinary, and then one of two things would happen. They'd be told to resume their patrol or, based on how concerned Frank sounded, would be asked to make a visual inspection of the dwelling. She'd been praying for the latter. Maybe, she thought, I'd better pray harder.

The thought of praying conjured up another difference between she and her husband. Her belief in God and his dislike of God. She remembered him joking about it early on their relationship. "God really packs a punch, should've seen what he had that guy do to his girlfriend." They weren't really jokes either, she'd realized that. It was Keely conveying his beliefs to her.

She did not go to church at all, nor was she devout in the traditional sense. She believed in God and didn't partake in the pomp and circumstance of religion to prove her faith. Keely had come home from crime scenes and made comments about how God was one sick bastard. How a baby is fed to a dog, or a four-year-old child molested was beyond him in the scope of simple humanity. Add the fact that an all-powerful, all-seeing God was watching it happen and doing, as he'd said, not a damn thing about it, made it impossible for him to have faith in a higher power.

It never came between them. They would talk about it, discuss it as mature adults, but never fight or accuse. Keely never made her feel as if she needed to defend her belief. He'd often say that he only wanted her to understand why he didn't have faith in a God. He loved her despite all her faults, but he never made her feel as if her faith in God was a fault. He'd tell her how sick he felt at seeing the things he saw and she'd hug him. She was surprised but brought to tears when her muscular, tough husband told her he felt secure in her arms.

How would he feel after learning of this breech?

Sweet rounded the door frame causing one of the saloon doors to slap against the wall. It made Elise jump in her chair and pain shot through her arms and legs.

"You're going to be getting new neighbours." He raised his arms as if in celebration for scoring a goal, letting his hands rest on the outside of the door frame. Elise stifled tears, but the pain she felt from guilt and remorse were difficult to mask altogether. "They'd be alive if you hadn't been such a bad girl." Sweet sucked in air through tight lips. "You have been such a bad little girl, haven't you?"

She wasn't good at mind games but it didn't take a genius to see where this was going. "Fuck you." *Bad choice, Elise.*

Sweet walked slowly toward her, a look of enjoyment on his face and a spring in his step. "Fuck me? Oh, no. Fuck you," he said and grabbing each side of her blouse pulled, popping all the buttons. Her blouse lay open revealing her black lace bra. "You owe me."

"I don't owe you anything."

"I shot my brother because you got him to like you." He spoke as if she were a child. "You wanted him to hurt me. Then I had to hurt him."

She saw movement outside the room and hoped her immediate plan would work. "You shot him because he's stupid."

He smiled, a yellow-toothed grin that made her queasy. "You got me there. He takes after his mother. But he's still my brother and you made me hurt him."

"So what? Guy's a moron."

He slapped her hard enough that she couldn't hold her head straight. It swung violently to the right and she felt a stab of pain in her neck to join the sting on her face. Slowly, only because it hurt if she moved too fast, she turned her head back to face him. Now Sour was beside him.

"I know he thinks I'm stupid, but you, too? I thought you were nice." Sour brought the knife up to where she could see it. He ran the point down her cheek then over her lips. She didn't flinch; passive aggressive was all she had to work with right now. "I get her first."

"Like hell you do." Sweet stepped up and grabbed his brother's shoulder, pulling him aside. They stood face to face in front of her. "She's mine."

"You fucking shot me."

"You made me shoot you. I didn't have a choice."

They stood there, two maniacs fighting over which one was going to rape her first. They were in for a very big surprise.

"We'll draw for it. Highest card," Sweet said, then turned to Elise. "Where're your cards?"

She scrunched her face to give the impression of thought. "Guest bedroom, box at the top of the closet."

This was not going to happen. It was one of those questions people ask at parties or in social settings where everyone is curled up and safe and enjoying a nice buzz. What would you do if someone tried to rape you? A sadistic question that Elise had never answered.

Sweet left the room and Sour glared at her with hunger in his eyes. He actually licked his lips and she shuddered.

Keely had given her the rundown about what the experts say to do. He was genuinely concerned for her and she'd listened. But here, now, none of what he talked about applied. She couldn't yell fire or get free and run while yelling fire. When the act started it wouldn't matter if she succumbed. They were going to kill her anyway. She realized in one brief moment that her husband was not going to save her and that she was going to die.

No man would ever understand what she was feeling at that moment. Her want to prevent such a violation had little to do with her virtue. It was all about possession which is tied to one's dignity and giving up her right to choose. She'd been with Keely for many years and freely given herself to him. It all stemmed from love. Through her inability to bear children he loved her. Through family crises, he loved her. It didn't matter what was happening in their lives, she knew that he loved her. She gave herself to him because she loved him. Her choice had been made and it was based on love. There would be no choosing. They were going to take her last shred of dignity. She swore that it would not happen. She refused to die that way.

Judging by the look on Sour's face, she may not have that choice after all.

* * * *

Numbers' gripped his head hoping to suppress the throbbing, but it did nothing. He leaned over the wreckage amazed that his little car had done so much damage. He walked around behind the crumpled mess and came up to the driver's side door of the sedan he'd hit. The Hyundai made contact with the sedan at the front wheel, collapsing the axel and crunching the front quarter panel. Part of the driver's side door had been bashed in. There was glass and debris all around the accident.

"No officer. I didn't see him coming. I was driving across the runway." Numbers laughed as the driver moaned. "Easy, buddy. Let's see who you are." Numbers put a hand lightly on the man's shoulder and leaned him backwards into the seat. "You're that guy wanted to help bail out Keely. You're the fucking boyfriend."

"Gotta get her." Bishop's voice was a raspy whisper.

"Easy, buddy. You've done enough damage." Numbers rubbed his head again.

"Don't understand. I was trying to stop him from getting on the plane."

"Keely was trying to help her you idiot."

Bishop's eyes opened looking instantly shocked. "He was going to kill her."

"What? No way. What makes you think that?"

"I was told to call in when she was dead. I couldn't let it happen."

"Okay. Just hold on. I need you coherent. If you're the inside guy then we have a lot to talk about." Numbers dug out his cell phone and dialed nine-one-one. "This is so fucked up."

Bishop tried his door then slouched back against the seat. Numbers thought the blood on his hands was probably from wiping his head.

"No cops. No."

"What? What's wrong?"

"No cops. They want her dead."

"I need an ambulance," Numbers said into his phone. "There's been an accident."

* * * *

The leather seat was so comfortable that Keely had to fight sleep. He'd only been sitting for a few minutes but his weariness was more powerful than he imagined. The pilot was mid-fifties, black, with salt and peppered tightly curled hair. His face had seen a few battles and the scars showed. He was of average height and from his physical encounter with the man, not a good fighter.

"I have my orders. Take the lady to Mexico. That's it."

"And I don't suppose you'll tell me who gave that order, right?"

The man shrugged and shook his head.

Kira was still crying and clutching her shoulder. Gone was the pink cycling jersey she'd worn the night she went missing. It had been replaced with a loose-fitting grey T-shirt and blue shorts. White socks clung to her calves above well-worn hiking boots. Her brunette hair was in a ponytail and she looked just like her posters. Round faced, fresh and pretty but somehow hard edged. Her body was obviously muscular, too muscular for Keely's liking since it gave her a manly quality.

"All I want is your voice on a phone for five seconds. That's it. I don't care about anything else."

"Why do you want my voice?"

He considered her for a moment. This whole ordeal started when he found Todd Watkins' dead body. Was she really just an innocent person in all this? Roberto said he'd met her and she said that Todd had fell and was dead. He'd asked her about it and she said it was an accident.

"Who killed Todd Watkins?"

She straightened in her seat, wrapping her arms tightly around herself. "It was an accident. He fell."

"You made him fall?"

"No, not me." She looked at Keely and knew this wasn't her old coach. This was someone who wouldn't gloss over the answer.

"Then who?"

"I didn't see—"

"Bullshit. You're protecting someone." Keely leaned forward, clasping his hands together, fingers intertwined. "And that means it wasn't an accident."

"It was. He fell."

Keely put up a hand and surprisingly Kira fell silent. "You can't say it was an accident unless you saw and I think you did. In fact, it was you that Todd was looking for at the top of the cliff. Not sure if he was supposed to go with you, or if he saw you and wondered what the hell was going on. But you saw it happen. You saw someone hit him in the head and watched him lose his footing and fall to his death."

Her mouth was open and she was losing colour in her face. She looked to the pilot but soon realized he was of little help.

"Who hit him, Kira?"

Keely's phone rang and he dug it from his pocket. "Yeah."

"It's Mick." Numbers' voice reverberated as if it was a long distance call on a very old phone line. "I'm watching the guy that tried to run you over being put on a stretcher. It's bike girl's boyfriend."

"Bishop. Is he dead?"

"Oh my God. No. Please." Kira screamed hysterically.

"Nah. Just banged up some. I got him good."

Keely looked over to Kira. "He's fine. Just a few bumps and bruises." It seemed to calm her down.

"Boy, do I have shit to tell you. Robitaille is in on it. Nobody searched the caves and he called off the search for Kira already. Park is now open for business."

"What? So, he knew she was running? Shit." Keely took the phone from his ear and stared at Kira for a few seconds. "How the hell did Bishop find us anyway?"

"Got one of his flunkies to bug my car. Tracked us the whole time."

"He was keeping tabs on us. Doesn't mean that Robitaille knew about us looking for her though."

"I know, but he did know about Elise. In fact, after you were supposed to bump off Kira, he was the one to make the call to the kidnappers. And, get this, he was to use her cell number."

"Mick, sit tight, I'll call you back."

"I ain't going anywhere."

Keely slapped the phone closed and turned on Kira. "Your boyfriend was the inside guy. He was to call the kidnappers who have my wife the second I killed you."

"Please. He had no choice. You don't want your wife to die. Do you?"

"Of course not."

"He didn't want me to die. He had no choice."

"Yes he did." Keely said. "Just like I did. I could have shot you when I was climbing on this plane and called them to say you were dead. But, I didn't. I want my wife back, but I'm not willing to kill you to accomplish that." Keely pulled the gun from his belt and tapped his head. "You're going to help me. And you're going to tell me who killed Todd."

Kira's body seemed to shrink and she lost her hard edge. She sniffled and tears dripped into her lap. "It was an accident. She didn't mean it."

"She?"

"Amanda. She was trying to help me. She didn't mean it."

Chapter 26

Keely swivelled the large, supple leather chair so he could look out a porthole-shaped window. The lights of the airfield were in full bloom now only a half hour after they'd taken off. Thoughts careened through his mind and his vision went blurry. He had a few more questions before calling Numbers back. He snapped himself out of his self-induced haze.

"Kira," he said sounding as friendly as possible under the circumstances. "You knew you were doping and wanted out. Right?" She nodded. "Why not just go to the media and tell them what was happening?"

Her shoulders slouched and she took on the physical attitude of a teenager. She glanced at the pilot, who gave her an understanding look as he continued to dress her arm.

"You deal with a different type of criminal than the kind you don't see or hear or ever touch," the pilot said. "But there are criminals who can see you and hear you and definitely touch you. Do you understand, detective?"

Keely had a very tingly feeling in his stomach, the kind of feeling he used to get when closing in on the solution to a case. "I think so. The kind of criminal that can pull strings and never get their hands dirty. Like the government."

The pilot touched his nose with one hand and pointed to Keely with the other.

"You're telling me that you couldn't just say you didn't want to do this anymore because you'd be in danger from the government if you did?"

"Yes. That's right." She flinched when the pilot tied off the dressing.

"Hey Pilot, what's your name anyway? And don't say Captain because that's taken."

"Joe."

"Joe. You're working for someone that you've never met?"

"Yep. It's the corporate life for me. I get a call from my supervisor who gets a call from his boss who gets a fax from an unknown number that changes every day. That kind of shit."

Keely tilted his head and looked up as if to peer over the frames of imaginary glasses. "You a spy or something?"

He laughed and grabbed his belly. "I wish. Gotta be better pay. No. I'm just a corporate pilot that this morning is working for Body Fuel. I pick up and drop off. Sometimes people, sometimes packages, sometimes documents, but always very secretive."

Keely looked out the window again. Morning would be here soon enough. The plan to have her speak to the kidnappers was moot, he knew that. He was to kill her, but there was no way to do that. Unless...

"Kira, Steven was going to let you get on this plane and disappear, right?"

"Yeah. He said to call him when I got wherever I was going."

"Why the hell didn't I think of this before? He was just going to call the kidnappers and tell them you were dead. I'll just do the same thing. You get to go to Mexico or wherever, Joe gets the job done and I get my wife back."

Keely didn't realize she was shaking her head. "Why not?"

"I'm so sorry. He really had no choice. He didn't want your wife to get hurt but he loves me and—"

"They wanted visual confirmation didn't they? A photo or video?"

She nodded her head and began sobbing again. Keely felt as if a giant snake was wrapping itself around him constricting his every move. He had to find out where Elise was and to do that he had to let the kidnappers visually confirm Kira's dead body. Without the help of some very talented people he couldn't pull off a fake. The kidnappers would easily see through it.

He stood and took the few steps necessary to reach Kira and knelt in front of her, his hand on the arm of her chair. "I need you to be completely honest with me, because my wife's life could depend on it."

She nodded and wiped at her wet face with the back her hands.

"Amanda knew you were doping because you told her. Everybody at Body Fuel knew it too, right?"

She gave another nod. "I think so."

"Are you certain?"

She thought for a moment, biting her lip, then said, "Yeah. They knew."

"That means that the cops are working with the government and they can't be trusted. How do I make you dead and show it? I can't." Keely sat back down in his comfortable chair. He'd figured out who was on which side – a very good start but not nearly close to the end of the game. "I just don't know what else to do other than kill you."

"You wouldn't."

"Relax. I could never do that. I'm just trying to figure out what kind of leverage I have to get my wife back."

"Excuse me," Joe said. "I'm no detective and I'm sure as hell no bad guy, but what is it that the government is trying to protect itself from and what is Body Fuel, to a lesser extent of course, also trying to prevent?"

Keely and Kira exchanged glances of uncertainty.

"They don't want the young lady to expose their little secret. Trust me, people pay a lot of money to keep other people quiet." Joe beamed a guiltily happy smile at them.

Keely flipped open his phone and speed-dialed Elise's number. The phone rang twice and a male voice answered. Keely didn't let him talk. "Listen to me very carefully. I want my wife back or I call a press conference in the next hour." He flipped the phone closed and squeezed his eyes shut. His whole body constricted with fear but he had no choice. He couldn't let them threaten him. He needed to make them think about the consequences of such an act or at the very least, contact the person to whom Keely's threat would hurt the most.

"Man," Joe said getting out of his chair. "You got balls."

* * * *

"I gotta go make a call," Sweet said, grabbing Sour by the arm. "I'm first."

Sweet pounded up the stairs and Sour threw the deck of cards towards the back wall. They flew in all directions, a few of them landing on the window sill. One, the ace of spades, landed in Elise's lap.

"You're going to pay."

"I'm going to pay? Me?" she said seething. "You kidnap me and I'm going to pay?"

"You lied to me. You were nice but only to get away."

"You think I don't like you?" She asked it as incredulously as possible. "Really?"

Sour trudged over to stand in front of her and she knew he no longer believed a word out of her mouth. She had no choice and secretly apologized to herself and to her lover.

"Undo my bra. Please," she said seductively.

Sour stiffened, unsure of her sincerity. His movements were at chameleon speed, his hand slow and jerky on its course to the clip at her bra. He had the look of a teenage boy surprised by success in the backseat of a car. Though his face was lined with distrust, his eyes hungered for sex.

"It unhooks in the back."

Her statement, though spoken softly, startled him and his hand stopped. He considered his options and reached into his pocket coming up with his knife. He rounded the chair and in a two quick slices, freed her arms.

"Stand up," he demanded.

She tried but it was impossible to clear the back of the chair with her hands tied. At the very least he'd have to cut the ties on her legs. He realized that without her saying it and came around to stand in front of her.

"If you do anything stupid, I'll stick you," he said and traced a line down her chest with the tip of the knife. She bent her head back to give the impression that it felt good and moaned slightly to sell it even more. He dove for her legs and she was soon standing free of the chair.

His hands were on her breasts, kneading them through the light material of her bra. He was clumsy and she felt him pinch her several times before sliding his hands behind her and fumbling to release her bra. Finally the last clasp was unhooked and he stood back to admire his handiwork as if he had actually created her breasts.

He lifted the bra up letting the underwire rest on top of her chest. She was fairly large, a 36D, but age and gravity made them seem smaller because they sagged. Sour planted his hands on his hips and scoffed. He eventually took one of her breasts in his hands like he would pick up a melon. He tested it, squeezing and crushing, petting and pinching until he finally settled on twisting her nipple like the dial of a radio. He looked pleased as he bent down and took her now erect nipple into his mouth.

Her body was reacting naturally but that didn't mean she was aroused. On the contrary, while he noisily lapped at her bosom she calculated her moves, going over them like a dancer visualizing her steps. He wrapped his arms around her while dropping to his knees allowing him full access to her exposed flesh. She nearly burst out laughing when he squeezed her breasts together and made a motor boat sound between them.

She scolded herself for almost blowing a great opportunity but quickly refocused, leaning down to whisper in his ear. "Untie my hands, baby. I want to touch you, too."

She was airborne, his hands grabbing her under her arms, her tensing muscles not enough to stop the pain of his tight grip. Her head slammed into the shelf above the washing machine. She squirmed and kicked at him but caught nothing but air. He twisted her by grabbing one of her arms and pulling up hard. She was helpless to stop the spin onto her face, the cold metal against her chest shocking her.

"No," she said in a growl.

His hand gripped her hair and pushed her face into the hard, sheer surface of the machine. Pinned by the weight of his body, feeling his growing erection against her butt, his other hand searched to unbutton her pants. Instead of pushing back against him, she leaned forward into the front of the machine to make it more difficult for him. It wasn't hard at all. He pulled away from her slightly, grabbed one side of the waistband and pulled. The button popped off easily and her pants and panties were around her thighs in a second.

Every time she tried to speak or made any noise, he drove her head down hard into the white, shiny metal now smeared with blood from her head and face. She heard him spit into his hand and felt him rub himself. She wanted desperately to vomit in hopes that it would stem his urge, but her adrenaline wouldn't allow it.

He entered her roughly and she felt herself tear from the dryness. His saliva lubricant had failed miserably. It burned as he thrust into her, grunting and groaning with each push.

"Keely." She heard herself say his name and began to silently cry. It wasn't his fault. It wasn't her fault. The sick monster would be finished soon. It would be over soon.

* * * *

The phone in his hand, Keely let it ring several times before answering. "Yeah."

"My employer says that we can meet and exchange our goods." Sweet's voice was tight, as if he was talking through clenched teeth.

Keely smirked from the satisfaction. He had gained a modicum of control. "I'll call you back with the location," he said and hung up.

Joe rolled his eyes and whistled. "You are one cool cat. Either that or you're a whacked-out nutjob."

Keely couldn't help but laugh. "I'm a bit of both right now. If this was anyone else, we'd have landed by now and I'd've informed the cops of everything I knew. Only thing is, this is not just anybody we're talking about. I have to throw the playbook out the window."

"A whole new ballgame, eh?"

"Ah, no offence, but shouldn't you be flying the plane?" Keely asked not really expecting an answer.

"Junior is good enough to fly in circles. Now landing, we'd have a problem."

The phone rang and Keely ignored it.

"I'm going to the bathroom," Kira spoke softly, sounding afraid of her own voice.

She got up and Keely touched her hand lightly.

"I'm sorry I shot you."

She looked down at him with sorrow-filled eyes. Her ordeal was too big even for her, a cycling superstar. "I'm so sorry about your wife. I hope she's okay," she said and headed for the rear of the plane.

"So what now, detective?" Joe asked, and Keely could hear the tiredness in the man's voice.

Keely hadn't stopped thinking about it. He couldn't go to them, not because of transportation restrictions or timing. Hell, he was in a plane. He couldn't give them home-court advantage. He needed them to come to him. But where?

If they travelled it might give Elise a chance to escape. Or maybe she'd get killed trying to escape. Dawn was coming. The sky was still dark but there was a light tinge to the horizon. He could go home and wait for them there. That would certainly give him the advantage. He knew his house and they'd be in the dark.

Keely picked up his phone and dialled.

"Where do you think they are?" Joe asked.

"I don't care where they are. I'm getting them to come to me."

* * * *

Sour froze, one hand gripping her side, the other in her hair.

"No. Brother—"

The bang was so loud she stopped breathing. The echo of the gunshot lingering in her ears like the endless buzz from a loud rock concert. Sour gently released her hair and as she stood up, he fell backwards, slamming the floor hard. His pants were at his knees and he was still erect. There was a small red dot in the middle of his forehead, his brains in a puddle of blood behind him. She grabbed her clothes, covering herself as she looked at Sweet, the gun still pointing at his brother as if he may have to shoot him again.

Sweet turned the gun on her, pointing it at her chest. He smiled and she suddenly didn't care.

She was with Keely, the day she was photographing their niece, Jessica. Little Jessie. She was only four years old that day. Cute as a button in her little floral dress. What was she now, sixteen? Twelve years had flown by so quickly. Keely couldn't stop laughing that day. Jessie just didn't want to have her picture taken. She was bound and determined to find the muddiest spot in the park. Keely pretty much encouraged her. Rose was thrilled with the photos though. All those pictures of a little girl scowling in a pretty dress and a whole lot more of the little girl smiling brightly playing in the mud in a pretty dress. Keely managed to get his mug in a few shots.

Sweet smiled at her. "It was my turn."

One down, one to go, she thought and cursed her own callousness. God only helps those, she thought, who help themselves. She silently asked for Keely's forgiveness then looked at Sweet and dropped her clothes.

Chapter 27

"Boss."

"What is it, Junior? Arms getting tired?"

"Bogie!"

"A what?" Keely asked.

Kira was walking back up the center isle to her seat when Joe jumped up heading for the cockpit. "Sit down and swivel the chairs to face forward. Lock them in position with the little handle on the bottom," he said now talking through the tiny cockpit doorway having strapped himself in his chair. He yelled for them to do the same. "Hold on tight, kiddies. This could get ugly."

From Keely's vantage point he couldn't see anything but a sky coming to life. A few of the stronger stars were visible high in the sky but the horizon was struggling to breath light into the day already. The plane jerked to the left the straightened abruptly. Keely felt sick and was suddenly concerned about the location of the air sickness bag. He didn't want to mess up this beautiful upholstery or carpeting.

"Is that a missile?" Junior asked.

"You gotta fucking be kidding me," Keely yelled to no one in particular.

"No joke," Joe yelled. "Hang on."

Keely shot a panicked but accusatory look at Kira who was white-knuckling the armrests of her seat. She looked over to Keely and mouthed the words, 'I'm sorry.'

Instantly Keely was aware that Kira had somehow given away their position. What was more incredible was the swiftness and severity of the reaction by whomever was pulling the strings on eliminating her. The plane flipped, diving right and throwing everything that wasn't nailed down onto the ceiling. Keely hung from his seatbelt as if on a carnival ride, only there was no thrill for him at all. He looked out the window and saw something whiz by so quickly he couldn't possibly identify it. Though it did leave a trail of smoke in its wake.

"Evasive manoeuvres," Joe yelled. "We're going to ground."

Keely didn't want to know what that meant but he didn't have a choice, he was living the definition. As the plane continued out of its roll, Joe guided it ground-ward. Keely watched the horizon travel far too high over the front window of the plane and noticed something besides their radically steep descent. There was no engine noise. They were gliding toward the ground.

"Good move," Junior said. "Heat-seeking missiles."

"Can't hit us if we ain't hot," Joe retorted then he said, "We're going to land on the highway so I need you guys to be prepared for anything. Okay?"

"Right," Keely said and saw Kira nod. "We're ready."

He secretly wished his wife was with him then scolded himself for the thought. No matter how horrible it sounded, on some level he wanted her with him. She would make everything okay. She would make him feel safe. Bad jokes would stream from her like yelling, "Watch out, children of the corn" or "Wonder what kind of crop circle we're going to make?" He had to get a grip on himself. Kira needed him.

Keely watched out his window as the horizon slowly evened out to become parallel with the plane, distant forest, then a few farmhouses, and finally telephone poles all making close-up appearances in his little window. He didn't know why, but he felt confident in Joe's ability to land his plane anywhere. The man not only looked the part, he played it well. He was going to need nerves of ice to drop the plane safely on the two-lane highway. Those telephone poles were going to be very close to the wingtips.

The phone. She'd used her cell phone in the bathroom. Keely was no expert on espionage but it seemed logical enough. She disappears for ten minutes and someone starts shooting ground-to-air missiles at them to shoot them out of the sky. Felt very spy-like to him. Who would she call?

"No more bogies, we must be out of range. We have another problem."

Keely didn't want to hear what Joe had to say. He'd had enough problems.

"We have a bit of light traffic."

Keely craned his face against his window but he couldn't see ahead of the plane. He leaned sideways and looked out the front windows through the open cockpit door but the plane was gliding nose up and he saw only sky.

"Two-hundred. You got her, boss?"

"Putty in my hands. I just hope I don't make that car putty."

"One-fifty. I flashed our nose light at him. Should do the trick."

"They don't brake soon, it's going to be close."

"Shit. I mean, one-hundred. C'mon, man. Get the hell out of the way."

We're going to need some special kind of traffic controller now.

"Brace yourselves for impact," Joe yelled and Keely watched telephone poles slide by the tip of the wing by what looked like a few inches. He felt a thud and the plane's nose dipped making Keely's stomach rise. He looked out to see a car skid out from under the plane. He didn't see where it went but heard a muffled crash.

The nose hit the ground first and Joe struggled to pull it up to give the rear wheels a chance to catch up. It was no use. He cursed and the plane slid sideways. Keely heard Kira scream and Joe swear a dozen times before the plane stopped skidding sideways, its wheels digging sharply into the ground to send the plane skyward again. Keely felt his body soar and looked down on Kira curling up into a ball.

Metal bent and groaned. There were deafening scraping sounds as part of the plane continued its journey down the tarmac. Keely saw sparks outside Kira's window and then a massive boom deafened him for several seconds. Now the plane was sliding on its right side the wing having been snapped off. Glass all along the cabin shattered and for an instant the sounds of the crash reached a fevered pitch, only to die off into thuds.

We're really winging it now.

They'd stopped and Keely wasted no time popping his seatbelt but lost his grip on the seat and fell, feet first, against the side of Kira's seat. He felt a slap of pain from the dog bite, something he'd forgotten all about. Kira was screaming uncontrollably that they were all going to die. Keely tried to get her seatbelt unfastened but she fought him, her eyes as wide as the ends of binoculars.

"I don't want them to kill me." She slapped at Keely's hand and he finally had enough.

He grabbed her arms and screamed, "Stop!"

She looked wounded, not physically, but emotionally, as if his words had made her feel inferior. He spoke more gently, getting her to realize the situation. She relaxed enough to let him undo her belt. Once she was free he pulled her up from the chair and headed for the cockpit. They walked on the wall that was now their floor, scraped up windows showing the asphalt of the road. The plane was canted on the side with the exit. He had no idea if there was a second door on the other side of the plane.

Joe was popping his restraints, and struggled not to fall, placing his feet against the console for support. He looked wearily to his right. He turned to them, waving them forward. "Through here. Come on, we'll go out the window."

He disappeared for a second and Keely heard a loud bang, like a door hitting a wall. He shoved Kira into the cockpit and watched Joe's hands reach out and guide her. He followed her and felt Junior's hand on his back.

"Keep going, sir, we're almost out."

Kira was climbing out a small side window that had been pushed from its frame. Of course, an emergency window, Keely thought. He climbed up and out of the cockpit right on her heels. The moment his head hit the air outside the plane, he could smell the fuel, strong and biting. He used his bent arms to pull himself up, then planted his hands on the fuselage and pushed himself the rest of the way out.

He stood on top of the plane straddling the open window below and helped both pilots escape. Keely smelled smoke but saw no fire. Thick black skids marked their path down the highway and the deep gouges in the asphalt showed the exact place the plane had decided to flip. Keely felt a push on his back and they slid to the ground on the rounded fuselage, where another stab of pain shot from his foot. Joe screamed at them to run. They got a hundred yards from the plane when it exploded, spewing glowing orange and red fire high into the sky. The heat was intense and they continued to back away, unable to take their eyes from the carnage.

"Bye, old girl. You served me well," Joe said wiping his sweaty hands on his black-spotted white captain's shirt.

"Joe, we'd—"

"Go," the captain said, and turned to face Kira. "I'm sorry we didn't make it."

Kira nodded and her wet eyes reflected the glow of the massive fire. "Thanks for trying."

Keely grabbed her by her uninjured arm and dragged her into the ditch, scrambled up the other side then helped her over a shaky wooden fence. He wished for night again, but he'd have a long day before the dark would be their cover. For now, he had to get Kira into the woods a ploughed field away. Night was dying and soon they'd be easily spotted.

* * * *

She wanted nothing more than to cry. To curl up in her nice warm bed, pull the covers around her and cry. That was not going to happen because all she had left was decorum. How she acted would determine her fate. She would not be a victim.

The rounded metal edge of the dryer pressed hard at her hips but she wouldn't make a sound. He was still inside of her, flaccid, unable to get erect or just not aroused enough. She believed the latter since he slapped her ass hard a dozen times, calling her horrible names and when she didn't respond in any way, he hit her harder. Her kidney felt swollen from the punch he'd landed. He needed a woman to submit. She wouldn't give him that.

Sour couldn't defile her to his ultimate pleasure thanks to the hole in his head. She wasn't going to let a little thing like pain change anything. If Sweet wanted an orgasm, he'd have to get it the old-fashioned way. He grabbed a handful of her hair and yanked her head back. She felt something hard jab at her head.

"How's this, bitch?" He dug the gun into her temple and cocked the hammer. "Beg me not to kill you."

Was it worth it? Was staving off rape worth dying for? What would Keely have her do? He'd love her no matter what, she knew that. She was looking long past this day, when this would be over and they'd be together and he would reach to touch her and she…What would she do? Could she let him inside her after…? Of course she would. She wanted her husband still. After all the years of marriage, the ins and outs of daily life, their lovemaking was fantastic. It wasn't porn-film, yoga-tested, gymnastic fantastic. It was honest and real.

"Explain that to the boys." She said it so callously she frightened herself. "Killed the bitch because I couldn't get it up." She giggled.

The gun rained down on her as if there were ten of them. She put her hands behind her for protection but the pain in her hands from the strikes was too much. She felt the crack of the metal and the sting of his hand as punch, slap and hit came one after another. She was losing consciousness, unable to keep track of where her body hurt most. Her head spun from a rush of blood – her body's final attempt to keep her conscious. Her eyes closed and her final thought before passing out was that laughing at him had been the wrong thing to do.

* * * *

The mud was sloppy and yielding to their feet slowing their progress. Keely had no choice and shoved Kira down and lathered her with the thick muck. He rolled in it then stood to apply it where he needed to blend with his surroundings. He got Kira to do his back. It would make their travels even more sluggish, but since speed was out of the question, camouflage was the new imperative.

A light breeze floated past them and Keely blew hard out of his nose.

"This mud's been fertilized," Kira said, plugging her nose. "It smells like shit."

"Trust me, this is nothing compared to what I was wearing a few hours ago. Keep moving."

He pulled his foot out of the endless field of mud using more energy than he thought he had left and plunked it down in front of him to take a foot-and-half-long stride. Just then the wind shifted and he smelled the burning fuel. He could still hear it clearly, crackling loudly like some great bonfire. Being in camping country he expected sticks and marshmallows any time now. He turned to see a few cars stopped on both sides of the road well back from the burning plane.

Keely heard the sirens in the distance and turned to see a row of flashing lights coming from the north. He grabbed Kira's arm. "Let's go, it's not much farther."

They clamoured into the woods a few minutes later and Keely grabbed a tree, panting, feeling like his heart was trying to escape from his chest. Kira stood inside the tree line, leaning casually against a tree, breathing evenly and looking rested; she could easily make the trip again, Keely thought.

"I gotta get on the juice, man."

Kira sighed. "Not funny. That shit killed Todd. Might've killed Steven, too."

"I'm not sure I follow you. I figured Todd was doing it, but Bishop, too?"

She pushed off the tree, her easiness gone. "For a detective you're an idiot. Todd was on it, yeah, but I meant that because of that stuff all of this is happening." She walked over to Keely's tree and leaned her back against it, looking down at him bent over, still struggling to breathe. "I can't believe Todd's dead. He was a really good guy."

"Not how I hear it," Keely said and was finally able to stand up but still held onto his tree. "I heard you guys were fighting and broke up and hated each other. All that end of relationship stuff."

"You heard wrong."

"Yeah, so why'd you shut down and stop talking to Sarah and Todd after they got together?"

"Because they got together," she said, her voice raising an octave. "It was weird enough, so I just let them be, you know."

He regarded her for a moment, standing in the dullness of the forest wiping mud from her shirt. "You were mean to her. You turned on her." He faced her for effect. "Don't bullshit me."

"I was pissed at her, yeah," she said and backed away a few steps. "Not because of Todd, though. He and I ended it amicably. We just weren't meant to be together."

Keely peeked through the trees and saw several men with hoses training water on the wreckage. He waited a few moments longer, giving her a chance to tell him without being asked again, but he realized she needed pushing. "Why were you so mean to her then?"

It was obvious to him by the way she ducked her head, averting her eyes, her posture slouching that she was ashamed. She sounded how she looked. "If it wasn't for her, I wouldn't have started the treatments."

Treatments? Interesting word choice. Not exactly how he'd refer to doping, but okay. "After the Olympics?"

She nodded. "She kicked my ass. We were on separate pro teams but were both riding for the U.S. She showed me up bad. I admit I was having an off day and the team wouldn't let Pepe wrench me, which made my bike feel like a fucking brick. When I found out she was coming to our team I knew I had to do something. They came to me a few weeks later and we talked about this new treatment that would increase my muscle without me working out. I jumped at it."

Keely's phone rang. "Hold that thought," he said then flipped open his phone. "Yeah."

"Thank Christ. I thought you were an overdone steak."

"Mick, where the hell are you?"

"In a stolen car about a kilometre south of the crash. And you?"

"Woods to the west of the crash, top of a short hill at the end of the ploughed field."

There was silence but for some heavy breathing. Apparently Numbers was deep in thought. When he spoke it was with vigour. "Just checked the map. Go through that forest and keep traveling west, you'll come to a dirt road. I have no idea what it's called, but that doesn't matter. I'll be waiting on the other side for you."

Keely thought about it for a moment, then said, "Not so fast, okay? They may be following you, so just take your time. How far is the road from here?"

"Fuck if I know. About half a centimetre on the map. Maybe a couple, three kilometres. I'll try and line up with the forest, but it won't be easy. If you have to look for me, I'm in a dark blue Monte Carlo. Okay?"

"Okay, see you in about two hours. Be careful." Keely said and hung up turning to Kira. "You good to go?"

"Yeah. I could go all day."

"Cheater."

Chapter 28

The worn trail indicated that others had hiked through these woods. Probably a shortcut from one road to the other, Keely thought. With the discovery of the trail he decided he'd rather be biking it and by the looks of things, he was sure Kira agreed. They had made a lot of progress through the forest but Keely knew they'd be faster on their bikes, not that he'd be able to keep up with her.

He desperately wanted to hear his wife's voice and thought about calling the kidnappers to talk to her. If he did, he might lose the advantage he'd gained and as he negotiated a stand of pines residing close together on a short climb, he decided to maintain the silence. His biggest concern was getting to his house before the kidnappers. He told them tomorrow by noon, so that gave him more than twenty-four hours to get there and prepare for their arrival. That should be more than enough time. It would take another hour to meet up with Numbers, then it was a matter of a few hours' drive.

Pine scent mixed with dry dirt replaced the manure-laced mud he'd smelled, which certainly buoyed his spirits. It didn't help his energy level at all. Even struggling for footing in the dim forest, Kira was moving at a superior pace and looked fresher with every step.

"You were telling me the reason you doped." Keely wiped sweat from his face and hoped she'd see he was struggling to keep up. "Something about Sarah kicking your ass in a race."

He wanted her to slow down, but had no idea that his statement would bring her to a standstill. Or was the sight of him panting and wheezing why she'd stopped? She sat down at the base of a big spruce, the roots so high out of the ground that she could use them as a chair. Keely slid down against the trunk of a tree on the opposite side of the trail. He felt thick with sweat, and tired enough to sleep on the hard ground.

"She's good ya know." She took on the air of a proud sister. "Amazing technique, fantastic body and the best work ethic of anyone I'd ever ridden with. She was my Ullrich."

"Jan Ullrich. German cyclist that finished second to Lance what, four times. Only won the Tour when Lance wasn't there. That Ullrich?" She nodded. "How do you figure?"

"No other cyclist pushed Lance like Ullrich. He was always nipping at Armstrong's heels. Only difference is that there's only *one* Lance Armstrong and he always made sure to have the best team on the tour. I am *not* him and I never got to have a great team working for me, they all wanted to win themselves. Screw the team game."

Keely blew out air as if it were smoke from a cigarette. "No offence, but it sounds like a copout to me."

She threw her head back and forced out a laugh. "No offence, but you sucked and should've stepped down."

"I didn't say that—"

"You didn't have to. Everybody looked at me with the same sad face. 'Poor thing, she's at the end of her career.' 'Go on now like a good horse. Go out to pasture.' " She stiffened. "Fuck you and all of them. You don't know shit."

"Hey, I've been nice. Watch it."

"Oh, I'm sorry," she mocked. "Did I hurt your feelings? Was I disrespectful?"

"Is one of the side-effects from doping being a prick? Age catches up with everyone, athletes included. What makes you so fucking special?"

"Man, do you hear yourself? You know why guys dope in the Tour de France?"

Keely stared at her. He knew, but if he said why, she might somehow take that as acceptance.

"Fine. They cheated because they needed the job, the money."

"There are other jobs, other ways to make money."

"Tell that to the sponsors," she yelled. "Did you have a little chat with Leila, huh? She was so fucking blind by it all. I'm a goddamn product, not a person. I bring in the bucks from females in the twenty-five to forty-five category. I'm good for business."

"Actually, that sounds more like your boyfriend talking. Leila thinks of you as a friend."

"You know what?" she said, getting to her feet. He could tell she was trying not to cry. "Fuck you."

He was on his feet faster than even he believed possible. He leapt across the skinny trail and landed with his arms outstretched, hands slapping the tree above Kira's head. He looked down at her but inside he was looking down *on* her.

"Because you couldn't stand the fall from grace my wife is being held hostage. Show some respect. Swear at me again and I *will* leave you on your own."

"Go to hell," she said and pushed him aside to climb to her feet. She was walking away but he didn't chase her.

"Whoever is after you wants you dead enough to shoot you and innocent people out of the sky. You really don't care about that, do you?"

She stopped as if hitting a wall and dragged her hands through her hair. Her head was shaking and soon her whole body was convulsing. She dropped to the forest floor, crying uncontrollably. Keely ran to her and tried to comfort her but she'd have none of it. She slumped onto the ground and cried until there were no tears left. He stood there, dumbfounded, just staring at her.

When she finally gained her composure her face was puffed and her eyes were red and watery. She sniffed and wiped her nose with her shirt.

"I'm sorry. I'm so scared. And I just want to see Steven, to make sure he's all right. I didn't know your wife would get kidnapped."

"It's okay. I'm sorry, too. You were trying to tell me something and I wouldn't hear it." He sat down on the dirt in front of her and crossed his legs. "You know, I loved being a detective. Busting bad guys, getting them off the streets. It's a real high. And a lot of guys, they thought I quit because of this incident that happened. I let them think that because I didn't want them to know the truth."

She perked up at that and propped herself up on an elbow. Even the trees, grey, lonely stanchions reaching for any sign of light, seemed to crowd around them, listening.

"I've seen some terrible things. Horrible things."

"I can't imagine."

"Good. Because you'd stay awake nights. You'd see a little baby in a carriage outside of a store and hunt down the parents to give them shit for leaving their child exposed. You'd lock your doors at night and know that the monster you'd just put away had a dozen more like him to take his place. I would hold my wife so damn tight when I was asleep she'd stop breathing, hit me to get me to let go. I'd throw guys to the ground and feel too good when I heard their nose break or their wrist snap. I couldn't take it anymore. A man killed his own daughter. It was blood-coloured icing on a sadistically vicious cake. I just couldn't take another slice."

She sat up and slid over to him, her shorts making a swishing sound in the dirt, crossed her legs and took his hands in hers. "Pressure. It hurts."

He smiled at her and she responded with a toothy grin of her own. "Yeah. It does. I've never had a whole company rely on my performance and don't know how that feels. But yeah, I do know pressure. It builds until you just pop. I got out before that happened. You doped to stop it from happening. I get that now."

She bowed her head and spoke to her feet, but Keely could still hear her. "It's absurd, isn't it? I ride a bicycle for a living and they pay me half a million dollars to do it. You have to see a man shoot his child. Whatever they paid you, it wasn't enough."

* * * *

"Rise and shine, porcupine."

It took several seconds for Elise to remember where she was. The mental image hurt her mind to view but her body hurt worse. There wasn't a place on her that didn't hurt. The worst was her head. It pounded in several places, not the least of which was where it attached to her neck. The slightest motion ignited fireworks from her neck up and down her spine.

She ran her tongue over her lips and teeth. All of her teeth were present and accounted for but her lip was split in two places. She couldn't lose the coppery taste of her own blood. She couldn't breathe through her nose and wasn't about to blow out whatever was blocking it. Considering the pain she was quite sure the blockage was nasal cartilage. Her nose was broken.

"You look a little different this morning. Have you done something with your hair?" Sweet said and laughed hysterically. "I'm making breakfast. I hope you're hungry. You should be after that great night." He winked then dashed through the swinging doors out of sight.

She realized she was naked; she'd never felt so exposed in her life. She thought about looking at herself and that's when she felt the throbbing around her eyes, then her ears, chin, shoulders and chest. She stopped there, mentally probing each rib, counting the ones causing her pain when she breathed. She thought eight of them had been damaged. Not broken, but damaged.

Her hips seemed okay. Her ass cheeks burned where he'd slapped her. Her back was burning like her ass cheeks and as she readjusted her sitting position she felt bumps, most likely welts, around the shoulder blades and down the right side of her spine.

She dared a look at her crotch and gasped at the blood dried crusty on her thighs. An image of her attacker pushing something inside of her formed in her mind but she shut it down. She couldn't bring herself to examine that any deeper with either her mind or eyes. She wasn't feeling any pain there so that would have to keep her going for now.

She could see welts, cuts and bruises all down her legs. She was alive. That's what was important. She'd lost a battle last night, but was way ahead in the war.

"Hey, did I tell you?" Sweet yelled from somewhere out in the basement. "Hubby is coming home tomorrow. He won't even recognize you."

Her body clenched sending pains shooting to all directions. What had happened to her captors? She glanced down at the dead body looking up at the ceiling. The blood from his head now dark like dried paint. She tried to take a steadying breath but the pain brought tears to her eyes. They'd started off so professionally. Now one was dead and the other was completely unpredictable. Keely was walking straight into her hell. She had to warn him.

* * * *

They cleared the trees and looked out over an empty field that descended at a gentle angle to even out where it met the dirt road. They had less than a kilometre to go. The first signs of early morning light brightened everything helping Keely to find new strength.

They bounded down the gentle slope, the grass tickling Keely's legs. He ignored the sharp pain in his ankle where Daisy had sank in her teeth. He was almost at the road and that meant he would be on his way home to Elise. More energy surged from some unknown furnace inside him to fuel the final few hundred metres.

Kira stopped and put out her arm like a gate to hold back Keely. "Listen," she said tilting her head to the right. "You hear that?"

Keely had gotten far too familiar with that sound and grabbed Kira, throwing her roughly to the ground. "Sorry. Stay still. Hopefully the grass will hide us. Stay still."

They waited for a few minutes as the sound grew louder. Keely was sure the chopper had hovered over them, but there had been no indication they'd been seen. *What would that have been, a flare?*

The chopper headed north and when the sound was just a whisper, Keely chanced a look. He tapped Kira and they both got to their feet.

"We have to hide. It could come back anytime." The only place he could see to hide was a farmhouse not far from the other side of the road. He put a hand on Kira's back and they ran for it.

They ended up at the side of a barn behind the farmhouse. Keely felt it would be safer to stay clear of the house. He wasn't about to add breaking and entering to his list of crimes. Loitering on private property was fine with him, he thought as he led Kira into the rundown structure full of holes.

Light streamed in from all directions and lit the floating dust from the mounds of hay covering half the floor on the far end. It was several stories high with dark, grained rafters. Farm equipment, some modern and some more rustic, occupied the corners on either side of the big doors.

Keely reached for his phone and called Numbers. There was no answer. He walked to the front door, careful to stay out of sight and peered around the corner. He watched the road in hopes of seeing any sign of his big friend. The helicopter was back and that could be why Numbers hadn't shown yet.

Kira's phone rang and Keely cursed. He'd forgotten to throw it away. He rushed to her and grabbed it from her, throwing it with all his might to smash on the cement floor of the old barn.

"Don't you move, motherfucker."

Keely whirled around to see a young man in his late teens, wearing a black, baggy track suit and a white hat turned sideways. A medallion of some kind, big and shiny, dangled on his chest. He held a rifle on Keely whose leg was in the air, waiting to stomp down on the what was left of the phone.

"Easy, big man. I just needed a place to protect the lady."

"Yeah, that's why you're smashing her phone, punk."

"You got it all wrong. I'm a cop."

"And I'm fucking Eminem. Shut up," he said and turned his attention to Kira. "Miss, you okay?"

"I'm fine. He's telling the truth. I swear."

He looked bewildered, as if he'd been asked a difficult question. "You got anything to do with that crash over there? It's been on the radio. Two pilots died."

"What? They were alive—"

"We have no clue what you're talking about." Keely shot Kira a glance that said he'd do the talking from now on.

"They were both shot in the head, but you probably know that. Right, you motherfucker?"

Keely put his foot down and took a few steps toward the boy upon noticing Numbers moving cautiously toward the barn. "You know what? There's no call for that kind of language. There's a lady present for crying out loud."

The guy raised the gun to rest the stock on his cheek, eyeing down the sight. "You step back or die, fucker."

"Let's not do anything stupid, sonny." Numbers held the gun pressed against the teenager's ear. "Lower the rifle." When the boy didn't respond, Numbers leaned closer to his ear and said, "I'm the motherfucker who's gonna put a cap in your ass. Cool?"

He lowered the gun and when Keely stepped forward to grab it the kid said, "It's cool. No big."

"Chopper spooked me," Numbers said, "so I parked in this young man's garage. There is a beautiful Cadillac Escalade in there that's perfect for our needs."

"That's my parents' car," he said in a high-pitched voice, sounding more like a normal kid than a gangster. "They'll kill me."

"Hey, if you like, I can knock you out," Numbers said. "Then mommy and daddy won't be so pissed and would probably be all worried about their little boy."

"Yeah, and your homies will think you're the bomb," Keely added.

The kid screwed up his face as if thinking was a chore, then he smiled. "Big points for me, man. Yeah. Whack me."

"Oh, no," said Numbers. "There will be no whacking today."

Chapter 29

Numbers was behind the wheel of the large black SUV now cruising down Highway 94 towards a little town called Callander. Keely was keeping a very close eye on Kira in the backseat.

Once they'd tied up gansta rapper boy they made their way to the garage. Numbers had parked the stolen Monte Carlo inside and traded up. The kid had been quick to give up the keys but before they could leave the house, Kira ascended to a rage and began slapping and kicking at Numbers.

"You could've killed him," she'd screamed. "Asshole."

It was harder to stop her tirade than he'd imagined, but eventually Keely got her settled down. He had explained that both Mick and her boyfriend were under the impression that each was trying to hurt someone they cared about. It seemed to do the trick, but now, Kira looked like a sulking child, the size of the Escalade's backseat added to her immature standing. Her shoulders were lower than the back of the tan, leather seat. She seemed to be swallowed by the interior. Keely thought that when she spoke, her voice would likely echo.

What Kira Bremner didn't know was that once Mick Moyer decided you were his friend, he'd do anything for you. Like drive his car straight into another car to protect you. Numbers learned quickly that others might not appreciate his friendship in quite the same way. Like earlier when he'd been beaten up by a girl.

It was almost comical and Keely had to stifle his laughter. Numbers' face was full of surprise and not wanting to retaliate his only course of action had been to cover up and let Kira's blows land on his hands and forearms. Keely'd heard Numbers' muffled cries for help from inside his rope-a-dope.

The day was bright and cloudless and even at six in the morning, it was hot. Keely silently thanked the farmer for his taste in fine automobiles and for choosing the air conditioning package. The truck rolled on and Keely barely felt the largest bumps in the road. They'd be in Callander in a few more minutes and Keely promised Kira he'd try to find out how Steven was doing. Mick said the kid was a bit banged up but fine.

Numbers had walked away with only a bump on his head from that crash, but he'd lost a little dignity to Kira. She hadn't hurt Numbers. Keely would never have let that happen. Sitting in the passenger seat of the massive SUV, more comfortable than he'd been in days, Keely thought Kira either insane or fearless. Those two things, he suddenly decided, were not mutually exclusive. There are times when you have to remove yourself from reality to stave off the results of fear.

Regardless of how she'd done it, Kira had taken on Numbers and would live to tell the tale. Or, at least Keely hoped that would happen. He wasn't being smug when he'd told her someone with deep pockets of power was out to end her life. Keely had seen how string pullers could manipulate people and change the course of an investigation. Never had he seen such power wielded to end an investigation before it began. Anyone who could order a private plane shot out of the air must feel they were above the law, of that there was no doubt. Add to it the murder of that plane's pilots on the ground and you've got someone who not only thinks they're untouchable, they might very well be just that. Not only did this kingpin care nothing for the people around their target, they were thorough in silencing witnesses. It meant Elise was disposable, a back-up in case things went awry.

How do you fight person you can't even see? He tilted the vents and directed the cooled air away from his face. Keely watched a gas station and car dealership get closer and felt something familiar about the scene. He dug into his memories and realized that Elise had dragged him this way a few years ago to take a tour of Lake Nipissing. She'd talked about great blue herons nesting by the hundreds and trumpeter swans in flocks big enough that you'd swear they were a cloud. They'd seen none of that of course because they never left their hotel room.

"We can't stop." Numbers looked nervously around the car. "This is one of the first places the cops are going to be. We gotta keep moving."

"I said she could call her boyfriend."

"To hell with her boyfriend."

"To hell with you," Kira screamed and kicked the back of Numbers' seat.

"If she has to call let her use your phone." Numbers furrowed his brow. "Hell, she can use my phone. Anything is better than stopping."

The only phone that had been tracked was Kira's. However, technology existed to find and track a cell phone by simply knowing the number. Once you had the number you needed to know the general area in which it would be used. After that it was easy. The moment the phone went hot, you could track the signal to the user. "No way. Payphone or not at all."

"That little corporate weasel is with those fucking guys who kidnapped your wife and you're telling me you want sunshine back here to have a chin wag with him. There is no damn way I'm stopping this car."

"Numbers, he was looking out for her, just like you're looking out for me."

The big P.I. shook his head vigorously. "Are you fucking blind? You've been off the job too long, man. That little shit tried to kill you, remember?"

"He was trying to save me," Kira said sternly.

"He was going to contact two kidnappers the moment you were dead," said Numbers. "That makes him a bad guy and it makes you," he pointed at Keely, "stupid."

"Let's not get carried away here, Mick."

Numbers' face calmed as if a bad headache had just gone away. "I'm sorry that I'm seeing things a bit differently here. I want you to get Elise back in one piece. But we have a corporation trying to kill her and us, and we have cops that are either helping or at least looking the other fucking way."

"He's not trying to kill me," Kira said but the strength in her voice had ebbed. "He loves me."

"McAdam, at the very least that idiot boyfriend of hers was going to make that call after she fled the country on that plane. We both know what would have happened to Elise if he made that call."

There was no denying it, Elise would have been dead since Bishop wouldn't have had the visual confirmation they wanted. He must love Kira because that would have put a tag on his toe for sure. The only thing keeping Elise alive was Kira Bremner. If Keely lost her, showed up at the meeting without her, then Elise was dead. There was far more going on than he had the time or inclination to figure out. Why was Amanda Zandestra trying to help Kira get away? Was Steven Bishop playing both sides? He wanted Kira but had to answer to a higher corporate power that wanted any evidence of doping erased? Why were the cops letting them get away? Was Body Fuel capable of wielding such power?

It didn't take long for them to pass through Callander whose biggest claim to fame was an annual highland festival. The Blockbusters and Starbucks would bring in more business, Keely thought.

A familiar-looking SUV appeared from around a sloping bend and Keely's senses tingled with recognition. He'd seen something similar somewhere. A newspaper article or a website on vehicles. Military vehicles. *Armoured* vehicles. Just as he made the connection the passenger window behind the driver went down and an automatic rifle's muzzle poked out. "Down!" Keely shouted. "Get down!"

The windows exploded in, glass shards raining down on them. Kira screamed and before Keely could sit back up, he heard the car's engine rev louder. Numbers was up and dividing his time between mirrors and looking at the road ahead. It was fairly straight, sided by forest and fields with the occasional small body of water mixed in. Kira had slipped her arm and shoulder free of the shoulder portion of her seatbelt. That would allow her to stay down and hopefully out of the line of fire. Only one problem with that theory.

"Those bullets are gonna rip through this car like it's made of paper," Numbers said finishing Keely's thought.

"Fast as you can, big man, until we can figure out what to do."

"Don't have to tell me twice."

Keely chanced a glance behind him and saw their pursuers had turned and were now traveling in the same direction a few hundred metres behind them. They wouldn't be able to go as fast, but the moment the Escalade slowed or stopped, it was over. No doubt they'd have explosives to take care Kira. And there was that nasty point about not giving a shit about who they took with her.

"I don't suppose you brought that map?" Keely asked.

"Glove box. Don't go anywhere without it, especially when I'm running for my life."

Keely scanned the map and wondered if they could get far enough ahead of their pursuers to simply lose them. He knew that wasn't possible. They might be able to get far enough ahead to ditch the car and either run or swim for it. Again, he knew that the people in that vehicle were specially trained personnel who could track a mouse through a jungle. There was really only one choice. "You're not going to like this."

"Try me," Numbers said eyes flipping between mirrors.

"We gotta call in the cavalry."

He shook his head and gave an honest light laugh. "And who exactly is the cavalry? Can't be the OPP 'cause they're the bad guys now."

"They can't all be bad."

"They're getting closer," Kira yelled.

"Keep your head down," Keely warned. "Numbers. We don't have a choice. Can you get us to Pawasson?"

They flew by a car and Keely chanced a glance at the speedometer – they were going one-ninety. A popping sound made Keely turn to look back and just as he did the passenger side mirror shattered. "Can you go faster please?"

"Not like we have a choice. Right?" Numbers said and drove his foot down on the gas pedal. Keely watched as the speedometer rose steadily to just over two-thirty. He glanced back at the black SUV with its black windows and guards over the wheels, to see it fall slightly behind.

"At this speed I'll get us there in a few minutes. What then?"

"Just get to the OPP station. It's our only shot."

Powassan was on them faster than Keely expected and he loved it more than any town he'd ever visited. Numbers had no choice but to drop his speed drastically just before they hit the city limits. There were people milling about in pockets, some on their way to work, Keely expected, and some just out to enjoy a beautiful summer morning. Seeing the little town take its first lively breaths of the day made him feel good. Even better was that the bad guys were nowhere in sight. Keely was constantly checking behind them to ensure they'd be unimpeded to the station.

"Hey, if they're gone, why not just keep going?" Numbers asked looking more tired then Keely had ever seen him look.

"We can't chance it. They're definitely on to us so there's no place to hide. Can you guarantee she'll survive?" By the look on his big friend's face

Keely knew the answer. The problem would be getting them to believe their story. He had to get to Elise. Surely Robitaille would understand his motivation.

Numbers took a sharp right and Keely almost found himself in the big man's lap. He regained his composure and straightened ready to confront him about his dangerous driving but Numbers didn't give him the chance.

"Another one was coming north through the town. God knows how many of those tanks they got on us."

"Please. I don't want to die." Kira had her feet up on the seat, her knees to her head, looking like a sloppy ball.

"Nobody's going to die. Just a minor setback." Keely scanned the small streets lined with little houses that reminded him of cottages. "Gotta ditch this car, Numbers."

"I'm going to hit the gas in a few seconds and round a corner and if we're lucky, another corner after that. We're not going to have a lot of time, so pick a house and we bust in quick. Okay?"

"Did you hear that, Kira?" She didn't respond. "Hey! Did you hear that? We gotta run fast when the car stops, okay?"

"Whatever."

He undid his seatbelt and reached back, giving her leg a loud slap. She unfolded herself and Keely could see she'd been crying. "This is for you. We're doing this to keep you alive. The moment you want to give up, I'm out of here. Because when you give up, you're going to get us all killed."

They stared at each other for what seemed like minutes until Kira wiped her face and nodded. Keely looked out the back window of the Escalade which seemed a football field away and caught his breath when an OPP cruiser shot out from a side street and blocked the big SUV. He could just make out another cruiser pulling up behind the black truck and in moments the occupants were out and showing badges to each other.

Two men had emerged from the truck and both were armed with rifles. Keely thought they looked like M16s but he couldn't be sure. "They might be RCMP or military. Whoever they are they've got credentials."

As Numbers guided their SUV around a corner Keely saw the first shot. One of the OPP officers dropped and after that all of the men scrambled to find cover.

"Armour piercing bullets. We have to help them."

They'd made the turn and Numbers increased speed a bit. He'd still had to be cautious since a number of people were emerging from their homes to see what the noise was all about. They roared onto the street opposite the gun fight and Keely watched as one of the cruisers exploded. The SUV shuddered, Numbers fighting for control, and instantly Keely felt the heat of the blast through the shattered windows.

"We have to help them." Keely watched an old man struggle to his feet and then help his wife do the same. The force of the blast had knocked them right off their feet and they were more than a block away.

"And do what? Get ourselves blown up?" Numbers' face was backlit by the glow of the red fire and his hair sticking out at odd angles made him look devilish.

"We can't just leave them."

They were back on the main street that ran through the town and Keely noticed first the helicopter hovering a few hundred feet above them then, in seconds, police cars seemed to emerge from every side street. There had to be ten cruisers, all with their cherries flashing and sirens blaring.

"I think they want you to pull over," Kira said from the back seat, sounding distant.

"Looks like we're saved," Keely said.

Numbers stopped the car and turned off the ignition. "Looks like we're arrested," he said putting his hands in the air. Keely did the same.

* * * *

It had been difficult to eat but she'd managed. Sweet may have split her lip and made it tough to chew but she knew keeping up her strength was important. She'd need it for whatever Keely had planned.

Sweet re-ziptied her hands and stood in front of her, leaning down as if to scold her. Instead his face seemed to be all smile and he chuckled. "I can't wait to see him. Can you believe it? He's coming tomorrow. It's like Christmas." He turned and practically skipped out of the room.

Sweet had snapped and beaten her to within an inch of her life but nothing could crush her spirits now. Keely was coming. Her husband was going to save her. She smiled then grimaced as her lip split opened anew.

Chapter 30

Some guys kept a physical count of their collars, but it wasn't Keely's style. He'd kept a mental photo album of serious offenders, the murderers, rapists and such, that he'd had a hand in putting away. The steps involved in apprehending, arresting, trying, convicting and jailing a criminal were complicated, bureaucratic-laden and time consuming. The initial step of processing an alleged perpetrator had, over Keely's twenty-year career and with a glance at his mental photo album, become rote. Only this time, he'd been the arrestee.

It had taken a few hours to go from being slammed up against the stolen Escalade, frisked, handcuffed and informed he was under arrest for a shitload of things, to being in one of the only two tiny holding cells in Pawasson's OPP station. From the moment he'd been put in the back of a cruiser he'd been asking to see Robitaille and no one would answer him. He tried to think of a way to escape but was too damned tired to fight any of the cops for a gun. Even then he'd probably just end up shot and that wouldn't do Elise any good. He'd have to speak with Robitaille.

There was a *Barney Miller* feel to this station since it was on one floor, the holding cells were at the back tucked behind a wall running half the length of the room. Keely was in the cell closest to the wall so he could only see an older officer sitting at his cluttered desk, but the sounds of the squad room were clear. The occasional phone rang above the din of what must have been more cops than that station had ever seen. Keely was big news.

He squeezed against the bars separating his cell from Numbers'. "Hey, what's going on out there?"

"Us, I guess. I can't see anything special." He leaned against the bars at the left of his cell for a better look. Keely figured his cellmate could probably see about two thirds of the squad, the rest blocked by the wall of hiding.

"Where's Kira?"

"They took her out a few minutes ago. Probably for a lie down or maybe to debrief her." He stretched out his back like some massive, overfed cat.

"What about our mercenary buddies? The boys in black? The warlords—"

"I get it." Numbers shot him an annoyed look. "I figure they're in cells somewhere else in the building. Probably in the basement."

"Why the hell aren't they letting us talk to Robitaille?" Keely saw Numbers' red face and wanted to take back the question.

"Who the fuck do you think I am, Ken Jennings?" He paced in his cell. "I don't fucking know, okay?"

Keely sat on the thin bed along the right side of his cell, the springs creaking eerily. "I'm sorry I got you into this, Mick."

"I swear at you a few times and you get all mushy on me. You are not the man I once knew. Too many trips into the forest, my friend."

"Okay, I'm glad they've charged us with kidnapping. It'll put hair on your chest."

"That's better." Mick smiled and lost some of his hardness. "We're going to get out of this and I'm telling you, the publicity is going to bring me so much work I won't have to spend a minute with Nancy. Don't be apologizing to me, kid. I should be thanking you."

If the circumstances were different, if they were in a bar or they were lounging on Keely's deck nursing some beers, he'd talk frankly with his friend about getting out of his marriage. He liked Nancy, hell, he knew that Numbers liked her too. But that was it, he *liked* her. Certainly not the basis of a good marriage. Though many of Numbers' generation 'stayed together for the kids,' Keely didn't see the sense in living such an existence. If it's broke, fix it. If you can't fix it, get out. It would be better for Mick and it sure as hell would be better for Nancy.

"Speaking of Nancy," Numbers said, pulling Keely from his thoughts. "I'll give her a call and she'll set the wheels in motion for our release. We won't see any quick bail hearings on this puppy. If Robitaille doesn't get us out of here today, we're here for long time."

Keely's stomach tightened and he burped. When was his last shower? When last did he brush his teeth? He wanted to sleep so badly but the thought of Elise sent burning sensations through him, shots of adrenaline that made him feel energized but riding the edge of his sanity. It was as if every incident had pushed him closer to a meltdown and telling himself he needed to stay calm and rational for Elise's sake had lost its meaning. He needed to speak with Robitaille, now.

Just then a young Asian officer who looked half Numbers' size stepped around the half wall. He stopped in front of Numbers' cell and held a key a fraction of an inch from the lock.

"You are now getting your phone call." He sounded bored. "You may call whomever you choose but as an officer of this province it is my duty to advise you that it would be in your best interest to contact legal representation. Your call may be monitored in compliance with Canadian anti-terrorist acts. Please turn around and face the back of the cell."

Numbers complied and did the same when asked to place his hands behind his back. The officer cuffed him then walked him out of the cell and around the wall just as another officer led Leila Marques toward Keely's cell. Her white sundress looked completely out of place in the bland surroundings. She looked as if she were going out on a date in her perfect hair and makeup, heels and a clutch purse.

"I'll give you a few minutes," the older officer said and walked back to his desk.

"Keely."

He stood up and walked to the bars, crossing his arms, leaning his forearms against his cage. "You are liar." It had the desired effect. Keely heard her breath escape quickly and watched her face tense. "You knew about the doping. You probably knew who killed Todd and you sure as shit knew that Kira was running."

"I didn't know any of it."

"Don't fucking lie to me. I've had enough of that thanks."

She stepped guardedly to the bars. "I swear to you that I had no knowledge of any of this. I got a call from Detective Sergeant Robitaille and came here as quickly as I could. Kira is here and I came to see her, to make sure she was okay."

"Yeah, make sure your asset is in one piece. Thanks for stopping by, now go away."

"Keely, please."

"Do you know what's happening, Leila? Do you know that my wife is being held against her will and that I was to kill Kira? Did you know that? Huh?"

Her face wrenched and she squeezed her eyelids closed. "Oh, God. I didn't know. I'm sorry. What can we do?"

"Did you know that your boy Steven tried to kill me because he truly thought I was going to kill Kira? And he says the cops were in on it. Were you aware of that little tidbit of information, you lying sack of shit?" Keely slammed his fists against the bars then turned away from her and walked to the back of the cell. He stretched out his arms and pushed against the wall.

"I feel so foolish. I…I want to help you. Please."

"Excuse me, ma'am." The short cop was back with Numbers. Keely glanced over his shoulder to see the big guy scowling worse than usual after speaking with his wife. He was face first against the bars and when the cell door was opened the cop ushered him inside and unlocked one of the cuffs. He never got a chance to unlock the other one.

Numbers spun right and drove his elbow into the smaller man's temple. The officer crumpled onto the bed and before he could make a sound Numbers hit him hard with his fist several times.

"Mick, what the fuck?"

"I gotta go buddy. I'll get to Elise as fast as I can," he said while removing the cuffs and collecting the cop's gun. "This is a one-man job for now."

The older cop was moving from his desk as Numbers leapt out the door. Leila screamed when Mick grabbed her, spinning her around so her back was pressed up against him, the gun at her head. "I won't hurt you if you stay quiet."

She shot Keely a look of desperation – who wanted to help who, now?

"Back off. Everybody back the fuck away or she's dead." He slowly moved forward and, keeping his back to the wall, slid around it. Keely could hear him yelling for the other officers to stay back. Then he yelled for someone to bring him a car with Kira Bremner in it.

In that instant Keely knew what had happened. The same thing that was happening to him and Elise. Someone was holding Nancy and wanted Mick to bring Kira as trade. Worse, he'd been told to leave Keely behind, which made his heart stop for several beats. Was Elise even still alive?

"Hey," he said poking the little groaning cop through the bars. "I want my phone call now."

* * * *

Robitaille leaned against the end of the half-wall silhouetted by the bright fluorescent lights of the squad behind him.

"It's about fucking time," Keely said and darted up to the bars. "We need to have a conversation."

"I really don't know where to start," he said and waved for the older cop to bring him a chair. When it arrived he sat casually, legs crossed, head tilted slightly, as if at a coffee shop amongst friends. "I know everything now. Your wife, the bicyclist that was killed, the men that were after you. All of it."

"The men? The guys that tried to kill us? Where are they now?"

"I asked you to stay away from the case and you got involved. Granted, it was out of love. That I can forgive. I would kill for love. Do you understand?"

"What the hell are you talking about?" Keely felt the edge he was on sharpen and it was getting harder to balance on it. "Where are those men?"

"Listen to me. Just for a few minutes. Okay?"

Keely was so surprised by Robitaille's calm, almost gentle demeanour that he sat down on the edge of his bed, surprisingly calm himself now. The slender French Canadian leaned forward in his chair, his face a few feet from the bars.

"Nine-eleven was bad for everyone and it created new legislation to help protect every person in this country. It was this that allowed us to listen in on Mr. Moyer's conversation. He first spoke to a man calling himself Sweet."

"No. God no." Keely felt his head gain weight and in an instant it felt empty, light. He strained to breathe and to keep Robitaille in focus. Sweet had moved. He'd learned what was happening and had changed his tactics. After all, two hostages are better than one. Mick wasn't thinking straight when he kidnapped Leila to get to his wife. If he'd taken just a few more minutes to think about it, he could have regained the control Keely had established over Sweet. They had what he wanted most, a live Kira Bremner.

Even if Numbers had decided to take Keely with him, Sweet had to know that they would disagree on the tactics. He'd get them fighting, a sure way to create sloppiness. It would all but guarantee Kira's murder and that of their wives.

"Where's Mick?" Keely breathed it out then regained some composure. "We have to clear this station, right now."

"He had your wife and you didn't trust me to tell me this?"

"This is not about you and me. This is about my wife. It's about keeping everyone alive."

"You call me an idiot, but it's you who's the idiot here. I knew Bremner was running. I had orders to let her go and that she would be safely cared for. I had to maintain my position. I had to let those who wished to harm that girl think we had no idea where she was, that way they wouldn't have a clue where to look." He stood up and shook his finger at Keely. "You fucked it up. You led them right to her."

"Oh my God. Would you get your fucking head out of the playbook? They knew you'd follow orders and you'd keep everyone away from her. You made it easy for them to grab her."

"Who? Who did I make it easy for? That Body Fuel company?"

"They were trying to get her out. Don't you see?" Keely wrapped his fingers around the bars and tried to shake them, but all he did was move his body back and forth until he looked like a madman. He took a deep breath and levelled his gaze on Robitaille. "Whoever gave you the order to let her go, that is who's responsible for trying to kill her."

"We have her and we have your big friend. We heard the conversation with the man called Sweet. He told Mr. Moyer to go home. That he'd be waiting with his wife and yours to make the exchange for the cyclist. We are going to be there, but not you."

It was so clear to Keely and he wondered what possibly could be blocking Robitaille's logic and reason. "Who do you think Sweet was talking to, Mick, or you?"

Robitaille stepped close to the bars and gave Keely a smirk. "I know who he was talking to. That's why those men are being detained right now. We let them go to see what the next move would be. These men don't work for the OPP or RCMP. They are not with our military. My orders came from my boss who got them from his boss and so on up the chain of command. These men were hired by the drink company to kill the bicyclist."

"What's going to happen to her now?"

"She will be protected."

"By who?"

"Not your concern anymore."

"Keep her here and she's dead." Keely lowered his head to rest his forehead on the bars. "Take out Sweet now. Bring in the military to question those men. Most of all, clear this building because there was a second truck full of guys who're probably on their way to rescue their buddies."

Robitaille shoved the chair out of the way with his knee and that caught the older cop's attention. He waved the desk jockey over and instructed him to open Keely's cell.

"Unlike you, I follow orders. You are to be released and a helicopter will take you home where you will be guarded until this matter is settled." Keely opened his mouth to speak but Robitaille cut him off. "I swear to you that your wife will be fine."

"Forgive me if I don't put a lot of stock in that."

"Cuff him."

"What?" Keely said, incredulous at the increasingly bizarre situation. "Why?"

"Flight risk."

"From a fucking helicopter?"

The building shook as if a thunder cloud was inside of it. Keely grabbed the grey-haired cop to stop from falling and Robitaille was holding onto Keely. Rubble, like bricks falling on other bricks, rolled through the building. There were gunshots, then yelling and screaming. Keely heard the distinctive rapport of handguns and rifles. Water hissed, spraying up from the floor near the far corner of the room. Windows were breaking and Keely smelled smoke.

The floor slid sideways beneath his feet and Keely went down hard, the old cop and Robitaille landing on top of him. The room exploded with gunfire and Keely desperately scrambled out from under the policemen to take cover behind the half-wall.

He sat back against the wall and reached his hand out to pull Robitaille to safety. Before his hand could fit into the old cop's, the man froze, his arm extended, hand open as if someone had taken a photo of the men before they could shake hands. His old smoky blue eyes dimmed then his lids closed. He collapsed to the floor and Keely dove beside him to grapple with the man's holster.

He felt several bullets whiz past his body, one ricocheting off one of the cell bars behind him, chipping the paint. He finally freed the gun and felt Robitaille's hands around his feet, pulling him until he slid backwards on the shaking floor back under cover. He got to his knees and faced Robitaille, who now had his gun in hand. "Thanks."

"You see," the Frenchman said, "everything is under control."

Chapter 31

He'd gone out a few times but it had been useless to even try to free herself. God knew where he'd gone and all that kept her going was the thought that by this time tomorrow, Keely would be here. This time, Sweet had decided to take her with him on his outing.

Something was sticking into her back, most likely the jaws from the set of jumper cables she'd seen when he'd made her climb into his trunk. She didn't beg or even ask not to be shut in the dark space. She was through pretending. She began showing her contempt of him whenever possible. Every time he'd remove her gag so she could eat, she'd spit at him and call him every despicable name she could conjure.

She took great pleasure in reminding her rapist of his inabilities. Keely was going to be upset at her for that. Goading her attacker was not a smart thing to do. She'd paid the price a few times receiving a slap or punch. To her, it took less energy to absorb Sweet's abuse than to play his damned games.

The sock in her mouth was clean, she knew that because Sweet had taken it right out of the dryer. It was one of Keely's little white riding socks. It soaked up all the moisture from her tongue and tasted so drab that she fought hard against gagging. There was no way she was going to choke on her own vomit. Sweet was not going to win.

The car backed up and she felt the bump of it leaving the driveway. It stopped then swung left and accelerated. She had no idea where they were going but in a small way she was glad to be out of the house. She could hear the engines of other cars as they passed by, some were isolated but then other times there seemed to be dozens of them. Horns blared, tires screeched, people talked and yelled. Life was happening all around her and she told herself that she would soon be back in the game.

What made the journey even more difficult were the musty smells, and gasoline and carbon dioxide fumes. She tried to reposition her body so her head could be closer to the rear of the trunk, but it was no use. There was something taking up room at the back of the trunk and she was bound, hands behind her back, feet together. Wherever they were going, she wished he'd get there soon.

* * * *

"Where's Mick and Kira?" Keely held the brushed silver gun between praying hands and bent knees, his back against the now vibrating half-wall. Regardless of how he felt about Robitaille, he had no choice but to work with him, otherwise they were dead men. Keely put the gun in his left hand and rolled the back of his shoulders across the wall to point the gun around the end. Without aiming, he fired several rounds.

"Not where they think." Robitaille smiled showing dingy teeth. "You see, I knew there'd be more of them to come." His accent was thicker now, in the heat of battle.

Cement flew off the wall in a cascade of little chunks just beside Keely's head. He poked the gun out and fired off a few more rounds, this time moving the gun from side to side. "Where are they?"

"There are two officers in their place in the cells downstairs. Guns are hiding under their beds. Plus, many more cops are in the building. I just didn't expect them to use explosives. You know?"

"Where the hell is Kira?" Keely jumped at the loud gunfire. His assailant had changed weapons or had changed altogether and now it might be a completely different person.

"They are going under guard to your friend's home as this Sweet person requested. We have the entire place surrounded and are just waiting until your friend can show up so the kidnapper thinks everything is fine. Then, when he least expects it, we pounce."

He'd heard this plan before and it hadn't turned out so well. Keely did think there was a very big difference between Sweet and Harper – he'd investigated Harper, tracked him down and then encountered him in that house. Sweet was an unknown. He had no idea what the man was capable of or his history, his personality. He had no choice but to go by the book now.

"Hey, you ever play one of those shooting gallery games they have at carnivals?"

Robitaille screwed up his face and shook his head.

"I'm going to dive over there, you're going to wait until our guy returns fire then put a bullet in his head. Okay?" Robitaille smiled and nodded. "Make sure you aim at his head. He's probably wearing a Kevlar vest."

"Okay. Go."

"What? No. On three. Ready?" Keely spun free of the wall and crouched. His hands were shaking and rivulets of sweat tickled his skin. Fear was good, he thought, since it motivated him to concentrate on performing his task perfectly. "One." He shuffled backwards to give up his position to Robitaille. He pushed an image of a happy Elise from his mind and leveled his breathing. "Two." Keely visualized what he needed to do, like when he'd ride his bike and pick a line on the trail. "Three." He took several steps out into the open and fired two shots then dove to the floor, sliding head first towards the old cop's desk.

At the far end of the room a man dressed in dark blue coveralls, a black Kevlar vest puffed out of his chest like a life jacket, popped up from behind an overturned desk. Keely's head disappeared under the desk just as he heard a shot being fired. He felt no pain and wondered when the fire would burn in his body and where it would start. He tensed and lay motionless until someone kicked his foot.

"He's dead."

Keely put his hands on the outside of the desk and pushed against it, forcing his body to slide out from underneath. Robitaille was looking at where the shooter had been positioned and that motivated Keely to scramble to his feet. The room was in shambles. Bullets had penetrated the concrete a dozen times on the opposite side of their hiding place. Keely silently thanked the builder for using really strong bricks or having a magical touch when building the structure that protected them.

With a nod they moved cautiously forward, slaloming around undisturbed desks and approached the overturned one. Keely was careful not to step on any of its contents that had spilled to the floor. If the gunman was still alive, the noise would give away how close they were to him.

There was gunfire elsewhere in the building and as far as Keely could tell, outside of it as well but he pushed those sounds aside. Again, concentration was what would keep him alive. They approached from opposite sides of the desk and once Keely saw a pair of legs sticking out at an odd angle from behind it he knew Robitaille had hit his mark. He was amazed after turning over the shooter's body. Robitaille had shot the man with almost perfect accuracy. A little red hole was slightly off centre an inch above the man's brow between his closed eyes.

Keely spun to his left and reached for a phone, picking it up and cradling it between his head and shoulder. Before he could dial, Robitaille was beside him, his hand on Keely's shoulder.

"No need. I've informed every OPP station of our situation and the RCMP are most likely already outside involved in the fight." He backed away and looked carefully out of a window frame now devoid of its glass. "This struggle is almost over."

The gunfire had all but ceased, Keely hearing a last barrage before a lot of yelling. He went to the window and looked out on a parking lot that was filled with OPP cars and several RCMP cars. There was even a special task force truck parked down the street, its back doors open, one man in black sitting on the floor of the unit. Men were running all around the building and once they'd hit an assigned area and cleared it, they'd walk slowly away, eyes searching their surroundings for anyone hit in the firefight or trying to hide.

He'd thought they were battling for an hour but it had lasted less than fifteen minutes. His body refused to believe these facts and once again he felt drained. Every muscle ached, his head pounded and all he wanted to do was lie down. He searched the room and decided a chair would suffice, a nice, padded office chair. It sank down a few inches when he sat then sprang up again – he hoped he could do the same.

"I don't understand what's going on. Why did you suddenly call in all this backup?" Keely asked.

Robitaille needed only the time it took to sit on the edge of the desk in front of Keely to consider his answer. "Rockets and dead pilots and a bad cop and kidnapping and doping. These are a lot of reasons, yes?" Keely scrunched his brow. "Detective, I know when I'm in over my head. I needed help."

Keely felt the warm rush of understanding. "Are you telling me that you're ready to listen to me?"

"I will hear what you have to say, yes."

* * * *

The little media room at the Burk's Falls OPP station had been filled with high-ranking cops from all forces. Hell, Keely recognized officers from Toronto and Ottawa. He'd told them what he knew, described his ultimate theory, that it was the government that was trying to erase any signs of gene doping. For some reason they didn't want it getting out. When asked why, Keely said he had no idea, but when did the government need a reason to do anything? He'd gotten a laugh at that one. Something he could use right about now.

The helicopter was more comfortable than Edgar's seaplane, and for that Keely was thankful. He didn't need stomach-lurching turbulence at the best of times, but now, with thoughts of his wife and Nancy in the hands of Sweet and a task force of cops, it would send his stomach over the edge. Numbers sat beside him and Robitaille sat directly across from him. Both men rested their heads against their respective windows, blank looks on their faces.

They'd been very understanding, something Keely hadn't expected at all. He'd broken more laws than he could list in his attempt to free his wife but in the end they all felt certain they would have done the same thing. He would, however, have to pay for the repairs to the cruiser he'd smashed up and an apology to its occupants might be nice, too.

Steven Bishop, it turned out, was not connected to Sweet and Sour in any way. Quite the opposite. He'd been contacted by them and told that the moment Kira was dead, he must contact them or a list of his loved ones would never be seen again. He had no idea that they'd kill Elise McAdam when he did. He was scared and didn't know what else to do. Given the choice, he was going to help Kira escape by way of their corporate jet, then call Sweet and let him know that Kira was dead. He was not on the inside feeding them information. All he was trying to do was find and protect Kira, just like everyone else.

Keely felt a surge of fright when the helicopter dropped fifty feet. The pilot looked back and gave them a wink instead of an apology. The blades whirred overhead and when he concentrated on the sound, Keely felt better, more relaxed. He thought about Elise and how he was trusting others to save her. He really had no choice. Just like he had no choice but to go after Kira.

And where was Kira now? Robitaille had done what he'd set out to do, he'd helped her survive. Two lookalikes housed in the basement cells gave up their uniforms so that Kira could get away. She drove out in the front seat of a cruiser. Genius. Robitaille and only a handful of officers knew her current location. If need be, they'd have her near Mick's place in case Sweet wanted confirmation before the exchange.

There were a few unfinished pieces of business to take care of from where Keely was sitting. First was to get Elise and Nancy away from Sweet. Numbers stared out his big window at the passing landscape. Keely was pretty sure what he was thinking about – Nancy.

What worried Keely most was that an organization powerful enough to call in a ground-to-air missile attack could easily intervene on Sweet's behalf and take care of things. In fact, Keely had stopped asking himself why this mysterious government operation hadn't stepped in yet and started thinking how fortunate they all were that it hadn't.

One of the more unfortunate things to happen in this entire episode, the event that had initially attracted Keely's interest, was the accidental murder of Todd Watkins. No one had been able to locate his body yet, nor could they find Amanda Zendastra. Keely had informed Robitaille and the rest of the law enforcement representatives of the situation. He made it clear that it was an accident and that Kira could corroborate that which, he was immediately informed, she had. They surmised that Todd's body had been taken to hide any evidence of gene doping. Every Body Fuel employee involved with the cycling team was being questioned, even Paulo Chagas. Edgar had been forced to land in Niagra Falls. Keely was told he'd get a chance to speak with the old pilot soon enough. That brought a brief smile to the ex-detective's face.

A coverup, but why? It was probably a question Keely would be asking himself for months afterward. For now, all he wanted was his wife back.

Keely thought he heard a phone ring and watched Robitaille pull a little cell phone from a holster on his hip. He looked odd in street clothes and Keely fought to put his finger on a good description. He settled for almost approachable. Robitaille mumbled a few things into his phone then dropped it from his ear.

"Your house is clean. There is no one there. They found some blood and evidence of where your wife was being held, but other than that..." Robitaille shrugged. "We're still waiting for a visual confirmation at Mr. Moyer's house."

"How the hell do you know he's there?" Numbers asked, unable to disguise the displeasure in his voice.

"We don't. We have to assume until we have absolute confirmation. Best we can do."

Numbers' face was stone, and just as grey. He turned back to the window and his thoughts.

"Look, Mr. Moyer, we have a team of men around your home and the moment they have a clean shot, they take it. That order was issued when you were walking to that cruiser with Ms. Bremner. They've seen nothing yet. I stress, yet."

Keely put a hand on his big friend's shoulder and squeezed.

Numbers shook his head then looked at his feet. "I'm sorry, Keely. I took off and left you, but he said he'd kill Nancy if I didn't leave you behind. I panicked. Put the ball back in his court. I'm sorry."

Keely said nothing in response. Instead, he gave Numbers' shoulder another squeeze and smiled at him. It was going to be okay. He wouldn't dare let himself think any other way.

* * * *

The car finally stopped after what seemed like hours and Sweet climbed out. She could feel and hear the door slam shut. She waited for what seemed like a few more hours before Sweet got back in the car and they were once again on the move.

It had taken about the same amount of time to stop again and Elise hoped she'd be getting out of the trunk soon. Her entire body was cramping from lack of motion. Her wrists and ankles were raw and she swore that eventually, if he kept using zipties, her hands and feet would fall off.

The trunk opened and she stared up at him.

"We're home."

By the looks of things, she had no idea where home was.

Chapter 32

They landed on the football field of a high school that Keely was told was a few kilometres north of Numbers' place. They scurried from the chopper bent over from paranoia that the blades would somehow bend or drop six feet to chop through them.

Once clear of the aircraft they were escorted to a home economics classroom with one major island at its centre, its surface flat and uncluttered save for the sinks at the workstations. The spigots were turned to the right looking like an army unit's choreographed parade. The neat room was on the second floor at the corner of the building with windows running the length of two walls. Posters of food boasting nutritional facts ate up most of the wall space.

It looked like any other classroom in any other school he'd ever seen, a detail not lost on him amongst his trepidation. They were near the border of North York and Scarborough, two suburbs north and east of Toronto, sections of town Keely rarely visited outside of his work or to see friends. Most Torontonians kept to their side of the dividing line of the city, Yonge Street. Keely used to refer to it as their Berlin Wall. It was natural, of course, for anyone living in the east to *live* in the east and vice versa for westerners. Keely didn't get up and do his shopping in the east end of the city. Why would he? Everything he needed was on his side of the dividing line. Like everything else in life, people saw it in extremes. They had no idea what extreme meant.

The tallest man Keely had ever seen walked into the room and Keely felt like standing at attention. He was obviously in charge of the tactical squad. Everything on him was black, including his gun, boots and hat, a stark contrast to his pale white skin. *Nothing a little camo-paint wouldn't cure.*

Two men stood on either side of the island over laptop computers. Each had a phone and radio sitting beside him. That was where the similarities ended. In fact, they could be polar opposites: one white, one black, one short and beefy, the other taller and lanky. The biggest difference was that the short white guy was in street clothes and the taller, black guy was in a black RCMP uniform complete with snappy hat.

A television sat on a rolling stand and under it was another computer. The screen was split into two views; on the left was the front view of Numbers' house and on the right, the back. The picture changed to an aerial view of an entire neighbourhood then zoomed slowly down until the frame was filled with an overhead view of Number's house. It quickly changed again, and Keely watched the feed from a tactical officer's head-cam as he slowly looked around a yard, then ran for its back fence.

"Rene," the man in black said, his voice deep and strong. "Say the word and we're a go."

Robitaille gave the man an almost imperceptible nod then turned his attention to the big man in black. "Sergeant Richard Rolland, this is retired detective Keely McAdam and private investigator Mick Moyer."

They shook hands in turn then Rolland said, "Everything here is under control. Your loved ones *will* be safe."

Rolland's commanding presence and confidence eased Keely's apprehension, if only slightly. Still, any relief from the long-standing tension he'd felt from the moment Elise had pleaded for him to help her was welcome. Rolland did not seem like the type who would do anything rashly. He'd hold his men until there was no other recourse but penetration.

"Snipers?" Numbers sounded so wired that Keely thought the question was more a demand.

Rolland wasn't rattled. "Four. Every side of that house is locked down. A mouse moves and we'll know it. Hell, it moves and we'll hear it. Meant to tell you, Rene, we've got the place miked externally." He looked at Mick and Keely, then reached out and pulled Robitaille to the corner of windows where they spoke privately.

"Guy looks like he knows what he's doing." Keely was tired of the sound of his own voice.

Numbers turned to show Keely his pallid face. "I've never been so fucking scared in my whole life. I've been shot at, beaten, chased, cornered and never once was I this scared. She doesn't deserve this. However we feel about each other, the last thing I wanted was something like this."

Numbers wasn't saying something he didn't already know. The big man just needed to say it out loud. Keely completely understood that. Innocent bystanders always became involved, it was inevitable when someone wanted to dole out the ultimate in hurt and humiliation. As cops they never forgot the fact that revenge started away from you and worked its way towards you. "You said it, brother."

Robitaille trotted over to them. "We've got cops set up at every available street leading out of this neighbourhood. Two SWAT teams are already in position. Now, we need you to make a call, Mr. Moyer."

"What about Kira? He's going to want to talk to her."

"Taken care of. Kira Bremner is under guard by men I trust with my life. No one else will see her until this situation is resolved. Even then, it will only be when I believe her safe. I've been duped once, I will not be duped again, even if it means my job. She will be given a cue to speak and patched into our phone here."

"That's traceable," Keely said.

"Scrambled. Not to worry."

"Not to worry. Are you fucking serious?" Numbers barked revealing his lack of confidence in the operation. "My wife is in that house, asshole. I can't _stop_ worrying."

Robitaille's demeanour changed instantly to soothing. "I'm sorry if I sound trite. I did not mean to insult you." Robitaille had been shaken enough for his thicker accent to make an appearance. "I mean only that every, *every* precaution is being taken to ensure the safe return of both your wives. Please, both of you, sit over here and I will have someone bring you something to drink."

He directed them to a sofa on the same side of the room as the door, only in the opposite corner. There was a pantry beside it and a series of cabinets that lead to a full fledged kitchen complete with stove and fridge.

"All I need now is your phone, Mr. Moyer."

Numbers dug out his cell phone and handed it over to Robitialle who practically ran over to the short white guy at the island. A few minutes later, a young cop in uniform brought them soft drinks and asked them if they wanted to eat. They declined.

They'd been waiting for almost a half hour and impatience was fostering anger in Keely. By the look on Numbers' face, the big P.I. was ready to snap. The white computer tech, wearing jeans, a white buttoned shirt, untucked, and a brown corduroy jacket, came over to them and crouched in front of Numbers, introducing himself as Anthony. His hair was like a curly black wig, the colour matching his eyebrows. His dark eyes were brown, but despite all the darkness, Anthony was upbeat.

"First off, sorry about the situation. I'll do my best. I can deliver on that." Robitaille joined them and Anthony gave him a nod. "I'm almost ready to go. Another few minutes then I'm going to have you call the guy. You're going to see some weird cables attached to your cell phone and it's necessary scientific shit, okay?" Numbers nodded. This was the kind of person that Mick Moyer could relate to, a straightforward, off the street, genuine guy. Anthony ran his hand through his tight black curls and took a long breath. "Okay, so when you got the guy on the line I'd really appreciate it if you could drag the conversation a bit, you know, keep him on there for a while."

"How long's a while?" Numbers asked.

Anthony cocked his head. "Seriously, as long as you can keep him on the line that would be great. If that works out to thirty seconds, so be it. A minute, two minutes, whatever you can manage. I want to be able to pick up any background noises and then we'll be playing the conversation for the shrink, maybe they learn something, maybe not. Okay?"

Numbers nodded. "And if he asks to speak to Kira?"

"She's already patched into your phone, so when we call the guy, she comes along for the ride. We got someone on her phone listening in and when you say hold on, he counts to two and hands the phone to her. I'll block outgoing at that point and you can listen in, then when you supposedly take the phone back, I open up outgoing and you start talking. Make sense?"

"Anthony, you've made more sense to me than anyone else today." Numbers reached out his hand and Anthony shook it. "When this is over, I hope you'll do some work with me. You're good."

"I'm great. And you can't afford me."

Numbers chuckled a little and Keely felt more confident. Anthony turned to Keely and winked.

"Listen, when that phone goes live, this room is silent. I know you've got a shitload invested in this, detective, and that's why I'm letting you stay, but you gotta keep it together, no matter what you hear, okay?"

"Not a problem. I'm with Mick, you're doing all right."

"Okay, gentlemen. One minute and we're good to go," he said and shuffled back to his computer.

Keely hadn't noticed how crowded the room had gotten in the last few minutes. There were cops of every rank, shape and size. Keely recognized a few of the top dogs who had been in his debrief. He baulked at the sight of them. One thing he remembered clearly about his days as a detective was that anytime the big kids were around, something always went wrong.

"Mick." Anthony, now wearing a headset, waved to Numbers who literally jumped from the sofa and ran to him. It didn't take long before Numbers was holding his cell phone. Robitaille gave the nervous P.I. a last pep talk and reiterated his instructions, then Anthony hit a few keys on his computer and asked Numbers to indicate when the phone was ringing.

Keely thought Numbers looked jittery, like a lion after a kill surrounded by hyenas. He kept looking around the room, his head darting one way and then another, as if trying to catch someone sneaking up on him. He hoped his good friend could regain his composure since there was more than one life on the line. Numbers nodded at Anthony who deftly executed a few more key strokes.

Keely watched a tiny blue dot appear on a map on the computer screen. Anthony seemed happy to see it as well. Numbers kept his eyes locked on the little computer specialist and Keely could tell he was concentrating to find the place where he had to be in order to seem real to Sweet. But something was wrong. The phone kept ringing.

"What the fuck," Numbers said. "You dial the right number?"

Anthony pointed to a place at the bottom of his computer screen, just below the map. "That's your wife's cell number, right?"

Keely's cell phone rang and every head turned in his direction. He couldn't believe how naïve they'd been. No one even thought that Sweet would contact Keely again. As far as Sweet was concerned, Keely was locked up in a cell in Burk's Falls.

* * * *

He'd let her use the bathroom, the half bath on the lower level. She checked out what she could in her short trip. It was obvious to her they were in an abandoned house. Though it had boards on the windows, it was fairly clean inside. A Victorian-style home if ever she'd seen one. It had ornate mouldings, including floral plinths and a fantastic ceiling medallion that mirrored the floral motif. The worn oak floors creaked but in a familiar way, as if to say they wanted you to stay.

There was little furniture and the few pieces were all crowded into the dining room, covered in an old, paint-stained tarp. She was in the living room, a fireplace to her right that probably hadn't seen a fire in years but showed it had once been well used. The space was large but not enough to think it unmanageable. It could be cozy if decorated with the right hands.

She was still smarting from all the abuse she'd taken. Sitting was probably the worst position she could be in with the bruises and cuts she'd suffered to her back, butt and legs. Still, she sat stoically, never looking away from his gaze and always keeping her chin up, head held high.

He flipped open her phone and hit a few keys. He'd changed, she thought. He was once smartly dressed and even-tempered – a Wall Street broker on a job. How easily he'd slid down so low.

"Ah, detective, so nice to hear your voice again."

He was pacing slowly in front of the boarded up bay window, sliding a foot along the floor and placing it directly in front of the other foot as if on a tightrope. She knew that in another few hours she'd not be able to see him without some kind of light source. *Was the electricity still connected?*

"No doubt all of your friends are trying to get you to hook up some contraption to you phone. Doesn't matter. Tell Mr. Moyer to take Kira into the house, now." Sweet hung up and turned to Elise.

"Were you good friends with Nancy Moyer?"

* * * *

"Let me speak to my wife." Keely fought to listen over the commotion in the home economics room. He put his hand over the receiver and yelled, "Shut up."

"No doubt all of your friends are trying to get you to hook up some contraption to you phone. Doesn't matter. Tell Mr. Moyer to take Kira into the house, now."

The phone went dead.

"What did he say?" Anthony asked. "How did he sound?"

Keely shook his head at Numbers.

"McAdam, what the hell did he say?" Robitaille asked.

"He's not in your house, Mick."

"What?" the RCMP officer began to pound the keys on his computer. "I have a heat signature of someone in a chair, likely tied. And, there is a slight signature of a prone body at her feet. Sound of a person breathing heavily through their nose. He's in there."

"No, he's not. Robitaille, you have to believe me."

"Tell me why. What did he say?" Robitaille almost yelled it.

"He said to *take* Kira into the house."

Anthony jumped from his seat. "Not to *bring* her? He said take, not bring?"

Keely nodded.

"We need to get visual confirmation," Robitaille said to Rolland. "Can you get a team close enough to poke a video camera in there?"

"Of course—"

"No," Keely said loudly. "He wants you to go in. He wants Mick to go in with Kira. He's not there but he wants them to go in."

Everyone in the room looked blankly at him and he was amazed that even with the level of experience the policemen in the room shared, none had figured it out. "Holy shit, people. I'd be calling in the bomb squad if I were you."

Chapter 33

"Smelled gas so we pulled out. Least little spark will blow that house." Keely watched a corner of Anthony's computer screen where a man with a helmet, shield lifted to look like a clear hat brim, spoke into what must be a camera on his own small computer. The image was jerky and blurry as if it had been filmed with an old eight-millimeter camera. "We've called the gas company to turn it off. I'll let you know when it's clear."

"Out," Anthony said and used his mouse to close the box containing the image of the bomb specialist then turned to Numbers. "He must have opened up the gas line and then left the house. Wanted you to unlock the door. Might have caused a spark."

"I'm betting on the matchbook in the doorframe," Numbers said and shot Keely a knowing look. "Had a case where a guy opened the gas line then folded a match back so it rested against the rough strip. Then he squeezed it between the door and frame. Neighbour comes over a few hours later to bang the guy's wife, who he'd conveniently tied up in the bedroom. Guy opens the door causing the match to strike and boom."

"Make sure nobody goes near that house until the gas company says it's clear," Keely said loud enough for anyone in the room to hear.

"You don't have to worry about that," Anthony said. "These guys don't shit unless they're told. We'll get your wife out of there in one piece, Mr. Moyer."

"Numbers, please, you make me very nervous when you talk like that."

"Uh, yeah. Sure." Anthony looked like he was about to ask a question.

"Apparently I'm cheap and everything comes down to numbers with me."

"I was thinking you might be some kind of math whiz."

Numbers' face reddened. "Not on my best day, kid."

The room was crowded and hummed like a party. Pockets of conversation broke out between the different police services and units; tactical talked with the Mountie, Robitaille talked with a group of local cops and every so often they'd merge, mingle and depart into cliques again.

Keely felt lost all of a sudden. Somehow, the murder of a pro cyclist had turned into a government coverup of gene doping. Why? What would the government gain by hiding this new form of cheating? Regardless of the answer to that question it was obvious that someone was going to great lengths to silence anyone holding evidence that gene doping existed. Worse, Keely had drawn his wife and best friend into the fray. Now Nancy was involved, too. What must happen for all this to stop? Kill everyone?

In three short days so much had happened and the one thing he was trying to accomplish seemed farther and farther away with each step he'd taken in its direction. Elise was still missing and undoubtedly in the hands of Sweet, a man willing to commit murder – the deadly trap for Numbers was the only proof Keely needed. If nothing else, Sweet was trying to get rid of what might very well be the last piece of physical evidence in existence that gene doping worked – Kira.

Anthony had been adamant that Keely give as much information to him about Elise's phone as possible – its make, model, service provider and number. All Keely could tell him was the phone number. He'd barely glanced at her cell phone and she kept separate and very strict records on her business dealings for tax purposes. The number would have to suffice for now.

Nancy's phone had shown up on Anthony's computer screen, the blue dot, when it was activated, but knowing Sweet wasn't in the house they had to assume he'd left with Elise. Anthony wanted to track Elise's cell phone but warned Keely that it was literally like finding a cell phone in an entire city. The only advantage they might have is if Keely had a general idea of where they might be.

"Any ideas yet on where he'd take her?" Anthony was, Keely thought, also a mind reader.

"Nah. Only place I can think of is my house and you guys tell me it's clean."

"I've already used satellite tracking and found nothing. Unless of course the phone is off."

Keely felt a stab of anxiety. "You're telling me the only way you can track it is if it is on and someone is using it?"

"Yeah. Or if someone is at least calling the phone and it's on. Then I can get a signal. But even then I have to be looking in the right area to locate it. I've got access to some heavy duty satcom shit. A few hundred satellites are at my disposal. I only have me and a few buddies willing to track though, so I could map the planet but I'd need a few weeks to do it. Narrow the search area and I can find your target."

"If the target is on." Keely shook his head.

"I promised you my best. *This* is my best."

"Gas company says we'll be safe inside of an hour." Rolland looked disappointed that he didn't get to storm the house. "Mr. Moyer, may we poke a few holes in windows please? It'll help dissipate the gas and we'll get some cameras in there."

"My wife isn't choking or anything, on the gas?"

"No. She's been exposed and is probably passed out, but the worst she'll have is a headache." Rolland waited anxiously while Numbers crunched the numbers.

"Come on, Mick. It won't cost that much and it means getting Nancy out of there faster." Keely had his hands on his hips and felt like a father lecturing his big son.

"I'm thinking."

"Mick. For fuck sake, man."

"Okay. Do it."

"You're a good man, Mick Moyer. Cheap, but good."

Upon considering the matchbook scenario, the gas company representative refused to go through any of the doors and cut a hole in the sliding patio door to gain entry. Once inside, he was accompanied by two officers who went about the task of securing the home and opening every window. The bomb squad used dogs to check the entire house and called it clear in minutes.

It hadn't taken long for the tactical team to enter the house once it was cleared.

Nancy was in a chair in the centre of the living room at the front of the house, a squat two-bedroom bungalow. On the floor in front of her, his head between her feet, face looking up at her, was Sour, dead and greying. Once the tape had been removed from her mouth, Nancy couldn't stop yelling and crying.

Female officers were the first to attend to her, Robitaille thinking she would be less shocked by women. It wasn't to be. The cops on the scene described Nancy as a wild woman. When Keely finally saw her, he agreed. Her mid-length grey hair jutted out like thick fingers, her makeup was running and her wide, fright-filled eyes gave her the stereotypical look of someone who was insane. In the back of the ambulance a few houses down the street from their home, Mick hugged his wife and was the only person able to calm her. It took another hour before they could speak to Nancy about her experience.

She sat on a bed in a small room in the emergency ward of Scarborough General Hospital sipping a coffee. She looked small and frail in her wrinkled, pale-blue robe. Keely took a mug from her shaking hands. She gave him a thankful nod and slumped forward slightly as if fighting stomach cramps. Robitaille, Numbers and Keely were by her bed while several other officers waited in various spots throughout the emergency ward.

Numbers slid onto the bed beside her and Nancy fell into him. Keely had never seen Numbers so affected emotionally. He'd always held it together, but now Keely could see the obvious signs of a man not wanting to cry or kill someone. He wrapped his arms around his wife and she almost disappeared. "When you're ready, okay?" he said and angled his face back from hers to give her a reassuring look.

She started without taking a breath. "He knocked on the door early this morning and woke me up. I saw him through the window and he held up a badge, looked exactly like yours," she said pointing to Robitaille's badge hanging from a chain around his neck. "I opened the door and before he said anything, he grabbed me by the neck and pinned me to the stairs."

"What did he look like?" Robitaille asked.

"White. Tall, about six feet. Thick hair, wavy. Medium build. Wore a suit. That's it."

"There's nothing else you can think of?" Robitaille asked.

Keely brushed him off with a glance. "Nance, what happened after he pinned you on the stairs?"

"Pulled a gun, told me if I made a sound he'd kill me," she said and her voice went high and she began to cry.

"It's okay now. I'm here. No one will hurt you ever again." Mick sounded stern but level, his voice reassuring and threatening at the same time.

Nancy composed herself and continued, her voice changing pitch when she had trouble with the vision of her memories. "He gagged me then taped me to the chair and put my back to the front window. I heard him close all the drapes and blinds. Then he went out the side door and dragged this body inside. He put him in front of me. Then pinned that note to him."

The note was a single, small piece of paper from a note pad on which was hand written in blue ink, "It's personal." She reached out for her coffee and Keely gave it to her. She took a few calming sips before going on. "He stayed for about an hour and talked to the dead body a lot. After a while he disappeared for about two minutes and then he said goodbye from the side door. I turned to see him doing something to the side of the door and then he closed it and left."

Robitaille leaned forward to speak but Keely put up his hand to stop him. The emergency room was busy, even on a Tuesday night. The noise of nurses and doctors going about the business of trying to stay ahead of the crunch in the waiting room was almost leveling to Keely. Life was happening outside of the madness.

"I gotta tell ya, Nancy, you've done absolutely incredible." He stepped forward to lean his thigh against the side of the bed and put his hand on her shoulder, squeezing it gently. "You've made it through some tough stuff and I admire you for it. Shows how strong a person you are. Thanks."

She put her hand on top of his. "Thank you, Keely. I feel better."

He leaned down to bring his face level with hers. "Did you hear any of what he said to the body?"

She was calm in thinking about it, exactly what Keely had hoped. He didn't want her frantically searching her memory for what Sweet said. She needed to relax a bit, let the memory come to her. He'd learned that technique a long time ago and Numbers must have recognized it because he smirked at Keely.

"Yeah. I heard him say, 'eye for an eye.' Ah, he called the dead guy lots of horrible names, too."

"Like what?" Keely asked it in the tone he'd use to ask her how her day was.

"Like asshole and shithead and mother…you know?"

"Oh yeah. But did he use a name?"

"He blamed the guy for screwing something up," she went on as if Keely hadn't spoken. "Too nice, he said. Something about dad not approving of it. He said something really weird about how he was supposed to be first. Not sure what it meant. But he got really pissed off about it."

The events of the day had taken their toll on Nancy and Keely thought she looked far older than her fifty-odd years. He wanted nothing more than to hug her and tell her everything would be okay. He needed as much information as possible and Numbers nodded at him, obviously understanding the situation and recognizing that Keely had been getting good results.

"Anything else? Names perhaps?"

Keely's phone rang. He glanced at Robitaille with a look that said he'd be right back, don't open your mouth. "I have to take this, but could you give that some thought." He said it so gently that he could see Nancy unwinding, relaxing. He dug out his cell phone and glanced at the display. He didn't recognize the number. He flipped it open and said, "Yeah."

"It hasn't been on the news. I can't tell you how much that disappoints me."

"Sorry, Sweet. I guess I'm just smarter than you are."

"Not a good thing to say to someone who has a gun at your wife's head."

"She'd be dead by now if that's what you wanted." Keely felt his body tighten. "You want Kira Bremner dead, then let's trade women once and for all. You can fucking do whatever you want after that, you sicko. Just give me my wife back."

Keely heard the silence as if it were an intrusive noise. He looked up to see Numbers, Nancy and Robitaille staring at him. Down the row of curtains on both sides of the room, at the nurses station, out in the hallway, everyone within earshot had stopped and was staring at him. He closed his eyes and took a deep breath. He cursed himself for losing his composure.

"I have a better idea." Sweet's voice oozed through the little speaker at Keely's ear and it made him gag. He clenched his hand into a fist and began to dig it into his thigh. He was tired of the games. He wanted his wife.

"No. You obviously want me in the game, so here's what we do. I'll come to you and you get me for my wife."

"You were thinking what I was thinking. Good. Go home and wait for my call."

"Only if I can speak to Elise, now."

"Or what? You won't play anymore?"

He looked over at Numbers holding his wife and for that moment, he hated him. The P.I. wasn't in love with his wife, but they were together. Then Keely chastised himself for what he was thinking. His longing for Elise was making him irrational and that was dangerous. He had to keep his wits about him or he'd never see his wife again. He tore his gaze away from his friends and said, "No. Don't hurt her. That's how you get me to play your fucking game. Let me talk to her, I have to know she's okay because without the prize, there's no reason for me to play anymore. Right?"

Silence was quickly becoming Keely's nemesis – it meant uncertainty.

"Keely, I love you." Her voice was soft and he could feel her will sagging.

"I'm coming, sweetheart. Where are you?"

"Old house. Fire—"

"That's cheating," Sweet interrupted. "Go home and wait for my call." He hung up.

Keely listened to the dial tone and wished he could keep his emotion as monotone. A man was moaning somewhere in the room and a doctor was talking gibberish about someone's blood pressure. A bong sounded and a metallic voice mumbled something over a loud speaker. There were little coloured dots floating in his vision and his stomach felt as if someone was filling it with air, trying to expand it like a balloon. He locked eyes with Nancy and she blurred then the center of his vision was black, as if someone had cut a hole in the middle of a photograph.

Bile burned all the way up his chest until he tasted it in his mouth. Hands were grabbing him but he couldn't fight. He had no energy left to fight. He heard his phone bounce on the floor, then the circle of black expanded and everything went dark.

Chapter 34

If the burning taste of a habanero pepper could be translated to a smell, that was the odour Keely was experiencing — hot, pungent and painful. He whipped his head to get away from it. Eyes watering, he opened them on a glossy scene.

He was in a chair and a nurse was standing in front of him with smelling salts cracked open. The nauseating scent still lingered in his nose as she stepped aside to reveal Nancy sitting on her hospital bed, the light around her angelic in its glow. Sound traveled to his ears as if he were under water. Keely blinked and the hard-edged world of reality snapped clearly into view.

He felt a hand on his back and turned to see Numbers standing beside him. "You're okay, Keely? You just passed out. Nothing a shot of B-12 wouldn't cure."

"We'll let a doctor decide that," the nurse said sharply.

"He's right." The sound of his own voice made Keely cringe. His headache was an inside job. "I'm exhausted. I've barely slept since Friday night."

"You've been busy, too," Robitaille added. "I know it is probably useless for me to say this, but you should get some rest. Then we can talk about what Sweet said."

What Sweet said? He was on the phone with the man that had Elise. He had to get home. "You're absolutely right. I need to go home and sleep for a few hours at least. It'll be back at it in no time." *Damn. Made it too easy for them.*

Robitaille eyed him suspiciously.

"I'm at the end of my physical rope, man. But I don't want to stay in a hospital. I want to go home. That's all."

Robitaille's face looked jovial, as if he'd caught Keely in a lie. "Fine. I'll send two officers home with you." He raised a hand before Keely could complain. "Your home was very recently a crime scene, and though it is now cleared and can be cleaned, I'd be considered a very bad policeman if I let you, the husband of a kidnapping victim, go home all by himself." He took a few steps toward Keely then bent down to look directly into his eyes. "After all, Sweet will only talk to you."

Any energy Keely had regained since waking evaporated.

"Sorry to disappoint you both," the nurse's voice sounded as curt as when she first spoke, "but Dr. Farkas will decide when this gentleman can go home."

They got him a gown, transferred him to a bed and took his vital signs every fifteen minutes. Keely was a patient in emergency and he felt it was worse than being a prisoner – at least they could walk around their cells. Every time he slid a foot outside of his covers a nurse pounced on him to "get back in bed."

More frustrating was that his cell phone had been broken and somehow they were going to get him another one and set it up so that it would have the same number. It hurt his head thinking about the red tape they'd have to cut through just to make that happen.

Cops were stationed at every major entrance to the hospital and there was one in the emergency ward. It was obvious to Keely that the young Metro cop didn't like hospitals. He sympathized. Keely had pulled guard duty in his first year. A boy band was in town and he was part of crowd control at their hotel. He felt then the way this cop looked now.

Nancy was resting and Keely was thankful but jealous. They'd been friends shortly after Numbers had taken Keely under his wing. He wanted her to feel better but the pang of missing his wife coated his feelings with resentment. Long ago he'd realized, with Elise's help, that he was human. A man cannot see the horrific things he'd seen and not feel anything. He can hide them in a variety of ways, but they will always be there. If he was able to simply recognize them, he could more easily deal with them. He had to admit his humanity or he wouldn't last. It was okay to feel things. It didn't make him a bad person, it made him human.

Recognizing that he was just experiencing what any human being would feel also helped wash away the guilt. He didn't want to see Nancy hurt or have had Elise back instead of her. He was simply yearning for his wife and that manifested itself in strange ways. What he had to do more than anything else at the moment was get home. Unfortunately that wasn't going to happen anytime soon.

Anthony dropped by to explain how the new cell phone setup was going to work. They had his new phone hooked up in the same way Numbers' phone had been, only this time they were going to keep it and patch another cell phone into it so when Sweet called Keely, the phone he had would ring. That way they could monitor everything and try to locate Sweet at the same time.

"Clear," Anthony had said.

"As mud," Keely had responded.

He picked up the little cable wrapped around the bed frame and pushed the red button on the end. A minute later a nurse arrived. He had to go to the bathroom but he was not using a bedpan. She got the uneasy looking cop to escort him and his pole with its intravenous drip attached to the washroom at the other end of the emergency ward.

"We wouldn't want you escaping on us now, would we," she'd said so pleasantly that Keely wanted to punch her.

He was comfortable enough physically, but his mind was doing acrobatics. Sweet said to go home, which probably meant he was going to call him on his land line. He'd never been told, at least that he could remember, that he'd have to be alone, so maybe getting a few cops to tag along was okay. All he had to do was convince the doctor to let him go.

"Thought you could use this." Numbers handed him a steaming hot cup of coffee.

"Black?"

"As midnight."

"Have I ever told you that I love you?"

"Yeah, and it makes me uncomfortable." Numbers stepped over to Nancy's bed and for a moment watched her sleep. Satisfied, he went back to Keely. "We'll find her. You know we will."

Keely studied the coffee cup. "What did they find out about the dead guy?"

"It's the damnedest thing," Numbers said enthusiastically, happy to change the subject. "It's like the guy never existed. We matched his blood to the blood they found at your house, but that's it."

"It what? How do you mean?"

"I mean, it's like this guy has no identity. They ran his prints and got nothing. They ran his DNA and came up empty. They even checked his photo for anything in the system and he's a zero. Not on the books anywhere."

"What about dental records?"

"Pulled."

"They pulled his dental records and what?" Keely took a gulp of coffee forgetting how hot it was and grimaced from the burning sensation. A second later, he thanked the coffee gods for the feeling.

"No. You don't get it." Numbers sipped his coffee and looked to Keely like he was enjoying it, too. "He had all is teeth pulled. Just a bunch of bloody holes in his mouth."

"Guy gets whacked at my house. Obviously he's Sour. But was he wiped clean from the system before or after he gets killed?"

Numbers shrugged. "No clue."

"So Sweet kills Sour and leaves a note that says it's personal. What the hell is he trying to say, Mick?"

"Okay Mr. McAdam, let's have a look." A tall man in scrubs and a white coat was at the side of his bed and Keely hadn't even noticed. "How you feeling?"

Dr. Farkas was nothing like Keely thought he'd be. He was no Marcus Welby. More like George Clooney. "I'm great. Sign me out."

He checked Keely's chart while pressing his finger into Keely's wrist, then flashed a small penlight into each of Keely's eyes. "Okay, we've cleaned and dressed your puncture wounds so you're good to go. I urge you to get lots of sleep. You're exhausted, man." And the good doctor was gone.

Keely whipped the covers off his body but before his feet left the bed Robitaille rounded the curtain. "Not so fast."

"I'm cleared to go home."

"We need to talk first. About your last conversation with Sweet."

The Detective Sergeant had a way of sucking the energy out Keely. "He was telling me how disappointed he was that Mick's house didn't blow up.

He said he'd have seen it on the news but hadn't and that is how he knew we were on to him."

"And."

"And what?" Keely was starting to lose his patience with Robitaille.

"He has your wife, you want her back. So what does he want you to do?"

Keely tried to burn a hole in Robitaille with his eyes. "He said he'll contact me soon. Okay?"

"You're tapped into his phone so you'll know when the guy calls." Numbers stepped between Keely and Robitaille. "Leave him alone for now. Let him go home and get some rest."

Keely didn't have to look to know that Robitaille had left, he could hear his shoes squeaking as he walked away. Numbers grabbed the curtain and, with a single tug, closed them in. A brown paper bag was under his bed and he pulled out his clothes and got dressed. He noticed the fresh dressing on the cuts Daisy had made with her teeth and the plane crash flashed through his mind. He'd been through so much in such a short time, he was looking forward to sitting in his living room, rejuvenating. He knew that he was going to need his strength for the last leg of the race.

* * * *

The drive had taken about a half hour and when the police cruiser pulled into the driveway, Keely laughed at the sight of his beat up Explorer. The OPP had obviously towed it to his home and left him to get the damage repaired. Fair enough, he thought. It was my choice and I'll pay the consequences.

One of the cops, a pleasant veteran with a round face named Hall, went into the house and came out about ten minutes later. Keely had watched lights go on in several rooms as the cop had checked to make sure there were no surprises waiting for them. Both of the officers stayed in their cruiser, declining Keely's offer to come inside. He didn't press the issue since all he could think about was getting inside and sitting down.

He entered by the front door and saw nothing out of the ordinary. The house looked and smelled as it always had. He passed from the entranceway, through a main hallway to the kitchen in the back of the house.

A few dirty dishes cluttered the sink were the only sign that someone other than his wife had been in the house. She would have immediately put the dishes into the dishwasher.

He looked through the patio doors to a yard falling prey to night. He glanced at the clock on the microwave: 9:18 p.m. How the day had flown by since passing out. He took a deep breath and held it, waiting for some sign that life other than his own was present. The fridge hummed, a car drove by the house, but there was no other sound barring his beating heart. He exhaled, grabbed the counter and fought back his emotions.

He spun left and walked into the dining room, then swung left, avoiding the table so he could continue into the living room. He had to sit down. Officer Hall had cleared the house. It was safe but he didn't feel safe. His skin burned as if being stretched. Sweat darkened his T-shirt. He needed to clear the house himself and ran for the stairs.

He took the stairs three at a time and checked the bedrooms, guest room and bathrooms. He opened every closet, not only to ensure the bad guys were gone but also to see what they'd soiled, what they'd touched. He flew down the stairs and didn't stop at the landing, moving to his right and continuing to the basement. The lights were burning bright in the family room and the yellow tape that stretched from the banister at the bottom of the stairs all the way to a lamp in the corner to his right. The room had been cut in half by the tape and what was most disturbing was what it housed.

The dark green carpet had a copper stain the size of a coffee table on it just to the right of the laundry room entrance. Keely ripped down the caution tape, growling the entire time, tearing it into shreds and whipping it across the room. He couldn't catch his breath. The pain in his stomach and chest was too much. It wasn't like a stab wound or like being shot. It was far worse. It was fear.

Bent over, hands on his knees, he controlled his breathing and pushed his emotions aside. He raised his head to see that someone had propped open the swinging doors to the laundry room, the bare bulb casting a harsh light that spilled onto the blood stain. She'd been here. This was where they'd kept her. Did she see Sweet murder Sour? Did they hurt her?

Trembling, he inched toward the room, tears welling in his eyes. He stepped through the doors and immediately spotted the chair beside the water heater on the left. He stepped to the chair and saw blood stains on it.

He grabbed the back of it and with all his might threw the chair against the shelves just above the washer. It crashed with a sound like thunder and the shelves emptied their contents. Soap floated into the air, bleach guzzled onto the metal of the machines below it, cups and bottles bounced making clapping sounds.

"Where are you?" he screamed and couldn't contain the tears any longer. He reached out to the water heater, leaning on it. His body convulsed as the tears flowed. "I love you," he said softly.

His new cell phone chimed and he instantly pulled himself together. He found the talk button on the phone and pushed it. "Fuck you."

"Nice to hear your voice, too."

"Regardless of what happens to my wife, you're dead. You have to know that."

"Kira Bremner. Put her in a car, drive to Humber Bay Park, the west side. Drive out to the farthest point. Have her get out of the car, walk around it slowly and get back in the door she came out of. You have two hours. You got that?"

"No, asshole. Tell me again. I'm slow from lack of sleep."

Keely heard mumbling in the background then two sharp slaps. There were a few more moans then Sweet was back. "I made her bleed. She was good, you know? Tight. Like a little girl's. You must have a little pecker if she's that tight."

"You are fucking dead! I'm going to kill you!" Keely screamed it over and over until Hall and his partner rushed into the room and took the phone from him.

"He's off the line, Keely," Hall said and snapped the phone closed. "He's gone. Relax."

Keely felt his face twitch and sweat sting in his eyes. His breathing was erratic and it made him feel lightheaded. He collapsed to the floor, his back against the water heater. Hall leaned down and put a hand on his shoulder. "I'd kill him for you if I could."

He played the slapping sounds over in his mind and they rolled into her voice saying she loved him. Hall's big red face loomed closer and Keely felt the cop lightly slap his cheek. Elise's voice was as clear as if she was standing in front of him.

"Help me, Keely. I can smell you. I don't want to end up like Janet. Old house ... "

Everything stopped as if Keely had bent time. Hall and his partner looked down at him with concerned faces. The bleach stopped dripping from the top of the washer. There was no sound. Keely's heart stopped beating. He knew where to find Elise.

Chapter 35

I don't want to end up like Janet. Old house. Fireplace!

It had taken several minutes for Keely to recover from his angry tirade. The two officers sent to babysit him kept looking at each other for some sign of what to do next. They paced, talked soothingly to him, paced some more and finally, Hall had had enough.

"Look, we were told to guard you, but we don't have to do it from inside. If you need something, we're in the cruiser." Then he shoved his young partner out of the room and Keely heard them leave the house.

Inside he was burning up but his skin felt as if he was submerged in ice. His head ached and his body was stiff. He had so little time left, he was certain of that. Once Kira was dead, Elise would be, too.

Robitaille wouldn't possibly think of complying with Sweet's demands.

The phone was in his hand faster than the thought occurred to call someone.

"Nine-one-one. What's the nature of your emergency?"

"I have to speak to an idiot."

He'd been more forthcoming the second time he called and was told that Robitaille would call him. While waiting he felt the bubble of animosity rising with the memory of Janet Harper's death. His hands were shaking and he was careful not to spill the coffee he was pouring.

He took his cup to the front room window and checked on his sitters. They were drinking coffee from a flask and eating sandwiches from plastic bags. Must be dinner time, Keely thought.

"You are going to stay exactly where you are." Robitaille was in a talkative mood. "If you move, I swear I shoot you myself."

"Don't listen to him," Keely said on his way to the kitchen. "If Kira Bremner does what he wants, you know she's dead."

"It is none of your concern now. We're going to find Sweet. Anthony is close. You stay there and don't move."

Keely slammed his cup down on the counter too hard and lost half his coffee. He was amazed that he couldn't feel the steaming hot liquid as it splashed all over his hand. "If they can shoot down a fucking plane they can kill someone in the open. They'll be waiting. You have to know they'll blow up the car she's in if they have to."

"Keely." Robitaille's voice was quiet, soft. "I know you will never fully trust me, but I am good at what I do. *I* trust me."

"The moment she steps out of that car, they'll make her. That's all they need. Once they know it's her, they'll kill her."

"Trust me," he said, and the line went dead.

"Fuck!"

Who could he trust beside Numbers? He couldn't tell anyone where he was going, least of all Robitaille. *I don't want to end up like Janet.* He was playing by the book again. This time it was going to get Kira killed and if he told Robitaille that he knew where Elise was, he'd get her killed, too. He couldn't chance a repeat of a few years ago. Janet Harper's death was the last piece to a very ugly puzzle. If he lost Elise, he'd have nothing left.

He thought about calling Numbers, but what could he say? Anything he said would be heard by Anthony or someone like him. They'd record it and play it for everyone to interpret. He couldn't take the chance. He'd call when Sweet was dead. And he'd have to kill him before they killed Kira, otherwise he'd be too late to save Elise.

He wiped his hand on a dish towel and turned off the downstairs light. Then he climbed the stairs and put on the bedroom light. Hall had seen the upstairs layout and would hopefully remember that their room was in the front of the house. He quickly put on fresh clothes, a dark blue T-shirt, light-coloured buttoned shirt over top and khaki pants. He needed cover for the guns, one on his ankle, another holstered under his arm and the last tucked into his belt at the base of his spine. His running shoes would suffice and he slipped them back on.

Keely waited for several agonizing minutes, time he could sorely use to get to his wife. It was necessary to fool his guards into believing he was going to sleep for a while. He'd even thought about asking them for a wakeup call, but they felt uneasy around him and he welcomed the distance.

After what felt like an hour but was only two or three minutes, Keely doused the bedroom light and dashed down the stairs. He kept his body bent avoiding every window, walking Quazimodo-style to the patio door. He quietly escaped from his own home, running full-tilt at the back fence and climbing it easily.

The night felt hot but damp, the mugginess clinging to his exposed skin and making what was covered overheat and sweat badly. He darted between the houses and emerged on the opposite street to his own. It was early enough that getting a cab should be easy. He turned left and trotted down the street toward the main intersection of the neighbourhood.

* * * *

Humber Bay Park was essentially a manmade spit. Sometime in the late Seventies an MP or a city councilman or even the mayor had the bright idea to extend the mouth of Mimico Creek and build parks on either side. Ingeniously, they used landfill from local construction sites to create the terrain, making it a popular park and boat launch since its completion in the Eighties.

Robitaille sat in the back of the sedan watching a bird's-eye view of a convoy of dozens of cars roll towards the park on the west side of the creek. He swore at the person responsible for its construction and hoped he'd covered every possible scenario.

The sedan pulled into the park well ahead of the line of cars several kilometres behind and drove along a winding road, slowing every so often for speed bumps. He'd wanted a close enough view of the area without being close enough to draw any fire.

"There," he said and pointed to a utility building sitting out in the middle of the spit but several hundred metres back from the farthest point of land. His driver pulled the car beside it and shut off the engine. Robitaille adjusted his jacket and straightened his tie. Yes, he was nervous. Of course he was, two lives depended on his timing.

He no longer needed the laptop to see the convoy, it whizzed past him toward the point. He watched the black SUV with its dark tinted windows negotiate the rocky ground and park facing west. Then a similar vehicle, next in line, pulled in front of it, parking so its nose pointed south. The other cars in line began to park nose to tail, forming a circle around the first SUV. Kira Bremner was nowhere near that car. She was still safely guarded by those officers Robitaille knew were loyal. The lookalike officer only needed a wig to complete the ruse. It didn't matter. He would comply with Sweet's demand, only slightly modifying it.

Finally, the helicopters arrived in a V-formation. The only way he could tell they were in any kind of formation was thanks to the lights on the bottom of their fuselages. Once they reached the area above the SUV, they turned on powerful search lights. Six lights bore down on the cars, land and water around the SUV. If anyone moved, the tactical squad would know immediately.

Sirens and flashing lights indicated the final piece of Robitaille's modifications. A dozen firetrucks streamed past him and parked in a circular formation to form an outer ring of protection around the SUV. Once the final truck was in place, he ordered one last sweep of the area. If someone was going to try something, they'd have one hell of a time pulling it off. His only worry now was Keely McAdam.

* * * *

Keely paid for the cab. Normally, he'd flash his badge on such an occasion but today he didn't want any red flags popping up anywhere that might ruin his chances of saving Elise. He recognized the neighbourhood immediately; the pawn shop and strip club were his first reminders. He walked east on Queen Street and turned left at the next corner. He could already see Harper's old place a few blocks up on the right.

"Think like a crook."

The big Victorian was a few houses from the corner and Keely took a quick right. He walked the length of the house that was situated on the corner of the block until he could see over fences into the Harpers' old yard. The back of the house was taller than it should have been for a two-story home, but with the high-pitched roof and turret-like structures at each corner, it gave the impression of height.

All the windows were boarded except for one on the upper floor. Someone, most likely kids, had pulled off the board and it lay on a slim metal balcony below the gaping hole. Keely climbed several fences without incident and thought maybe his luck was changing. He got to the Harpers' yard and stood looking up to where he had to be and glanced around the yard. There were no ladders or grappling hooks to use so he dug into his youth and decided the only way was to climb.

He quietly approached the window on the first floor and again his heart soared at his good fortune. A few holes had been punched into the board and they made excellent holds for him to at least get his feet onto the sill. With the fingers of his left hand curled into the hole, he looked up to judge the distance to the bottom of the small balcony. It was easily five feet above the top of the ground-floor window, a leap he couldn't make.

Examining the bricks he realized they'd been staggered; a row of bricks ending with one jutting out an inch, the next row flush, then the next being another jutting brick. His only problem was that the window arched. He chanced it and spreading his legs he used both sides of the window frame to climb to where he was a foot from the rusting metal bottom of the tiny terrace. He could go no further.

He'd need to perform a static jump. He remembered the climbing move well since he'd enjoyed attempting them any chance he got. In fact, he'd used the move to impress a young Elise. A static jump was leaping up to a target while only having one point of contact with the wall. He forced himself to relax and placed his left hand, palm up, under the arch of brick. He could now push up with his hand and down with his feet for stability. Only problem was, this static jump was going to require that he leave the wall completely on the way up.

He bent his knees then straightened them again a few times, then counted to three. He thrust hard from his feet, driving his body up as he let his left hand drop free from under the arch. He reached up with his right hand for any purchase and found it, hooking his fingers over one of the rusty slats of metal, dangling a dozen feet in the air.

He threw up his left and hooked his fingers over metal, then tightened his stomach to raise his legs to the wall. Pain gripped him harder than he gripped the metal, making his stomach ache and piercing into his fingers. He shook it from his mind and concentrated only on sliding his hands back so his legs could walk up the wall to bring his body horizontal with the ground. Once there, he hooked the tip of his foot through the slats and was able to reached a hand to a thin, square baluster.

He managed to get himself up and over the railing and as he landed on the slats that had cut into his fingers, they gave way. He flailed for the railing as his feet dropped from beneath him. He hung there as metal clanged loudly to the ground below. Only problem now was that he was sure Sweet knew someone was coming.

* * * *

He'd taken every precaution and even now, minutes until she was to walk around the SUV and get back in, he had men scouring nearby hiding places. The roar of choppers had taken over from the sirens since they had been silenced when the firetrucks went into position. Lights drew lines over every surface around the strange arrangement of cars and officers stood at the ready from their hiding places surrounding the spit. He could see no way anyone could get to her and yet he had complied with the demand.

The laptop screen was active once again and Robitaille heard a tinny voice say it was time. He watched the shaky image of a modern day circle of wagons and silently prayed that the officer playing the part of Kira and all those involved would be alive and well at the end of this oddity. The door of the SUV swung open and the lookalike stepped out. She had to partially close the door in order to get between it and one of the cars parked close by. Robitaille smiled at that; the closer the better.

Her hair whipped in the artificial wind of a low flying chopper and the ground must have been uneven or soft under her feet since she reached out every so often to touch the big SUV for support. She rounded the front and made her way along the closest side of the truck to his position. He glanced out his window and was ecstatic at not being able to see her at all. Back on the screen he watched her round the rear of the vehicle, again grabbing the edge for support.

"Water. Eleven o'clock. Five hundred meters," someone yelled into his earpiece.

It happened so fast that Robitaille had no way to see what had popped out of the water. He only saw the ripples caused by the helicopters dropping down to take a closer look. Whatever or whoever it was, they were gone. Out his window Robitaille watched as four divers dropped from a helicopter into the water.

"Stay alert," Robitaille said calmly into the tiny microphone curving across his mouth. "There may be a counter attempt from another direction. Stay alert."

* * * *

The room was once a bedroom, Keely was sure of that from its size and location. It was completely devoid of any furniture and only had garbage strewn across one side. The door was open and he stood completely still inside the window, listening. He heard a muffled moan from somewhere downstairs. His heart pumped extra blood to his head and he felt like his face had swelled. She was alive. He'd gotten to her in time.

A phone rang only once and Keely finally heard the clear voice of a man he'd only heard over the phone say hello.

"You gotta be kidding me. Too bad." There was a pause and Keely took the opportunity to cross the room. He kept to the edge of the floor, as close to the walls as possible, thinking there'd be less chance of any floorboards squeaking. "I'm done, right? Full pay? A flight out of this shithole?"

Keely made his way to the top of the stairs and pressed his back against the wall. He twisted slightly left so his head could clear the corner and he could hear better.

"It was a pleasure doing business with you. Never call me again."

He heard Sweet doing something. Punching some buttons on his phone perhaps. Keely's cell phone rang.

* * * *

A man in a dark grey sweatsuit strolled casually up the walkway and placed a briefcase on the doorstep of the McAdams' home. Hall and his partner were long gone. The man walked away and two minutes later, the case exploded, taking the house with it. Fire lit up the night sky for ten kilometres in every direction.

* * * *

He didn't answer the phone. Instead, he drew the gun from his ankle holster and walked down the stairs. Every ache, every pain he'd felt was gone. He had boundless energy and couldn't be killed. He could take a bullet and keep firing at Sweet. Nothing was going stop him. He rounded the newel post at the bottom of the stairs and raised his gun. Sweet's head filled the sighting.

"Not a good idea," Sweet said, crouched beside Elise who was tied to a chair. His thick hair lay in tendrils across his face and he held a gun to Elise's temple. "Remember this, huh? Remember how you shot Curt Harper?"

Keely heard the words but his ability to comprehend had been impaired. He held the gun on Sweet, barely noticing his badly beaten wife.

"Imagine my surprise when I take a job that not only erases me from existence, but that connects me with the man who killed someone important to *me*." Sweet was shaking and his voice was becoming loud and gruff. "Though I thank you for giving me the opportunity to get rid of the dead weight that was my little, illegitimate bastard of a brother. I thank you most for allowing me to seek my revenge."

Sweet whipped the gun up and there was a huge bang. Keely registered the flash and Sweet disappeared into white. Keely struggled to see anything in what was like the worst blizzard whiteout he'd ever experience. A loud buzzing ripped at his eardrums and he tried hard to orient himself. He hadn't moved, his gun was still trained where Sweet should be. He began to squeeze the trigger when someone tackled him to the floor. He pulled the trigger but never heard the shot.

Epilogue

"Nancy is still at her sisters?" Keely asked dropping onto the sofa.

"Yep. She said she needs space and time to sort things out." Mick shrugged.

There was an awkward silence then Keely said, "Anthony called. Said it'll be on the news at noon."

"He wants you to call him Tony," Numbers said from his side of the couch.

"And I want insurance to pay full price for my blown-to-smithereens house. Can't have everything." Keely smirked and ruined his act. He'd forgiven Anthony for giving him a phone with a tracking device in it. That didn't stop Keely from enjoying torturing him though. "Hey, you using him on that banker case?"

"Might need him. I'll see."

Keely put his feet up on the coffee table in Numbers' basement and leaned back to stretch out his spine. Though it was a month after the flash-bang in Harper's old house and the tackle that followed, Keely still felt aches and pains. He knew it was the culmination of the four days leading up to him shooting at a SWAT officer, but the tackle was freshest in his mind.

"You need an office, Mick. More professional."

"More expensive."

"I'm going start calling you Cheap instead of Numbers."

"Not when I see the bottom line my friend."

Keely laughed. "Why can't we be there?"

"Cop you shot will be there. Might want to shoot you back."

"I hit his flack jacket. He barely had a bruise."

"You're lucky it was him and not me. I'd definitely have shot you by now." Elise had come down the stairs and was almost at the couch. Keely was amazed at how quickly the physical wounds had been healing. Her mental and emotional state were lagging behind but knowing his wife, she'd get through it. She leaned down and kissed Keely softly on the mouth. "What's the big deal with the news?"

"Rene told Anthony—"

"So, it's Rene now?" she said with a lilt.

"He told us to watch the health minister's news conference on the grounds of that new hospital they're building. Said it would be interesting."

Keely wrapped his arm around Elise's waist when she sat on the arm of the couch. He liked Numbers' big-screen television but lamented the loss of his own in the explosion. They could shoot a damned plane down but couldn't track Sweet. They had no idea he'd left the McAdams' house for Harpers'.

"Here we go." Elise leaned over and her breast lightly rested on Keely's head. He knew she was aware of it but said nothing. "What, my boobs don't do it for you anymore?" she asked.

"Not when I'm watching TV."

They laughed and Elise swatted Keely's arm. She slid down to squeeze between him and the arm of the sofa just as a stocky woman with black hair and too much makeup approached a bushel of microphones.

"Good afternoon," she said and a loud commotion made her step back from the mics. The camera swung around to show Robitaille, a dozen cops trailing behind him, walking purposefully across a red carpet laid in front of two big, yellow, stationary bulldozers.

"Excuse me, Madam Minister, I am sorry to interrupt but I must be heard." Robitaille stepped up to the microphone after a few of his posse squeezed by RCMP officers in full dress uniforms. "There is a situation that involves the government of Canada, specifically, the health minister and the defence minister."

"This is outrageous. I demand—"

Robitaille silenced her with a well-placed look. "There was a young woman who should have been here today, but I am so sad to tell you, that she cannot. She was murdered."

All three people on the sofa leaned forward. Keely glanced over at Numbers who shrugged. Robitaille was struggling to keep his composure and finally stemmed his emotions enough to continue.

"A very brave woman by the name of Kira Bremner thought she was extending her cycling career by cheating. She thought she was gene doping as a means to enhance the human body's strength. For the most part, she was. However, what she did not realize was that this procedure was also a long-term experiment by the government. The gene doping caused tumours to develop in her brain and they were not caught in time to save her life."

The health minister looked shocked. "I had no knowledge of any of these experiments."

The cameraperson was doing a great job getting to the speaker but decided to pull back and include both the minister and Robitaille in the frame.

"We have discovered a trail of paperwork that leads to the ministers in question. Place her under arrest."

"You gotta be kidding me?" Keely stood up. "Rene, you got some balls, man."

Through the commotion of the arrest, Robitaille continued. "We all know that Todd Watkins' death was an accident but we suspect that his body was stolen from the morgue to hide evidence that he, too, was suffering from these tumours, again as a result of the experiments."

Keely was awestruck by the way Robitaille was handling himself. The man was calm and in complete control.

"We aim to prove that the government has exposed thousands of military personnel to this procedure and we have been able to save many lives thanks to the courage of Kira Bremner. My office will issue a statement by this evening. I thank you for your time."

They watched two of Robitaille's crew escort the minister from her press conference in handcuffs leaving the media on hand in a frenzy. The remaining officers were obviously there for crowd control.

Keely felt numb. He had no idea that Kira was sick and it made him feel ill that he'd not spoken to her since her rescue. He looked at Numbers and could tell he felt the same shame. The big man struggled off the low sofa and walked to a bar on the far side of the room, lifting part of the counter and slipping behind it. He reached for a bottle of scotch, then grabbed three shot glasses from below the bar.

Elise and Keely joined their friend as he cracked the seal on the bottle and filled the three small glasses.

Keely felt a lump grow instantly in his throat when Mick Moyer raised his glass and looking directly at Elise said, "To very brave women."

THE END

www.authorianoneill.blogspot.com

ABOUT THE AUTHOR

Ian lives in Oakville, Ontario, Canada with his wife and daughter.

BookStrand

www.BookStrand.com

CPSIA information can be obtained at www.ICGtesting.com
Printed in the USA
LVOW091925260212

270484LV00019B/145/P

9 781606 011720